D1738285

COMPULSION

COMPULSION

J. Lance Erikson

JLE BOOKS
Puerto Vallarta, Jalisco

COMPULSION

For My Family
Suzie, Chip, John, Jay, Catharine

ONE

Maximilian Van Zuylen

I am Maximilian Arthur Van Zuylen, born to Beatrice and Frederick Arthur Van Zuylen in San Francisco on July 1, 1989. It was not a convenient time for my parents as it spoiled their summer stay at our estate in Napa. My christening was delayed until November first so my parents could be certain family members and social friends would have returned from wherever they go in the summer.

Of course, I know nothing about the christening, but I have been taken through the album again and again, and it does seem impressive if you are into that kind of event. The ceremony took place at Grace Cathedral on Nob Hill in San Francisco. The service was limited to two hundred guests because my mother wanted to be sure each guest could be accommodated at the celebratory cocktail party and dinner which was to follow at L´ Etoile, the famous restaurant in the basement of the Huntington Hotel, diagonally across the street from the Cathedral.

There are pictures of the Bishop holding me above the font and pouring water over my nearly bald head. There are pictures of my parents´ guests mingling in the bar at L´ Etoile while Peter Mintun played his signature music from the 1930´s and 1940´s. There are also pictures within the restaurant showing the two hundred guests dining at twenty tables for ten. There are no more pictures of me, however, as I had grown fussy and was whisked away by my nanny in one of our two limousines to our penthouse in Russian Hill where, presumably, I was given a bottle and put to bed after an all too exhausting afternoon.

Four weeks later, my future roommate, William Mortimer Radcliffe IV, underwent a similar, if slightly more elaborate, christening at St. Patrick´s Cathedral in New York City. I was not to learn of this until my first visit to the Radcliffes´ townhouse at age thirteen when Mrs. Radcliffe showed me, much to her son´s displeasure, his christening album. Six hundred guests, I was told, came from New York, Newport and Palm Beach. She insisted on showing me photographs of the most well-known guests, although none was known to me, and telling me it was the society event of the season. The post-christening dinner was held in the ballroom of the Pierre Hotel, just around the corner from the Radcliffes´ townhouse. Mrs. Radcliffe even read to me from the society columns, each describing the event in the most glowing terms.

William, I remember, was particularly annoyed because we had only Saturday and part of Sunday in New York before returning to Deerpark, our boarding school in Connecticut. His plan had been to take the Madison Avenue bus to Harlem where we would find young Puerto Rican girls who would "do it" for five dollars. He even gave me a condom, the first one I had ever seen, in preparation for our adventure. Alas, we did not go to Harlem. Instead, Mr. and Mrs. Radcliffe accompanied us to a matinee performance of some thoroughly forgettable musical and then to dinner – just the four of us – at La Caravelle, their favorite restaurant in Manhattan where they could be assured of the center banquette in the main section of the dining room, visible to all and every patron who entered the restaurant. The following day, as a special treat, Mr. Radcliffe took us to Yankee Stadium to watch the Yankees play, which was pretty cool if not quite the same excitement William and I had hoped for on our weekend in New York. But I am getting ahead of our story.

TWO
Maximilian Van Zuylen

We lived, as I already mentioned, in Russian Hill. Our home was the penthouse of The Pinnacle, a forty-four story condominium which was built between 1982 and 1987, notwithstanding the consternation, complaints and threatened lawsuits of our Green Street neighbors, particularly the residents of The Summit, which until that time had been the tallest building on the hill and above which we now soared an additional eleven stories, blocking their view to the east. To be fair, the best view from Russian Hill was always to the north which gave on to vistas of the Golden Gate Bridge, most of the San Francisco Bay, and the hills of Marin.

Our apartment occupied the entire forty-second, forty-third and forty-fourth floors of The Pinnacle and had wide, wrap-around terraces on each floor. The main entrance was on the forty-third floor where we had our living room, a double height space facing north with floor to ceiling windows of thirty feet. There was also a north facing dining room, a red lacquered library, and the west facing kitchen. A circular stairway connected the floor above and the floor below. Upstairs was my parents' private space. Overlooking the living room was the den, a masculine space which was where my father spent most of his at-home time. A low, onyx-topped bar allowed my parents to enjoy cocktails from above the living room while admiring the evening view. The west end of the forty-fourth floor was their suite. There were two large bathrooms, two dressing rooms and a master bedroom which had both north and west views. I was rarely invited into this inner sanctum.

My floor, if I can call it that, was the forty-second. Here, there was a large great room, as it was called, and my bedroom, both facing north, a servants' kitchen and sitting room, and six servants' bedrooms – two for The Nannies – more about them in a minute, two for the chauffeurs, a large corner room for the couple who cooked and served, and one for the maid who helped the couple keep everything clean and tidy.

Perhaps my first real memories are of The Nannies. There were always two so that one could spell the other. These are good memories. I am told I was a pretty docile child, not subject to tantrums or major disobedience. I suppose it helped that The Nannies – six in all, I think, between my birth and age eight when my father decided another kind of supervision was in order – treated me as a kind of toy or pet. They played with me during all my waking hours, inventing games which a young child could comprehend, reading to me either inside or, when the weather was fine, outside on the forty-second floor terrace.

They took endless delight in dressing me, sometimes several times a day. We took walks in Russian Hill, at first in my stroller – they called it a perambulator – and later on foot, one or both of them holding my hand. Often, one of the chauffeurs drove us to Huntington Park on Nob Hill. It is not really a child's park, but there are lots of walking paths there which I ran around, sometimes kicking a rubber ball.

One routine never varied. At seven each evening when my parents were in town, I was bathed, dressed in fresh clothes, hair brushed and combed, and thirty minutes later, taken by elevator to the forty-fourth floor. There, my parents would be midway through their cocktail hour. I sat on one of the low chairs at the white onyx bar while they enjoyed their cocktails. When I was old enough to converse, my mother invariably asked "How was your day" and I would tell her about a game The Nannies and I played, or a story that had been read to me, or our adventures in Huntington Park or, sometimes, Golden Gate Park. The interview always drew to a close ten or fifteen minutes later with my mother saying "That's nice, darling." Then, my Nanny and I would again board the elevator and descend to the forty-second floor – home.

My favorite time during those years was the summer when we moved to our estate in Napa. Here, I could run around and play outdoors without having to be driven to some park. We lived on a fifty-five acre knoll which overlooked the Napa Valley. Unlike most owners of large Napa properties, we did not have a vineyard. My mother loved wine, but hated the ugly little vines which were "ghastly looking" most of the year. Instead, our property rather resembled a park: there were acres of rose and cut-flower gardens, lawns that covered probably thirty acres, a tennis court and viewing deck and a pool and spa. It was here, at age five, I learned to swim, and I also took tennis lessons on our court around the same time. Our house was a massive stone pile, one of the oldest in Napa, built to look like some chateau in the French countryside. My father bought it two or three years before I was born, then spent several more years renovating it. He added the pool and tennis court and also built a pond which had lily pads and frogs – my favorite place. My mother's contribution to the pond was a nearby "folly", as she called it, a small, white-washed pavilion where you could sit and rest away from the sun. I often had a picnic lunch there and regularly fell asleep on one of the chaises in the pavilion afterwards under the watchful eye of one of The Nannies.

Happy as I was in Napa, I did not see much more of my parents there than I did in the City. My parents were avid golfers and left most days after breakfast to play. Often, they would return home with their golf foursome partners to a late lunch on the stone terrace which overlooked the swimming pool and the Napa Valley. They did a great deal of entertaining and had large luncheon parties for thirty or forty guests almost every Sunday. These generally started around one and lasted until four-thirty or five o'clock. Occasionally, I was trotted out at one of these luncheons – perfectly dressed, of course – to say hello to the guests, then led away by one of The Nannies. Despite these rare intrusions into the adults' world, I was pretty much left to whatever The Nannies wanted me to do, so I swam a lot, looked for frogs by the pond and had pretty much idyllic summers.

At age five, I was enrolled in St. Mary's Country Day School in Pacific Heights. Apparently, I had applied to St. Mary's a few days after my birth. My parents would probably have applied sooner, but I think you actually have to be born first. I was to stay at St. Mary's through grade six. The school was run by a strict order of Catholic nuns who brooked no nonsense from any of the students, even those of us in kindergarden. This was a big, rather unhappy change for me. I had gone from days spent with playful nannies who were, I admit, somewhat indulgent to days spent with scary women who demanded absolute obedience and – most of the time, anyway – silence. Fun was never part of the curriculum. Tears were never tolerated so I learned to be fairly stoic as I watched the clock move from nine until noon when I could return to my forty-second floor cocoon and the affectionate care of The Nannies.

Apart from school, the biggest change came in my young life when I was eight years old. My father, as I mentioned, decided I needed a different kind of supervision, so he dismissed the last of The Nannies and hired Michael Smith to come live with us. No one knew exactly what to call Michael. He was part tutor, part babysitter, part companion. During the day, while I was at St. Mary´s, Mike attended San Francisco State College, studying English literature and hoping one day to become a lawyer. Our classroom hours didn´t exactly link up, but by mid-afternoon, we were both back in the penthouse doing homework at a partners´ desk in the great room. Mike was a bit like an older brother, I suppose, although I never had siblings, older or younger. At least, I never thought I did. Best of all, he was fun and probably a little mischievous. To be sure, we did our homework, Mike checking my assignment book each night so the nuns wouldn´t discipline me for failing to complete an assignment. But we did things – guy things, especially on weekends – that were infinitely better than playing with The Nannies.

We went to the movies at least once a week. Mike took me roller skating at a rink in San Bruno, a town just south of San Francisco that I am sure my parents would never set foot in. We went to Golden Gate Park, threw footballs and sometimes baseballs and had water balloon fights. Of course, I always lost the balloon fights and ended up soaked, so Mike brought along a towel for me to dry off in the unlikely event we ran into my parents in the garage.

In hindsight, the trouble began with water balloons. I have no idea why or how the thought came to me, but somehow I had this vision of Sister Margaret sitting on a water balloon, water running down her legs. She was, without doubt, the most dour faced, unkind nun at our school. I often wondered if she hated her habit, hated being a nun, or just hated children. Anyway, you could see the hate in her face as she marched into our room at the beginning of period one, checking to be sure each of us was in our seats, notebooks open, hands in our laps. If she couldn´t find any student to discipline, she took her seat behind a table which served as her desk and began the day´s lesson, banging as she always did with the pointer she used to underscore lessons on the blackboard.

So, I did the unthinkable. I got Julius, one of our chauffeurs, to drive me to school a few minutes early, feigning something important which I needed to do before classes began. Mike was not the wiser, as he had already left for classes at San Francisco State. In my pocket was a deflated water balloon which I filled in the boys´ room, then placed under the cushion on Sister Margaret´s chair.

At precisely eight – it was always exactly eight – so all of us could be seated and ready to start our lesson for the day – Sister Margaret came into the classroom. She glanced around the room looking for any dress code or behavioral infractions. Seeing none, she walked to her chair and took a seat. Immediately, the balloon burst and water began running down her leg. It sounded like she farted and looked like she had pissed herself at the same time. There was a snicker from somewhere which, of course, only made the situation worse.

Sister Margaret was beyond furious, whatever that next level is. It was, in fact, impossible to understand her first few words. Finally, she demanded *"Who is responsible for this outrage? Who among you dared such a dastardly deed?"* No one spoke and no hand was raised, including mine. "All right," she said, "unless I am told who the culprit is *immediately*, I will beat every one of you. Is that understood?" Later, I realized she would do no such thing, but it was too late as my hand was already in the air.

"Come up here!" Sister Margaret commanded. She then told me to face the blackboard and take down my pants, both my school pants and my underpants. Immediately, she began to beat me with her pointer. I shut my eyes as tight as I could so I wouldn´t cry, but I´m afraid some tears leaked out anyway. Finally, exhausted, I think, she stopped and ordered me to sit in the corner of the room for the rest of the hour and pray to God for forgiveness for my sins.

I did sit in the corner, but I didn´t pray. Instead, I thought about what went wrong and why. Three things occurred to me that hour. First, honesty is not always the best policy. My second thought was don´t ever get caught. My third thought, even better than the second, was don´t even become a suspect. So, those were three lessons I learned at St. Mary´s Country Day School. They have stayed with me and served me well.

After that, I kept pretty much out of trouble except for a couple of incidents which hardly merit telling. I did put dog shit in an upper classman´s locker, a big bully who used to pick on almost everyone. And, I took one of the Sister´s sack lunches from her locker and put it in another Sister´s locker. That caused a bit of a stir, but most of what happened was out of earshot of the students. Best of all, I was not a suspect in either of these misdeeds. I thought about repeating the water balloon prank at our graduation ceremony, imagining the nuns walking out on stage and taking their places in the chairs arranged there, but I knew I´d get blamed so I reluctantly let that one go.

THREE
William Radcliffe

You already know about my christening because Max told you. He also told you my name, of course, William Mortimer Radcliffe IV. My father is number III and my mother is Sybil *Peabody* Radcliffe. She is never just Sybil Radcliffe; she is always Sybil *Peabody* Radcliffe. This looks better in the social pages, apparently.

Our stories, mine and Max´s, are remarkably similar even though they took place nearly three thousand miles apart. The main difference is that my earliest memories are mostly unhappy ones whereas Max had a pretty happy childhood even if his parents were somewhat distant. Our home – the Radcliffe home - was on East Sixty-Second Street, just off Fifth Avenue, in New York City. It was designed and built beginning in 1905 by Horace Trumbauer, a noted and much admired architect of New York townhouses in his time. Ours was, and is, the only triple wide Mr. Trumbauer ever attempted. "Triple wide", in New York-speak, means that the townhouse takes up the horizontal space usually reserved for three separate townhouses, thus occupying sixty feet of frontage along East Sixty-Second Street. The David Rockefellers, as my mother is wont to point out at every opportunity, live a few blocks away in a – pause here for effect – "double wide" townhouse.

The Radcliffe townhouse is large, obscenely large by any standard. Perhaps most obscene of all is the gallery which runs from the front to the back of the house on the first floor just past the purposely small scale foyer. Here in this space you are confronted – and I think confronted is the right word – with a marble-floored space twenty feet wide and about fifty feet deep. There are double staircases – marble, of course – ascending to the five upper floors and, worst of all, a gold leafed, cage elevator centered at the rear of the gallery between the sets of stairs. To say that jaws drop when guests first glimpse the gallery is an understatement. My mother always demurs – "Oh, we never use the elevator". Of course, she used it all the time, especially when guests were waiting in the gallery.

Because the house was so large and because we were a small family, whole sections of the place were closed off. We did spread out, though. The lower floor was reserved for the kitchens and staff rooms, except that the rear garden space was used for al fresco dining when the weather suited. Upstairs, on the first floor, a fifty foot drawing room ran from the front to the rear of the house along the east side of the gallery. Opposite the drawing room were two very large rooms, a library, and behind it, the dining room where our meals were served after being sent up from the kitchens by dumb waiter. Actually, my parents ate there. Except for holiday dinners, I lived and ate on the third floor. More about that in a moment. The second floor was my parents´ private space. On one side of the gallery were my father´s and my mother´s studies and, on the other side, their private quarters.

The third floor was really my home. Here I lived with Adolphus and Margaret Schwimmer, the German couple whose sole job it was to take care of me, something most mothers and fathers seemed to manage on their own. They were humorless people who lacked any affection for each other, much less for me. They had their own apartment on one side of the gallery. The other side was my space, so I had plenty of room but really no one to spend time with other than my sour faced keepers. This is probably why I was so unhappy. Max had his playful nannies and, later, Mike Smith. I had the Schwimmers.

The fourth and fifth floors of the townhouse were largely empty. There were some guest rooms and a spa, of sorts, on four where my mother had her massages three times a week and her hair done. On five, there was an elaborately equipped gym, which was never used until I was about eleven or twelve and began to work out, more out of boredom than anything else.

The one really cool place in the house was the roof garden which occupied the nearly three thousand square foot space. It was beautifully planted with trees, plants and flowers and had nice garden furniture. It was a wonderful place to play, especially when I was young, and a nice place to escape the Schwimmers when I was able to go there by myself. My parents never used the roof garden because my mother hated the idea that people in the high rises on Fifth Avenue could look down on her. I think the only reason they paid for the garden's upkeep was to make sure people who did look down wouldn't see a shabby roof, regardless that it was never used.

Summers we left the City, almost always a few days before the Memorial Day weekend, and traveled to Newport, Rhode Island, where my parents owned one of the summer "cottages" on Bellevue Avenue. These were the massive piles built mostly in the late 1800's by men with names like Vanderbilt, Astor, Duke and Radcliffe. Ours was not the biggest "cottage" on the Avenue – much to my mother's consternation, I am sure – but it was certainly grand enough. The house had three floors in about thirty thousand square feet. Behind the house, on the ocean side, there was a pool, pool pavilion and two or three acres of lawn which ran to the cliff giving way to the sea. The cottage was originally named Land's End by some distant Radcliffe. My mother changed the name to Wit's End which she had emblazoned on the iron gates marking the driveway. I am sure she thought it very clever; I just thought it was dumb. Our next door neighbor, Doris Duke, named her place Rough Point which I always thought was a pretty cool name.

The first floor of our cottage was devoted to public rooms – drawing room, dining room, library, a music room and the kitchens. Running the length of the house at the back was a covered loggia with a fireplace, several seating groups and tables for outdoor dining. This is where my parents and their guests spent most of their time. The grandest space in the house was the second floor ballroom, a fixture in nearly all of the original Newport cottages. I don't ever remember it being used for anything other than tours which the Newport Historical Preservation Society was allowed occasionally to arrange. The ballroom was lined on the ocean side with huge French doors which led to a terrace overlooking the garden and the ocean. My parents did take their morning coffee there sometimes, but otherwise the ballroom and its adjoining terrace were vacant.

The family quarters were also on the second floor. My parents´ rooms were there on one side of the ballroom; mine were on the other side along with the Schwimmers´ apartment. Upstairs were guest rooms, the staff quarters and at least four or five storage rooms. Some of these held wines, liquors and other provisions for the house. Two were more interesting. They held some of the items installed in the house when it was first built. Chandeliers, old sofas and chairs – most of which were uncomfortable - other furniture, and lots and lots of old photographs. These I liked to look at, imagining what their lives were like in the early years of the house.

Newport, Rhode Island, at least the part of Newport where we lived, is really an adult world. Oh, we had the pool, to be sure, but that was off limits when my parents were entertaining on the terrace as they often did. We also had the Beach Club nearby, but if you´ve ever swum in the water off New England – even in the dead of summer – you know it is way too cold to enjoy. There were no kids in our neighborhood, the Schwimmers paid as little attention to me as possible, so, if anything, I was lonelier in Newport than in New York. Simple boredom is probably what started me down the road to trouble.

The only place I really liked as a boy, and even as a young teenager, was our place in Palm Beach, Florida. Unlike our homes in New York and Newport, it was a contemporary structure with lots of glass offering views from the Intracoastal to the Atlantic. We always spent Thanksgiving there and the whole month of December. Best of all, the Schwimmers did not join us in December because that was when they took their annual vacation in some town in Germany whose name was impossible to pronounce. Even if my parents entertained, which of course they did, it was on the terrace between the house and the ocean, leaving the whole back - or front, depending on your point of view - between the house and the Intracoastal a playground for me. I even found a few friends among the children of my parents´ friends who vacationed in Palm Beach in the winter.

I mentioned that boredom was probably the root of all the trouble I caused. I was cleverer than Max, though, at least in the beginning, and was neither caught nor suspected. It started with thefts in Newport. I would take things from the purses my parents' guests deposited in the cloak closet, but rarely enough to be noticed. For example, if I found five twenties in a purse, I would take one, making sure not to disturb anything else in the purse. This soon bored me as it is not much fun to steal something if no one knows it is missing. So, I began to take small objects – a lipstick, a comb, a compact. Occasionally, from my vantage point above the entrance gallery, I would hear one of the women say "I *know* I put my lipstick in here before we left home". Her husband would reply irritably, "Well, I guess you just *thought* you did," further annoying his wife.

Most often, though, my thefts went unnoticed, or at least unremarked upon, which was disappointing, so I began stealing things which had to be noticed while our guests were still in the house. One rainy night while my parents and their guests were having dinner in the dining room, I stole two of the six umbrellas in the cloak closet. These I hid in an old trunk in one of the storage rooms, then waited in my hiding place above the gallery. This was excellent. I heard phrases like *"Where the hell could an umbrella go?"* and *"I know I brought the damn thing in from the car,"* and on and on. Other treasures included two ladies' evening wraps, and a man's straw hat, all of which joined the umbrellas in the trunk in the storage room. Some of the guests became very annoyed, one of whom said "Well, we can't come here if our things are going to disappear!" My parents were mortified and suspected one of the servants but couldn't pin anything on any of them. That I was responsible was never even considered. So, that was my beginning. It came to an end soon enough, though, as summer was over and we moved back to New York.

Max talks about school being a big, unhappy change for him. For me, it was an escape. My school was The Brook, a private school for boys which dated back to 1870. Like Max, my parents applied for admission within days, or maybe even hours, of my birth. Because there is so much competition for available spaces in the top New York City private schools, my father sent large contributions to The Brook every year and even endowed a new library. The Admissions Committee had little choice but to accept me. Later, the administration would find it impossible to expel me even if I caused mischief, which I certainly did. Getting rid of a troublemaker was just not worth watching the money dry up.

While I escaped the Schwimmers, if only for a few hours a day, my first years at The Brook were a bit daunting in their own right. There were one hundred fifty boys spread among six grades, or classes. My class had twenty students until one of the Kennedys wanted in, then there were twenty-one. I suppose it is always intimidating being the newest, youngest and smallest group of boys at school. It certainly was for me, although the sixth graders generally just ignored us. There were a couple who would bump into us on purpose in the corridors or knock books out of our hands, but the proctors and teachers were pretty observant and that kept bullying to a minimum.

I didn´t start causing trouble at school until I was about ten, just after the summer I started stealing stuff from my parents´ friends in Newport. Again, I credit myself with being smarter – or at least cleverer – than Max at this point because I was never caught, although I was certainly under suspicion repeatedly. My first target was two seniors who were best friends and the two biggest boys in school. They were also mean and would often punch younger boys in the arm if they thought none of the faculty was looking, or knock over your milk at lunch, or whisper "fag" as they walked by. None of this was ever reported, of course, for fear of having the crap beat out of you outside school. The boys were Mark Rogers and Frederick Stapleton.

One afternoon, I stole an expensive science textbook out of Mark´s locker. My heart was racing as I left school with the book and hid it away in my bedroom in our townhouse. I kept it there for several days. In the meantime, there was a hue and cry at The Brook about the theft with instant expulsion promised for the thief. Three days later, I put the book in Frederick Stapleton´s locker where it was discovered on what was then a daily search of all lockers. Mark and Frederick actually got into a serious fist fight in the corridor, which I watched until the proctors broke it up. Frederick was never expelled, but the incident ended his friendship with Mark and both boys left The Brook with unfavorable references. Years later, when Max told me about hiding one nun´s lunch in another nun´s locker, I just couldn´t believe the similarity. Maybe that´s when I knew how much in sync we were.

My greatest triumph at The Brook came when I was twelve years old, just a few months before graduation. In that last year, our class was organized like a junior high or high school so that we moved from classroom to classroom throughout the day studying different subjects under different teachers. We were also introduced to subjects not usually taught in grammar school, the better to prepare us for what was next in our academic lives. One of these classes was An Introduction to Science which covered a little bit of everything – chemistry, geology, astronomy and biology. Nothing in much depth, obviously. The biology piece involved dissecting a frog. There was one for each of the twenty-one students and we worked on them for probably ten or fifteen minutes three times a week. Each frog had a tag on its left leg identifying the student responsible for its dissection. This made it possible for the teacher to grade each student´s work at the end of the project. When the frogs were not being worked on under the direction of Mr. Minasian, they were kept in a huge jar of formaldehyde on his work table.

My best friend in the sixth grade was Bobby Maxwell, the son of a newspaper and magazine publisher who lived around the corner from us on Park Avenue. My mother encouraged this relationship because Bobby´s father owned the newspaper in which the society columnist Aileen Mehle ("Suzy") appeared and which my mother read before she did anything else at all in the morning. If her name appeared in that day´s column – Sybil *Peabody* Radcliffe – we had a very good day at the Radcliffe home.

Anyway, Bobby and I were fast friends and, it so happened, seat mates in Mr. Minasian´s science class. Bobby was a good student overall, but science eluded him, particularly our biology assignment.

His frog looked like it had been attacked with a meat cleaver instead of the small scalpel we were given for the dissection. And each day it looked worse. When Mr. Minasian handed out the frogs, he always looked at Bobby's with disgust. I wanted to help my friend because Bobby had been provisionally admitted to Choate, a very fine prep school in Connecticut, and an "F" in science could have wrecked his chance of going there. So, I did what a good friend would do.

I snuck into Mr. Minasian's class early one morning, opened the formaldehyde-filled jar and cut off the left leg of each frog, thereby separating the ID tag from the body of the frog. Afterwards, I went into the boys' room and spent fifteen minutes scrubbing my hands and forearms to make sure no trace of the foul-smelling liquid could be detected on me. I then went to my first period English class and my second period math class before going to Mr. Minasian's third period science class. I didn't learn anything about English or math in those two hours, but I was able to calm down and get myself under control for what was sure to follow.

Bobby Maxwell was pretty dejected that day. This was our last day with the frogs and he knew he had no hope of a passing grade. As he always did on Monday, Wednesday and Friday, Mr. Minasian opened the frog jar and removed the first frog, minus its left leg. I could tell he was stunned, but he had not yet recognized the reality of what he would find with each frog he extracted. Mr. Minasian is Armenian and, like many Armenians, dark skinned. It is hard for dark skinned people to turn purple, or even to blush, but turn purple he did. To this day, I have no idea what he said when the carnage was revealed. It could have been Armenian or it could have been jibberish following a small stroke, but whatever he said was not something any of us understood. That was probably for the best because he was in no condition then to question us about the mutilations.

Mr. Minasian did manage to leave the classroom on his own and to return soon thereafter with the head master and two proctors so his language skills must have returned quickly. After pointing out the "heinous crime" – his words – to the head master, one of the proctors led Mr. Minasian out of the classroom to the teachers' lounge. I did not see him again that day. The headmaster, Matthew Worthington, gave us a stern talking to and demanded to know who was responsible for mutilating the frogs. Again, I remind you that I was, at least then, smarter than Max, because I did not raise my hand. Of course, no one else did, either, and there was really no way for Mr. Worthington to pry the truth from one of twenty-one boys who all denied responsibility.

Days later, it was decided that the frog dissections would not be counted as part of our final science grade. Bobby Maxwell had received passing grades – some just barely – on the other science components so he graduated from The Brook and went on to Choate. We saw each other with some frequency over the next few years as Choate and Deerpark are not far apart and we also spent time together on school holidays. He knew what I'd done but we never spoke of it. I think he also suspected I was responsible for some of the mischief which occurred at Deerpark during my time there and later at Columbia University, but we never spoke of that, either.

FOUR
Maximilian Van Zuylen

My graduation from St. Mary´s Country Day School, in June, 2001, was pretty much a non-event. Mike went with me and we left just as soon as the little ceremony was over. Both my parents, together with Denise Hale and Ann Getty, were in New York at a luncheon Graydon Carter, the editor of *Vanity Fair*, was hosting at his restaurant, the Monkey Bar. The *San Francisco Chronicle* published pictures of the group the following morning which I was told to save in a phone call from my mother. She didn´t mention the graduation.

A few days later, just shy of my thirteenth birthday, we moved, as we did each year, from San Francisco to Napa for the summer. When I say "we", I mean my parents, Mike and me. Even at almost thirteen, my parents felt I needed supervision, or a companion, or both, during the summer holiday. Not long after settling in, we four had lunch together on the stone terrace overlooking the valley. This was an unusual occurrence as my parents usually entertained at lunch and even if they didn´t, Mike and I mostly ate our meals separately. Anyway, at this lunch, I was informed that I would be attending Deerpark Academy in Greenwich, Connecticut in the fall.

Applications to Deerpark, Choate and several other east coast boarding schools had apparently been made shortly after my birth to assure placement. I don´t know why Deerpark was chosen, but that is where I was headed and where I would live for the next six years. Mike would continue living in the penthouse, at least for the foreseeable future, so he and I could spend time together on school vacations. I was grateful this news was given to me at the end of lunch because it certainly took away whatever appetite I had left.

Later, Mike came to see me in my room. "Did you know about this?" I asked.

"No. Of course not."

I am glad he didn't hug me because I might have started to cry. "I really wish I could stay home."

"And I wish you could, too, buddy. Just remember, if you do well at Deerpark, and you will, you are almost guaranteed admission to any university in the world. And, there are lots of school holidays when you will come home."

"I still have to pass the interview. Maybe I could tank that."

"Don't think that way, Max. Give it your best shot. This may be the best experience you ever have." I didn't think so.

In any event, three weeks later, the four of us flew on my father's plane to New York. Why Mike had to come along, I didn't know, but I was glad for his company. My parents owned a two bedroom apartment in the Sherry Netherlands on Fifth Avenue, so we stayed there that night. Mike and I had room service from the hotel dining room while my parents went around the corner to La Grenouille, their favorite restaurant in the city.

"I must seem like a big, fucking nuisance to them," I said to Mike while we ate hamburgers at the window overlooking the park.

"No, Max. They're just trying to give you the best education possible. Not everyone gets to go to such a good school."

"Bullshit. One kid was one too many. Back here, I'm outta sight, outta mind, not that they ever paid any attention to me in San Francisco." Somehow, my language went south when I turned thirteen.

That night, I lay in bed in the room I shared with Mike wondering if I could burn down the place, or whether I should jump out the window, or just run away. Running away seemed like a good idea except that I didn't have any money and didn't know where I could go. So, after these ruminations, I went to sleep thinking *fuck it!*

We left the hotel shortly after eight the following morning for the drive to Greenwich. Actually, Deerpark is not in Greenwich. I guess you could call it Greenwich-adjacent. After learning I would be attending the school, and living there, I had spent quite a bit of time on the school's website. Among other things, I learned that Deerpark had places for six hundred fifty students on its four hundred thirty seven acre campus. All were boys and all were boarders. Students, according to the site, came from all over the United States and from over thirty foreign countries. Photos of the campus showed a spectacularly beautiful country setting on the north shore of Long Island Sound. Then, again, they wouldn't publish ugly pictures, right?

I learned that students lived in halls – many named after trees, some, apparently, after Catholic saints – with twenty-eight lower form students and four upper form students to each hall. Here, we lower form students would live, sleep, study and eat under the watchful eye of four masters who would undoubtedly do whatever was possible to make our lives miserable. Deerpark offered all the normal junior high and high school courses, plus optional immersion courses in foreign languages and environmental science. There were also extensive sports programs in every sport I had ever heard of. Deerpark, according to the website, stressed both academic excellence and athleticism for its students.

I had time to think about all this on the way to Greenwich as there was little conversation in the car. For the interview, my mother had packed a blue blazer, grey slacks, a stiff white shirt and black loafers. Very preppy. As we drove onto the campus, I had to admit that the place looked pretty special. It was really like a giant park with buildings set among the trees. There was more lawn here than I had ever seen in one place, except maybe for Golden Gate Park.

The administration building, Deerpark Hall, occupied pretty much the geographical center of the campus. The bas relief above the door said "Founded 1860". We were met at the building entrance by one of the masters who was working on campus for the summer. He explained to my parents and Mike that they might like to take a stroll around the campus – he actually used the word "stroll" – as I would be meeting with Mr. Morrison, the head of Deerpark admissions, alone. My parents could join us in about an hour.

Stephen Graff, the master, walked me into the building, one hand on my shoulder as he led the way to Mr. Morrison's office. This irritated me, although I couldn't say why, exactly. The admissions group occupied the west wing on the first floor of Deerpark Hall. There was a reception area outside the offices where another master sat behind a desk checking in arrivals.

"Name, please."

"Max Van Zuylen." He put a check mark on the paper in front of him, presumably by my name. "Take a seat, Van Zuylen."

Stephen Graff and I sat down in two of several chairs in the waiting area. It was a pleasant enough space, very masculine, with dark paneled walls and dark stained hardwood floors partially covered with oriental-looking rugs. Leaded glass windows on one side of the room looked out to a well-manicured garden. Stephen had little to say. He was probably bored stiff showing prospective first term boys into and out of the building. After a few minutes, the door to a corner office opened and a couple came out with their son in tow. They spent a moment saying good-bye to someone inside I could not see, then left.

"Okay, Max. Let's go," Stephen said. He led me to the door, knocked once, then opened it and indicated I should go inside. A man in his early sixties, or so I thought, walked across the room and held out his hand.

"Charles Morrison," he said, "and you are Maximilian Van Zuylen." We shook hands and then Mr. Morrison led me to a pair of leather chairs beside a large, stone fireplace. The office looked like one of the rooms at San Francisco's Pacific Union Club, again very masculine and comfortable. Mr. Morrison's desk was in front of more leaded glass windows looking into the garden.

"What do you like to be called, Maximilian?" he asked.

I decided not to be a dick. "My parents call me Max, sir, and the boys at school usually call me Z."

"Z it is, then." He seemed nice enough. He was glancing at some papers in his hand. "Very fine academic record at St. Mary's, young man." It was a good record and I could thank Mike for always helping me with homework when I needed it.

"Thank you, sir."

"What prompted your interest in Deerpark, Max?" He seemed to have forgotten Z.

"Actually, sir, my father thought boarding school would be a good idea for me …"

"And, what do you think of the idea?"

"To be honest, sir, I´m not sure. It´s a long way from home and I´ve always lived at home."

Mr. Morrison smiled. "We have boys here from all over the world, Max. I always ask them that question, and the ones who tell me the truth tell me exactly what you just did. Boarding school is a tremendous adjustment for every student, but it can also be one of the best periods in your life."

"I hope so, sir."

"Now, tell me about this incident with Sister Margaret." This came out of nowhere and I am sure I stammered as I tried to answer.

"Well, it was a prank and I know it was wrong. I was punished for it."

"Yes, that´s in here, too." Was he trying not to smile? I couldn´t tell. He went on. "Whenever you have six hundred fifty boys together, as we do at Deerpark, there will be pranks from time to time. Sometimes it´s a joke played by one boy on another; sometimes it´s stretching school rules. When that happens, and we know who is responsible, the student is punished. We don´t beat our students but we take away their privileges."

He paused. "Here´s what I want you to understand, Max. Serious infractions of our rules can and do result in either suspension or expulsion, depending on the gravity of the offense. It´s very important to understand that, Max, because an expulsion from Deerpark is a mark which stays with you and may well prevent your admission to another quality secondary school or later to the university of your choice. You have a fine record from a very good primary school. I hope you realize how important it will be for you to continue that record here at Deerpark."

I wondered if the water balloon incident would stay on my record forever. "Yes, sir. I understand."

"Good then. Max, I am pleased to tell you that the Admissions Committee of Deerpark is offering you a place in our first form class.

Congratulations and welcome!" Mr. Morrison stood and I followed suit. We shook hands, and then Mr. Morrison turned to his desk and retrieved a thick notebook with Deerpark Academy emblazoned across the front.

"Have you looked at our website, Max?"

"Yes, sir."

"Well, this binder has much more detailed information than the website and should answer many of the questions you have now, or may think up later, about our school. Anytime you think of something which you don´t find in the binder, pick up the phone and give us a call or send us an e-mail. We want our new students to have answers to as many questions as possible before their first day here. It will help with the adjustment, believe me."

Mr. Morrison gave me the binder, and said, "Let´s invite your parents to join us for a few moments, then one of our masters will give you and your family a guided tour of Deerpark." With that, he turned again to his desk, pressed a button and asked the master at the reception desk to invite Mr. and Mrs. Van Zuylen to join him in the office.

I don´t remember much of the conversation we four had in Mr. Morrison´s office. Pleasantries, mostly. What I do remember is that my mother scraped, bowed and fawned as she might if meeting Queen Elizabeth II. For a moment, I wondered if Mr. Morrison regretted his offer to accept me. Apparently not, as we were soon escorted into the reception area and a master by the name of James Fairfield, a junior from London, asked us to join him for a tour of Deerpark. Mike Smith met us in front of Deerpark Hall and we all boarded a stretch golf cart for the tour. I sat in front with James so I could hear his explanations of what we were seeing.

We rode mostly on gravel paths, sometimes on the grass. We did not go inside any of the buildings, but James told me about many of them. The majority were residence halls. There were twenty one, each housing about thirty two boys. All of the buildings, except for the athletic complex, were old looking – Tudor architecture, my mother said. We passed other buildings which James said were classrooms. He explained that the average classroom size was twelve students and told me with so few students in each class, there was no hiding from the professor. Actually, I was used to that at St. Mary's. The athletic facilities were apart from the rest of the campus and consisted of a full-size soccer field and baseball diamond and multiple tennis courts. Inside the sports complex, James said, were an Olympic-size swimming pool, gymnasium, weight room – which he said was awesome – basketball court, lockers, showers, "etc., etc."

We also passed by the student union where students could just hang out and where mixers with girls' boarding schools were held. In this building were also held school assemblies and graduation ceremonies, James explaining that the theatre inside the building held seating for seven hundred.

It *was* impressive and I began to feel a little better about going to Deerpark, although I was still mightily pissed at my parents for simply deciding I should be sent there without any consultation or opinion from me. I did not sulk in front of James, though, as I did not want him to think I was an asshole in case we met up in the fall.

The tour lasted a little over an hour. James let us out of the golf cart in front of the administration building and we walked to our waiting car. From Greenwich, we drove directly to Westchester Airport in New York where my father's plane was waiting to fly us back to San Francisco. Because of the time change traveling west, we landed at San Francisco International Airport at four-thirty which was fine with my parents because they had an eight o'clock dinner engagement at their friends the Wilseys in Napa.

Both limousines were waiting for us at Butler Aviation, the general aviation facility just north of the main airport. Apparently, we had had enough togetherness and my parents didn't want to spend the ten extra minutes it would take to drop Mike and me at the penthouse where we were going to stay for a couple of weeks. I had a fair amount of required and suggested summer reading from Deerpark and my parents thought it would be easier to find the books I needed in San Francisco than in Napa. Also, there would be fewer distractions in the

City and I could concentrate on the binder Mr. Morrison had given me plus the books I was to buy.

In truth, I was glad to be alone with Mike and the staff on the forty-second floor. I had a lot to sort through, a lot to think about, after my brief visit to Deerpark. Mike and I ate dinner at a little bistro on Jones Street, then went to a movie in the Marina. Afterward, Mike bought me an ice cream cone. I could tell he felt sorry for me, although neither of us talked about the events of the day.

Back home, I went to my room, undressed and climbed into bed. I actually liked what I saw of Deerpark. Mr. Morrison seemed like an okay guy, although I wasn't sure how much I would see of him at school. Stephen Graff, the first master I met, seemed like a bit of a jerk, but I liked James Fairfield, the upper classman from London. I fell asleep trying to decide whether to follow Mr. Morrison's recommendation about maintaining a good record or to be a dick and get thrown out. Tough decision.

FIVE
William Radcliffe

The summer before I started at Deerpark was a mixed bag. We were in Newport, Rhode Island, as usual, and the Schwimmers weren´t with us. They had been dismissed – "retired," my mother said – and were now back in wherever-the-hell they lived in Germany. I did enough damage to their apartment in our townhouse – nothing really serious, just enough to require a plumber and painters – to guarantee they would never again be part of the Radcliffe household. My mother actually sent them a letter in Germany complaining about the condition in which they left their rooms. Served them right.

That was the good news. The bad news was that that asshole Morrison from Deerpark admissions had loaded me down with this humungous binder "which I *strongly encourage* you to study carefully" and a lengthy summer reading list which was "*required* reading". What a prick! I might as well be in summer school. I also received envelope after envelope from Deerpark. One of them told me I got to choose one elective for my first term year. *One!* Spanish, French, German or Arabic. *Arabic! What the fuck!* Another told me my first term roommate was Maximilian Van Zuylen. *What kind of a name is that?* I would obviously be rooming with some German or Dutch immigrant for whom English was a second language. Worse, he lived in San Francisco, home of the fruits and nuts. Undoubtedly a fag.

This same envelope told me I would have a different roommate for each of the first four years at Deerpark in order to spend time with many different students; then, as a junior and senior, I could choose who I wanted to room with. At least I would only be stuck with this Van Zuylen prick for one year.

A third envelope informed me Van Zuylen and I would be sharing suite twelve on the second floor of Cedar Hall, where we would live with thirty other boys, including four upper classmen, or masters.

Each "suite" consisted of two rooms – one for living and studying and one for sleeping, plus a private bathroom. In addition, Cedar Hall, like all the other residence halls, had a big recreation room on the first floor and a dining room where we would take all our meals together.

I had actually been to Deerpark a couple of times as my cousin, Alex, went there and graduated in June, so much of what I read about the place I already knew. I actually liked the place if it was possible to like school. Maybe I could ask for a different roommate – sorry, *suitemate* – so I wouldn't have to room with some stupid foreigner who might even be a terrorist.

I didn't steal anything out of the cloak closet that summer. There were probably two reasons: first, it got boring repeating myself over and over again; and second, I was pretty sure my mother had asked one of the servants to keep an eye on the closet, so there was a good chance I would be caught if I tried to take anything. That didn't mean the summer was mischief free, though.

The husband of one of my mother's friends, a man named Walter Winger, was a big show-off. He loved to brag about how much money he had and spent – a new fifty thousand dollar watch, a painting he bought at auction for a huge price, and on and on. One evening the Wingers showed up for dinner driving a Rolls Royce convertible, the special edition which had the doors opening from the front instead of the rear. A real beauty. What I wanted to do was key the car but that was too dangerous because our gates were always kept closed and that would mean the key job had been done by someone on the property. No, I was too clever for that. Instead, I snuck into the garage and found a tool which allowed me to let the air out of his tires. Not all of them, just one.

When the party was over, Mr. Winger was anxious to show the car to all of the departing guests so they left mostly as a group and went into the motor court. And there it was, his gorgeous Rolls Royce with the left front tire flat as a pancake. You would have thought someone had been shot. I never heard such bitching and moaning and, of course, he got no sympathy from any of the other guests. "You paid *how much* for that thing, Walter, and it only came with *three* good tires?"

This went on for some time until our butler called a twenty four hour tow service to fetch the car. Twenty minutes later, a big flat-bed truck came down our driveway. Then things just kept getting worse. Mr. Winger and the tow truck driver got into a heated argument about how the car should be hitched up and winched onto the flat-bed and where the car should be taken once it was on the truck. Finally, the tow truck driver got so pissed off he got back in his truck and drove away, leaving the Rolls Royce in our driveway. Since our butler could not find another twenty four hour tow service in the phone book, there was nothing for Mr. and Mrs. Winger to do but hitch a ride with one of the other guests and leave the car where it was until the Rolls Royce people could be summoned in the morning. This was excellent! The best time I had all summer.

Just after Labor Day, we packed up our things and headed to Manhattan so I could get ready for Deerpark. My mother made a big deal of organizing my things for boarding school, but, really, there wasn't much to do except pack my clothes and the personal things I would be allowed to take, iPad, iPod, PC. Cell phones were strictly prohibited so the one I had would have to stay in New York.

SIX

William Radcliffe

Deerpark Academy opens its fall term with an orientation weekend for first term students. The only other students on campus are some of the seniors – kiss-ups, probably – who volunteer to show us around and explain what we already know from reading Mr. Morrison´s binder. Boring as hell. Plus, I would have to meet my faggot foreigner roommate, Maximilian.

On the appointed Saturday, we left Manhattan for the drive to Greenwich. I wanted to go alone with Jacob, our driver, but my mother insisted on going, too, so she could make sure I got properly settled in my new rooms. *Great! Thirteen years old and my mother has to unpack for me.* I just hoped the Van Zuylens would arrive after she left and not see any of this. In the end, my father came, too, so the four of us arrived at Deerpark and were greeted near the administration building by one of the volunteer seniors who helped Jacob load my luggage onto a golf cart and then drove us to Cedar Hall.

Most of the student rooms, including suite twelve, were on the second floor of Cedar Hall, with the first floor space taken up by the large recreation room, dining room, kitchen, and suites for the four seniors, or masters, who would watch over us. The second floor was organized in a "U" shape with all the rooms opening onto a central hallway. Suite twelve was on the northeast corner of the building and the door was standing open. This meant only one thing – the Van Zuylens were already there. We walked into the sitting room which was a nice room with plenty of windows. Two desks faced one wall which was surfaced in cork board so you could pin up notes, pictures, schedules or whatever. On each desk was yet *another* welcoming letter from Deerpark Academy. There were also two lounge chairs separated by a table near one of the windows. No television, I noticed.

My parents and the Van Zuylens introduced themselves. They looked normal for foreigners and spoke without any accent I could detect. "Max is just through there," Mrs. Van Zuylen said, indicating a doorway which led to the bedroom. I walked in to find Max with his back to me hanging up some clothes in the closet. He turned around and for a minute I thought I was looking into a mirror. We were both about the same height, big for thirteen at just under 6´. We had slim builds, short brown hair, blue eyes and light complexions. Max spoke without an accent, and he didn´t look like a fag or a terrorist. I couldn´t believe it.

"Max," he said, holding out his hand.

"Will ... I guess we´re roommates," I responded, sounding dumb and stating the obvious.

"Yes, I think so. Good to meet you, Will."

It was awkward, and I can´t really say we bonded at that first meeting, but we weren´t apart that weekend except when one of us used the bathroom. I know we were both relieved when our parents finally left. There we were, in a suite we would share for the year. It felt okay.

The weekend schedule was spelled out in a sheet on top of the welcome folder on our desks. We would have dinner with our hall mates downstairs at 6:30 p.m., then meet in the student union at 8 p.m. for a formal welcoming to Deerpark and an introduction to the senior administration members and the professors who would be teaching the first-form students. Sunday was "open" and we were encouraged to explore the campus, meet as many of our hall mates and other first-termers as possible, and make use of the athletic facilities. Classes were to begin at eight a.m. – sharp – on Monday.

Max and I sat together at dinner in Cedar Hall. We met, or at least said hello to, most of the other hall residents, including all four of the seniors whose job it was to look after us. They seemed cool except for one, Andre Obregon, who seemed like a tight ass. After dinner, we walked together to the student union and listened to a rehash of the stuff we had been "*strongly encouraged*" to study carefully in Mr.

Morrison's binder. We then went back to our suite in Cedar Hall, finished unpacking the little of our things that remained packed, and climbed into our beds around 10:30 p.m. That's when we bonded, I think. We told stories of our lives before Deerpark, our families, the schools we went to, even some of the mischief we caused. I loved Max's story of the water balloon and Sister Margaret and gave him a full "10" for that. He, in turn, gave me a ten for what I did to the frogs in Mr. Minasian's class and a ten-plus for the Rolls Royce mischief. We were definitely going to be best pals. I felt badly thinking he was probably a foreign faggot terrorist, my last thoughts before falling asleep.

SEVEN
Maximilian Van Zuylen

I couldn´t believe how much Will and I looked alike. More than that, we *were* alike. He had that "edge" New York boys have, but otherwise we could have been brothers. We had two classes together, first period Spanish, our one elective – "gotta be able to talk to the spic chicks, man" – and fourth period algebra, right before lunch. We also had gym at the same time, right after study hall, but we were assigned to different sports. Will played soccer; I was in gym class.

All in all, I liked Deerpark though I never gave my parents the satisfaction of telling them, not that they would have cared much one way or the other. I missed Mike, my parents not so much. Will was cool, though. Mike was ten years older, Will was my age, and with classes plus our meals plus living together, we spent more time with each other than with anyone else at Deerpark.

Will was obsessed with getting laid, thus our first trip to New York together where instead of meeting girls in Harlem, we attended a Broadway musical and a Yankees game. Not the same at all. He kept telling me we were going to be the oldest virgins at Deerpark even though we both knew the stories many of the other boys told about their conquests were pure crap. Anyway, one afternoon, I came back to our suite to find Will hunched over his desk copying his mother´s signature onto a letter he had written authorizing him to take the train from Greenwich into New York City and for me to accompany him as the Radcliffes´ guest. So, I called my mother and asked her to write a letter giving me permission to go to the Radcliffes. I asked her to sign it, scan it and e-mail it to my computer. She was only too happy to oblige as she thought the Radcliffes were quite acceptable socially and very much approved of my associating with Will and with his parents.

Even though we had one good forgery and one legitimate letter from my mother, we turned them into the administration mid-afternoon on Friday when the staff was thinking more about the weekend than anything else and not likely to scrutinize the letters too thoroughly. We were admonished to get them in sooner next time but were nevertheless given signed passes for the weekend. The next morning, just before noon, we were picked up from the administration parking lot in a taxi and driven to the Greenwich train station.

It was a cold, gray day in late-October. Will would never admit it, but we were both extremely nervous and I was sweating. We each had a condom in our pocket and the required amount of cash. Will thought it would cost us five dollars each, but we had ten dollars each for the girl, just in case, plus taxi fare to Deerpark once we were back in Greenwich. We took the train to the One hundred Twenty Fifth Street station, then started walking west toward Broadway. It didn´t take long. A girl – young woman about eighteen or twenty – had us pegged and approached us before we had covered a full block.

"I´ll handle this," Will said.

The girl stopped directly in front of us, blocking any further progress along the sidewalk. Before Will could open his mouth, she said "fifteen for the two of you, my place upstairs". Will and I looked at each other. Seven-fifty apiece was okay, right in the middle of what we had with us. So, Will said okay and the girl turned, beckoning us to follow her. We entered a building a few doors down the street and climbed to the fourth floor where she led us into a room at the back of the building. She must have lived there, although the only furniture was a card table with two chairs and a mattress on the floor.

"Okay, who´s first?" she asked, all the while unbuttoning her blouse and removing her clothes. Will and I looked at each other. Despite his earlier bravado, Will said "You first, Max." Somehow we both got it done, although the entire experience – the entire time we were in the room – could not have been more than fifteen minutes. So, technically, we were no longer virgins.

We retraced our steps to the train station feeling about as proud of ourselves as two young men could. We didn´t talk much at first, just remembering what had happened and imagining it to have been much more awesome than it actually was. Once back at Deerpark, we couldn´t help bragging to our hall mates about what we had done. The story quickly found its way to one of the masters who lived with us in Cedar Hall. He figured we probably did not have parental permission to leave campus, particularly after we returned to Deerpark in just a few hours. One call to the Administration and a call from Administration to the Radcliffe home and our deception was discovered. For this we lost our school privileges for two weeks which meant we could only leave our rooms for meals and classes. Lesson learned: keep your mouth shut.

EIGHT

William Radcliffe

Max and I didn't get into any other trouble that year, although we should have. We pulled two pranks for which we could have been suspended or maybe even expelled. One involved two of the masters who lived in Cedar Hall. Most of the masters, including all four of ours, were scholarship students. Scholarships were awarded strictly on financial need, not academic merit because everyone at Deerpark was superior academically. These were the students who couldn't afford to go there without help. In return for serving as a master in the residence halls and watching over the younger boys, these students' tuition was reduced. Many of them didn't receive spending money from home, either, so the school offered part-time jobs on campus for which they were paid an hourly wage. The masters in Cedar Hall were Andre Obregon, a senior from Mexico City, Charles Washington, a junior from Oregon, and Steve Benson and Pierre Balaise, both seniors. Steve came to Deerpark from New Jersey, Pierre from France. Steve and Pierre were both pretty cool guys, although Pierre was the one who turned us into the Administration for our unauthorized exit from campus. Andre and Charles, on the other hand, were generally assholes, particularly Andre who was always looking for some rule infraction so he could take away school privileges.

Max and I were determined to screw with Andre and Charles. This would require careful preparation and execution. Our plan was to put deer shit in four locations in their rooms: just inside the door, in one of Andre's running shoes – Andre was the worst of the two – and under their pillows. Finding deer shit was the easy part, as at least two families of deer roamed the park-like campus. The gardeners spent part of their time picking up and disposing of deer droppings. We just had to get to some of it first.

Andre and Charles both had campus jobs. Andre worked the campus switchboard from four to six p.m. Monday through Friday. Charles picked up mail from the Administration building and drove it around in a golf cart to each of the twenty one residence halls. His hours were variable but usually about four to six p.m. Thursday through Saturday. Another student delivered the mail Monday through Wednesday.

We had a window of time when both Andre and Charles would be out of Cedar Hall. We had to put the deer shit in their rooms on either a Thursday or Friday between four and five, just to be sure Charles didn't finish the mail delivery early and catch us while we were still in their suite.

The most difficult part of the plan was going to be access to the suite. For this we would need a key. Getting it would be the risky part. In the end, it was easy. Like most of the Cedar Hall residents, Andre and Charles only locked their door when they left Cedar Hall for class, their jobs or for some other reason. Nobody much worried about thefts and they were practically unheard of at Deerpark. So, a couple of nights after we devised this part of the plan, Max and I went into the dining room at seven p.m., as usual. Andre and Charles were already there. Watching over us at mealtime and making sure everyone behaved was one of their responsibilities as masters. After everyone was seated and into their dinner, I got up to go to the bathroom which was located just off the recreation room and next to Andre's and Charles' suite. Instead of going into the bathroom, I walked a few more feet down the hall and tried the door to their suite. It was unlocked, as I thought it would be. I walked in, closed the door and opened the center drawer in the first desk I came to. There, in a little tray, was a key to their room attached to a Deerpark key chain. I took the key, left the room and returned as quickly as I could to the dining room. No one, it seemed, paid any attention to my leaving or returning.

It turned out that the key I took belonged to Charles. We heard him asking several of our hall mates if they had seen a key lying around in the dining room or the recreation room. No one had, of course. Within a couple of days, he gave up looking and got a copy from the administration. Now we had access. All that remained was to collect the deer shit and put it in their suite on a Thursday or Friday afternoon. We waited until Sunday because that was the one day of the week the gardeners did not work and we didn´t want to run into any of them while collecting the droppings. We found what we needed in a field quite apart from the main parts of campus and deposited the shit in four zip-lock bags which Max had pilfered from the store room at Cedar Hall where kitchen supplies were kept. We added a bit of snow which had fallen overnight so the droppings would not dry out, sealed the bags and hid them in the back of our closet.

We decided to place the deer shit in Charles´ and Andre´s suite on Thursday. There was usually more activity in the hall on Friday with boys just hanging out or preparing to leave for the weekend. The hours we had available were pretty good ones as most boys were in their rooms studying in the afternoon, usually not coming out until just before dinner time. At just after four, we put on our winter coats and each of us put two of the zip-lock bags in our pockets. We walked downstairs, then into the short corridor where Charles´ and Andre´s suite was located. Had anyone seen us in the corridor, they would have assumed we were either going into or just coming out of the bathroom located there. We saw no one. We tried the door to the suite and found it locked. Max used the key we had and unlocked it. We intended to leave it unlocked so the boys would think it had been left unlocked all along, and not that a stolen key had been used to gain access. Depositing the droppings took no time at all. Andre´s running shoes were by the foot of his bed. I filled the left shoe with the contents of one of the bags and deposited my second bag under his pillow. Max put his first bag´s contents under Charles´ pillow and then emptied the other bag very near the door to the suite where someone might easily step in it. We left the suite, again seeing no one, and walked out of the hall.

Our plan was to walk to the student union and deposit the soiled bags in one of the trash bins there. We also wanted to get rid of the key and decided to just drop it on the ground somewhere along the way. If it was found – and it probably would be – it would be turned into the administration and no one would think more about it. Max was extremely nervous, I could tell. We had to keep walking until he calmed down or we would risk becoming suspects when the deed was discovered. By the time we had thrown away the bags, lost the key and were walking back to Cedar Hall, Max seemed to calm down quite a bit. We got back just before six and went straight to our rooms. Now all we had to do was wait.

It didn't take long. Andre had returned to the suite first and had, indeed, stepped in the shit. You could hear him all over the hall, cursing and yelling. Many of the boys opened their doors and went out in the hall to see what the commotion was all about. We went out in the hallway, too, to avoid suspicion. A few of the older boys, who were not afraid of Andre, were laughing, the younger ones not so much. From the upper story, we could look down into the recreation room. Andre had grabbed one of the two boys who happened to be there by the shirt, dragged him to a standing position and demanded to know if he had put shit in his room. The boy stammered no and looked like he was about to cry. Andre pitched him back into the chair in which he had been sitting. He then did the same thing to the other boy before stomping off to his room, leaving deer shit tracks in his wake.

Andre and Charles were both furious at dinner, telling us they would beat the shit out of whoever did this, then make sure the guilty student was expelled from Deerpark. It was pretty quiet in the dining room. It was also pretty clear they had not found the other piles of deer droppings. Later, in our rooms, Max and I did our best to stay awake once we got into bed about ten. We needn't have worried. Shortly before eleven, there was an explosion from downstairs unlike anything I had ever heard. Apparently, both Andre and Charles had gotten into their beds and discovered shit under their pillows. Everyone in Cedar Hall was awakened by the outbursts and then by security officers who were called to the residence. All of us were rousted from our suites, most of us in pajamas, and ordered to assemble in the recreation room by the senior security officer. Andre and Charles were red-faced and pissed. They couldn't stand still and demanded to know who was responsible. The senior security officer kept trying to take charge but was constantly interrupted by one of the two boys. More than once

I had to bite my cheek to keep from laughing. We had screwed with them but good, and, as far as I knew, Andre still had not discovered the shit in his running shoe. A perfect plan, perfectly executed. Max and I were awake well past midnight, laughing quietly and congratulating ourselves on seriously fucking with these assholes.

The best part was undoubtedly the following afternoon. Andre often went running around two or two-thirty before he had to go to work on the campus switchboard. It turned out that both Andre and Charles were in their rooms when Andre tried to put on his running shoes. I was sure, even from upstairs, he was having a stroke or heart attack, or maybe both. He actually threw the shoe through his bedroom window and followed that with his desk chair. Utter insanity. Max and I locked our door and kept quiet. I don't think either one of us had felt this good – ever. Well, maybe with the Puerto Rican chick, but otherwise this was the best.

NINE

Maximilian Van Zuylen

Actually, Will did *not* tell you the best part. That was when Andre, who would positively smirk when he took away some resident's school privileges, lost his for two weeks. Yes! *He* was confined to his room except for meals, his job and classes, and he was ordered to pay restitution for the broken window and damaged chair. We had definitely fucked with him. After that, Will and I decided a breather was in order. No point pushing our luck.

For the Thanksgiving holiday, we each joined our families. Will flew to Palm Beach where he and his parents spent both Thanksgiving and Christmas. I was driven to the Westchester Airport where my father's plane was waiting to take me to San Francisco for the Thanksgiving holiday. I think what I looked forward to most at Thanksgiving was seeing Mike who I talked to regularly but hadn't seen since September. He was in his first year of law school at Hastings College of the Law, just ten minutes south of Russian Hill near San Francisco's civic center. Mike and Julius met me at Butler Aviation. I was really glad to spend some alone time with Mike. I had missed him a lot and loved listening to his tales of law school. He talked about his professors, some of whom were quite famous in their fields, and the "shitload" of work he had 24/7. His words, not mine. After a brief reunion with my parents in the penthouse, we got back in the limousine and headed to Napa Valley where my parents planned for us to spend our Thanksgiving holiday.

I enjoyed the four days I was there. My parents spent more time with me than I could remember. We four were like a family, and in some ways we really were. Mike was like an older brother to me and an older son to my parents. The weather that weekend was near perfect – warm and sunny during the days and cool in the evenings, but not cold. Mike and I played tennis and swam in the pool which my father had had heated for the weekend. My parents visited friends two of the nights I was home, but we were together the other two and Mike and I spent that time together.

Sunday morning we drove back to San Francisco, and to my surprise, my parents continued on with me to the airport. I had expected that we would drop them off at the penthouse and that Mike and I would head to the airport alone. There were hugs all around before I boarded the plane with my mother saying it would only be four weeks before Christmas vacation. They were planning something for the four of us, but it was a surprise and I was not to know what we were doing or where we were going. If Mike knew, he didn't let on.

When I got back to Deerpark about six hours later, Will was already there in our suite and he was pissed.

"Worst fucking Thanksgiving ever!"

"What happened, Will?"

"For starters, the weather in Palm Beach sucked big time. It was fucking cold, man, windy as shit, and it rained every goddamn day. Might as well have been in New York. Thanksgiving Day was the worst! We went to the home of one of my parents´ friends. Everyone there was my parents´ age or my grandparents´ - everyone except an eight-year old girl who wouldn't let me out of her sight. Followed me everywhere, the little bitch. I thought seriously of drowning her in the pool except she wouldn't go outside because it was raining. *Shit!*"

I started laughing. Couldn't help it and, of course, it only made Will madder. I thought he was going to take a swing at me, but then he started laughing, too.

"Aw, shit, Max. If I didn't have you as a buddy, I probably would off somebody." I thought he was joking, but now I know he wasn't.

The next three weeks passed quickly because we spent all our waking hours either in class or studying for mid-terms which we would take the week before Christmas vacation. Will and I were both good students, but I think everything came just a little easier for him.

TEN

Maximilian Van Zuylen

The week before Christmas vacation was pretty intense. Will was especially uptight, but in the end we both aced our exams although we would not know that for sure until we returned to school in the new year.

My Christmas surprise turned out to be two surprises. The first was that Will wanted to ride with me to Westchester Airport where my father's plane would pick me up. Will usually was driven into New York City by his family's chauffeur who then took the Radcliffes to Teterboro Airport in New Jersey for their trips to Palm Beach. Much to my surprise, Will walked out on the tarmac with me and started climbing the steps to my father's plane.

"What the hell are you doing, Will?"

"Going with you, bro. Your mom invited me, so here we go."

I couldn't believe it.

"So, where are we going?"

"Can't tell you, but you'll know soon enough."

I wanted to throttle him, but I was also thrilled we would be spending the holiday together – at least I assumed that was the plan. I watched the cabin monitor a few minutes after take-off, and it was clear we were not going to San Francisco, but somewhere to the south. It wasn't Los Angeles, either. My parents hated LA and anyway our course was taking us toward Texas, not California. Not Texas, either, because four hours into the flight we flew right over Texas and crossed the US – Mexico border, heading southwest.

"C'mon, man, where are we going?"

"Okay, Max, keep your pants on. We're going to Puerto Vallarta, Mexico. It's a beach town on the west coast, kind of in the middle part of the country."

I had never heard of Puerto Vallarta and couldn't imagine why my parents chose that place for our Christmas vacation. "Don't we need a passport to go to a foreign country?"

"I'm sure yours is on board. Mine is in my pocket." He pulled out the blue covered booklet from his rear pants pocket, showing it to me.

"How long have you known about this?"

"Since Thanksgiving. That's when your mom called us in Palm Beach and invited me. I've never heard of Puerto Vallarta, either. It's probably some little shithole, but anything is better than Palm Beach even if I have to spend the time with you." He reached across the aisle and punched me in the arm. I tried to hit back, but he moved forward just enough that I missed.

I was, of course, very glad we would be able to share the holiday even if it meant going to a place neither of us had ever heard of. It was on the beach, according to Will, so how bad could it be? Besides, my parents weren't likely to choose some dump for the holiday.

And they didn't. We flew out over the Pacific and made a big left turn. From the windows, Will and I could see a huge bay on our right – the Bay of Banderas according to the flight monitor – and land to the left with a combination of what looked like hotels, housing and agricultural fields. After a few minutes, we made a right turn and headed straight for the Bay before touching down at Diaz Ordaz International Airport. The pilots parked the plane in an area which appeared to be reserved for private aircraft. The co-pilot told us over the inter-com to keep our seats until the immigration and customs people could come aboard and check our travel documents. Max pulled out his passport and my father's steward, George, gave me mine. We filled out some little customs cards which George provided and waited.

It was only a few minutes before two uniformed officials boarded the plane, stamped our passports, collected our immigration cards and told us we were free to leave. Mike was waiting on the tarmac not far from the plane. He hugged me and shook hands with Will who he had spoken to on the phone but never met.

"What are we doing here, Mike?" I asked.

"Christmas in Mexico, buddy, and this place is awesome! Beautiful beaches, a nice little town, cobblestone streets and hot chicks in bikinis.

And, the place your parents rented is amazing. Right on the water. Two swimming pools, one built out into the ocean. Wait 'til you see it."

We settled into the back of a dark blue minivan for what turned out to be a forty minute ride south to Casa Cherokee. We passed modern looking hotels and condos not far from the airport. Then everything changed and we were in older sections of Puerto Vallarta. Here were the small bars, restaurants and shops, many of them open air, and the cobblestone streets. There was a huge boardwalk which I later learned was called the malecon. People were strolling everywhere and music was playing. Best of all, all along the ride on our right was the ocean, blue and inviting in the afternoon sun.

"What do you guys think of the weather?" Mike asked. It was about 80 degrees and sunny. "It stays like this all day and most of the night."

Will and I were thrilled. We had left Connecticut in freezing weather with snow falling. The heavy jackets we wore to the airport were still in the plane and could stay there until we flew back just after New Year's Day. After driving through the town, we continued south on the highway for two or three miles until the minivan driver turned right into a driveway and stopped in front of a very nondescript-looking house. What we saw was a beige stucco wall with a couple of carved wood doors in the center. *This was it?*

What we saw when the doors opened, however, changed everything. Past the double doors we walked into a flagstone courtyard with another pair of doors just ahead. On our left was some sort of dining pavilion and to the right what looked like an entrance to staff quarters. The courtyard, itself, was planted with yellow hibiscus. To get to the second set of doors, we crossed a small bridge over a waterfall which cascaded away to our left and disappeared into the house. Passing through the second set of double doors, we found ourselves in a reception area or entrance gallery with a wet bar on one side and stairs on the left leading to a sunken living room of such immense proportions Will said it would impress even his mother.

"Come down here and see this," Will called from the living room.

I walked down the half flight of stairs to the living room and joined

Will on the broad terrace just outside the room. Looking down, we saw the pool sixty or seventy feet below with water from the waterfall near the front door spilling into it.

"It wraps around the stairs and ends up down there," Mike said.

My parents were seemingly asleep on lounges beside the pool. Further down, maybe another twenty or thirty feet, was the ocean pool. Mike was right. It was built of large boulders in a semi-circle with small waves pouring over the top of the boulders.

"C'mon," Mike said. "Let's take your stuff down to your room. Then, we can hit the pools or the beach. Whatever."

The guest rooms were one floor down, directly below the living room. Mike had one; Will and I were to share the other. We stowed our stuff as quickly as we could and changed into bathing suits. Mike came into our room just as we were changing clothes. "We can take the stairs or ride that little train over there," he said. The 'little train' was actually a four-person funicular which connected all five levels of the estate. We chose the train and rode down two levels to the swimming pool where my parents were still asleep, then down one more level to the salt water pool built into the ocean. Last stop. The pool was on our left and a beautiful sand beach to our right.

The three of us got into the pool and just sat there with the waves splashing over the tops of the boulders. "Beats the shit out of Connecticut," Will said.

In the distance, along the beach, board surfers – maybe ten or twelve of them -- were riding the rollers to shore. Not big crashers like the ones at Bailey's Beach in San Francisco, but three to four foot waves which rolled gently toward shore giving the surfers nice, easy rides.

"I want to learn to do that while we're here," I told Will and Mike. "It looks awesome."

"There's apparently a great surfing beach about an hour and a half north of here in a little village called Sayulita," Mike said. "I read in a *Vallarta Lifestyle* magazine that surfer dudes there will rent you boards and teach you to surf for about twenty-five bucks a pop. Want to take the car one day and go there?" Mike got an enthusiastic 'yes!' from both of us.

"I'd like to do some snorkeling, Mike," Will said.

"Water in the Pacific is not as clear as it is in the Caribbean or Hawaii, but snorkeling's supposed to be pretty good down there," he said, pointing to some rocks sticking out in the water a mile or two down the coast. "Los Arcos those are called. You can take a panga there, go snorkeling and then have lunch at one of the beaches you can only get to by boat."

"What's a 'panga'?" I asked.

"There are a couple now," Mike said, pointing to two small boats passing in front of us. "You rent them at the main dock in town and they take you to any of the beaches inside the Bay."

"Awesome. Let's do that, too," Will said.

And so began the best vacation I ever had. I was with my two best friends in the world, Mike and Will. We were in an absolutely fantastic place. My parents went off most days to play golf, so it was just the three of us free to do whatever we wanted. We did go to Sayulita and rented boards and took lessons from three surfer dudes. Mike and I caught on much more quickly than Will, but he would never admit it. Another day, we took a panga from the main pier and went snorkeling at Los Arcos and ate shrimp for lunch at a beach called Las Animas, or the spirits.

We also explored the town, walking along the malecon where everyone seemed to gather to walk or relax on stone benches among the flowers or admire the brass sculptures by Colunga and Bustamante. We stopped in some of the tourist shops and bought souvenirs. I bought a tee-shirt for my dad which said "I Don't Need Google – My Wife Knows Everything". He loved it; my mom, not so much.

Some of our meals, usually breakfast or lunch, we ate in a small pavilion next to the pool. Dinners we ate on the living room terrace because it offered the best views of Puerto Vallarta and the Bay. We had dinner out a couple of nights to give the staff some time off. Once my parents took us to an Austrian restaurant, Kaiser Maximilian. *Austrian in Mexico – who knew?*

One night, Will and I were in bed when he said "I have a plan." That could only mean one thing. We were going to look for trouble.

"So, tell me, Will."

"Well, have you ever wanted to have some real money of your own, not just the crappy allowances our parents send us?"

"Of course, but robbery is not an especially good idea in Mexico. I don't think we would like the jails."

"Not robbery. A trade, kind of."

Then he told me. The house was full of masks. There were probably a hundred of them spread among the various rooms of the villa. A lot of them appeared to be quite old and depicted figures from Mexico's past, especially Aztec. Will said the old ones were very valuable and would be coveted by museums in New York, especially the Museum of Natural History and the American Heritage Museum.

"But, Will, we're *thirteen*. We just can't walk into a museum and ask how much they would give us for a couple of masks. They'll know the masks are stolen and call the police."

"I know that, jerk-off. We'll take them to a pawn shop. Those guys will take anything from anybody. They'll only give us half – or less – of what they are worth and then sell them for a big profit to one of the museums when we don't redeem the pawn ticket. It's fool-proof, man."

I wasn't so sure. Will's plan was to buy a couple of cheap masks sold at the tourist shops and "trade them" for two of the masks in the house. He said the staff would never notice and, anyway, the house was rented all the time so even if they noticed the switch, they would not know who did it.

I promised to sleep on it, but even then I knew we were in. And, I liked the plan.

The next morning, my parents left early for golf. Mike was still sleeping, so we took a taxi to the malecon and visited three tourist shops before we found one with the masks we wanted. They were cheap imitations, of course, but they looked old and authentic. We bargained a bit and got both for four hundred pesos, or about thirty-five dollars. Mike was swimming in the ocean pool when we got back to the villa so we had a window of opportunity, although undoubtedly a brief one. Will chose the two "trades", one in the library and one in the living room where there were so many masks it was hard to believe the staff would notice the change. If they ever did, we never heard about it. A perfect crime, Will kept telling me.

Our Christmas holiday ended three days later. Mike had flown to San Francisco commercial the day before because he didn't have any more time off. Will and I flew in my father's plane to Westchester Airport in New York while my parents stayed on at the villa for another week. Once we got to our suite at Deerpark, we stashed the stolen masks in the back of our closet and began settling in for the new term. Our first quarter grades were waiting for us in envelopes on our desks. We both got all A's in our academic subjects. I got a B+ in gym class and Will got an A- in soccer. He said his superior grades meant I had to be his errand boy for the next quarter. Good luck with that!

ELEVEN
William Radcliffe

Max and I were much more relaxed at Deerpark our second term. We knew the routine, we got excellent grades, although I beat him in total grade points which I pointed out until I was sure he was going to punch me, and we didn´t feel like the new boys, even though we still were. Maybe the best part was that Max and I were going to spend spring break together in New York because his parents were going to France for some big party and he wasn´t invited.

We could sell our masks in New York over the holiday. I spent several hours of free time on the computer looking up masks, their history and use in various cultures, and especially their values. I couldn´t be absolutely sure, but it looked like at least one of ours – the Aztec mask – could be worth a lot of money, probably more than ten thousand dollars. I printed some of these materials to show to the pawn shop owners. I also took a look at maybe a dozen auction house catalogs. In one of them, I saw photos of several masks to be auctioned in New York next month, one of which had an estimated value of twenty five thousand dollars. We were definitely going to pocket some serious change, even though I knew the pawn broker would screw us but good.

The weather was terrible throughout January, February and even into March. Very cold and lots of snow, a big, unwelcome change from the sun-filled days we spent in Mexico over Christmas. There was really very little to do but stay indoors and study. Our PE class was fun, though. Since sports outside were out of the question, our class divided into teams and played volleyball and basketball in the gymnasium. Max and I were on opposite teams. My team went undefeated in volleyball, but honestly that was mostly because I got the better players on my team. Basketball we pretty much split, winning some and losing some. Toward the end of the term, we went into serious study mode and both Max and I thought we did okay on our exams. It was a relief to have them over before spring break so we could kick back and enjoy our ten days in New York and make some money with our masks.

We had intended to take the train into the City, but since we were staying for over a week and had luggage, my mother sent the car for us. Just after our last exam, Jacob met us in the small parking area next to Cedar Hall and we set off.

"I'm surprised your parents are in the City, Will. I thought you guys always spent holidays in Palm Beach or Newport."

"Not this time of year. My mother likes to be in New York for the 'spring social season' as she calls it. The good news is they'll be out most nights so we'll be on our own. I already told them I'll be taking you around the City during the day. We're going to have a blast, man!"

Just the week before, around the first of April, the weather had gone from snow and/or freezing rain to spring. It was like someone had pulled a switch, and the days were now warm even though the nights remained cool. Jacob drove us south on the FDR Drive to midtown Manhattan where we started across town to our house on East Sixty Second Street.

"This is so cool, Will. I've only been to New York a couple of times and never for very long. We have the whole vacation here!"

My mother greeted us at the front door and invited us into the drawing room for tea while Jacob took our things upstairs to my rooms.

"I'm so glad you could join us, Max," she said. "Your parents are in Paris for a party?" *Here we go, I thought.*

"Yes. My Aunt Marie-Helene is throwing a big birthday party for my uncle. His seventy-fifth, I think."

"Did you say *Marie-Helene*?

"Yes, ma'am."

"Marie-Helene *de Rothschild*?" *I thought my mother might swoon.*

"Yes, that is her. Do you know my aunt, Mrs. Radcliffe?"

"Well, not really, but I have seen the Baroness at a couple of charity events here in the City. Does she ever come here to visit you?" *I could see the wheels spinning.*

"Not really, Mrs. Radcliffe. Sometimes, she comes to San Francisco to visit, but mostly my parents see her in France." *Oh, the look of disappointment.* I knew my mother was already planning to open our house to the Baroness so she could visit her beloved nephew here in the City and not have to trek to Greenwich.

We must have endured a half hour of questions from my mother about the Rothschilds, their seventeenth century hotel particular in Paris, and Ferrieres, their country estate where the Baroness de Rothschild had last year thrown a Proustian Ball, whatever that is. For some reason, that party received world-wide press. All this according to my mother. Max said he had only been to the Hotel Lambert once and never to their country home and seemed to know nothing about any balls. More disappointment. Finally, we were allowed to escape to my rooms and unpack our bags.

"What was that all about, Will?"

"My mother is the world's biggest and most obvious social climber. Just wait: In a day or two we will read about the Baroness' nephew staying with the Radcliffes while your parents are attending a 'spectacular' birthday party for the Baron. *Such bullshit!*" Max laughed, which I was glad to hear because I thought he might be pissed off at all the questions.

TWELVE
Maximilian V lan Zuylen

Will was right. We had a blast. I remember that first afternoon after we got settled at the Radcliffes in Will´s rooms. He had a big bedroom plus a sitting room, a dressing room, bath, and even a little balcony overlooking the street. We actually had the whole floor to ourselves as the Schwimmers, his caretakers, were long gone back to Germany. This was better than the forty-second floor at the Pinnacle because we had the space completely to ourselves. No nannies, no servants, no one.

After unpacking, we took a long walk in Central Park. As I mentioned, my parents had an apartment at the Sherry Netherlands, but I had only been there twice and had only seen Central Park through a car or hotel window. It is an incredible place, running fifty or fifty one blocks from south to north and two very long blocks east to west. Inside the park, there are a couple of huge ponds – maybe they are called lakes – great lawns (one of them is actually called the Great Lawn), trees, rock formations, and even a skating rink. There is also a zoo! Imagine a zoo in the center of New York City. Seals, monkeys, penguins and even a huge white polar bear swimming in a frigid enclosure. Pretty awesome!

That first evening, we stayed in with Will´s parents. At dinner, Mrs. Radcliffe kept asking me questions about my aunt and seemed quite disappointed that I didn´t know more. In truth, I had seen her once at the Sherry Netherlands, once at the Hotel Lambert in Paris, and maybe three or four times in San Francisco. She was nice enough but not all that interested in a young boy she didn´t know very well. So I am sure I was disappointing, and we didn´t see a lot of Mr. and Mrs. Radcliffe after that which was fine because Will and I could be on our own.

We did a lot of walking. New York is a great walking city, unlike San Francisco, because it is flat and you can spend hours walking around without much exertion. We visited some of the tourist spots which, I am sure, bored Will, but he never complained. We went up in the Empire

State Building to the roof deck where you can see three states - New York, New Jersey and Connecticut; to the Statue of Liberty, which Will had never seen; and we rode the subway to Greenwich Village. That was the best.

We bought hotdogs and cokes from a street vendor and sat on benches in Washington Square Park next to the bums who seemed to have taken up permanent residency there. We watched the pretty NYU coeds cross the Park going to and from classes in the surrounding NYU campus. Will said they would be hard to score with, especially since we were still thirteen, almost fourteen.

One afternoon, we crossed the Park and took the subway north on the Broadway line to a stop near Columbia University. This trip was at Mrs. Radcliffe's recommendation, or really at her insistence. She thought Will should consider the University for college. Will's complaints that we were five years away from going to college did not deter her. In the subway, Will insisted his mother had visions of our living together at Columbia, of my aunt visiting, and of her becoming BFF with the Baroness de Rothschild. I don't know if that's true, but Will was right: we did read in the *Post* about my staying with the Radcliffes while my parents were attending the Baron de Rothschild's birthday party in Paris.

The campus at Columbia, at One Hundred Sixteenth Street and Broadway, was like a self-contained space. All the buildings surrounded, and sort of enclosed, a park-like commons. There were grassy areas where students sat and talked and even studied, walkways connecting the four sides of the campus, and some benches where students sat reading, talking or just waiting for their next class. I liked it immediately and Will didn't rule it out even though his mother recommended it.

The very best day of our vacation, though, was when we sold the masks.

"Look. We're not going to pawn with the first guy, okay?" Will said.

"Okay." I was along for the ride and knew it. This was New York and Will was New York through and through. I was not.

The first pawn shop was on Fifty-Third Street near Seventh Avenue. We got there by walking down Fifth Avenue, then turning right at

Fifty-Third Street. Will had found the pawn shop in the yellow pages. It had one of the biggest ads so Will thought it was worth a try. We rang a bell on the street and entered when a buzzer announced that the lock had been released.

The owner /proprietor/whoever was a very old man, kind of hunched over, with no hair at all on top of his head and very long side-burns. He wore wire framed glasses which perched on the end of his hose and coughed frequently into a handkerchief which he held in his hand.

"What can I do for you young gentlemen?" he wheezed.

Will marched up to the counter and produced the two masks from a satchel he had with him. He explained to the old man that the masks had been given to us by our grandmother and that we needed to pawn them in order to pay for school tuition. Will produced some of the internet materials he had found and informed the man that the masks, together, were worth at least fifteen thousand dollars. "This will keep us in school," he said with a catch in his voice. I had heard him practice that little speech before so I managed not to smirk.

"Fifteen thousand dollars you say," the man said. "I can only loan you half their value, and I think they are worth more like fifteen hundred dollars, so seven hundred fifty is all I can do."

"We will just have to try someone who will be fair to us," Will said in his most crestfallen voice as he put the masks back in the satchel. "Sorry to have troubled you."

"*Asshole,*" he said as we left the shop. "*Fucking asshole*".

We visited three more pawn shops until we found one on West Forty-Sixth Street where the proprietor, a Jewish guy about thirty, allowed that the masks might be worth eight thousand dollars and agreed to loan us four thousand, actually more than we expected. "Best regards to your Grandma," he said as we walked out the door, the proprietor knowing we would never return. So, we each pocketed two thousand dollars, and in the process committed our first felony, or maybe our second: stealing the masks in the first place, then selling stolen property. I don't think either of us felt the least bit guilty.

THIRTEEN
William Radcliffe

Spring term at Deerpark was definitely the best that year. The weather was great so we spent as much time as possible outdoors. Max and I swam in the school pool and played tennis against each other almost every day. A couple of times we snuck off campus at night and went skinny dipping in the Long Island Sound. After, we would lie on the grass near the shore and stare at the stars, if it was a clear night, until we dried off.

We had two mixers that term with Smithfield Girls Academy in Guilford, Connecticut: one there and the second one at Deerpark near the end of term. At the first mixer, I met Sylvia Marshall, also a first-year student from Manhattan. Sylvia´s family lived at One Sutton Place South, a cooperative apartment building overlooking the East River, just a half-dozen or so blocks from our townhouse on East Sixty-Second Street. I could tell she wanted it. At the second mixer, we spent the whole evening together. Nothing happened, of course, because it seemed like there were two chaperones for every student. *Shit!* We did, however, exchange phone numbers and made arrangements to get together in Manhattan. Now that I had two thousand dollars in cash in my pocket that my parents didn´t know about, I could get a hotel room. Max also found a girlfriend at the mixers, a very pretty girl, Louise something or other, but she was shy and much less likely to do it as I kept reminding him.

Three weeks before the end of term, we found envelopes on our desks from Mr. Morrison, the admissions prick at Deerpark. It had *another* suggested summer reading list. *What is the matter with that asshole?* Included was a book of Spanish short stories (we were studying Spanish) and an introduction to philosophy, a class we would take next year and which Mr. Morrison said the professor would expect us to have read before class began. *Could he possibly be any more of a prick?* I was determined to fuck with him and began thinking of a plan for Max and me.

In bed in our room one night, I said "Look, Max, *I have to do this. Are you with me?*"

He said ´of course´ after pointing out that if we were caught we would be thrown out of Deerpark and probably couldn´t ever get into any school other than some New York PS for me and some equally lame public school in San Francisco for him - assuming our parents didn´t disown us first. So, he wasn´t enthusiastic, but we were "bros" and would do this together.

Our options were somewhat limited. We had never seen Mr. Morrison arrive on campus, so finding his car and keying it – or worse – was not possible. We had no idea where he lived, so sneaking off campus and doing something to his house was equally impossible. That left his office in the Deerpark administration building. The admissions group occupied the west end of the first floor in the building with Mr. Morrison´s office located in a corner in the west end overlooking the garden through stained glass windows. Sunday was the best day to do some damage because there were no administration people around, no gardeners and only a small security staff. Still, breaking into the building was out of the question because the building was alarmed and any forced entry would bring down security staff right away.

My plan was simple: break a small section of the stained glass window behind Mr. Morrison´s desk, insert a garden hose in the opening and flood the room. I could only imagine the damage! Desk, papers, rugs all ruined. *Yes! It was perfect.* I thought about going into the little hardware store in the village near school and buying one of those hoses you see on television which expand when water flows through them and retract when you turn the water off, but I was pretty sure there were none of those on campus, and I didn´t want to use something which could possibly be tied to us later. So, the only alternative was to use one of the gardeners´ hoses.

This proved not too difficult, at least in concept, because the hoses were often left in place on the lawns or flower beds when the gardeners quit for the day. The problem was they were really long – maybe one hundred feet or more – so stealing one and hiding it was not so easy. Max came up with the obvious solution: steal a hose from the gardens late on a Sunday night, connect it to a faucet at the administration building, break the little glass panel and turn it on. Instant flood! For this plan, the longer the hose the better because we could connect it to a faucet even if it was not close to Mr. Morrison´s office windows. Yes, Max was definitely in!

Max even scouted the administration building one day and noticed a faucet not all that far away from Mr. Morrison´s office. Now, we just had to wait for Sunday. We decided that sometime between eleven thirty and midnight on Sunday would be perfect. There were very few guards on campus late at night and those who did walk patrols all carried flashlights so you could spot them from some distance and disappear before they saw you. On the appointed evening, we snuck out of Cedar Hall just after eleven and walked toward the administration building. We kept a close watch but saw no one. There might have been the beam of a flashlight three or four hundred yards away, but Max thought it was probably a window light. Anyway, we got to the administration building without incident.

It took a while, but we found a hose at the far east end of the building, lying in the grass. It was long, for sure, but not long enough to reach all the way to the west end, so we disconnected it and dragged it behind the building until we were just opposite the northwest corner of the building. Here was the faucet Max had spotted days earlier. We connected the hose and pulled it around the building until we were outside Mr. Morrison´s office. We used a knife I had copped from the dining room to force a small break in one of the stained glass panels, inserted the hose several feet so it wouldn´t fall out when water began to flow, then walked back to the faucet, turned on the hose – slowly at first – and checked to make sure it was in place before walking back to our residence hall.

Through the ground floor windows of Cedar Hall, we could see the television on in the recreation room. Not good. We did not want anyone to see us coming in at this hour especially with what was going on in the administration building, so we sat down on a nearby bench and waited. It was a warm night so being outside was no problem as long as we could eventually get inside without being detected. Our chance came about twenty minutes later when the television was turned off and the only lights on the ground floor were the security lights which stayed on all the time. We snuck in as quietly as possible, climbed the stairs and went down the hall to our suite. No one was around. We closed the door and gave each other a high five. Another perfect crime!

Climbing into bed, we fell asleep pretty quickly only to be awakened about two hours later to the sound of sirens on campus. In the distance, we could see what appeared to be fire trucks in the area near the administration building. There were maybe half a dozen vehicles of different sizes all with lights blazing. Some were police cars. Awesome! It didn't take long for the whole residence hall to be awake with many of the boys wandering into the corridor asking what was going on. Finally, one of the seniors came out of his room and told us a fire alarm had gone off in the administration building, that everything was under control, and that we should all go back to sleep NOW! Max and I went back to our rooms but had a hard time sleeping, imagining the scene in Mr. Morrison's office.

The entire campus was summoned to an emergency assembly in the student union the following morning at eleven a.m. That was fine with Max and me because we got to miss algebra. When everyone was seated, Mr. Morrison approached the podium and told us in a very solemn voice that a "deeply disturbing incident" had taken place on campus the previous evening. Can you believe it? *Deeply disturbing?* He talked on and on about a serious crime having been committed involving the destruction of tens of thousands of dollars of property. *Really, that much? Even better than I had hoped.* He said students were unfortunately and sadly suspected because there were no known visitors on campus last night.

He talked about honor, about Deerpark's tradition of fostering honesty and integrity, and asked the guilty party or parties to identify himself or themselves. No one stood, and since Max and I had talked about honesty not always being the best policy, we kept our seats, too. Mr. Morrison looked dejected. *Did he really expect some student out of six hundred fifty was going to stand up and confess to a crime which would get him thrown out of school?* Get real, asshole.

This wasn't the end of it, though. Campus police and an administration official interviewed all six hundred fifty students individually. Can you believe it? What a joke! Max and I had appointments, separately, the following afternoon. They started with the first term students, probably thinking that the bad seeds were in the newer students as opposed to those who had been at Deerpark longer.

Where were you on Sunday night? Was anyone with you? Did you go to the administration building? Blah, blah, blah. It was like a fucking TV show. Max and I stuck to our script: we were at Cedar Hall in bed by eleven p.m. until we were awaked by all the sirens at two or three in the morning. No, we hadn't heard anything else. No, we hadn't seen anything. *What dicks!* Did they really believe either one of us would stand up and say "I did it, sir".

FOURTEEN

Maxilmilian Van Zuylen

Will and I were unhappy to see the term end. Not that we wanted to stay in school. We just didn´t like our prospects for the summer. And we *really* didn´t like the fact we couldn´t room together next year.

My parents and I were spending the summer at our estate in Napa. I had liked it a lot when I was young and The Nannies would take me swimming and to the pond to look for frogs and keep me entertained pretty much all the time. Then, Mike was with us and it was even better. But, The Nannies were long gone and Mike wouldn´t be with us – maybe not at all – because he was now a summer associate at a big law firm in San Francisco and was "working my ass off 24 / 7" to quote him. He still lived in his room at the Pinnacle but told me he was only there a few hours a night to sleep. He said he even had to carry a firm cell phone with him at all times – "even in the can" – in case one of the partners wanted to heap more work on him. So, I would be on my own in Napa with no one to hang with and basically nothing to do.

Will wasn´t any happier. He thoroughly disliked Newport. "Nothing for me to do there, man. The water´s freezing, nobody anywhere near my age. You go to the Beach Club, look around and wonder why they don´t have an ambulance parked outside. Surely, one of those old farts will die at dinner." What was worse, if anything, for Will, was that Sylvia Marshall, his hoped-for girlfriend / conquest, was sailing to Europe with her grandparents on the *SS France* two days after the term ended and spending the summer at their home in Marbella, Spain.

We were bummed, to say the least. We did have one last weekend in New York at a little celebration Mrs. Radcliffe arranged to mark the end of our first year at Deerpark. My parents flew in from Napa so they could collect me and my belongings and take me back to California after the weekend. They stayed at the Sherry Netherlands. I opted to stay with Will. The first night, we had a rather stiff dinner in the

Radcliffes´ dining room with Mrs. Radcliffe asking what I thought were too many questions about my aunt and the birthday party she threw for my uncle earlier in the year. Anyway, Will and I escaped as soon as we could and spent most of the night playing video games on his TV.

The next night was better. My parents invited the Radcliffes for cocktails in our apartment and then for dinner at La Grenouille. Will and I were allowed out on our own as we were now "young men" of almost fourteen, so we went to PJ Clarke´s and ate hamburgers and chili. Awesome! It was hard saying good-bye when my parents came for me in the morning. Will and I had been inseparable at Deerpark. We looked alike – everyone said so – we pretty much liked and disliked the same things, and we were best buddies, no doubt about it. The worst part was that we would not be living together for the next three years in order to experience "diversity" at Deerpark or some such bullshit. Anyway, my father was anxious to leave so we reluctantly said good-bye, promising to talk by cell as often as we could.

FIFTEEN

Beatrice Van Zuylen

What an odd woman Sybil Radcliffe is, I thought as we flew across the country. Such an obvious social climber. God, all those ridiculous questions about Marie-Helene. But there was something more. She seemed nervous, frightened even, as though something ominous were about to happen. Oh, well, we shall see very little of her, I suppose.

Poor Max. He is sound asleep on one of the couches. I covered him with a cashmere shawl a few minutes ago and he didn´t stir. I suppose he´ll sleep all the way to San Francisco. His father and I really have to come up with something for him to do this summer. Mike is just too busy with his new job and there are really no other young men we know in Napa who might pal around with him. The Wilseys are either too young or too old and I can´t think of any other boys in the valley to invite over.

He was so unhappy to leave Will. The boys are really remarkably alike. From the back, I am not sure I could even tell them apart. Same height, same build, same hair color, and from the front, same eyes, even very similar mannerisms. Maybe that comes from living together. The only noticeable difference was Will´s distinct New York accent. That you couldn´t miss.

Frederick and I will just have to figure something out. Otherwise, I am afraid our son is in for a pretty unhappy summer.

SIXTEEN

Maximilian Van Zuylen

Julius was waiting for us at Butler Aviation when we landed in San Francisco. The plan was to spend the first night at the penthouse so I could dump my school gear and then pack for the summer. Mostly tee shirts and shorts and "one nice dress up outfit, darling," my mother said. I never saw Mike. The next morning, one of the maids told me he came in very late and left again before dawn. Well, I thought I could certainly cross lawyer off my list of possible careers.

Napa was every bit as boring as I knew it would be. Will and I talked every day by cell, mostly trading complaints about the summer. That first week, I swam every day and played tennis twice with an instructor my parents hired. Then, everything changed.

"Max," my father said one day at lunch on Sunday. It was unusual for my parents to be at home on Sunday unless they were entertaining, but it was just the three of us on the terrace. "How would you like to take a bike trip through Europe?" He went on before I could process what he was saying, much less offer an answer. "Abercrombie and Kent. You know the travel company?" I shook my head up and down although I didn´t really have any idea who or what that was. "Anyway," he said, "they are offering a six week biking tour from Amsterdam to the south of France for boys thirteen to sixteen. The group is small, only ten boys. I booked two spots in case you wanted to ask Will to go along."

I was beside myself. *"Yes! Yes! Definitely! Yes! I need to call Will,"* I said, jumping up from the table.

"Well, you better take a look at this first," my father said, handing me what looked like a travel brochure. I ran up to my room and glanced quickly through the folder. Amsterdam to the Cote d´Azur. Almost one thousand miles. Mostly biking, but some travel by train and river boat. Six weeks with an option to extend for a seventh week at a hotel on the beach in Monaco. Ten boys maximum and four tour guides. Good hotels, not hostels, all meals, etc., etc. I couldn´t wait any longer.

"Will, Will" I practically shouted into the phone, immediately launching into an apparently incoherent description of the trip.

"Max, my man, slow down. I can´t understand anything you are saying."

I started over, more slowly, and described the trip or at least as much of it as I could from my all too brief glance through the travel brochure.

"Do you think your parents will let you go, Will?" I finally managed to ask.

"I think they´d be glad to get me out of here, Max. I´ve been pretty much a shit ever since we got to Newport. Can you fax me the brochure?"

"Sure …Wait. There´s a web address. Yes, here it is. You can pull up the brochure at AKBIKE.com. Call me when you know if you can go, okay, Will?"

"Of course, but my parents are out on a boat right now with some friends so I won´t be able to talk to them for at least a couple of hours. I´ll pull up the brochure in the meantime and have it for them when they get back."

We talked some more and then hung up so Will could print the brochure and look it over. I was super excited. The last two weeks of July until Labor Day. What unbelievable luck!

It took almost four hours until Will called and I had begun to lose hope. Then, the phone call. "My dad wants to talk to your father, but bottom line, I´m in." I let out a bit of a whoop and ran downstairs to tell my father he needed to call Will´s dad. It turned out Mr. Radcliffe was with guests who had been invited for cocktails and dinner, so they didn´t connect until the next day. But, they did connect and made the arrangements they needed to make for us to join the tour.

SEVENTEEN
William Radcliffe

I was so *fucking* glad to get out of Newport, I would have gone anywhere. It turned out there was a pretty long list of recommended clothing and other gear for the trip so we made a special trip into Manhattan to buy what I would need. The bikes were provided and they looked really cool in the photos, but that was all. I couldn't tell if my mother was pissed that she had to waste the day in the City shopping for me or relieved that I would be out of her hair for most of the summer. Anyway, we bought three sets of biking shorts and matching jerseys, all red "so the cars can see you, dear," she said, and a matching helmet. We also bought special biking shoes and some other clothes for the trip. All of our belongings would accompany us in a van or be brought along in the train and river boat, the brochure explained. Laundry would be taken care of at the hotels where we were to stay.

I was a little disturbed by the recommendation that we bring at least one "conservative" sport jacket, whatever that means, and two dress shirts plus ties. For a bike trip? Nevertheless, I couldn't wait for the trip to start. I tried not to be too much of a shit at home in case my parents decided to cancel the trip to punish me, but I was really anxious to go. The plan was for Max to fly into Westchester Airport the day before our departure and spend that night at our townhouse. We had to stay over so the pilots could rest before taking us to Europe. Amsterdam is six hours ahead of New York and the flight time is about nine hours, according to Max, so it was decided we would leave Westchester Airport at nine the next evening for an arrival in Amsterdam about noon local time.

"This is going to be *maximum awesomeness!*" were the first words out of Max's mouth when we met each other on the Westchester tarmac. Jacob drove us to our townhouse while Max and I sat in the back seat and talked non-stop. It had been little more than a month and we talked by cell almost every day, but it was like much more time had passed since we´d been together. We´d both cut our hair very short – almost buzz cuts – for the trip but had never mentioned it to each other. "Fucking strange," I told Max. "Great minds," he said.

We got home just as cook was putting our dinner out. My parents came into the dining room on their way to some engagement or another to say hello to Max. My father said they wanted to take us to lunch tomorrow to wish us a wonderful, safe trip. *Good riddance*, more likely, I thought. Then, they would return to Newport for the rest of the summer.

EIGHTEEN

Maximilian Van Zuylen

We did have a nice lunch the following day. A send off, I guess. The Radcliffes took us to "21", the famous former speakeasy, now a popular bar / restaurant at – where else? -- Twenty-One West Fifty-Second Street in midtown Manhattan. I think even Will enjoyed himself. We sat at one of the first few tables past the entrance and just opposite the bar. It was Friday, about one p.m., and the place was packed. Two tables away sat the society columnist Aileen Mehle, who Mrs. Radcliffe greeted pretty effusively, Nancy Reagan and King Juan Carlos of Spain. I recognized Mrs. Reagan, but not Mrs. Mehle or the King until Mrs. Radcliffe told me, somewhat breathlessly, who they were. *Almost as good as meeting my aunt Marie-Helene,* I thought. Security was everywhere, but it was still a lively crowd and it was fun to be there. Mr. and Mrs. Radcliffe had the restaurant´s famous – I was told by her – chicken hash and Will and I had "21" burgers. I think we made the better choice.

We were pretty much at loose ends the rest of the day, waiting to go. We played some video games and talked about the trip. "It looks like there will only be eight of us, Will, plus the four guides, unless someone else signs up at the last minute."

"Yeah. The two brothers from Atlanta, who else?"

"Two Dutch guys from Amsterdam plus one guy from Mexico City and another dude from France, I think. They´re all older than us, right?"

"Yeah, everyone except the Mexican, but not by much. Everyone else is fifteen except one of the brothers from Atlanta is sixteen. Not to worry. We´re bigger than most sixteen year olds at school and I can protect you if anyone gets on your case."

"*Dipshit.*"

Finally, it was time to go. We had sandwiches for dinner, still pretty full from the big "21" lunch. Jacob drove us to Westchester Airport, and by nine p.m. we were "wheels up", as my father always announced on take-off. Will and I settled on the two couches in the rear of the main cabin, pulled blankets up and went fast asleep. We were talked out, for the moment anyway, and tired from all the excitement about the forthcoming trip. George, my father's steward, woke us about an hour from our destination and put out breakfast for us at the dining table near the front of the cabin. Eating breakfast, we watched land come into view as we made our descent into Schiphol Amsterdam International Airport. We went through immigration and customs in the plane, as we had done in Mexico, and then walked across the tarmac to the private terminal waiting lounge. There, we met Rolf Donaldson, one of the four guides / chaperones who would accompany us on the trip. Blonde hair, short stubble on his face, probably early twenties. Turned out he was a senior at some university in the Netherlands whose name was so unpronounceable I couldn't begin to say it, much less write it. This was the second summer he had conducted these bike tours for boys our age, and I knew Will and I were going to like him a lot.

We climbed into an Abercrombie and Kent van and started toward the center of Amsterdam. Almost everything we saw was old, really old. But not in a bad way. Some of the business buildings seemed newer, but the houses and apartments looked like they could be two or three hundred years old. Very cool, actually.

We stopped in the valet zone in front of the Hotel Krasnapolsky, near the very center of Amsterdam at Dam Square and directly across from the Queen's Palace, Rolf told us. My parents knew the hotel because they stayed there a few times when visiting our Van Zuylen relatives who still lived in the Netherlands. When my mother had reviewed our itinerary, she was surprised Abercrombie & Kent would choose such a lavish hotel for a group of boys who were traveling on bicycles. "I'm not," my father said. "Have you seen the price for this excursion?" Anyway, it was a beautiful, old building with an ornate lobby. Rolf took us to our room, which was located on the third floor overlooking the Square. He gave us each Abercrombie & Kent cell phones with his cell number and the cell numbers of each of the other guides programed into the address book.

"This is how we will keep track of each other on the trip, boys," he said. "You're on your own this afternoon. Walk around, have a good time and stay out of mischief. We'll meet the others at seven p.m. in the lobby and take a short walk to a bistro where we are having dinner. Wear a dress shirt, tie and nice pair of slacks, okay?"

I was surprised we were allowed to be on our own right away in a strange city, but Will and I thought it was a good sign.

NINETEEN
William Radcliffe

Max and I unpacked some of our clothes – those we thought we might need here in Amsterdam – and then walked out into the Square. Everything was old, as Max had noticed, but nothing looked neglected or run down. The buildings were beautiful, some of them very colorful, and there were flowers everywhere – along the street, in containers on apartment and office terraces, and everywhere you looked in Dam Square. We hadn´t had lunch, but neither one of us was particularly hungry. We stopped at a shop which sold ice cream and bought two dishes which we ate at a very small table on the sidewalk.

We walked around the central area for a bit, not wanting to venture too far from the hotel on our own because if we got lost we weren´t sure we would find any English-speaking person to direct us back to the hotel. At the entrance to one street, we saw women, many of them topless, at their windows beckoning to the men who passed by.

"Amsterdam could be interesting, Max. How long are we supposed to stay here?"

"Two days to see some of the local sights, but I don´t think those women will be part of the tour. Besides, you like the Puerto Rican chicks, right?"

"I like all the chicks, but some of those babes look like they´ve got an awful lot of mileage on them."

We laughed and began walking back to the hotel, which we found easily enough. We still had two hours to kill before meeting the others so we stretched out on our beds, tired even though we had slept on the plane.

It was not hard to identify our group when we went downstairs shortly before seven p.m. The four guides, including Rolf, all wore dark green Abercrombie and Kent blazers. The other boys were easy to identify, too, because they were the only young people in the hotel lobby. William Davis, from Abercrombie and Kent´s New York office, was the senior guide and the person in overall charge of our group. He introduced us first to the guides. Rolf we already knew. The others were Sven Johanssen, from Sweden, and Andres Strauser, a German. The three younger guides were all college students working for Abercrombie and Kent for the summer.

We also were introduced to the other boys. Mark and his older brother David Stedman from Atlanta, Miguel Sanchez from Mexico City and Philippe d´Uzes from Paris. We also met Paulie Marks and Georges Oberman, both from Amsterdam. It seemed like a good group, although I couldn´t tell about the senior guide, William Davis. "Could be an asshole," I told Max.

We walked about three blocks from the hotel to a bistro Max and I had seen earlier in the day. It was crowded then and it was crowded now. There were tables set up on the sidewalk and the inside was pretty busy, too. We were led to the back of the restaurant, past the bar, to a private room which had already been set up for us. It was a cheerful room, wood paneled with sconces on the walls which looked very old. The table was set for twelve. Four guides and eight boys.

"Take a seat, boys," Mr. Davis said. "Dinner will be sent in soon. In the meantime, I want to talk a little about our trip." He went on. "Tomorrow morning, we will go by A & K van to our warehouse here in Amsterdam to pick up our bikes. Amsterdam, by the way, is considered the friendliest biking city in the world. There are cars here, of course, but bikers and drivers are courteous and respect each other´s space. We may find that kind of courtesy less often as we journey south through a bit of Germany, Belgium and France.

"You have maps of our route showing where we will go by bike and also by train and riverboat. We will stay together on our daily rides, but once we reach our destination for the night, you are free to do some exploring on your own as long as you keep your cell phones with you.

"A word of caution. We are treating you like young adults, which you are, and expect you to behave like it. Any boy found causing serious trouble or failing to follow instructions from the guides will be sent home immediately, most likely to an unfriendly welcome. We all clear on that?"

Heads nodded all around.

"Now, here comes our food. Eat up. Tomorrow will be a very full day."

One waiter brought in a tray of mixed soft drinks and some glasses. Another carried a bowl of ice. More waiters brought in trays of food. I couldn't believe the quantity or the variety. There was fish in some kind of sauce, two different kinds of pasta, sliced roast beef, baked chicken with potatoes, a veal dish, mixed vegetables – some of which I didn't recognize – and fresh fruit. "This is going to be okay, Max," I said.

I don't know why I remember this particular meal so well. Probably because it was our first together. Anyway, we were off to a great start. Newport, Rhode Island seemed a million miles away. Here I was with my best friend, Max, and a bunch of guys about to take off on an adventure. Not an asshole in sight, not even Mr. Davis.

The plan was to meet at nine a.m. in the hotel lobby, drive to the warehouse for our bikes, and then spend both tomorrow and the next day touring Amsterdam before heading south. We were to be divided into two groups: Max and I drew the Stedman brothers plus Rolf and Sven. That seemed like a really good draw to me and it was.

TWENTY
Maximilian Van Zuylen

I thought we would have trouble sleeping when we got back to our hotel. I was wrong, though. Probably a combination of all the food we put away at dinner, plus the excitement, plus crossing the Atlantic. Whatever it was, Will and I hit our beds and were gone until seven when Will's cell phone rang and Rolf told him we should both get up, dressed, and be down in the lobby by eight in order to get breakfast before we set off. We grabbed showers, got dressed and were among the first in the lobby. One of the guides, the German Andres, pointed us in the direction of a room off the lobby where a breakfast buffet was laid out. The others joined us soon enough and we sat down to eat and listen to more information from Mr. Davis. We would meet again in the hotel lobby at seven in the evening, but the two groups into which we had been divided would go their separate ways to see some of the sights in Amsterdam after we got our bikes.

The A & K van was waiting for us in the loading zone in front of the hotel. All twelve of us piled in for the short ride to the warehouse where our bikes were waiting. The bikes were cool. They weren't racing cycles but they weren't bikes that Granny would ride, either. The handlebars were chrome. The aluminum frames were painted either metallic red, blue or green. Mine was blue, Will's red. Just behind each bike seat was a satchel in the same colors as the aluminum frames. It wasn't real big, but it could hold a couple of bottles of water, energy bars and any other small items you wanted to store there. Our last names were printed on the rear portions of the satchels. Van Zuylen for me, Radcliffe for Will. Rolf stuck a couple of water bottles in our satchels and also the Stedmans', and a few minutes later we were off, biking through the streets of Amsterdam.

Mr. Davis was right. This was a bike-friendly city, and there were hundreds, maybe thousands, of them in the streets. Those of us on bikes tended to stay to the right while the cars drove past on our left. No one seemed in a hurry. We rode along ancient canals, built in the seventeenth century, according to Mr. Davis, and we also saw the defense line, built in the nineteenth and twentieth centuries to keep the sea from flooding the country. We made two stops in the morning, one to see the Anne Frank house which the Stedman brothers, who were Jewish, wanted to see. We also went to the Rijksmuseum. In the early afternoon, we parked our bikes in a very small park next to one of the canals. Rolf and Will walked to a grocery store and came back with bread, cheese, sausage and fruit which we ate on the grass while watching the small boats float along the canal.

In the afternoon, we went to the world's only floating flower market, which my mother had told me not to miss, and the Hermitage Amsterdam. Will said to me, "What is this shit? *Three* museums in one day. WTF?" Still, it was a good day – a great day, really. Amsterdam was beautiful, we biked at a nice, slow pace and could really see the city. We rode back to the hotel – around back, actually – where our bikes were put in one of the hotel's storage rooms for the night.

We ate dinner that night at another bistro not far from the hotel. Mr. Davis tried to lead the conversation into a discussion of what we had seen that day. I just hoped he wouldn't call on Will to talk about our visit to the museums. Among the boys, Philippe d'Uzes pretty much dominated the conversation. He didn't want to talk about the day's adventures, though. Instead, he decided to talk about his family. "Oldest noble title in Europe … family traces its history to Charlemagne … two castles … fortune founded in chemicals." And on and on and on.

"I knew there had to be at least one asshole in the group," Will said to me. Mr. Davis kept steering the conversation back to today's bike ride and Pierre kept interrupting to say something else about his family.

Finally, Rolf said, "Philippe, I don't think we need to hear anything more about your family unless you want to tell us the brand of fertilizer your father makes." This produced laughter all around the table. Even Mr. Davis, a bit on the serious side, laughed.

One of the Stedmans said "He´s in the *shit* business!" More laughter while Philippe sat there fuming.

Later, in our hotel room, Will told me "I think we´re going to have to fuck with Philippe. What an asshole!"

"Let´s not get kicked off the trip, Will."

"Not a chance."

The next day was more of the same. We did more biking through Amsterdam and visited the Van Gogh Museum. Even Will thought that was cool. At one of the Stedman´s urgings, we biked through the red light district. "Don´t tell Mr. Davis," Rolf warned. The women made catcalls and whistled, but I don´t think any of us really wanted to stop as most of the women we saw were clearly our mothers´ ages, or older.

TWENTY-ONE
William Radcliffe

At dinner that night, everyone was a bit restless as we were all anxious to head south on our ride through The Netherlands. Philippe was pretty quiet for a change. What an asshole! Anyway, Mr. Davis handed out our itineraries for what he called the first leg of the trip. We would travel from Amsterdam to Hoofddorp to Leiden to The Hague, then Rotterdam, and finally Breda before crossing the Belgium border and stopping at Antwerp. Mostly these would be eighteen to twenty-five mile trips each day. Mr. Davis said anyone who became tired could ride in the van. Fat chance! After we signed up for the trip, Max and I spent every day cycling – me in Newport, Max in Napa -- and fairly quickly worked up to 40 miles without much of a sweat, so we were ready. We would spend two full days in The Hague, another two in Rotterdam and two in Antwerp, so it seemed really easy.

And so we began our bike trek south. Each day we were rousted out of bed at seven by one of the guides, ate breakfast together in the hotel and were on our bikes by eight or eight-thirty. The van driver brought along packed lunches from the hotel which we ate in a public park or some other public space, usually around one o´clock. After lunch, we resumed our bike rides until we reached our day´s destination, somewhere between three and four o´clock. Most days, that gave us a couple of hours to look around the city where we were staying, or another whole day if we were spending a couple of days there which we did several times.

Not all of the hotels lived up to the Krasnapolsky and some of the cities we visited were not very interesting, but there wasn´t anything I could complain about except Philippe d´Uzes who continued to act like an arrogant asshole. The only boy who had trouble with the rides was Miguel Sanchez from Mexico City. He rode in the van sometimes and even put up good naturedly with the shit the other boys gave him.

He was the youngest of the group and said he didn't have a chance to take practice rides back home. Max and I both liked him and hung out with him at lunch and often at the end of our daily rides.

We had dinner each night either in the hotel where we were staying or, more often, at a local bistro. Mr. Davis, who was the oldest man in our group and who never rode in the van, talked to us about what we had seen that day and what was in store the following day. It was a kind of mixed history / geography lesson, but Max and I didn't mind. I had to admit it made the trip more interesting even if it was somewhat like school.

The Hague was the most interesting city we visited in the Netherlands apart from Amsterdam. It is the third largest city in the country, behind Amsterdam and Rotterdam. Mr. Davis told us the International Court of Justice and the International Criminal Court, both of which are located in The Hague, have played very significant roles in world affairs, especially since the end of World War II. The Hague is also the seat of the Dutch government and we were able to visit parliament during our two day stay there.

It took us another week or ten days – it's hard to keep track of each day on a trip like this – to reach the ancient city of Brussels, Belgium. Here we planned to stay at the Hotel Metropole for two days before boarding a train to Paris. At dinner the first night, Mr. Davis told us Brussels was founded in the tenth century as a fortress town by a descendant of Charlemagne. That last part was unfortunate because it set Philippe off again about his family and their ties to Charlemagne. *We have to fuck with him, we really do.* We took a half-day tour by coach one morning, visiting a number of sites in the city, including Grand Place, a huge square with its world famous market where if you can't find it, it probably doesn't exist, as our guide said. Brussels became an important center for international politics after World War II and we drove by NATO World Headquarters which is located in the city. Our last stop was at the outdoor café at the Hotel Metropole which we learned was one hundred ten years old and the only nineteenth century hotel in the city left standing. We ended the tour there with coffee and Belgian chocolate in the café.

Two days after our arrival in Brussels, we boarded a first-class train for Paris. Nobody bitched. I think we were all glad to be sitting on something other than a bicycle seat, at least for a while. The A & K vans, which left Brussels a day before we did, met us at the central rail station in Paris and drove us to the Hotel La Tremoille near the center of the city where we would spend one week. Like the Krasnapolsky, Hotel La Tremoille was among the older hotels in Paris and very near the Champs-Elysees.

The A & K people arranged a number of tours for us that week, most of which Max and I liked. We went to the Louvre and although we spent *way* too much time there, some of the paintings were pretty impressive. We saw the Arc de Triomphe and visited the Eiffle Tower. Miguel wasn't sure he wanted to take the elevator to the top, but Max and I coaxed him and we all thought it was really cool until the guide told us the tower sways with the wind. *Shit! We didn't need to know that.* We took a half-day trip to see the Palace of Versailles which is pretty spectacular. Our guide told us there wasn't a toilet anywhere in the palace even though the settlers of ancient Ephesus had invented flushing toilets more than two thousand years ago. It gave me a chance to tell Philippe how dense the French are.

One day, Max's aunt invited us for lunch at her house in Paris, a hotel particular called the Hotel Lambert. I have never seen such a place. It sits on the edge of the Ille Ste. Louis and looks more like a palace than a private home. You could put a couple of hundred people in there and they probably would never see each other. In the car on the way, Max told me his aunt and uncle bought the place in 1975, kicked out the tenants who lived in several apartments and then completely reconverted it to the private residence it had been when built in the 1600's. No wonder my mother wanted to know the Baroness. She would gladly have killed for an invitation to this place. The chauffeur drove us through the front gates into a huge central courtyard. From there, we were taken to a formal reception room and told by a butler to wait while he informed La Baronne of our arrival.

It didn´t take long. Max´s aunt came into the room within a matter of minutes, hugged Max and introduced herself to me. I have to say she is beautiful and very charming. She saw me looking around at the massive reception room and told me she had great fun "fixing up the place". On our way to lunch in a secluded garden off the courtyard, she took us through the Galerie d´Hercule, maybe the biggest room I had ever seen. This is the formal dining room or banquet hall and, according to Max, seats one hundred eighty people around the enormous dining table. There are paintings on the ceiling depicting some of Hercules most impressive mythical feats. Marie-Helene asked Max if he remembered being there for his cousin Eduoard´s wedding dinner. He said he did, although he was only about six at the time. We walked through an archway in the courtyard to the garden with a table set for just the three of us. "Guy and Eduoard are at our house in Deauville," she explained, "meeting with our breeder." Max later told me his uncle is big in horse breeding and racing, at least in France.

At the table, Max and I were given glasses of lemonade while Marie-Helene drank champagne. Lunch was some sort of soufflé which I couldn´t identify but liked and dessert was peach ice cream and cookies. After lunch, Max´s aunt took each of us by the arm for a walk around the garden. It wasn´t large as it was inside the grounds of the Hotel Lambert, but it was carefully and symmetrically laid out.

"Such handsome boys," she said. "You could be brothers, maybe even twins. Which one is taller."

"I am," said Max.

"Only if you stand on your toes," I replied. The Baroness laughed while escorting us both to the car. She kissed me on both cheeks and hugged Max. She told us we were both welcome at the hotel whenever she was in Paris. I liked her a lot.

Even with the tours arranged by A & K and the lunch with Max´s aunt, we still had plenty of time to just walk around and explore Paris on our own. We walked up and down the Champs Elysees and also along the Seine. We had a picture taken at the Hotel Lambert with Max´s aunt and took more pictures of each other, or together when we could find someone to snap the photo along the Seine. All of these we e-mailed to our parents. I was sure my mother would go crazy when she saw the one with the Baroness.

From Paris, we traveled south through the Loire Valley. We mostly rode our bikes, but we also traveled by river boat with Mr. Davis pointing out sights of interest near the banks of the river. On our bikes and on the boats, we could see castles, or chateau, throughout the valley. "Most of these," Mr. Davis explained, "look better from here than they do up close." One night, we camped under a canopy of trees beside the river in sleeping bags A & K provided. Max and I loved it after so many nights in luxurious hotels with way too many shirts, ties and jackets. Everyone else loved it, too, except for Philippe d´Uzes who complained that the A & K brochure promised luxury hotels throughout. *What a dick*!

It was Max who came up with the plan just a few days before we were scheduled to ride into Cannes and our final destination, the Hotel Carlton. There, on the steps of the hotel, Mr. Davis would present us with commemorative jackets with A & K Bike Tour printed on the front and a map of our travels from Amsterdam to Cannes on the back and the names of all the cities we visited.

Throughout the trip, each boy was required to take care of his own bike. A & K provided the tools, which we kept in the packs behind our seats, but we were responsible for checking tire pressure, looking for any punctures or leaks and checking the sprockets with a special tool to make sure the wheels were properly attached. Max´s idea was to mess with Philippe´s front wheel just before our ride into Cannes so his bike would be disabled and he would have to make the final trip to the Carlton in the van where his father, the Duc, was to meet him. It was brilliant!

Our last night before Cannes was also spent camping in sleeping bags. Again, Philippe bitched about it and said his father would want money back because the trip was not as advertised. Finally, Mr. Davis had had enough. He said he was looking forward to meeting the Duc and telling him what a nuisance his son had been. *Hooray for Mr. Davis!*

I almost wanted to clue him into our plan, but of course I couldn´t. Camping out made it easier to get to Philippe´s bike than if we had been in a hotel. Max and I waited until everyone was asleep – the hard part was staying awake – and then found Philippe´s bike and loosened the front sprocket. Now, all we had to do was distract him until it was time to go. That was easy once Max asked him where his family´s home was in the south of France. He didn´t shut up until Mr. Davis told us to mount our bikes for our ride into Cannes.

We were only about ten miles from Cannes when we left our campground. I think we had ridden less than half a mile when Philippe´s front tire came loose and the bike collapsed on the roadway. Philippe scraped up his left side which one of the guides treated with iodine and applied some patches. On inspection, it appeared the bike´s front frame was bent so there was no possibility of Philippe riding it into Cannes even if he had felt fit enough to do so, which he did not. Another crime perfectly planned and perfectly executed!

The best part, of course, was arriving at the Carlton Hotel and the presentation of the jackets. Each of us, except for Philippe, arrived riding our bikes. Some members of the hotel staff came out on the steps and applauded us as we arrived. Philippe exited the van looking dejected. The Duc d´Uzes was there, taciturn and unsmiling, especially after his conversation with Mr. Davis. The Stedmans´ parents were also there as they planned to vacation in the south of France with their sons for a couple of weeks.

After the presentation, A & K put on a lunch for the boys, the guides and the boys´ parents who were there on the hotel terrace. The Duc and his son declined to attend. Mr. Davis congratulated the rest of us on completing our one thousand mile journey and we were each given a half-glass of red wine with lunch to toast the occasion. Max later asked me if I felt sorry for Philippe. "*Fuck no,*" I told him. Max gave me a high five.

TWENTY-TWO

Frederick Arthur Van Zuylen

Max is coming home in two days' time after his six week bike trip through the Netherlands and France. The Radcliffes' plane is picking up the boys in Nice and flying them to New York where our plane will meet Max and fly him to San Francisco. It is little more than a turn-around as Max and Will have to be at Deerpark in just ten days for their second term. Max has e-mailed several pictures, mostly from France, including a couple taken at the Hotel Lambert with Marie-Helene. Although I have let Beatrice's comments about how similar the boys look and act go without comment, Max and Will could certainly pass for brothers, even fraternal twins since they are obviously the same age.

God, I keep thinking back to Malcolm Forbes' party aboard The Highlander fifteen-plus years ago. Beatrice stayed behind in San Francisco because she thought she had the stomach flu. Instead, It turned out she was newly pregnant with Max. That evening, the yacht circled Manhattan while the guests – there must have been at least fifty of us – drank and dined celebrating some Forbes' event I can't recall. I actually remember very little of the evening, although I do remember getting very drunk and I *think* I remember being below deck in a cabin with one of the guests at some point during the evening. *Good god!* I will not think any more about that. *I will not!*

TWENTY-THREE

Maximilian Van Zuylen

The second year at Deerpark was not as memorable as the first, probably because I was familiar with the school and the routine there. Will and I were both assigned to Maple Hall – *what is with the tree names?* – although we were not, of course, roommates. Will's roommate was Yoki Harari from Tokyo. He was on the smallish side, very thin and extremely serious. According to Will, he was terrified of scoring anything other than perfect grades and said his father would beat him if he did.

"The dude's kind of a stiff, Max," he told me. "Probably doesn't say ten words a day to me, but at least he's not a loud mouth like that prick d'Uzes."

I didn't have a roommate and stayed alone in my suite that year. It turned out the student assigned as my roommate withdrew from Deerpark the Sunday before classes started after all the room assignments had been made. It was okay, though. Most afternoons and evenings, Will and I hung out together in my suite, so we continued to see a lot of each other.

I remember Will complaining about Thanksgiving in Palm Beach again. *"What global warming? The place is like a fucking iceberg."* It didn't help that I started to laugh. The only school holiday we spent together was spring break. My parents flew into New York because my mother wanted to meet with a decorator about making some changes to our apartment at the Sherry Netherlands, so we stayed there for the ten day break. I spent most of my time with Will and we bummed around New York as we had done the previous year. We were pretty much free to come and go as we pleased since none of the parents seemed concerned about where we went or what we did.

As a treat, and probably because my parents didn't know what to do with me that summer, my mother invited Will to join us in Napa for six weeks during July and August. Will's parents, it seemed, were always happy to have him out of their hair and mine were just as glad that I had someone to pal around with.

For the past two years, I had been pestering my father to teach me to drive. He always said no because he didn't want to take the chance of an accident on a public road with me at the wheel. That summer, though, he talked to Denise Hale, my parents' friend who owned a twenty thousand acre cattle ranch just outside of Cloverdale and not far from Napa. There were roads, mostly dirt tracks, all over the ranch so it was a great place to learn. Mrs. Hale said yes and told my father her late husband, Prentiss Hale, had taught her to drive on the ranch only a few years earlier.

"Just don't let the boys hit any cows, darling," Mrs. Hale told my father.

Will and I were super excited and never once imagined the trouble ahead.

The day we went to the ranch, we drove in my father's beat up old Jeep which he loved and my mother hated. He only drove the Jeep in and around Napa and only when he wasn't going somewhere with my mother because she refused to ride in it. Both Will and I wanted to learn to drive a stick shift, so the Jeep was perfect. Plus, it was probably indestructible. Mrs. Hale, it turned out, had returned to her apartment in San Francisco for a few days so we were met at the ranch by Rusty, her foreman, who pointed at some track near the ranch house where he said we should start. He gave my father a hand-held GPS so we could find our way back. Twenty thousand acres is a lot of property, and Rusty said it is easy to get lost if you don't know where you are going. "I'll come and get y'all around dinner time if you aren't back," he joked.

My father drove the Jeep a ways down the track, then stopped so I could trade places with him. Will sat in the back seat. The Jeep had four forward gears plus reverse and neutral, all marked on the gear shift knob. With the motor off, my father told me to shift into first gear, then the other forward gears, each time depressing and then slowly releasing the clutch at the same time I pressed down on the accelerator. After a couple of tries, I thought I had the hang of it. My father told me to start the engine with my foot on the brake and the gears in neutral. Then, he told me to depress the clutch and shift into first. This I did without a problem, but when I started to let the clutch out and press on the gas, the Jeep immediately lurched forward and died. Once more, same result.

"You need to let the clutch out more slowly and apply more throttle," my father said. Will sat in the back laughing and telling us he thought his neck had snapped.

"Shut up, asshole! Wait 'til you try it!"

"Boys, stay calm and concentrate," my father said.

The third time we actually got going, and I managed to shift from first to second with only a minimum amount of gear grinding. The steering part was easy, but, of course, if I went slightly off track it didn't matter. I got to drive for about forty-five minutes before my father said it was Will's turn.

I have to admit Will caught on more quickly – which he, of course, pointed out – but he had the advantage of watching me and listening to my father since I went first. Will also drove for about 45 minutes before we stopped near a shade tree, drank some cokes and ate sandwiches from a cooler my father had brought along. We each got two more turns that day so by the time we left the ranch, we had driven most of the day. I never thought of my father as particularly patient, but he sure was that day. It was definitely the best time we had that summer.

TWENTY-FOUR
Frederick Arthur Van Zuylen

I poured myself a whiskey neat in my study and tossed it back.

My god, I think I just taught my two sons to drive today. No! I can't think that! I won't think that! I won't!

TWENTY-FIVE
William Radcliffe

That summer in Napa was just the best! The Van Zuylen estate was awesome. Lawns, tennis courts, pool, even a pond, it seemed to go on forever. Not like Mrs. Hale´s, of course, but it was vast. We explored the little town of Napa, which was kind of funky, and wandered around the area as much as we could on foot and on bikes.

One Sunday, we went to their friends, the Wilseys, for a lunch party. We met Todd and Trevor Traina, Mrs. Wilsey´s sons who were probably in their late teens or early twenties. Both seemed really impressed with themselves and not at all interested in either of us. We also met Mr. Wilsey´s young son, Sean, who might have been about ten and seemed not to fit in with any of the older group. Mostly, though, we skipped the adult stuff and just hung out together.

Mike Smith had an apparently rare weekend off so we went to stay with him in his apartment in the city. He took us to Golden Gate Park where we had water balloon fights and threw footballs. We went to Tommy´s Joint – aptly named – for dinner and out to a movie in the Marina after which we gorged on ice cream. Max shared Mike´s room and I slept on the couch in the living room of his apartment. A very cool day and night.

The best time of all was when Max´s dad taught us to drive. Of course, that also caused the trouble which followed. It happened about a week later when Max´s parents went into San Francisco for the night to attend a dinner at the restaurant L Étoile which Mrs. Hale had organized for the musician and conductor Zuben Mehta who was passing through San Francisco on his way to a concert in Japan. They would be gone for the night which gave us a perfect opportunity to take the Jeep out for a drive.

Mrs. Van Zuylen had given the staff the night off after the cook fixed our dinner so Max and I were the only ones on the property except for a couple of gardeners who lived on the north end of the estate quite away from the house. We planned to be gone for only an hour or two in case any of the staff returned early from wherever they went. The Jeep was kept in a separate garage away from the main house near a cluster of trees. Max let me back it out. Of course, I stalled it on my first try which allowed Max to give me a ration of shit. I made it out, though, and then turned the Jeep down the driveway and onto the lane which ran in front of the Van Zuylens' property. We drove away from town and really encountered no one. After about twenty minutes, Max and I traded places and he drove for a while, always on lanes, never the main roads. We each got the Jeep into fourth gear, something we hadn't been able to do on Mrs. Hale's ranch because the tracks were pretty rough and we couldn't get up much speed.

Neither one of us saw it coming. The road was dark, and even with headlights, it was difficult to see anything on the side of the road. Actually, we didn't see it at all. Instead, we felt a bump on the right side of the Jeep as we hit something. Max stopped the car and we looked back to see a body lying by the roadside.

"*Jesus Christ, we've killed someone,*" Max shouted.

"No, Max, maybe not. He's probably just dazed. You didn't hit him that hard." I wanted to believe that, but I wasn't sure.

"*What are we going to do?*"

"We have to find a pay phone and call 911!"

"Why can't we use a cell phone?"

"Because our phones can be traced and the police will know who called." Max was in no condition to drive anymore. I wasn't either, but I was better off than him. We kept going for maybe ten or fifteen more minutes until we found a gas station. It was closed, which was good, and there was a pay phone in the back near the bathrooms. Max made the call with part of his shirt over the mouth piece to disguise his voice. He told the 911 operator there was a body on the road along Napa Two just before the Beringer Vinyards, then hung up before the operator could ask him any more questions. I drove back to the Van Zuylens taking different lanes than the ones we had been on. We got the Jeep back in the garage and looked for damage. We couldn't see any, maybe because the Jeep was still filthy from our day on the ranch or maybe because there wasn't any. That's what I told Max anyway.

We went upstairs to our room and for some reason both of us wanted to take a shower. After that, we got into our beds to sleep. I thought I heard Max crying, but I am not sure. Anyway, it was a long night and neither of us slept very well. The next morning, just after six, we raced down the driveway to the mailbox on the street. This is where the *San Francisco Chronicle* and the local Napa papers were delivered each morning. Nothing in either of them, of course, because the accident probably happened well after the papers were printed. We went back to Max's room, not hungry for breakfast, and turned on a local radio station which played mostly dipshit music but also had periodic news bulletins. Finally, about eight, a newsman reported the accident:

Last evening, on Napa Route Two, just north of the town and near the Beringer Vinyards, a migrant vineyard worker was struck down by a motor vehicle as he walked along the roadside. The driver made no attempt to stop or to render assistance. An ambulance was dispatched after a 911 call from an unidentified person and the victim was found and taken to Napa Hospital where he is recovering from a broken arm and some mostly minor cuts and bruises. A hospital spokesman said the worker, whose name has not been released, is expected to make a full recovery.

"*Fuckin' A ,*" Max shouted, giving me a high five.

"Dude deserved it, Max. Shouldn't have been walking in the road."

"*A fucking migrant, too. Doesn't even belong in this country!*"

We got pretty worked up for a while. I think it was relief that the guy wasn't dead, but I am not sure.

TWENTY-SIX

Sylvia Radcliffe

We were having a rare dinner alone in our dining room at Wit´s End when I told William "I think we should consider sending Will to another boarding school."

"Why on earth would we do that, Sylvia? He´s going to one of the top prep schools in the country and getting excellent marks. What in the world are you thinking?"

"Frankly, I think he and the Van Zuylen boy spend too much time together, *way* too much."

"For god´s sake, Sylvia, they´re best buddies and Max is from a very fine family as you have told me enough times."

"Well, I think it´s unhealthy."

"If you´re suggesting they might be sissies or gay, forget it. You aren´t going to find two more red-blooded boys anywhere. For two years, Jacob has supplied them with condoms for their supposedly secret forays into Harlem.

"What? Harlem? For heaven´s sake, why would they go there?"

"To get laid, Sylvia. What do you think? Will and Max are perfectly healthy boys with perfectly healthy appetites and I won´t hear any more about separating them or sending Will to another school. End of discussion."

With that, William left the room. Manuel entered the dining room to see if I wanted anything more. "Yes, Manuel. More wine, please. Do fill the glass."

"Yes, ma´m," he answered topping off my glass.

God, I can´t think anymore. That party on the Highlander was more than fifteen years ago and I can hardly remember any of it. I do think I went below deck at some point because I was sick with all the liquor and wanted to lie down. I don´t remember anything else, or maybe I have just repressed it. Could Frederick Van Zuylen be Will´s father?

He was on board because I checked the guest list and recognized the Van Zuylen name. *No! Impossible! I will not believe it!* Oh, god, if this gets out, William will divorce me. I will be ruined socially here in Newport, in New York and in Palm Beach. Where will I go? What am I going to do?

"*Manuel!*"

TWENTY-SEVEN
Maximilian Van Zuylen

Our third year at Deerpark was the best yet. Will and I were lucky to be in the same house again – Elm this time – and we each drew good suitemates. Mine was a boy named Brian Adams, a hulk of a guy who transferred in from some school in his home state of Montana. Steve Swindle was Will's roommate, from Georgia. He had been at the school for the last two years, same as Will and me, but we had been in different houses and just never got to know him. Listening to the two of them talk – Will's New York accent, Steve's southern drawl – cracked up Brian and me. They sounded like they came from different planets.

"I can't understand either of you jokers. Why don't you try English," Brian told them. He could get away with it. Tall as Will and I were – we each pushed through 6'1" over the summer – Brian was maybe an inch shorter but outweighed us by at least fifty pounds and it was all muscle. He had played football in Montana and looked like he could eat hay and shit in the street.

"Hell, Max! Guy looks like he could walk through a wall," Will told me when we were alone. "Try not to piss him off."

We four were best friends that year. We spent two weekends together in New York at Will's family's townhouse. Will and I stayed in his rooms on the third floor and Steve and Brian stayed in what had been the Schwimmer's apartment and was now guest quarters. Brian had never been to New York and was a little awed by the city and all the people. "Why do they all want to live cramped up like this?" he asked.

"Best city in the world," Will countered. "Where else are you going to see all these chicks?"

"Okay, I get that."

On one trip, we went up to Harlem and picked up a couple of girls. "Maybe the city's not so bad," Brian offered on our way back home.

At Thanksgiving and again at Christmas, I gave Brian a ride in my father's plane to his family's ranch just outside of Missoula, Montana. It was just a drop off at Thanksgiving, but at Christmas I was invited to spend a few days at the Adams' ranch before flying on to San Francisco. The ranch was one of the biggest in the state, nearly two hundred fifty thousand acres. The Adams ran cattle mostly, but they also raised pigs. Both the cattle and pigs were sold at market. There were also chickens, thousands of them. They didn't sell the chickens, but they sold the eggs to one of the largest egg distributors in the country.

The first night at the ranch, we ate dinner with Brian's parents in their dining room. I don't know if you could call their place a ranch house. It was huge, built out of logs, "all from Montana," Brian's dad proudly told me, and what looked like about an acre of glass. The glass panels were thirty or forty feet tall and looked out on the lawns which surrounded the house and the northern end of the Rocky Mountain range in the distance.

After dinner, Brian announced, "Max and I are going to bunk with the boys tonight."

"Don't get into a fight with any of the hands, Brian," his mother said. "It's bad manners, especially in front of guests."

"Aw, mom, that was two years ago."

"Well, I mean it. Your dad and I don't want to be hauling you into Missoula for stitches like we did the last time."

"No worries, mom. No worries."

I had no idea what any of this was about or who "the boys" were. Brian told me to grab my toothbrush and a change of clothes and we were off. Outside, we headed to a big GMC SUV parked in the driveway. "You drive, Brian?" I asked.

"Been driving since I was eleven. Everybody drives young around here." We drove maybe a mile from the main house and parked in front of a cluster of nondescript buildings, all log construction like the main house. The largest building was in the center with two smaller buildings, four altogether, on each end. We walked into the center building which turned out to be a very large room with a massive stone fireplace, several couches and chairs, a kitchen area and several dining tables. There were maybe thirty men inside. Some were washing dishes, some were watching television, there was a poker game going at one of the dining tables. Many were just hanging around, relaxing with a beer. Brian got hugs, high-fives, slaps on the back and more than a few punches in the shoulder.

"Meet the boys, Max. These are the guys who work this place. Boys, my roommate Max. He´s from San Francisco but he ain´t no fag. That I know." There were cheers, catcalls, a few high fives and even a couple of shoulder punches. I was in, just like that. To say this was one of the most extraordinary nights of my life – so far – is probably an understatement. A bunk house in the middle of Montana with thirty or so rednecks. I couldn´t wait to tell Mike and especially Will.

We watched the poker game for a while, then pitched pennies with a couple of the men, quickly losing what change we had. Around nine o´clock, everyone started getting ready to turn in. The four smaller buildings were bunk houses, each of which held about twenty-five bunks. "Lots more boys here in the spring and summer, Max. Not so many now." Brian and I went into one of the bunk rooms with maybe eight or ten of the men and found a couple of empty bunks at one end of the room. By nine-thirty, it was lights out, the men apparently tired from whatever they did during the day.

The next morning, if you can call five o´clock morning, we were rousted out of bed and filed with the others into the bathroom. It resembled a locker room in a mid-sized gymnasium. There were lockers, multiple sinks and toilets and a communal shower with maybe twenty shower heads mounted around the space. When we were dressed and went back to the main building, at least half the men were already there sitting at the dining tables and eating breakfast. The cooks had put out large platters of scrambled eggs, bacon, toast with butter and jam and coffee which was served in honest-to-god tin mugs.

Brian and I ate our share, then joined two of the men in a four-passenger truck cab with an extended bed which had already been filled with bales of hay. We drove two or three miles from the bunk houses to an enclosure where some of the cattle had been rounded up and fenced in for the on-coming winter. It was still mild weather, unusual for Montana in December, but there wasn't much on the ground for the cows to eat. We drove along the fence line very slowly, three of us in the truck bed forking hay into the enclosure. We repeated this six times during the day while four or five other truck crews did the same thing at other enclosures. It was hard work forking the hay. "Good for you," Brian said. "Put some muscle on those skinny bones." That night, I actually fell asleep before dinner until Brian woke me up so I could get something to eat. I still think I was the first one in bed that night. The next day, we worked with the ranch hands again, this time collecting eggs from the hen houses. The hens were uniformly unhappy to give up their eggs and pecked at us as we robbed their nests. Fortunately, we all had thick gloves, but I could still feel the pinches from time to time.

Brian took pity on me and we moved back into the main house for my last night in Montana. During that day, we rode horses along a tributary of the Missouri River which ran through the Adams' property. "It's full of trout in the spring," Brian told me. "Usually frozen this time of year."

To tell the truth, I was glad to leave for San Francisco after three days at the ranch. Don't let anyone tell you ranching is an easy life. I wondered how the ranch hands put up with it day in and day out, but they seemed a pretty contented bunch. It's all what you get used to, I guess.

We spent Christmas in the city that year because my mother wanted to have a big holiday party in the penthouse. Decorators swarmed the forty-third and forty-fourth floor for at least three days, putting up trees, wreaths, garlands, lights, even a Santa complete with sleigh and two fake rain deer near the front entrance. With all the activity, I was pretty much ignored which was fine with me because it gave me a chance to do the reading assignments we were always given during every school break. The day of the party, caterers arrived and put out what looked like enough food to feed a small army. The food was set out in the dining room and also upstairs in the den. There were three bars, two set up on the forty-third floor in the living area and the one on the forty-fourth floor overlooking the living room. I had to admit it looked very festive, if *way* over the top. My mother told me two hundred fifty guests were invited and she expected about two hundred. "Always conflicts during the holidays, darling."

I was expected to dress and make an appearance, but with that many people in the apartment, I knew I could quickly slip away to my space on the forty-second floor. Mike came, of course. He grabbed a drink at one of the bars. We both collected plates of food and took them downstairs to the great room where we ate dinner at the partners' desk we used all those years ago to study together. He laughed when I told him about my experiences in Montana and the nights I spent in the bunk house. "Maximilian Van Zuylen, a ranch hand," he laughed. "I can't imagine you forking hay, or collecting eggs or doing any of it. Did you manage to avoid stepping in cow shit?" He was getting a real kick out of my stories which was okay with me.

I saw Mike twice more that holiday. He came to the penthouse for Christmas Eve dinner with just my mother and father and me, then spent the night so we could have Christmas morning together. Mike and Will. My two best friends in the world. I hoped that would never change.

TWENTY-EIGHT

William Radcliffe

Christmas break was okay. Palm Beach had finally warmed up so I could do some swimming in our pool and even in the ocean. I missed Max and Steve, though, and even Brian, the big hulk. We came from such different worlds, but I thought he was a really good guy. All in all, I was not unhappy to return to Deerpark and my best friends. Before leaving Palm Beach, I managed to work through the reading assignments that prick Morrison had *once more* laid on us *Maybe we need to fuck with him again.*

There was one other prick we needed to take care of, Robert Montgomery, one of the four masters at Elm Hall. It was always Robert, never Bob. He was tall, arrogant and had a mean streak. He didn´t much pick on Max or me, but he gave all kinds of shit to the younger boys, assigning some of them chores like making his bed and running personal errands in lieu of taking away privileges for alleged offenses. His birthday fell on a day in mid-January soon after we returned from our Christmas break. He was eighteen and for his birthday, his father gave him a brand new metallic blue BMW five series. It was gorgeous. Every time it rained or snowed, he made some of the boys in our house go out and wash it. Even when it didn´t rain or snow, one or two of the boys was pressed into dusting it off. *Prick!*

Once he came down on me and Steve for skipping an evening assembly and took away our privileges for a week. That did it. I talked to Max about it on our way to class one morning since I wasn´t allowed in other students rooms or to have visitors in mine for a week. "What are you going to do, Will?"

"I don´t know yet, but it will definitely involve his car."

"Is Steve going to be in on it?"

"No, Max. It´s always just been you and me and it needs to stay that way. Okay?"

"Yes, absolutely. You and me."

For the next couple of weeks, I lay in bed at night trying to come up with a plan. Not just *a plan*. It had to be *the perfect plan* and it had to involve damage to the car. Serious damage. Some things had to be ruled out. For instance, smashing the windows we couldn't do because it would set off the alarm. Keying the car had some appeal, but it wasn't enough. I knew Robert was going to the Caribbean with his family for spring break because he told everyone who would listen. That meant the car would be on campus while he and almost everyone else would be away. Would he leave his car keys behind in his room? I thought so but couldn't be sure until he left, and I still had to figure a way into his room to see if they were there.

My plan, if I could find the keys, was to steal the car late at night and drive it to the spot on the Long Island Sound where Max and I sometimes went skinny dipping. I would drive the car just three or four feet into the water and leave it partially submerged. One final thing: on a weekend trip to New York with Max, we found a novelty store in the Village which sold all kinds of crazy stuff. One item was a fake car license plate which said, simply, "FUCKED". I wanted to take off the rear plate of the BMW and replace it with the novelty one I bought. All I had to do was wait.

Max is a genius. Getting the key to Robert's room was amazingly simple. The janitors all had master keys to each room in case they had to go in in the event of some emergency, like a broken water pipe or even a fire. The keys were kept on a ring inside the janitors' closet. Max thought we could steal the keys on a Saturday night after the janitors went home, get the one we wanted copied at a hardware store in town on Sunday and return the keys to their proper place before the janitors returned to work on Monday morning. Brilliant! This we did one weekend in early March, more than a month before spring break.

"What if he takes his keys, Will?" Max asked.

"Then we come up with a different plan, but we *will* fuck him. *We have to!*"

Spring break began the second Friday of April. Almost everyone bailed out for the holiday that afternoon. Robert and his roommate, Glen, who was going with him to the Caribbean, left around three o'clock. Brian and Steve left around the same time, Brian to Montana and Steve to Georgia. Max and I were going to Acapulco – more about that later – but not until Monday morning. A perfect window of opportunity if only we could get the car keys. Meals were not offered in the residence halls during school breaks, so we went to the student center and bought hamburgers which we ate in the nearly deserted building.

We decided to look for the keys on Saturday in case any stragglers were still hanging around Elm Hall. We didn't see any. Max and I stayed in my suite that night, just to have some company. Saturday afternoon, absolutely no one was around. We used Max's passkey to go into Robert's room and started looking for his car keys. If he left them, it was not in an obvious place. Not in the desk drawers, not in the bureau with his clothes, not in the table next to his bed. We were both pretty discouraged until Max let out a soft whoop from the closet. "*In his jacket pocket,*" he said. And, yes, there they were. The arrogant bastard had attached the keys to a sterling silver key chain with "BMW" emblazoned on one end in metallic blue letters, the same color as the car.

"These have to go, Max."

"No doubt."

Now, we just needed to decide when to move the car. We knew it might eventually be dusted for prints, so we planned to wear gloves. The question was when. "I think we should do it Sunday night, maybe late," Max said. "The security around here on the weekend is minimal. What we should do is watch until one of the guards makes a pass around our hall, then take the car right after that. If it is missed at all, it won't be noticed for at least a couple of hours which is much more time than we will need." I agreed.

We waited in my room until just after ten o'clock when we finally saw a flashlight beam sweep the grounds near Elm Hall. We waited a few minutes to be sure the guard was gone, then went downstairs, out to the parking area and, using Robert's key, opened the doors to the BMW. Max had wanted me to drive, but I told him he should. "Forget the accident, Max. It was the fuckin' guy's fault." We took a minute or two to check out the dash, the steering wheel and the gear shift.

"It's automatic," Max said, "so it should be much easier than the Jeep."

Max was just about to turn the ignition switch when we saw a flashlight beam not fifty yards away.

"*Shit! What's he doing back here?*" Max whispered as we both slid down as far as we could in our seats.

The guard was not sweeping the grounds with the flashlight, as he usually did, but seemed focused on the ground in front of him. "*Max, he's retracing his steps. Maybe he dropped something.*" And, sure enough, about twenty yards further on, the guard stopped, bent over and picked something up off the ground. *Probably his keys*, I thought. We waited ten full minutes because we didn't want the guard to hear the car start. When we thought it was safe, Max started the car and drove it very slowly toward the Sound. The spot we used for swimming was no more than five hundred yards from Elm Hall. Max left the lights off and we literally inched along because it was very dark and we wanted to be sure we didn't hit a tree or something else.

We got to the Sound without incident. Max stopped the car short of the water. I got out and used a screwdriver we had taken from the janitors' closet to remove Robert's rear license plate which I replaced with the novelty plate that read FUCKED. I tossed Robert's plate into the Sound Frisbee style. I then got behind the wheel and nudged the car a few feet into the water where it promptly sank at least a foot in the soft mud. Our final act of destruction was to fill a Big Gulp cup we got from the student center when we had dinner with water from the Sound and splash it all over the interior. We repeated this four times to make sure everything inside was wet. *Perfect!* We started to walk back to Elm Hall before I remembered Robert's keys were in my pocket. I flung them into the Sound to sink along with the license plate. We were both stoked. I actually started getting an erection before I told myself to calm down.

TWENTY-NINE

Maximilian Van Zuylen

The following morning at seven o´clock, Will´s father´s driver, Jacob, showed up to drive us to the Westchester Airport for our flight in the Radcliffes´ plane to Acapulco. If Robert´s car had been missed, there was no sign of it and no police activity that we could see.

We had expected to spend spring break at our parents´ homes, me in San Francisco and Will in New York, until we each got letters just after New Year´s from our biking friend, Miguel Sanchez. He and his family lived in Mexico City, but they also had a villa in Acapulco and he invited us to spend the school holiday there. Neither of our parents seemed to mind when we were out of the way, so they readily agreed that we could go. My father did check out the Sanchez family and found that Miguel´s father owned a controlling interest in Cemex, the huge Mexican cement company. That did it for him, I guess. Anyway, we were now headed to Acapulco for spring break in the sun with our cool little Mexican buddy, Miguel.

When we landed at Alvarez International Airport in Acapulco, we went through customs and immigration in the plane as we had done in Puerto Vallarta and in Amsterdam. Miguel was waiting for us inside the terminal. No handshakes, just hugs and kisses on both cheeks for each of us. Mexican custom, I guess. We followed Miguel out of the terminal and to the curb where two vehicles were parked – a pink Jeep with pink fringe, no less, and a black SUV. I assumed the SUV was his, but he led us to the pink Jeep. WTF? We put our bags behind the rear seats and climbed in. We were introduced to Jorge, the Sanchez´s driver, who started the car and headed north out of the airport.

I soon realized why the pink Jeep. They were everywhere. "Must be the car of choice here," I told Will. I also noticed the black SUV which had been parked at the airport was right behind us. The windshield was tinted, but I could see two men in front. Maybe there were more in the back.

"Uh, Miguel, that SUV seems to be following us. Is that a problem?"

"No problem, Max. Those are my body guards. They are with me everywhere in Mexico."

"Why do you need guards?" Will asked.

"Kidnapping. The gangs often try to kidnap rich people, hold them for ransom. Sometimes they are let go when the ransom is paid, but usually they are killed so the kidnappers can't be identified."

"Why do you ride around in an open Jeep like this? Anyone can see you, maybe shoot you."

"That's true, Will, but these men don't want to kill me in the car. They want to kidnap me so my father will pay money and pray for my release. The guards make sure that doesn't happen."

I began to wonder if this trip was a good idea.

We drove north, the SUV right behind us, for about twenty minutes. The land was flat here and we could see the ocean on our left, sparkling in the afternoon sun. Turning left off the highway, we began to climb a hill. A roadside sign announced we were heading in the direction of Las Brisas Hotel. We actually climbed past the hotel, drove still higher and finally turned left again heading for the point where the hill appeared to drop straight down for maybe two or three hundred feet. The Sanchezes' villa was the only home on the point and it was behind heavy metal gates. We stopped in front of the gate and waited for a guard to come out from a little guardhouse. He checked the Jeep, even took a look at our bags, then walked back to the SUV and checked that. Satisfied, he returned to the guardhouse and pressed something which allowed the gate to open.

The villa was situated about fifty yards straight ahead. It appeared to be made of limestone and was pretty nondescript from the front. On either side of what could only be a massive front door, there were two double garages. We drove up to the one on the left, our driver pressed a button on the dash, the door went up and both cars went inside. The door immediately closed behind us.

"This is pretty scary, Will," I whispered. He didn't reply.

We walked to the front of the garage and through a door which led to a covered terrace connecting both garages and the front entrance. In the center was a stairway which led down to an enormous terrace built up to the edge of the hill. It was bordered with glass panels on the two sides which were open to the view. The two other sides were the villa walls with long covered verandas facing the terrace. Just spectacular. The most beautiful part was the swimming pool set in the middle of the terrace and covered not in tile, but in lapis lazuli. At the far end of the terrace, on the very edge of the hill, was a covered pergola, or palapa, with seating for eight or ten around a marble dining table. Here, just inside the palapa, Mr. and Mrs. Sanchez were waiting for us.

Tall, slender, patrician and extremely good-looking, they could not have been more charming or welcoming. "We usually serve lunch a little later in the day," she said, "but we thought you boys might be hungry after your flight." I must have looked puzzled, because it was just after three o'clock. Mrs. Sanchez laughed as she noticed my expression. "We usually have lunch, which we call la comida, around four in the afternoon. This is our main meal of the day. We then have a light supper around nine-thirty or ten, but we can accommodate any schedule you like."

"No," Will chimed in. "Anything is fine with us."

With that we sat down to a meal of tortilla soup followed by a green salad served with hot, sliced bread, sea bass on a bed of sour kraut and mashed potatoes and something called coffee flan for desert. It was shaped like a piece of pie and tasted like custard. Throughout lunch, Mr. and Mrs. Sanchez asked us about ourselves, our families and our school. They seemed genuinely interested, not just making polite conversation. After lunch, the Sanchezes excused themselves and went upstairs to their private quarters. "They each have a study up there. My mother likes to read and my father takes care of business. They also take siestas. They usually don't come down again until just before la cena. Sorry, I mean supper."

Miguel offered to take us downstairs to our rooms. This area of the villa was accessed through a circular stairway connecting the terrace level with the floor below. As we walked toward the stairs, a long lizard-like creature ran from one part of the garden to another. Will was in front. He stumbled backwards, nearly knocking me and Miguel to the ground. *"Holy shit! It's a gila monster!"* he shouted.

Miguel just laughed. "No, that's just Lulu."

"Lulu? What the fuck are you talking about. It's one of those poisonous things I've seen on Animal Planet."

Miguel couldn't stop laughing. "Lulu's an iguana. Wait until you meet her brother, Marcos. He's even bigger."

"Bigger? No way. What do they eat?" I seriously thought Will was going to have some sort of seizure. By this time, Miguel was laughing so hard he could hardly talk.

Finally under control, he told us iguanas are common throughout Mexico and are often kept as pets. He said Lulu and Marcos eat fruits and vegetables and any bugs they run across but they are not carnivores. He told Will he didn't need to count his fingers and toes each night.

"Wait here," Miguel said. He walked into the garden, picked up Lulu and walked back to where we were standing. "Want to hold her, Will?" he asked. "I can take a picture with my iPhone and you can e-mail it to your mother."

"No way," Will said.

"I'll hold her," I told Miguel. He placed Lulu in my arms and snapped our picture. I don't know what I expected, but somehow she didn't seem so intimidating after I held her. Will, of course, could not let that go.

"I'll hold her, too," he said. Miguel took another picture, this one of a grim-looking Will with the iguana held way out in front of him. Miguel returned Lulu to the garden and we climbed down stairs to the lower level. Here was Miguel's room, several guest rooms and two rectangular pools which resembled large Jacuzzis. "This one's a plunge pool, very cold and very nice on a hot day. The other one is a Jacuzzi. I use it most nights before sleeping." Both looked really inviting. Our room was next to Miguel's. We unpacked, put on swim trunks and went upstairs to the main terrace. The rest of the afternoon we spent swimming, lying in the sun and talking to Miguel about his life in Mexico.

"Don't you mind having guards tag along with you everywhere?" Will asked.

"Not really. It's what you get used to. Guards have been with me since I was born, so I hardly even notice them."

"But you didn't have guards in Europe, Miguel," I said.

"No, the gangs don't operate anywhere but Mexico."

"What if you want to be alone with a girl or something?" Will asked.

"They're very discreet and manage to stay out of the way if I need privacy."

I thought I would mind a lot if guards followed me everywhere, but I was glad it didn't seem to bother Miguel. As we sat around the pool that afternoon, I noticed how much Miguel had grown since our biking adventure. He was not as tall as Will and me, but he was honing in on six feet and had his parents' movie star looks. He was to become one of the most popular Mexican actors in the world, but, of course, I couldn't know that then.

We joined Mr. and Mrs. Sanchez on one of the villa's verandas for their cocktails before dinner. Servants were setting the table for dinner in the palapa. "That crescent of lights down there," Mrs. Sanchez said, "is from the hotels on Playa de la Condesa, Acapulco's main beach. Miguel will take you there one day. My husband and I remember when there was only one hotel, the Presidente, on the entire stretch of beach. The lights are very pretty to look at, but I think we preferred it when the beach was not so developed. Ah, here she is!" A nanny brought in Miguel's sister, two-year-old Maria. "She was sleeping this afternoon when we had la comida," Mrs. Sanchez explained, "so I couldn't introduce you." Maria clearly adored Miguel and sat in his lap the entire cocktail hour, then wanted her high chair next to his when we had dinner in the palapa.

The three of us - Miguel, Will and I – spent five of the next six days at the Las Brisas Beach Club, a private club on the beach almost directly down the hill from the Sanchezes' villa and just south of Playa de la Condesa. Guests at the hotel Las Brisas could use the club; otherwise, it was for members only, mostly families with villas in the Las Brisas area, Miguel said.

They offered everything. Will and I learned to water ski. Miguel was an expert and we were never as good as he was, but were able to get up on a single ski and to ski across the boat's wake, usually without falling. We rode jet skis north to Playa de la Condesa where we scoped out the yachts at anchor and at the marina. We learned to sail small sailboats. It is harder than it looks and one or the other of us had to be rescued from time to time by an instructor. Miguel was good at this, too, but he admitted he had been sailing since he was about eight or nine. Maybe most fun of all, we got to go parasailing. This is where you are fitted into a harness with a parachute laid out behind you on the beach and a tether line in front connected to a speed boat three hundred yards or so ahead in the water. When the whistle blows, the boat takes off literally forcing you into the air. Each ride was no more than ten or fifteen minutes, but they were awesome! We took iPhone pictures of each other in the air which we e-mailed to our parents, somewhat to their consternation, I imagine. When the ride is over, the speed boat coasts along the shore as the parachute descends and you end up caught by several beach boys waiting on the sand.

One day we went to Playa de la Condesa, just to see it. It is a beautiful beach, but way too crowded, and we were back the next day at the Beach Club. Most nights we had la cena with the Sanchezes in the palapa near the pool. Both Will and I were amazed at the temperature. It never got too hot during the day and never cooled off very much at night, so having supper outside, even at ten o'clock, was really nice. After dinner, we went down to our rooms and usually went skinny dipping in the plunge pool and then the Jacuzzi. With all the physical activity, we pretty much fell into bed after that.

One night, Mr. and Mrs. Sanchez were entertaining guests for dinner. She suggested that would be a good night for Miguel to take us to the Hotel La Caleta for dinner and to watch the famous Acapulco Cliff Divers. I had no idea who or what the cliff divers were, but we piled into the Jeep around eight-thirty that night and drove north past Playa de la Condesa to another hill which we climbed, Miguel's guards right behind us. The hotel appeared to be one of the older ones in Acapulco. The restaurant was around back on a terrace overlooking a cut in the cliff which filled with water when the ocean waves broke and went nearly dry when the ocean receded. After dinner, probably around eleven, some trumpets blared and torches flared on the opposite side of the cut. There, a half dozen boys – at least they looked very young from where we were sitting – were standing near the edge wearing colorful speedo trunks. "Miguel, tell me they are not going to jump into that gorge!" I said.

"Not jump. Dive."

"Shit. They will kill themselves," Will offered.

"Yes, that is possible if they don´t time the dive exactly right. They have to dive just before the waves flood the cut so they hit the water at its deepest. If they go too early or too late, they will kill themselves on the sand bottom."

I wasn´t sure I wanted to watch. Will looked a little uncomfortable, too.

There were more trumpets and drums and finally one of the boys came forward and was fitted with a light, colorful cape which he would wear on his dive. The boy stepped up to the ledge and then waited there for maybe four or five minutes while the drums continued to roll. I was convinced he wasn´t going to dive when all of a sudden he literally flew off the cliff, his cape trailing behind him as he fell at least two hundred feet into the water. There was a collective gasp from those of us in the restaurant. The boy hit the water and then didn´t surface right away. I thought he was hurt or dead when all of a sudden he surfaced waving his cape to the crowd. The applause, not to mention sense of relief, was overwhelming. We watched five more boys perform the cliff dive that night. On our way out of the restaurant, all six of the boys – some were older than they looked from a distance, but all were under twenty, I thought – were waiting by the steps of the restaurant for tips. Will and I gave each one $20 which Miguel later told us was probably ten times more than they got from anyone else. It was definitely worth it, but I can´t say it´s something I want to watch again.

We flew back to school on Sunday while the Sanchezes flew in their plane to Mexico Ciiy. It was a super vacation for which we thanked Mr. and Mrs. Sanchez and Miguel very much, promising to invite Miguel to one of our places for a school holiday very soon. "We should invite him to New York, Max," Will said. "Think of all the girls he could attract."

THIRTY

William Radcliffe

On the way to Westchester Airport, the pilots got a call from my father telling them to arrange a taxi to take us to Deerpark because Jacob was busy that evening. Robert Montgomery had arrived a couple of hours earlier and was in the Elm Hall recreation room talking to the Greenwich police when we got there. He was clearly agitated and royally pissed. I heard him tell one of the officers, "No, that is not my goddamn license plate!", so I knew he was looking at a photo of the rear of the car, maybe while it was still partially submerged. We didn´t want to hang around and maybe create suspicion, so we took our luggage and went upstairs to our rooms. We found Brian Adams in Max´s suite.

"Dudes," he said by way of greeting, "*did you see what´s going on downstairs? Somebody screwed with Robert´s BMW. Drove the fucking car into the Sound. I´ve never seen anyone so pissed!*"

"Do the police know what happened?"

"*It´s pretty obvious what happened. Somebody fucked with him. Even put a fake license plate on the rear of the car. It says FUCKED. I guess so!* Worst part is the BMW guys think it can be repaired so the insurance company won´t total it. Found it almost a week ago. It´s been in police custody and the shop ever since."

Brian had picked up a lot of information in the short time he had been back on campus, and it was all good. Max and I didn´t want the car totaled because Robert would just get a brand new one. We wanted it fixed because we knew for him it would never be the same, no matter the quality of the repair job. *Perfect!*

There was one problem we didn´t count on, though, and didn´t find out about until the following day. All students and all campus personnel who had been on campus the Saturday before last were ordered to attend a special assembly in the student union after supper

Monday night. Max and I relaxed a little when we got to the assembly, however, as there were at least thirty Deerpark students and fifty or sixty campus personnel – security staff, gardeners, janitors, several people from administration and even a few teachers who had not yet bailed out for the holiday. "There is safety in numbers," I whispered to Max as we took our seats. Mr. Prendergast, Deerpark´s headmaster, walked to the podium. Behind him, there were four uniformed police officers, all from Greenwich, I assumed.

"Gentlemen," he began, "a very serious felony took place a week ago Saturday when one of our student´s cars was stolen from the parking area near Elm Hall and driven into the Long Island Sound. The car was discovered by a resident who lives just east of Deerpark when she was walking along the Sound Sunday morning. The Greenwich police were called and arranged to have the car towed out of the Sound and taken to the police motor yard where it was inspected carefully for any clues it might reveal as to the identity of the thief. It is now at a BMW repair facility in New Haven.

"This kind of crime just doesn´t *ever* happen at Deerpark. We will investigate as long as it takes to find the perpetrator, and rest assured he will be prosecuted to the full extent of the law. This black mark on Deerpark´s reputation – and it is just that – *must and shall be erased!*

"Those of you in this auditorium are here because we believe you were the only ones on campus when the theft occurred. It is a sickening feeling to think one of our own could have done such a deed, but those are the facts we have. Let me repeat: *we will find the perpetrator and he will be punished!*

"Now I am going to turn this meeting over to Captain Marshall Davis of the Greenwich Police Department who will inform you of the next steps. Captain Davis."

The Captain was a big man who showed signs of liking donuts. He stepped to the podium and told us "We are in the very early stages of this investigation, but as the Headmaster said, we will find and prosecute the responsible party. Fortunately, Greenwich, Connecticut is a very low crime city, so we have plenty of resources to devote to this malicious theft.

"We will be contacting each of you in the next days and weeks, probably interviewing some in groups to start with, then individually. Headmaster Prendergast has assured us we will have Deerpark's full cooperation and that he expects full cooperation from each of you. That's it for tonight, gentlemen. You will hear from us soon."

The Headmaster closed the meeting by repeating that the culprit or culprits will be found and asking for – demanding, more like it – everyone's help and full cooperation.

Max and I weren't really worried. Even though we were among very few students at Elm Hall that night – there were only six of us, it turned out – we thought the investigation would likely turn pretty quickly to the janitors and security staff who were the ones with master keys to the suites. And that's exactly what happened. Someone had key access to Robert Montgomery's room and also found his BMW car key which was missing from its hiding place in his closet. We were kept very much up to date on the investigation because Robert Montgomerey, who must have been driving the police nuts, could talk about nothing else at meals. Max and I did meet with an Officer Griego at Elm Hall one afternoon about ten days later. I don't know how many others he had interviewed, but he seemed pretty bored with us. Why did we stay at Elm Hall over the weekend? Did we hear or see anything? Did we leave the Hall at any time on Saturday or Sunday? Did we notice whether the BMW was in the lot? Easy questions with easy answers. The interview lasted all of about fifteen minutes and then Officer Griego closed the little book in which he was making notes and left.

Robert never stopped talking about the investigation, which sounded like it was going nowhere. Soon school would be out for the summer and everyone except Deerpark staff would leave so the police couldn't talk further to the students until the fall, if at all. Robert's car was returned to him near the end of May. The FUCKED license plate had been removed and new plates had been installed front and rear because the original rear license plate was never found. Robert didn't want the car and kept finding little things he said were wrong, but the insurance company apparently paid no attention and refused to declare the car totaled.

Max and I congratulated ourselves on a job well done. "The prick deserved what he got," I told him.

THIRTY-ONE

Maximilian Van Zuylen

Worst summer ever! We were in Napa as usual and I had absolutely nothing to do. I tried to persuade my father to let me do some more driving, but he didn´t want me on public roads and wouldn´t ask Mrs. Hale if we could drive on her ranch again. Mike invited me into the City on a Sunday afternoon for dinner and a movie. He was otherwise stuck in his office, he told me, so we only had a few hours that Sunday night. I drove in with one of the chauffeurs and right back to Napa again after dinner and the movie. *Sucks!*

Will was having an equally bad time in Newport, Rhode Island. He hated the place and told me he would burn it down if it weren´t made of stone. I believed him. He apparently became such a shit that his parents sent him back to New York and the care of the two maids and the butler who were working there while the rest of the staff was in Newport.

"It´s better here, Max. Georges, the butler, never asks me where I am going or when I am coming back, so I am pretty much free to do whatever I want." He told me he went up to Harlem a couple of times and down to the Village where he ate in one of the little pubs there or sometimes bought a hot dog from a cart vendor and ate lunch in the Park where he said there was always something to see. Mostly, he was bored, though, just like me. Will did get to spend one week in Southampton with his friend from The Brook, Bobby Maxwell. Otherwise, the summer just dragged on for both of us, so it was with some relief that we returned to Deerpark for our fourth year.

It wasn´t an especially memorable year. We both had new roommates, of course, boys we had known from our earlier years there. They were okay, but nobody we really wanted to hang out with, so Will and I spent time together and also with last year´s roommates, Brian and Steve. Robert Montgomery was gone, having graduated from Deerpark in June. I'm pretty sure none of the boys who had been in Elm Hall last year missed him, prick that he was. There was no mention that Will or I heard about his car, so we assumed that investigation had just petered out, despite the headmaster's prediction that the culprit would be caught and punished.

I did get to spend Thanksgiving at Will's family's home in Palm Beach. The weather was good, so we did a lot of swimming and played some tennis. We also checked out Worth Avenue where all the shops are located and went one night for dinner to Mar-A-Lago, Marjorie Merriweather Post's former estate, now a club operated by Donald Trump. He was there holding forth at another table.

"Guy sure likes to hear himself talk," Mr. Radcliffe said.

"*William!*" Mrs. Radcliffe scolded. Will and I just laughed which probably pissed her off, too.

Winter term at Deerpark is always the worst because the weather sucks, and that year it was especially bad. We had snow, snow and more snow, so much that it was often hard to get to class even though the gardeners plowed the paths to keep them open. It was over spring break – Will was in New York, I was in San Francisco – that my parents came up with a plan for the summer. They apparently could not bear the thought of another summer with me in Napa with nothing to do and complaining about it all the time. The plan was awesome! They were sending me, and both Will and Miguel if their parents approved, on an African safari arranged, like our bike trip, by Abercrombie and Kent. The safari was for four weeks – the entire month of August. I was ecstatic! and phoned Will right away.

"*You know I'm in, man,*" he said. "Now I can stop reading about ways to off myself which I planned to do this summer." I don't think I believed him, but I am not sure. It was harder getting a hold of Miguel. I had numbers for him in Acapulco and Mexico City, but he wasn't at either of those places and my Spanish wasn't good enough to understand what the servant in Mexico City was telling me. Finally, I got one of our Mexican gardeners to talk to the man in Mexico City and learned that the family was at their country place in Cuernavaca.

When Will visited Miguel there a year or so later, he told me the Japanese-style house was built by Barbara Hutton, complete with Japanese rice paddies. The rice paddies were long gone, but the house was still there and used by the Sanchezes for weekends and part of the summer. Miguel sounded like he *really* wanted to go, but was unsure if his parents would let him. Two days later, he called back and said "*Yes!*" So we were set for the summer.

The plan was for Will to fly to San Francisco the last week of July. We would stay in the penthouse and buy what we needed for the trip at the Abercrombie store near Union Square in the City. We were cautioned against bringing too much and told it had to fit into the duffel bags they sent us early in the summer. Khakis and a warm jacket for night and early morning, shorts and tee shirts for day. Two pair of tennis shoes "in case a lion eats one pair" the brochure joked. At least, I assumed it was a joke. No dress shirts, ties, sports jackets. *Yes!*

The first part of the summer in Napa was as boring as last summer, but I had the safari to look forward to and I also had time to get the never-ending Deerpark reading assignments out of the way. I was pretty sure Will had some more mischief in mind for Mr. Morrison, but I didn't ask. He would tell me soon enough. When it was finally time to drive to Butler Aviation to pick up Will, I was surprised my father was coming along and even more surprised when he told me he would help us pick out what we needed at Abercrombie. The surprises kept coming. He gave Will a big hug when he came down the steps of the plane in San Francisco. We drove to the penthouse and after Will was settled in my room, my father took us to Ernie's Steak House in North Beach for dinner.

The next morning, we went to Abercrombie with our catalogue list in hand and bought everything recommended for the trip. It honestly wasn't all that much. Afterwards, my father took us to a camera store on Powell Street where he bought us Nikon pocket cameras with zoom features. He bought one for Miguel, too, so we could each take pictures of the animals we were going to see. I really didn't understand his sudden interest, but I wasn't complaining. After shopping, we went to The Big Four restaurant in the Huntington Hotel on Nob Hill for lunch. The final surprise of the day came when my father dropped us off at the penthouse, telling us he was heading back to Napa. "You boys probably have some catching up to do. Enjoy the City and try to stay out of mischief!" I couldn´t believe it! He was leaving us on our own in San Francisco. Well, not really on our own, of course. One of the chauffeurs was at the penthouse as was the couple who cleaned the place and cooked for us. There was also the building staff which tended to keep an eye on me as I was the youngest person to live at the Pinnacle.

"Your mother and I will be back Thursday morning to take you to the airport. Call if you need anything." And, he was gone. I spent the next three days showing Will just about everything in San Francisco. Will was fascinated by the cable cars which we rode for hours. On our first ride down California Street, Will asked the brakeman, a huge black fellow, what happens if the brakes don´t work. "Just jump for it," he said, pulling hard on the lever to slow the car as we began the steep decline down the hill.

"*No shit?*" was Will´s reply. The brakeman just smiled. We went to Fisherman´s Wharf to look around and have lunch. We walked along Pier 39 which is full of shops and restaurants. We went up to North Beach and checked out Coit Tower. We went to Chinatown one day and ate food neither of us could identify.

"You think we´re eating dog?" Will asked.

"Don´t know. Could be."

"*Shit!*"

On our last day in the City, Julius, our chauffeur, drove us out to Golden Gate Park where we went swimming in Fleischacker pool, supposedly the largest swimming pool in the world. Lifeguards patrol the pool in row boats.

By Thursday, we were stoked and ready to go. My parents showed up to drive us to Butler Aviation for the first leg of our trip which was to Mexico City to pick up Miguel. We would refuel there and fly directly to Gibraltar where we would again refuel for the flight to Maun. To avoid layovers for the pilots to rest, my father put on a third pilot so they could rotate time in the cockpit and keep within the maximum hour limit allowed by the FAA. At the airport, my father hugged both of us, a rare move for him. I kissed my mother good-bye and with that we were up the steps to the plane and on our way.

It was just under four hours flying time to Mexico City. We planned to meet Miguel and his parents in the terminal, so customs and immigration officers came on board and processed our passports to allow us off the plane. The pilots needed about an hour to refuel and service the plane, so we sat down with Mr. and Mrs. Sanchez and Miguel at a small table in the private terminal passenger waiting area. Miguel could hardly sit still, he was so excited about the safari. We all were. I gave him the Nikon camera my father bought for us. He had brought along a camera bag with a rather large looking camera and some lenses inside, but he decided the smaller one would be better for this trip and left the camera bag with his parents. We talked for a few minutes, promising to send photos and e-mails throughout the trip and to call whenever we could. I noticed the Sanchezes´ guards were with them and they actually stayed in the terminal until we boarded the plane and the stairs were raised.

We settled into club chairs in the front part of the cabin for the first part of the flight. Later, we would sleep as the flight to Gibraltar was ten hours long. Will and I had just celebrated our sixteenth birthdays in July and Miguel turned fifteen just four months earlier. Will thought the safari was about the best present any of us could have. Miguel had done more research than either Will or I, but we had all spent time on our computers checking out the camps we were going to, the accommodations – which looked nothing like a camp – and the animals we hoped to see. We talked about Botswana, Zambia, Kenya, Rwanda and South Africa, all of which we were going to see, until we actually talked ourselves to sleep. At some point, our steward, George, had reclined our seats to the "sleep" position and covered us with cashmere blankets. I woke up several hours later looking out into a very black sky. We ate dinner at the forward dining table, then watched a Star Wars movie on the plane´s monitor. Before long, it was back to sleep until we began our descent into Gibraltar.

In Mexico City, the chief pilot told me he wanted us to take a four-hour break in Gibraltar so everyone could walk around and stretch out before flying to Maun. Because of scheduling conflicts in Maun, it turned out we would have six hours in Gibraltar instead of four which was okay with Will, Miguel and me.

Once we passed through British immigration and customs – in the terminal this time instead of the plane – we found a taxi at the airport entrance and rode into the center of town to have a look around and also to have some lunch. Without any encouragement from us, the taxi driver gave us quite a rundown on Gibraltar. "We're a British Overseas Territory," he said, "located on the southern end of the Iberian Peninsula." He said Spain constantly tried to absorb Gibraltar into Andalusia, but "we're not having it. No sir!" The driver pointed out The Rock, which was actually hard to miss. A huge limestone uprising which, we were told, is Gibraltar's major landmark, marks entry into the Mediterranean and was for centuries a military outpost where sailing vessels entering the Mediterranean could be spotted and targeted. Today, The Rock is a nature reserve and home to about two hundred fifty Barbary Macaques.

We left our driver in the downtown area with the pillars of The Rock rising above us. "Big fucker" was Will's only comment. We ate lunch at one of the waterfront restaurants and then took a walk around the downtown. There were all kinds of shops along the waterfront, mostly for tourists, offering all kinds of trinkets, clothing, leather goods and assorted "stuff". There were back streets, too, with some homes and more shops. Miguel wandered into one of these shops looking for leather belts. Will and I walked ahead, finding nothing much of interest. In no more than a few minutes, Miguel came running up behind us.

"*Bastard groped me,*" he said.

"*What?*" Will asked.

"*Grabbed me,*" Miguel said, holding his crotch. "*Why would he think I'm gay?*" He was very upset and kept brushing at his fly like he was trying to rub something off his pants.

"You're a good-looking dude, Miguel. He was *hoping* you're gay. Don't let it get to you, man."

Still visibly upset, Miguel said, "I don't want to look around anymore. I want to go back to the plane."

"Sure thing, buddy," Will said. "You grab that taxi on the corner. Max and I will be along in a few minutes. Something I want to pick up for my mom."

"Uh, okay. You won't be long?"

"Twenty minutes max."

We walked to the corner with Miguel and got him into the cab. "Be right there, Miguel," Will said.

"You know what we've got to do, Max, right?"

I nodded as we walked back to the leather store. Inside, it was easy to spot the clerk who groped Miguel as he was the only person in the store. "You remember our Mexican buddy who was in here a few minutes ago?" Will asked.

"Sure do. *Sweet.* Did he change his mind? If not, I wouldn't mind a three-some with you two."

That did it. Will threw a punch to the guy's face that I don't think he ever saw coming. He fell backwards into a display case and hit his head on a corner of the steel base on the way down. I kicked him in the balls for good measure. Will bent over the guy and was prepared to hit him again when he stopped and pressed his fingers against the clerk's neck.

"He's dead, Max."

"*Holy shit. Are you sure?*"

"*I'm sure.*"

"*We've got to get out of here Will!*"

At the entrance to the store, Will thought to turn the "Open" sign to "Closed" as we left. Neither of us said anything all the way back to the plane. I kept thinking *we murdered him*, but I didn't find it as upsetting as it should have been. We didn't really *mean* to murder him, or did we?

THIRTY-TWO

William Radcliffe

The flight to Maun was almost as long as the flight from Mexico City to Gibraltar. We slept off and on for most of the way. Miguel, I noticed, slept with his hands folded over his crotch. *Poor bastard*! I wasn´t at all sorry we killed that sick faggot, and I was pretty sure Max wasn´t either. Lucky we got out of there, though. Even though the asshole deserved it, I figured we would have been in big trouble if we´d been spotted by the police or some customer of the store had wandered in.

I have no idea what the city of Maun is like, if there is one. We landed at a pretty small airport where Max´s father´s plane was to leave us. Everywhere else in Africa we would fly on small planes arranged by Abercrombie and Kent as the runways were too small to accommodate the jet. Inside the terminal, after going through immigration and customs, we met up with Sammy, our A&K guide. Actually, Sammy was more of a chaperone or companion as we had regular guides at each of the camps we visited who knew the areas where we would tour looking for animals. If Sammy had a last name, we never learned it. He was somewhere in his twenties, I guessed, rotund and never without a smile. He worked special group tours for A&K. "Never been out of Africa," he told us. "Never want to be."

Sammy led us to a prop plane sitting on the runway. There were four or five other people also waiting to board. "It´s like a taxi," Sammy said. "Goes around Botswana and Zambia delivering people to the various camps and then bringing them back to Maun after their safaris are over." Ground personnel tossed our duffel bags into a luggage compartment with everyone else´s. Everyone climbed aboard, probably about ten of us. There were a few empty seats, but not many. The propeller engines were very loud.

"There´s only one pilot," Miguel said. "I´ve never flown with just one pilot."

"Relax, Miguel," Max said. "He´s pretty young. Probably won´t croak today."

I wasn´t sure Max´s attempt at humor helped, but we were off before Miguel could decide he didn´t want to fly in a plane with only one pilot. As soon as we left the runway, our view from the plane´s windows was a limitless landscape. Below, there were no roads, no buildings of any kind, just endless land and water, some trees and herds of animals which were hard to identify at altitude. I know I saw zebras and some giraffe, but most of the others I couldn´t say. It was unlike anything I had ever seen, what the earth was like before people messed with it. Awesome, in fact.

The further into Botswana we flew, the more water there was. Our destination was the Vumbura Plains Camp in the Okovango Delta, the largest delta in the world. Most of the waterways were somewhat shallow as I could see animals wading out to what looked like the middle of streams. We landed on a short, dirt runway and were the only four passengers to leave the plane. An attendant asked us to identify our duffels, which we did, then found Joe Bronson, our Vumbura Plains guide who would spend the next six days with us. Joe grew up in Johannesberg, South Africa, worked at Vumbura Plains during summer vacations when he was in college, and now worked at the camp full-time.

The first surprise was Joe´s truck, our transportation for our stay at Vumbura Plains. It looked like a Jeep, only longer with more seats, and also wider. There was no top, and the only door was next to the driver. Everyone else climbed over the side and into the truck. No windows or posts to block the view of whatever lay out there. The next surprise was that the truck went through water, not real deep but above the side boards. "No bridges, man," Joe said. "You have to know the shallow spots."

"Isn´t it dangerous being so open like this?" Miguel asked. "I mean, the animals could come right up to us, right?"

"Absolutely, they could. But the thing is, they don´t pay any attention to the Jeep. It´s like we´re just part of the landscape – and probably not very good eating. Now, I don´t recommend you get out and have a walk around when we come upon a pride of lions, mind you, but if you´re in the Jeep, none of the animals pays much attention." It was the ´much attention´ part I wasn´t so sure about. Miguel didn´t say anything.

On our way to Vumbura Plains Camp, we passed several groups of Impala grazing on grasses and small plants. Joe was right. They paid absolutely no attention to us. "They´re the McDonald´s of Africa, boys. They´re everywhere!" We also passed some giraffes and a group of elephants. One of the elephants stopped eating and gave us a long stare, but he stayed where he was. Good thing, too. He was huge!

For two summers when I was younger, my parents sent me to a camp in the Adirondack Mountains in New York. It was for boys ten to thirteen, so I must have been ten the first year because I remember being one of the youngest campers. There was a nondescript structure on the property where we took our meals and also a building with showers and toilets. We were encouraged to pee out of doors and save the bathroom for ´number two´. We slept in four man tents on cots. I don´t know what I expected Vumbura Plains Camp to look like, exactly, but it was definitely not like the Adirondacks.

We drove up to a clearing where a couple of other Jeep-like trucks were parked. In front of us was the main Vumbura Plains pavilion. On one side of the large room were comfortable chairs and couches and lots of books and magazines on African wildlife. The other side of the room was the dining area with several round tables. Directly in front was a wall of glass looking out on a deck and a watery landscape. A lone hippopotamus was foraging for something in the water. Joe took us down a wooden walkway to our "tent". The walkway was elevated several feet above the ground except in one area it sloped down to ground level, then back up again. "This is for the hippopotamuses," Joe said. "They like to walk through here to the water. If we left this section elevated, they would walk right through it."

Our tent, if you can call it that, was a smaller version of the main pavilion. It had a huge living room with a deck beyond. The bedroom had been set up with three beds for us. There were two bathrooms, one of which featured a glass shower facing the deck. "The monkeys like to watch you shower," Joe said. "Be sure to keep the glass door closed; otherwise, you'll have company."

Joe said he would come back for us in twenty minutes for our afternoon drive and left us to unpack our stuff. A monkey sat on our deck staring at us through the window. "This is pretty awesome," Miguel said. Max and I certainly agreed. If this is what our African adventures would be like, we would have fantastic experiences. Before Joe returned, we managed to take a selfie of the three of us with the monkey in the background. Not a great shot, but we sent it to each of our parents anyway.

Once Joe returned, we walked back to the parking area for our first drive. He explained we would start each morning at six a.m. and drive for about four or five hours. Then, we would go out again around four p.m. for two or three hours. This schedule, he said, would allow us to find animals while they were up, awake and walking about. He said most slept in the middle of the day so there was no point in our being out then. Sammy never accompanied us on any of our drives, leaving that to the guides at each camp. His job, I figured, was to make sure we got safely from camp to camp during our stay. That first afternoon, we saw zebras, more impalas, – they *are* everywhere – a female lion with her two cubs, and more elephants. The best were the lions. The female, who was no more than about ten feet from the Jeep, was bathing the cubs with her tongue. She was completely unfazed by our presence and went about her business as though we were not there. Miguel turned out to be the best photographer among us, so we sent many of his pictures home. Max's mother wrote that she thought it irresponsible of the guide to take us so close to dangerous prey, and told him she planned to complain to Abercrombie and Kent until Max assured her we were perfectly safe in the Jeep and completely ignored by the animals. After that, we were more careful about the pictures we sent.

Dinner that night was a buffet barbecue set up on the deck of the main pavilion. There were space heaters at each table because the temperature dropped as soon as the sun went down and we all wore jackets. One of the choices from the barbecue was grilled impala which Miguel did not want to eat. It tasted like chicken. There was also beef, lamb, actual chicken, and bowls of vegetables and salads. There were several kinds of dessert laid out, mostly pies and cakes. No one at Vumbura Plains Camp was going hungry. The five of us ate dinner at one table – Sammy, Joe, Max, Miguel and me. Joe told story after story of his adventures on the plains, of the animals near the camp we would see, and one of a woman on safari here bitten in two by a hippopotamus after she refused to wait for the Camp staff to escort her back to her cabin. I don´t know if that story is true, but it was definitely enough to keep us from wandering around on our own. Max later said it was probably bullshit, but served its purpose.

And so our days at Vumbura Plains Camp followed a pattern. Every morning at five-thirty, the tallest, thinnest black man I had ever seen rang our doorbell and delivered steaming tea and biscuits. We dressed quickly in the warmest clothes we had and met Joe in the parking area. It was *fucking* cold before the sun came up. In the Jeep, at each of our seats, were hot water bottles and blankets. We wrapped the blankets around us, put the water bottles in our laps to keep warm, and we were off.

During our six days at the Camp, we went on two drives each day and saw an amazing number and variety of animals, including all of the Big Five one morning, something which Joe said was very unusual. We never saw a kill, but we did see the results of two. First, there was a lion finishing off an impala, and later we saw a leopard in a tree with the remains of an impala which he had dragged up the tree to prevent other predators from sharing in his feast. Maybe I remember so much about our first camp because the Okovango Delta was so spectacular or maybe it was the abundance of animals. Whatever, Vumbura Plains was a real stand-out.

Our next camp was Toka Leya Camp on the Zambezi River in Zambia. By the time we got there, Miguel had seemingly forgotten his groping experience in Gibraltar. Since we had no access to European newspapers where we were, Max and I didn´t know whether the murder had been reported anywhere. I suppose it is possible police thought the clerk had just taken a bad fall. That might have been likely if his only injury had been to the back of his head, but it wouldn´t account for bruises to his face from the punch I threw. Anyway, neither Max nor I thought much more about it and Miguel was once more his old self who no longer slept with his hands over his crotch.

We only stayed in Zambia a few days. Abercrombie and Kent included this camp on our itinerary primarily for two reasons: to see Victoria Falls which are the largest falls in the world based on width and height, according to our guide, and also to see white rhinoceroses. The rhinoceros is now a protected species in Africa as it is near extinction from poachers who value its horns, worth up to five hundred thousand each for the powder inside. Two rhinoceroses lived in a wilderness surrounded by armed guards. They were asleep when we hiked in to their location, but even lying down, they are fierce, intimidating beasts. There had to be an easier way to make money.

My other memory of Zambia is the monkeys. I don´t know what kind they were, but I do know they were everywhere and they liked to steal stuff. We ate lunch each day at Toka Leya on a large wooden deck surrounded by trees. As soon as any of the guests left their tables, monkeys would descend from the trees, jump on the tables and run off with whatever scraps were left. The braver ones didn´t wait for people to leave. One jumped up on our table in the middle of lunch. When the waiter tried to shoo it away, it jumped from the table onto Miguel´s head. I actually think the waiters spent more time trying to drive the monkeys off than serving food to guests.

THIRTY-THREE

Maximilian Van Zuylen

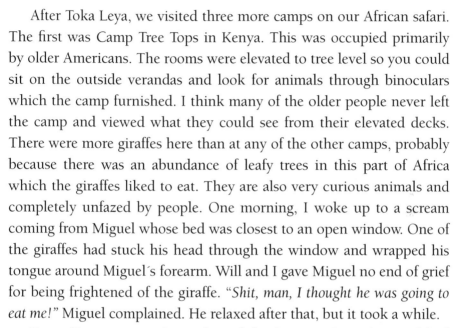

After Toka Leya, we visited three more camps on our African safari. The first was Camp Tree Tops in Kenya. This was occupied primarily by older Americans. The rooms were elevated to tree level so you could sit on the outside verandas and look for animals through binoculars which the camp furnished. I think many of the older people never left the camp and viewed what they could see from their elevated decks. There were more giraffes here than at any of the other camps, probably because there was an abundance of leafy trees in this part of Africa which the giraffes liked to eat. They are also very curious animals and completely unfazed by people. One morning, I woke up to a scream coming from Miguel whose bed was closest to an open window. One of the giraffes had stuck his head through the window and wrapped his tongue around Miguel's forearm. Will and I gave Miguel no end of grief for being frightened of the giraffe. *"Shit, man, I thought he was going to eat me!"* Miguel complained. He relaxed after that, but it took a while.

From Kenya, we took another of the "air taxis", as Sammy liked to call them, to Rwanda where we stayed in a small hotel on Lake Victoria which sits between Tanzania, Kenya and Rwanda. This was not technically a camp, but we were there to see the gorillas which live in bamboo forests nearby. To get to the forest, we drove in another open Jeep about half an hour from the hotel. This time, there were three armed guides, one for each of us. At the entrance to the jungle, we left the Jeep and began walking into the bamboo. The farther we went, the more dense the jungle became until there was nothing under foot but bamboo. At this point, we separated, each of us going with one of the guides. My guide, Jimi, who didn't look much older than me, told me I must be very quiet and make no sudden movements. We found a bit of a clearing and I sat down, Jimi sitting behind me with his rifle in hand. Here we saw about a dozen gorillas, including silverback males, females and babies. The silverbacks stayed mostly at the edge of the group, pacing back and forth and looking fierce. Jimi told me if one charged, I was to lower my eyes and head and make soft growling noises. This is supposed to calm the males. Fortunately, I was not charged, as I am not sure I could have looked at the ground with a several hundred pound gorilla running at me. The females were not aggressive, but did keep a close watch on the babies who approached me with no fear at all. One of them pulled my hair, another pushed at my stomach and a third one just sat in my lap and tried to steal my sunglasses. I managed to take a few pictures until Jimi told me he thought the flash might provoke one of the silverbacks. That was all the warning I needed.

In the Jeep on the way back to the hotel, we couldn't stop talking about the gorillas. Miguel might have been the most excited and began showing us the pictures he took. As usual, his were the best. He even got one up close of a silverback. "Did he charge you?" Will asked.

"No. Maybe he thought I was a relative. You know, dark skin, dark hair." Will thought that was hysterical and started calling Miguel "gorilla man".

Our last camp was Londolozzi in South Africa. In some ways, this was the best of all because we had the entire camp to ourselves. There were three cabins, each close to the central dining lodge. Will, Miguel and I stayed in one cabin, Sammy in one, and our guide, Jeff Bridges, stayed in the third. Here, we followed the same schedule we had in Vumbura Plains Camp. In our Jeep every morning by six, back in camp around eleven and out again at four for a couple of hours. The camp had originally been built in the 1920's as a hunting lodge for some wealthy English people. In the main lodge, there were maybe a dozen photographs of hunters with their dead prizes at their feet. Surprisingly to me, anyway, some of the hunters were women. The family still had a home on the property, but the camp was now run by a concessionaire under a long-term lease. Jeff told us you could get hunting permits for certain unprotected animals, but that most visitors just wanted to see the animals and photograph them.

On our drives from Camp Londolozzi we saw the now-familiar impalas, herds of elephants, giraffes (Will asked Miguel if he wanted to pet one which cost him a solid punch in the gut), more lions, hyenas, crocodiles and a massive herd of cape buffalo. These we encountered on one of our evening drives back to camp. As we came around a curve on the dirt track leading to camp, there they were blocking our way. There must have been about fifty of them. They seemed not the least bit surprised to see us and were definitely not inclined to get out of our way so we could pass. This might be the only time I was really scared on the whole safari. There were buffalo in front of us, on both sides, and eventually in back as well. We were indeed stuck until the animals chose to let us through. Cape Buffalo appear fairly docile, but they are huge animals with fearsome-looking horns. Any one of them could have easily tipped over the Jeep and stomped us to death. Jeff told us to sit still and be patient. "They're grazing," he said. "They'll move on when they finish here." He was right. They eventually moved away to our left, leaving an opening on the track for us. All three of us jumped out of the Jeep to take a pee as soon as the animals left. Not a moment too soon! Actually, it might have been a moment too late for Will, but he would never have admitted it, or admitted being scared for that matter.

THIRTY-FOUR
William Radcliffe

The flights home were nothing I ever want to do again. Nine plus hours from Maun to Barcelona. Max talked his pilots into flying through Barcelona as neither one of us wanted to land in Gibraltar, although I seriously doubt that would have been a problem. Eleven more hours to Mexico City where we said good-bye to Miguel and where my father's plane was waiting to take me to New York, and then five-plus hours to Westchester Airport. *Sucks!* Once in New York, I spent the last week of vacation in my room reading the required material Mr. Morrison had assigned us for the summer. *Prick! He needs to die!.* All that said, Africa was the best thing I ever did in my life! The animals were amazing; I was with my best friend and another good buddy; and I never had another experience to match that adventure.

One of the best parts of our junior year at Deerpark was we could finally choose our roommates, so Max and I were suite mates in St. Joseph's Hall. Finally, a residence hall named for something other than a tree. You would think I cared, but I don't suppose I really did. The important thing was we were back together again and could continue as roommates until graduation. The other good part was learning to drive. Not like driving on Mrs. Hale's ranch where it would have been nearly impossible to hit anything other than a bush along the dirt tracks, but really drive on real roads, with real traffic and real rules.

Deerpark offered optional driver's ed. classes for students sixteen years and older. This was good because you can't get a driver's license in Connecticut without passing classroom and driving tests given by state-certified instructors. Max and I signed up for classroom instruction on Saturday mornings. The classes were two hours long and went for five weeks. Much of the sessions were lectures about road safety, respect for other drivers, blah, blah, blah, but we also watched movies, some of which were kind of funny, although they weren't supposed to be.

These were films showing the effects of alcohol and drugs on drivers' reflexes in all sorts of situations. One film showed a driver by the side of the road trying to recite the alphabet to the policeman who had stopped him. "A, B… uh …D" and so on. *Hilarious!* Another showed a teenage girl, also at the side of a road, trying to touch her forefinger to the tip of her nose. I thought she was going to poke her eye out. Finally, our instructor showed us a drunk driver being processed at the local police station. He was strip searched (we only saw part of that), dressed in an orange jump suit and thrown into a cell with a bunch of men you would probably hope never to meet. *Okay, point taken!*

Much more fun was the driving part which Max and I did with separate instructors on Sunday mornings. No one was allowed to ride along with the instructor and student so there wouldn't be any unnecessary distractions. My instructor reminded me of the Schwimmers. He wasn't German, but he was certainly a humorless, dour old fart. The car we used was a Ford compact with driving controls on the driver's side and also on the passenger's side so that the instructor could take over at the first sign of trouble. Driving in and around Greenwich, Connecticut on a Sunday morning is about as easy as it gets for a new driver. Most residents were probably asleep, hung over or drinking bloody marys by the pool. Anyway, they weren't out on the road so it was easy to concentrate on staying in lanes, signaling for a left or right turn ("too soon is just as bad as too late," old sourpuss told me over and over again) and even parallel parking since there were rarely cars waiting behind us while I slowly – *very* slowly - backed into an empty space.

My biggest problem was the speed limit with my instructor forever telling me I was going too fast. "There are no signs around. How am I supposed to know what the speed limit is?"

"Didn't you learn anything in class?" he barked. "It is always twenty-five in a residential area and thirty-five in a business or industrial area unless otherwise marked."

Okay. Okay. What an asshole!

The best day was when he let me drive on the Connecticut Turnpike and I could give the little car some throttle. I think I got all the way up to fifty-seven miles per hour before the warning came.

Anyway, both Max and I got certificates of completion for the classroom sessions and also the road instruction, so now we were eligible to get licenses. Two problems immediately presented themselves: we had no car, and Max´s parents were not here to give their permission for him to get a license, something which is required in Connecticut.

We obviously had to have a car to take the driving test at the Connecticut Department of Motor Vehicles office. The only car my parents had in New York state was the limousine, and neither Max nor I thought we could pass the test driving that beast. After some haggling with my father, who didn´t think I needed to drive in the first place ("You don´t need to drive in New York, Will"), he relented and agreed to rent a car which Max and I could use for the test.

That still left us with the parental permission problem. Max´s father, who was somewhat more enthusiastic about our driving than my father, solved this for us. Or, rather, one of his assistants did. He learned that Connecticut would accept a signed parental consent form from an absent parent provided the parent´s signature was notarized. This was a great relief to my parents, as well, as it meant neither of them would have to trek to Connecticut and sign the form in front of a DMV clerk. So, within a week, we had the signed, notarized forms to take to the DMV.

Max and I made back-to-back appointments at the DMV on the last Saturday of October. Early that morning, Jacob drove the rental car from Manhattan to Deerpark. We each spent a half hour getting used to the car, which was a Chevrolet, but bigger than the Ford compacts we had driven with our instructors.

The night before our appointments, we read the Connecticut Driver´s Manual cover-to-cover and even tested each other on the questions we would need to answer. The written test was a snap. There were fifty multiple choice questions. It was easy to rule out at least two of the five choices because the answers were ridiculous. For example, "If there are pedestrians in a crosswalk, you should slow down until there is enough space to pass safely between them." I think you could miss five questions and still pass. Max and I got one hundred percent on our tests.

Then came the part where we had to prove we could actually drive. What a shit job it must be to sit in a car hour after hour with sixteen and seventeen year olds testing their driving skills. Nevertheless, the examiner we got was a young man, probably under thirty, who actually put us at ease. Max went first. He was gone about thirty minutes and I began to worry he'd had an accident or something. Instead, he returned all smiles and showed me his exam results: another one hundred percent. Now it was my turn and I was probably even more nervous because Max got a perfect score. I would never hear the end of it if I got a bad score or, worse, failed the test.

Traffic was light and I thought I was doing really well. I even nailed the parallel parking part, making it look easy, I thought. The last thing I was asked to do was turn right on the street leading to the DMV office. The light changed, I turned right and parked at the curb in front of the DMV. My instructor shook my hand, congratulated me on passing the test and gave me my test results with a ninety-eight percent marked on the top corner. I must have looked surprised because the examiner pointed to the comment section on the bottom of the form indicating I had signaled left for a right-hand turn. Two points deducted.

Max demanded to see my test and then the shit began. "Boy doesn't know his left from his right." "Come on, Will. Try again. Which way is left?" And on and on. I put up with it for a couple of minutes, then threatened to deck him. That didn't help. Max just continued to laugh and make left / right jokes. Finally, I laughed, too, although I tried not to.

"I swear, Max, if you start with this left / right shit at school, I'll kill you." Max just kept laughing. A few minutes later, we walked out of the DMV office with temporary drivers licenses which we proudly and carefully guarded in our wallets.

THIRTY-FIVE
Maximilian Van Zuylen

Will and I had our drivers' licenses, but still no car. Will's father pretty much made up his mind that a boy who lived in New York City didn't need one. No place to park, subways take you everywhere, blah, blah, blah. "But dad, I live in Connecticut. All the upper form boys have cars. Why can't I have one?"

"You'll only be in Connecticut one more year. After that, let's see where you end up in college. Then, maybe we will discuss a car."

"*Prick, bastard, asshole*". Those were just some of the words Will had for his father after these telephone calls. My father would not let me have a car in Connecticut because he thought I was too inexperienced to drive cross country at the end of term. He did, however, send me a picture of a bright red Chevy Blazer parked in our driveway in Napa. It had a big bow tied around it with a placard which read "Max's Wheels". I was beyond thrilled and could imagine myself driving through Napa in the summer and down to San Francisco to meet Mike. Awesome!

I think my Chevy Blazer is what got us a car in Connecticut. Oddly, there was some level of rivalry between my father and Will's. I have no idea why. Both men were enormously successful and wealthy in their own right and were not in any way business competitors. Nevertheless, both Will and I noticed it. Within a week of the photo of my car from my parents, Jacob showed up with a black Ford Explorer for Will. There was no note from his parents. So like them. I suppose that took some of the joy out of receiving the car, but not much. *We had wheels!*

Our junior year at Deerpark was also The Year of the Girls, or The Year of the Hot Chicks as Will called it. And, it was all made possible by The Wheels. As juniors, we were free to come and go as we pleased without parental permission slips, real or forged. The only condition was we had to maintain a three seven five or better grade point average, so we did keep up with our studies, but the freedom was awesome.

A week after Will got the car, he called Sylvia Marshall, the student at Smithfield Girls Academy in Guilford, Connecticut, he had hoped to nail a couple of years ago before she took off for the summer in France. Sylvia was now dating a freshman at Yale ("Can´t compete with that, man," Will told me), but Sylvia offered to introduce us to a couple of her friends at Smithfield. On the appointed Saturday, we drove to Smithfield, met Sylvia at her residence hall and were introduced to Mary Jacobson and Alexis Montgomery, both juniors and if not raving beauties, very nice looking. I don´t know how we decided to pair up, but I ended up in the back seat with Alexis while Mary sat beside Will in front. We drove to a pizza parlor which one of the girls recommended. It was a good choice because there were lots of high school and college students there, the music was loud and it was easy to relax.

Afterwards, Mary suggested we take a drive out to the Sound which was very close by. I noticed she had taken Will´s hand as we walked to the car. During the ride, Alexis had her hand on my thigh. I didn´t know what to do, but I needn´t have worried. Once parked near the beach, the girls were all over us. It was November then and too cold to be out on the beach, so we stayed in the car. Alexis and I had the better space (we were in the back seat), but Will and Mary seemed to have no problem in the passenger seat. I think we might have spent the night there, but the girls had to be in their hall by eleven p.m., so we managed to get back in our clothes and on our way before they would get late slips.

"*Holy shit, Will, did that just happen?*"

"I told you these boarding school girls are horny, Max." He had told me no such thing.

In any event, we saw the girls every week or two throughout the year and would have seen them more often except Smithfield kept a tight rein on how often and with whom their girls could leave campus. As Deerpark students, we were apparently considered more acceptable than the local high school boys so we were generally allowed to take them off campus at least a couple of times per month. At the girls´ suggestion, we quickly stopped wasting time at the pizza parlor and instead found secluded places to park. As the spring weather rolled in, we often took blankets down to the beach and had sex there, once changing partners at Mary´s suggestion. *Unbelievable!* At the end of that night, I heard Mary tell Alexis "Even their penises are the same." Will howled when I told him.

THIRTY-SIX

William Radcliffe

Max and I spent Thanksgiving with our parents, me in Palm Beach, Max in Napa. He sent me picture after picture of his new car, most with him clowning around: Max sitting on the hood, Max on the roof, Max standing beside the open front door, hands deep in his pockets. He was like a five-year-old with his first bike. I loved it!

When we got back to Deerpark, I was royally pissed. Once again, it was *fucking freezing* in Palm Beach. Why does *anyone* want to go there in November? What was worse, I was going back for Christmas. My parents stayed in Palm Beach, as they usually did, after Thanksgiving and would not return to New York until after New Year's, if then. *Shit!*

Then, I got a reprieve. Miguel wrote to invite both Max and me to spend part of the Christmas holiday with his family in Mexico City and Cuernavaca. Max could not go because Mike Smith had announced his engagement over Thanksgiving and would be married at the Van Zuylens´ penthouse Christmas Eve. But, I could go, and I knew my parents would be only too glad to get rid of me and my shitty attitude over the holiday. I spent a week with them in Palm Beach because I wasn´t invited to the Sanchezes until December twenty-second. Once again, I tried to behave so they wouldn´t punish me by canceling the trip. It was hard, but I managed.

On the twenty-second, I flew directly to Mexico City from the North Palm Beach Airport where Miguel and his parents met me in the private air terminal after I cleared customs and immigration on the plane. I don´t know if there is a more charming, or maybe the word is gracious, couple in the world than Mr. and Mrs. Sanchez. They welcomed me with open arms and actually seemed to care what a seventeen year-old boy had to say. If anything, Miguel was even better looking than the last time I saw him. Tall – almost my height at 6´2 ½" – he was maybe the most handsome young man I had ever known. *Must have to beat the chicks off with a stick. Lucky bastard!.*

Soon, we were off to the Sanchezes' home in Mexico City. No open Jeeps here. We rode in a black SUV with tinted windows, and were followed by another black SUV, presumably their armed guards. Somehow, they managed to ignore the security, although I don't know how. Once we cleared the airport and "el centro", we drove north on a broad, beautiful tree-lined boulevard. The street sign read "La Reforma" and this was clearly the area where the better homes and estates were located. The trouble was you couldn't see a single house. Every one was behind either tall walls or thick hedges or possibly both. Within a few minutes, we turned right into a short cul-d-sac with what appeared to be five homes – two on our right, two on our left and one at the end which turned out to be the Sanchezes' home.

"Home" is not the word which first came to mind when I saw the outside of their property. It was completely surrounded by a stucco wall, which Miguel later told me was fifteen feet high with jagged glass embedded into the stucco on top, razor wire all around the perimeter and cameras about every twenty-five or thirty feet. From the outside, it looked like a fortress or even a prison. *How do people live like this?* As we approached the gates, Miguel warned me not to say anything to the guards or even acknowledge them. Greeting them, which most people would expect, was their signal that something was wrong. *God!*

Once inside the gates, everything changed. There were fountains, trees, flower beds, lawns, all immaculately maintained, and statuary, including several pieces designed by Sergio Bustamante, the famous Mexican sculptor. As Miguel told me, I remembered seeing some of Bustamante's work on the malecon when Max and I were in Puerto Vallarta. The house, itself, reminded me of our cottage in Newport. It was probably about the same size or a little bigger, built of stucco, not stone, and there were very tall windows on the first and second floors, most of which opened to terraces or balconies. My mother would have called it enchanting. I thought *holy shit*!

We parked in the circular motor court and went up the steps to the huge glass and iron doors leading to the entrance. Inside, the space was cavernous. There was a large, single stairway which lead about half way to the second floor, then branched out left and right. *I could really be a shit and send my mother a photo.* I decided to think about it. Upstairs, Miguel's room was at the end of a long corridor. He actually had two rooms, a living room and a separate bedroom and bath. My room was across the hall. It was only one room, but a very large one with a sitting area, my own bathroom and a nice balcony which looked over the grounds.

I was unpacking when Miguel came in. "My mother said we will have la cena – excuse me, dinner – at nine tonight. Okay with you?"

"Miguel, anything is okay with me. I'm really glad to be here." *Anything but Palm Beach and my parents,* but I didn't tell him that.

We talked for a while, recalling our adventures in Africa and also our bike ride through Europe. Before we went downstairs, Miguel gave me a hug and a kiss on both cheeks. I recalled the customary greeting from our earlier times together, but it still made me a little uncomfortable.

Downstairs, we walked through the formal dining room to a less formal space outside. A fire burned in the fireplace. It was a cool evening, not cold, but the fire felt good. There were candles everywhere – on the table, in sconces on the wall, in free-standing holders on the terrace floor. There was no other lighting. A small fountain gurgled on the wall opposite the fireplace. *I would definitely send a photo to my mother, shit that I am.*

At dinner, I learned that Mr. Sanchez had a passionate interest in films. It turned out he owned a string of theatres in Mexico City, Veracruz and Guadalajara in addition to his cement business. Mrs. Sanchez told me she liked movies, but not as much as her husband, who, she said, saw every American and Mexican film that came out. I also learned that we would be going to a gala cinema awards show the following night which was the reason I was asked to bring a dark suit with me. I wasn't exactly thrilled with this news, but Miguel was obviously enthusiastic, so how bad could it be?

After dinner, the four of us walked in the garden, Mr. Sanchez and Miguel leading the way among the garden paths, Mrs. Sanchez and me following. "This is my most favorite time of day," she said. "Just smell the perfume. The flowers are so pungent at night, and the birds sing."

It was beautiful, and it did smell good, but I still couldn't help thinking we were in some kind of prison, however magnificent. After a while, Mr. and Mrs. Sanchez said good night, leaving Miguel and me alone in the garden. "Come, I have a surprise for you," Miguel said. I followed him into the house and up the stairs to his rooms, not sure what to expect.

"I want you to meet my girlfriend, Lola," Miguel said, "and her friend, Fabiola." Sitting in the room were two of the most strikingly beautiful girls I had ever seen. Lola came right up to Miguel and gave him a long, passionate kiss on the mouth. Any doubts I might have had about Miguel after his hugs and kisses on my cheeks dissolved that instant. *Lola was hot!* We talked for a few minutes, but it was obvious where this was going. Miguel fished in a cabinet in his living room and came out with two small bottles of brandy.

"Here," he said handing me one, "why don't you take this with you." And with that, Fabiola took my hand and led me across the hall to my room. Mostly, I remember being overwhelmed. The brandy, Fabiola's beauty, her passion. I don't remember her leaving. What I do remember is Miguel coming into my room the next day to awaken me at two in the afternoon.

"I see that Fabiola wore you out," he said. "You have to get used to Mexican women. They are much more passionate than Americans. Come on," he said. "Let's take a swim before lunch." I wasn't sure I could walk. Miguel just laughed as I made my way naked into the bathroom and got under the shower.

"Some surprise, Miguel. It may take me a while to recover. But thanks ... I think." He laughed again.

"Like I said, you have to get used to Mexican women." I was pretty sure I could do that. "Not to worry, Will. We leave for Cuernavaca tomorrow. I don't have any women there, so you'll get to rest."

After our swim, Miguel and I joined his mother and little sister, Maria, for la comida – lunch – in the outside dining room. It was after four when we sat down and almost five-thirty when we finished. I went upstairs to take a nap, still tired from the exertions – and probably the brandy – the night before. Miguel stayed downstairs to play with his sister. Around seven-thirty, Miguel came in my room to awaken me. It was pitch black inside and out. I thought I might have slept all night if he hadn´t rousted me. Dressed in my dark blue suit, and Miguel in his, we went downstairs to wait for his parents. They joined us right away and we set off for the theatre in three SUVs this time instead of two. Miguel said I would get used to the security if I lived here, but I am not sure.

We stopped in front of the Zocalo, or main square, in the center of the city. It is a magnificent complex with several two or three hundred year old buildings enclosing two sides of the square. All were lighted against the night sky. The centerpiece is probably the Palacio de las Bellas Artes, a bit like Lincoln Center only much older, grander and infinitely more interesting architecturally. Several of the guards got out of the cars with us while the others drove the cars away to someplace where they could park, I imagined. The four of us, accompanied by the guards, made our way across the square to the Palacio. We entered a large reception room where guests were milling about, drinking champagne. Miguel and I both passed on the champagne. I don´t know about him, but I thought better of it after the brandy the night before.

Mr. and Mrs. Sanchez obviously knew many of the people there and spent the time in the reception area chatting with them. Soon, an usher came to escort us to our seats in the auditorium which were right in front of the stage. I had not looked forward to this part of my stay, but, so far, it seemed pretty cool. The show began with a performance by Mexico City´s folklorico dancers, both men and women. They were accompanied by an orchestra at the back of the stage. This went on for some time with all the dancers performing at once, then just the men, just the women, and finally a couple. I had to admit it was spectacular. The master of ceremonies – I never caught his name – made his appearance and the winners of the various cinema awards were announced. My Spanish is not very good, so I caught only bits and pieces of what was happening, but it seemed to me it was like the American Academy Awards, only for Mexican films. Trophies were handed out for various categories, some of which like best direction, best actor and actress and so on, I understood. Interspersed with the awards, just like the Academy Awards, were song and dance performance and clips from the movies under consideration for awards.

The last award of the evening was given to Gael Garcia Bernal, then the most famous Mexican actor in the world. It wasn't for any particular role of his, as far as I could tell, but some sort of award for overall excellence. I am sure he knew about it in advance, but he seemed truly touched. Just as the show concluded, another usher appeared and escorted us back stage to meet the honorees. This was clearly for Mr. Sanchez who was introduced to many of the winners. Miguel was off in a corner of the room talking to Gael Garcia Bernal. They seemed to be talking like old friends. "Do they know each other, Mrs. Sanchez?" I asked.

"No, William. Miguel auditioned for a role in Sr. Garcia's next film a month ago. Miguel likes theatre, just like his father, and he did the audition as a lark. Apparently, the producers liked what they saw. I haven't said anything to Miguel, but if Sr. Garcia approves, Miguel will be offered a part in his next film which shoots in San Miguel de Allende."

I was floored! Miguel never said anything to me about auditioning for a role in a movie. As I looked at the two of them, though, I could see a bond there. They talked for some time, then Sr. Garcia gave Miguel a hug and kiss on both cheeks – that greeting again – and I assumed Miguel passed whatever test he needed to pass. The rest is history, but either Max or I will tell you about it later.

Miguel came into my room and woke me up not once, but twice during the night he was so excited about the prospect of acting in a movie with Gael Garcia. Finally, he stretched out on one side of my bed and fell asleep. I went right back to sleep and awoke the next morning late with Miguel encouraging me to get out of bed. We had places to see before taking off for Cuernavaca.

We had a light breakfast downstairs at noon, just coffee and fruit and set off on the tour Miguel had planned for us. Once again, a second SUV trailed us everywhere we went and at least two guards accompanied us whenever we left the car, and, as usual, Miguel paid absolutely no attention. First stop was Chapultepec Park and the Castillo of Maximilian and Carlota, Mexico´s short-lived Emperor and Empress. The two were sent from Spain by the Hapsburgs to rule the country in the 1500´s. Their reign lasted only a couple of years as Spain pulled the troops necessary to assure their authority and their lives. Carlota is thought to have gone mad and returned to Spain where she was confined to what we would call today an asylum. Maximilian was soon shot to death by a firing squad. Nevertheless, their history is still celebrated in an odd way in Mexico and they are very much remembered.

Next stop, the Anthropology Museum, which is a show place of Mexican history from the country´s earliest days up to the present. There are amazing artifacts there – Aztec and Mayan, principally, but much more. Here you will find history of the Conquistadores, statues of Aztec and Mayan Indians in their traditional garb, and even statues of Maximilian and Carlota in the fashion of the day. There are rooms devoted to maps showing the country when it extended into the United States, weaponry from all periods, other rooms depicting examples of Mexico´s wealth, from silver mines to agricultural products. It would have been easy to spend a week there.

Our last stop was the University of Mexico, an urban campus but very much apart from the industrial and commercial areas which surrounded it. The campus had been completed sometime in the 1950´s, so it was relatively new by Mexico standards. Mexican artists had been commissioned to create dozens of murals on the buildings´ walls, many depicting one aspect or another of Mexican history. There were also beautiful waterways throughout. Most were tiled and many sent up small sprays of water. Miguel had always hoped to go there, and I could see why. "Now, though, I am thinking of one of the major drama schools in the United States if I am successful in Gael Garcia´s movie."

"Would your parents agree?"

"My father would, I am sure. My mother might take some convincing since she has hoped I would follow my father into Cemex. Odd, no? It is usually the father who wants his son to follow in his footsteps."

I didn't say anything, but hoped Miguel would get to follow his dream, whichever way it led.

Leaving for Cuernavaca in the afternoon meant after la comida, which began after four p.m. and ended just before six, still "afternoon" by Mexican calculation. So, we set out for Cuernavaca in the dark about six-thirty. The city is fifty miles directly south of Mexico City. We were actually not going to Cuernavaca but to Juitepec, a small village a few miles farther south.

On the way, Mrs. Sanchez explained: "This has been a favorite project of mine since before Miguel was born. I met Barbara Hutton in the early 1960's just after she finished building Sumiya, her Japanese estate outside of Cuernavaca in 1959. It took five years, but was authentic in every detail, including the rice paddies and Japanese coolies she imported to work in the fields. Amazing, if you think about. I am not sure I particularly admired her," Mrs. Sanchez said, "but I do admire what she created. Sumiya is absolute perfection in every aspect, from the gardens, to the architecture, everything." She was obviously very passionate about this place.

"We come to Sumiya only a few weeks a year, but it is my favorite place in the world. The sense of peace and tranquility there are overwhelming." She went on. "After Barbara died, the estate was sold to the Camino Real Hotel chain. Mercifully, they did not tear down the original pavilions or destroy the gardens, but they did erect absolutely hideous hotel rooms on the property. My husband bought the property for me as a birthday present almost twenty years ago, and it has taken me nearly that long to demolish the hotel and restore the property to its original condition. Fortunately, there were lots of photographs and architectural drawings to help with the restoration. It is now almost exactly as it was when Barbara lived there, minus the rice paddies. I think she would be happy to know I preserved her dream."

I didn't know what to say, in part because I had never heard of Barbara Hutton. Nevertheless, I was anxious to see this place which evoked such strong feelings from Mrs. Sanchez.

Less than sixty miles from Mexico City, it nevertheless took us almost two hours to reach Juitepec, mostly because the roads weren't very good and seemed to wind around forever. Once the estate came into view, you couldn't mistake it for anything other than what it was – a Japanese palace in the middle of Mexico. Inside the red and gold gates, we stopped near a huge, central pavilion. The entire property, including several pavilions, was ablaze with lights, many of them inside colorful lanterns. Floodlights lit the trees and ground lighting marked the gardens and paths. It seemed magical, almost unreal.

"It is hard to see now, Will," Mrs. Sanchez said, "but every single plant and tree was shipped here from Japan, some by Miss Hutton, the rest by me."

I followed Miguel down a garden path, away from the main pavilion. It lead to a smaller pavilion, but still quite large. This was his bedroom which I would share. The structure was perfectly square and appeared to be made of teak, or something like it, and bamboo. There were no doors on three sides of the space, just shoji screens which had been pulled open. The two beds were hung with netting ("mosquitos," Miguel said, "but not this time of year"). There was a deck off one side of the room which extended into a garden and had a Japanese soaking tub to one side. The bathroom was on the one side of the pavilion which was enclosed, although upon entering, the shower was open to a small garden.

"No one likes this place quite as much as my mother," Miguel said, "but I like sleeping here. I leave the shoji doors open and it is like sleeping outside."

After we unpacked, Miguel showed me around the estate, at least the parts you could see at night. There were seven principal pavilions: the main living pavilion, the dining pavilion with an adjacent kitchen hidden behind bamboo, bedrooms for Mr. and Mrs. Sanchez, Miguel and me, and Maria and her nanny, and one extra guest pavilion. Fires were burning in sunken pits on the living and dining pavilion terraces. The swimming pool, behind the living pavilion, was guarded by four large golden buddhas, one at each corner. All four were lighted as was the pool, a rectangular structure with blue and gold mosaic tiles. At the rear of the property, mostly unseen behind a screen of bamboo, were quarters for the servants and the guards. A separate guardhouse was just inside the front gates and, once again, the compound was completely walled and there were cameras everywhere. A fortress of a different kind.

Miguel and I walked up the steps to the main pavilion and joined his parents who were having cocktails before dinner. Three sides of the main pavilion were open while the fourth side was enclosed and held a carved jade fireplace surround with television and entertainment cabinets trimmed in jade and gold on either side. We were offered our choice of green or mint tea. "We only have traditional Japanese dinners once in a while," Mrs. Sanchez said, "but I thought you might enjoy one while you are here."

"Wonderful," I said, imagining raw fish and other inedible food.

A short while later, we walked down the path leading to the dining pavilion. This one was completely open on all sides, although there were small cabinets at each of the four corners. Mrs. Sanchez took me to one of the cabinets and showed me a photograph. "This is Barbara Hutton in this very room in about 1960 with her seventh and last husband, Prince Pierre Raymond Doan Vinh na Champassak, a member of the former royal family of the Kingdom of Champassak, now part of Vietnam." She went on. "You can see Miss Hutton and the Prince sitting on pillows on the floor at the dining table which is right there in the center of the room." She laughed. "The one concession I made to comfort was to cut out the flooring under the table so you could sit western style." I noticed the table was no more than eighteen inches or two feet above the level of the floor and imagined it would be very uncomfortable spending much time there unless you could actually put your feet underneath.

"You still sit on pillows," she said, "but there is a chair back at each place so it is really quite comfortable. Miss Hutton would probably not approve, but she´s not sitting here anymore."

We took our places, Miguel and me on one side, Mr. and Mrs. Sanchez on the other. The centerpiece was a golden pagoda, probably three feet high and very delicate looking. There were also two smiling buddhas with very large stomachs facing the pagoda. *Extraordinary!* The meal began with shrimp tempura served in individual bamboo baskets. There was a red chili sauce which could be used to dip the shrimp. *Not bad. Not bad at all.* The main course was Japanese beef (how they got it from Japan to Cuernavaca, Mexico, I have no idea) with glass noodles, grilled Japanese eggplant and sticky rice. I pretty much played with the eggplant, but everything else was very good. Dessert was lychee coconut sorbet served with mango and lime. I would not have known what most of the food on my plates was except for a menu card at my place with hand-painted Japanese flowers in one corner. I took a picture of it and sent it to my mother. *What a shit I am!* Mr. and Mrs. Sanchez drank hot saki with their dinner while Miguel and I had more tea. For the main course, we were each given a very small cup of the saki. I am not sure I liked the taste, but it made me feel very mellow and relaxed.

Dinner lasted almost two hours, and we didn't leave the table until nearly midnight. When we got back to our pavilion, Miguel began to fill the soaking tub while we got undressed. The tub could easily have held more people. "Too bad Lola and Fabiola aren't here," Miguel said. He picked up a wooden ladle and poured some of the warm water over his head. I did the same and then laid back and looked up at the stars. The night was clear and with almost no ground lights in Jiutepec, you could see an infinite number of individual stars and star clusters. All my life in New York, I never saw a single star. *Amazing!* We got into our beds after the "soak" and I think I might have listened to the crickets for all of thirty or forty seconds before falling off to sleep. *I love this place!* was my last thought before sleeping.

For some reason, I was up before any of the others so I went around the property taking pictures, mostly of the pavilions but also of the gardens, the pool and the buddhas which were everywhere. These I sent to my mother and father, not because I wanted a memory book of what was here (I could remember well enough), but because I knew my mother would be envious and because deep down inside, I am truly an asshole!

We spent the late morning and early afternoon at the estate. It was Christmas Eve and we were going to have la comida at the hotel Las Mañanitas in the center of Cuernavaca. It is hard to get any feel for Cuernavaca because everything is behind high walls and closed gates. We drove into town with our usual security (I actually *was* getting used to them) and stopped in front of a white stucco wall with a non-descript wooden door. One of our guards knocked and the door was opened by a very dark Mexican – or was he black? – in what looked like a butler´s uniform and white gloves. We walked into a paneled room which looked like one of the private rooms at The Metropolitan, my father´s club in New York. Directly ahead were windows looking into the garden, probably an acre in size with groupings of wrought iron furniture on the lawn. We were led to unoccupied chairs near the center of the garden. A waiter appeared to take our drink orders – ginger ale for Miguel and me, wine for Mr. and Mrs. Sanchez. A second waiter appeared with bowls of sunflower seeds and other nuts. I thought this was strange until the birds and animals appeared.

"This is the charm of the place," Mr. Sanchez said. "You can sit in the garden, have a cocktail and feed the birds and monkeys. I don´t think there is anywhere else like it." I didn´t mention the monkeys at Toka Leya in Africa who jumped on the tables to steal whatever they could carry away. These monkeys seemed better behaved.

"The monkeys are Wooley Monkeys," Mrs. Sanchez said, "the cleanest monkeys in the world. If you give them a napkin, they will rub their hands together to clean them." And they did. Every time one of them took a sunflower seed or some other nut from me, I would hand him a napkin and he would scrub his hands. Amazing! The birds also came by, mostly parrots but some smaller birds, as well. All of them fed right from my hand with no fear whatsoever. *More pictures for my mother. Will I ever stop being a shit? Probably not.* I could have stayed there all afternoon, but soon it was time for la comida in the dining room inside the hotel. We sat at a table overlooking the garden, lighted now because of the encroaching darkness.

I don't remember much about the food, other than it was not Japanese. What I do remember is the fireworks show which started at dark. It came from somewhere other than the hotel, but many of the fireworks exploded right above us. It was spectacular. I thought the birds and monkeys might freak out, but they were unfazed, probably used to it.

Three days later, it was time for me to leave. Everything about my visit was awesome, including the nightly Japanese soaking tubs we took on the terrace of our pavilion while we lay back and watched the stars. Mrs. Sanchez invited me to go with them to Acapulco for New Year's, but my father's plane was already in Mexico City and I knew how pissed he would be if I kept the pilots waiting there. So, Miguel and I drove to the Mexico City airport while Mr. and Mrs. Sanchez were driven to their home there to get ready for the long holiday weekend in Acapulco.

It was hard saying good-bye to Miguel. He was a real buddy, not like Max, of course, but maybe my next best friend, and I didn't know when either Max or I would see him again. I thought about him on the plane as we sat on the taxiway and hoped his dream would come true. *So, there, maybe I am not an asshole all the time.*

THIRTY-SEVEN

Maximilian Van Zuylen

Will kept sending me pictures of his trip to Cuernavaca. The house looked, well, unbelievable. There were also pictures of him and Miguel at some restaurant with birds and monkeys sitting with them in a garden. Very cool! I wish I could have been there, too, but I could not miss Mike´s wedding. So, I spent Christmas vacation in San Francisco at our penthouse while my parents got ready for the Christmas Eve wedding.

A week before the wedding, Mike had his bachelor party in Cabo San Lucas, Mexico. Mike insisted I come along even though I was the "baby" in the group. There were ten of us altogether and my father flew us there in his plane. The party started before we left the runway, and I think at least a couple of his buddies were drunk before we landed. We stayed right on the beach at the Hotel Las Palmas. It was warm and sunny every day and we clocked a lot of beach time. One day we chartered five fishing boats – another gift from my father – to go marlin fishing. Each boat held the captain, his mate, and two of us. Mike chose me to go with him which was a surprise. "Hey, Max, we grew up together. Remember? I´ve known you longer than any of these other assholes. You´re in my boat, man."

We set out from the central pier in Cabo San Lucas around eight in the morning. As soon as we left the harbor, the boats separated and headed in different directions until I couldn´t see any of them. "Best to spread out," the Captain told us. The charters were for six hours and only one of our boats failed to score, although they did catch some albacore. Mike and I didn´t get a hook-up until almost noon and I thought we were going to head in with nothing to show. Not so. We were sitting in the fighting chairs on the aft deck when the line took off from the reel on the starboard side. Immediately, our deck hand flew down from the bridge and grabbed the reel in the port holder. As quickly as he could, he pulled in the line from that reel "so the fish can't get tangled up in it." Next, he grabbed the reel on the starboard side and released the drag "so the fish can run with it". He handed the rod to Mike, told him to put his feet up on the cap rail and just follow the fish with the tip of the reel. Back and forth the fish flew, sometimes jumping ten or fifteen feet out of the water. In twenty or twenty-five minutes, Mike was covered in sweat.

"Max, I need help with this!" The deckhand, Pepe, took the reel and placed it in the holder between my legs in the other fighting chair. He released the drag on the line while I took the reel, then tightened it a little at a time. I was taller than Mike, but not as strong and was completely exhausted after maybe ten minutes. We went back and forth for the next half hour, with Mike taking the rod most of the time. As the fish tired, we were able to reel in the line until the marlin was only ten or fifteen feet from the swim step. At this point, the Captain came down from the bridge to help us land the fish. Mike actually got the fish up to the step with a little help from the Captain, and Pepe used a gaffe hook to get the marlin up on the step. Awesome! Mike and I hosed ourselves down with water from the fresh water tank and collapsed into the fighting chairs. Pepe secured the marlin to the swim step with line from a storage locker and the Captain returned to the bridge to take us back to the harbor.

"Good thing tonight is not your wedding, Mike," Pepe said. "I think you're out of gas."

"You got that right, Pepe. You got that right."

It took us almost an hour to get back to the harbor at Cabo San Lucas. We docked at a weigh station where the marlin was hauled off the boat and up to the platform. Just over 130 pounds. It felt like 500 pounds. The fish was raised tail first into the air until its bill was just touching the platform. Then, Mike and I stood on each side for the traditional picture which I kept with me at school and later took to the apartment Will and I shared. It was one of the few possessions I really cared about.

We spent three days in Cabo San Lucas, then flew back to San Francisco for the wedding. Mike and his bride-to-be, Nancy Holland, worked at the same San Francisco law firm. She started there a year after Mike did so they had some seniority among associates, but not much. The firm gave them a week off for the wedding and honeymoon. Another gift from my parents, Mike and Nancy were going to the Mauna Kea Beach Hotel in Hawaii following the wedding.

Mike moved back into his old room in the penthouse when we returned to San Francisco. Nancy and her parents were staying in their apartment, and they both thought it best not to flaunt their living arrangement any more than necessary before the ceremony. As usual, my mother had taken over everything, which was okay with Nancy because she was working part-time that last week and her parents were from New Mexico and weren't in a position to make any of the arrangements. Her parents were very nice people who seemed a little overwhelmed. My mother does that to people.

The night before the wedding, my parents took over L' Etoile, the restaurant in the basement of the Huntington Hotel on Nob Hill where family and friends celebrated my christening seventeen years earlier. Some of the tables in the room had been removed to make way for a dance floor. A piano was placed at the far end of the room for Peter Mintun, the pianist who customarily played in the L' Etoile bar. A three-piece orchestra accompanied Peter during the evening.

My mother, grudgingly, I am sure, gave fifty places to the bride and groom, their friends and family. The rest she filled with her social friends. At my parents' table were the Hollands ("I have to include them", she told my father), Ann and Gordon Getty, Paul and Nancy Pelosi, Denise Hale and me. "It's taken *months* for the grass to grow back over the trails you left on my ranch," Mrs. Hale said. "You're not allowed out on the road, are you?" I didn't know what to say. Then, to my great relief, she laughed. "You're welcome anytime, Max. Maybe my foreman, Rusty, can teach you to drive a hay bailer." I told her I thought I should stick to my Blazer for now. She laughed again.

Toward the end of dinner, my father gave a very nice toast to his two "sons," Mike and me and also to the bride and her family. I didn't know the protocol for events like this, but there were an awful lot of toasts – from the Hollands, from a couple of Mike's friends, even from Nancy. Mike went last and included me in his toast ("my best friend and best man"). I was floored. Thank God no one seemed to expect me to say anything. The party lasted until midnight. We rode home in one of the limos. I think Mike was a little drunk or maybe a little overwhelmed. Anyway, my father told him to get a good night's sleep before the big day. I went into Mike's room to make sure he got his clothes off before going to bed. He almost made it, falling across the bed with his socks on. I put a blanket over him and went to my room.

The next day was one of those cold, crystal clear days San Francisco often gets in the spring. There was no sleeping in at our house. Workers - mostly florists and caterers - began arriving just after eight. Mike rousted me shortly thereafter. He seemed fully recovered from whatever over-indulgence he might have suffered the night before. The wedding was not until five, and he didn't want to just hang around until then, so we went out for breakfast and then out to Golden Gate park where we threw the football around for a couple of hours. We grabbed hot dogs at a stand near the park, then took in an early movie. My mother was in near-panic when we returned home just before four o'clock. *"Where have you boys been?"* she said. *"I nearly called the police. The wedding is in just one hour!"*

"Sorry, Mrs. Van Z. I just needed a little time off, and Max agreed to go with me. Don't worry. We'll be ready in thirty minutes."

She sighed. *"Boys! I could kill both of you!"*

Mike and I went downstairs to the forty-second floor, showered and changed into our wedding suits. There was some sort of flower on each of our beds which we were to wear in our lapels. I pinned Mike's on and he helped me with mine. Back upstairs by four-thirty, the bride-to-be and her parents were there posing for photographs. The photographer took one of Mike and me pretending to pin on the flowers, as they were already in place. He took shots of both families, together and separately, and several photographs of Mike and Nancy, who looked really beautiful in a short, white strapless dress.

The florist had placed huge stands of flowers on each side of the fireplace on the forty-third floor where the ceremony was to take place. It was to be a very small wedding, just family, at five o´clock with a reception beginning at six. Timothy Carlson, the presiding Bishop of San Francisco, performed the short ceremony. I stood beside Mike and Nancy´s sister, Janet, stood beside her. It was over in fifteen minutes and Mike and Nancy were married. More photographs followed the ceremony, some of them out on the terrace overlooking the Golden Gate Bridge and the hills of Marin.

Soon, the guests began arriving. I don´t know how many people my mother invited, but I think there were two or three hundred spread out over the three floors of our penthouse. There were bars and food stations on all three floors. Musicians had taken over the area behind my father´s bar on the forty-fourth floor overlooking the living room. By eleven o´clock, the party was beginning to wind down and Mike and Nancy were soon to be on their way to the Fairmont Hotel where they would spend the night before flying to Hawaii in the morning. Mike took me aside before leaving the penthouse and gave me a small package which he told me to open later. I put it in my pocket and watched as they went down in the elevator to start their life as a married couple.

Later, in my room, I took out the package and opened it. It was a red leather frame with a picture of Mike and me tossing a water balloon in Golden Gate Park maybe ten years earlier. Someone had taken it and given the photo to Mike. It is my other favorite possession, and I had it in my pocket when I went over the wall.

THIRTY-EIGHT
William Radcliffe

Winter quarter at Deerpark that year was fairly mild, so we weren't stuck indoors as much as we had been most years. Max and I saw the Smithfield girls a couple of times, but, honestly, I think we were somewhat bored with them. Early in the quarter, I started obsessing with what could be done to Mr. Morrison, who by then I truly hated. Max would probably have let it slide, but I could not. We had tried flooding him out; now I was going to burn him out.

It took a lot of digging on the computer – I used one of several in the library for my searches because I did not want any record on mine or Max's. I discovered Mr. Morrison was a widower whose wife had died about ten years ago. They had no children, and Deerpark appeared to be his only interest. Finding out where he lived proved to be so simple I couldn't believe I hadn't thought of it in the beginning: whitepages.com. There he was. Charles Morrison, 40 Ridge Drive, Bridgeport, Connecticut. Max and I drove by one day after class but before Mr. Morrison typically left campus. Ridge Drive was not in the estate section of Bridgeport and was nowhere near the water. The house appeared to be fairly small but on a heavily wooded lot which afforded privacy from the street and also from neighbors.

On a weekend trip to New York in my car, we bought a two and one-half gallon gas can from an auto supply store in the Bronx. I wanted to fill it while we were in New York, but Max told me that would be too dangerous because the gas could possibly explode in the back of my car so we decided to fill it in Greenwich when we were also putting gas in the car and hope the attendant did not notice. Timing was key because snow or rain could put out any fire before it had a chance to do damage. We needed a dry night but, hopefully, one with some cloud cover. We made one more trip to Ridge Drive, this one just after midnight. We drove past Mr. Morrison's house slowly, but not slow enough, I hoped, to attract attention. We need not have worried. There were no street lights in this part of Bridgeport and not a single house on Mr. Morrison's street had any exterior or interior lights on. *Bunch of old people probably in bed by nine-thirty*, I thought.

Choosing the night of the week was also key, Max thought. It should be either Friday or Saturday when neighbors might entertain and would not be suspicious of cars they did not recognize. We settled on a Saturday night in February. The first Saturday in the month proved impossible because the weather was the shits – it was alternately raining, snowing and hailing, if you can believe it. I refused to think this was a bad omen. The second Saturday was even worse, a major snow storm. *WTF?* Max looked a little down, maybe even dubious, but he didn't say anything.

Finally, we caught a break. The third Saturday in February was perfect. No moon, nice cloud cover, no storms in the forecast. We left the hall at nine, not wanting to cause suspicion by leaving at a very late hour. We filled the car's tank at a gas station in Greenwich and also the gas can we bought in New York, all without observation from the attendant who was inside the office and out of the cold. We then went to a movie in Greenwich, which we told some of our hall mates at dinner we were going to do so we had an excuse for returning late if anyone happened to notice. The movie was a loser, but it didn't matter. It gave us cover for a few hours.

Finally, at midnight, we started driving toward Bridgeport, the gas can in the rear section of the SUV, tied down with elastic cords. Max was still nervous about gas in the car, but it was fucking cold outside, so I figured nothing but a collision could make the gas explode. I did not mention collision to Max. Mr. Morrison's street was as dark as it had been the night we first cruised by. Not a single light burned in any of the houses, even though it was a Saturday night.

I drove to the end of the street and turned around because we wanted to exit the same way we had come. We drove back along the street with the headlights off until we were opposite Mr. Morrison's property. We got out of the car with the gas can and a length of rope we had also bought in the Bronx. This was Max´s idea, as he thought we could use it as a fuse. Max always thought everything through. We had dressed in dark clothes and must have been invisible in the dark night. I silently thanked my father for choosing a black car for me. It, too, would be nearly impossible to see from the houses on the street. We used the pour spout in the gas tank to spread the gas along the front of Mr. Morrison´s house, saving enough to soak the rope with one end near the house and the other trailing us toward the street.

Max got in the car with the gas can and I lit the match and touched it to the rope. As soon as I saw a spark, I got in the car, too, and we took off, afraid of being seen once the blaze started. We did wait at the end of the street, about two hundred yards away until we were sure the fire caught. And catch it did, probably burning some of the dead ground cover before starting on the house. We immediately headed north toward the turnpike and away from Bridgeport, Greenwich and the beach communities of southern Connecticut. Max was nervous with the gas can in the car so we stopped at a closed convenience store – 7 / 11, I think – and stuck the can in their garbage bin. I didn´t think the can could start a fire since there wasn´t much left inside but fumes, but even if it did, the bin was metal and well away from the store itself.

I wanted to use the GPS to find our way back to Deerpark, but Max didn´t think we should have a record on the computer of being in the area. *Maybe he is smarter than me.* Anyway, we drove for maybe fifteen more minutes until we found a familiar roadway and made our way back to school. We parked where I usually left the car and went into the hall. Except for security lights, it was dark inside and no one was around. We snuck upstairs to our room and once inside gave each other a near-silent high five.

News of the fire at Mr. Morrison´s house did not reach us until late the following afternoon when we heard two seniors we didn´t know well talking about it.

"*Holy shit, man.* Some sick fucker torched Morrison´s house last night. Totally destroyed it. He got out, but just barely."

"How´d you find out?" the other one asked.

"I walked by the Admin building on the way back from the gym. Police were all over the place asking questions. Morrison was there in some borrowed clothes, he told one officer, because everything went up in the fire."

"Must have been mightily pissed."

"More like shaken up. Afraid, even. He thinks someone tried to kill him."

"Whoa! Shit!" Serious stuff!"

"Let's check out the news at five. It will be the lead local story, for sure."

With that the two seniors walked upstairs to their suite with Max and me following.

"There's going to be a shit storm, Will," Max said once we were in our rooms.

"Yeah, but there is nothing to connect us. The asshole got what he deserved." I saw Max begin to smile, then we gave each other one more high five.

THIRTY-NINE

Maximilian Van Zuylen

Shit storm didn´t begin to describe it. News of the arson and attempted murder, as authorities called it, dominated southern Connecticut newspapers, radio and television for days. The story was picked up by most New York papers and was also reported at least once on the national nightly news. The *Bridgeport News* led with the story Monday morning:

ARSON AND ATTEMPTED MURDER OF DEERPARK ADMISSIONS CHIEF CHARLES MORRISON

Bridgeport, Conn. February 22. The Bridgeport home of Deerpark Academy´s chief of admissions, Charles Morrison, was destroyed by fire early Sunday morning. Bridgeport police are calling the crime arson and attempted murder and are apparently looking for two suspects based on evidence found at the scene. Security is heavy at the Academy and in Bridgeport where officers are canvassing the neighborhood looking for clues and talking to neighbors who might have seen the perpetrators...

"What evidence, Will? What could they possibly have?"

"Footprints, man. In his garden when we were spreading the gas and maybe in the street. That´s why they think there were two."

"Shit. We should have thought of that."

"Relax, Max," Will said. "We wear size 10 ½ shoes. Some dudes have bigger feet, some smaller. It gives them nothing. We wore Reeboks. Nothing more common than that."

"Just the same, let´s toss them. Maybe there is something peculiar in one of the treads."

That afternoon, we spent at least two hours mutilating the shoes. It was hard work cutting them up, but by the time we were finished, there were only little pieces left. Will and I both laughed at the result.

"These were expensive," Will said. "My mom would be pissed."

At night, we went to the Sound and tossed the pieces into the water, watching them float away with the light of the new moon. Another high five. I began to relax, but admit all the news coverage and all the activity on campus and probably in Bridgeport made me nervous. If Will were nervous, he never showed it.

That first week, the news was non-stop, but as Will told me, there was nothing new after the initial reports that the police were looking for two suspects. Bridgeport and Greenwich police were working the crime together, with Greenwich taking the lead at Deerpark Academy. Talk among the students, who really didn't know shit, was that the police suspected student involvement in the crime. Bridgeport, after all, is a sleepy coastal community of mostly upscale homes with virtually no crime. Mr. Morrison lived quietly alone and apparently had no beef with any of his neighbors, so the obvious place to look was where he worked.

Listening to student speculation in our dining room was interesting. Some thought the culprits were prospective Deerpark students whose applications for admission had been rejected. Others pointed out that made no sense because admission decisions were made in the summer and it was now February, almost March. Mr. Morrison was a big factor in recommending seniors to various universities. A few students thought students who weren't recommended to the colleges of their choice, or who didn't get in, would want revenge. On and on, with no one close to the truth: Morrison was an asshole who, with his unending reading assignments, made sure no vacation was really a vacation. Even I began to relax as the days and weeks passed with no new developments, at least none reported.

Every student at Deerpark, all six hundred fifty, was interviewed by detectives from the Greenwich and Bridgeport police departments. I began to wonder how any crime in Connecticut could be solved with such inept questioning.

"Were you in Bridgeport late Saturday night or early Sunday morning?"

Yes, of course. I went there to torch Mr. Morrison's house.

"Did you know of any Deerpark student who might have wanted to burn his house or kill him?"

You mean other than me and my roommate?

And on and on and on.

Still, I was glad when the quarter ended and we left Deerpark for spring break. If the investigation had progressed, there was no sign of it, at least not in the newspapers or the television coverage which seemed unending. Will and I had calls from both our parents about the crime, so it really was a national story. For the first time in all our years at Deerpark, there were no reading assignments during the vacation. Mr. Morrison was apparently still not organized enough to hand them out.

FORTY

Detective Stephen Olsen, Bridgeport Police Department

In late March, I went out to Ridge Drive to talk to Charles Morrison´s neighbors, Harriet and Paul Winslow. Their home was just south of the Morrison property, but not particularly close because the lots in this part of town were large. They were also heavily wooded which reduced the likelihood that anything could be seen from one house to the next. Still, every possibility had to be checked out. So far, we had two shoe tracks and nothing more. Worse, they were common athletic shoes owned by millions of people.

"Good morning, detective," Mr. Winslow said when opening the door. Mrs. Winslow stood just to his left. "Please come in." We walked into the living room which was nicely furnished if seriously dated. The Winslows appeared to be in their mid-to-late seventies and probably hadn´t done much to the interior in many years.

"Please sit here, detective. This chair is very comfortable. Would you like some cookies and coffee? They´re fresh."

"Just coffee, black, ma ´am, and thank you very much."

"Terrible thing what happened to Charley´s house," Mr. Winslow said. "Lost everything, poor man."

"Yes," Mrs. Winslow added, handing me a mug of coffee. "Do you know where he is? Paul and I have not heard a word from him, not that that is unusual. Charley and his late wife, Adele – God rest her soul – were very private people. She worked at the Academy, too, you know, right up until her death. Fundraising, I think, working with the alumni, something like that."

"Harriet, I am sure the detective has questions he would like to ask. Please go ahead, detective."

"Thank you. Yes, I have questions, but please don't hesitate to volunteer anything about the Morrisons. You can never tell where something might lead." Mrs. Winslow cast a satisfied glance at her husband.

"Now, on the night the house burned, you were home, correct?"

"Yes, we were here all night," Mrs. Winslow answered. "Of course, we were up just after the fire started and finally went back to bed around six in the morning when everything settled down."

"It didn't settle down for long," Mr. Winslow said. "Police were everywhere at first light, looking for clues, I guess."

"Did either of you hear or notice anything before the fire started?"

"Well, I got up to use the bathroom – weak bladder, you know ..."

"Harriet!"

"Anyway, I got up – it was right before the fire, just a few minutes before – and thought I saw movement in the street. Our bedroom is right over there and you can see the street from our room."

"'Movement,' you said. A person, two people, a vehicle, a dog?"

"I don't know, detective. Just movement. Paul told me it was probably the trees blowing, but there was no wind that night that I could tell, so it was something else. Movement."

"All right. And, did you hear anything?"

"No." Harriet volunteered. "We have double pane windows – protects against the cold, you know – so we don't hear much when we are inside and the windows are closed. They were all closed that night because it was very cold out."

"Couldn't hear a cement truck if one came by," Paul offered.

"Dear, trucks aren't allowed on Ridge Drive."

"Just making a point, Harriet."

Do old people always bicker? I wondered.

"Anything else you can think of? Any trouble in the neighborhood? Anyone upset with Mr. Morrison?"

"Oh, no. This is a very quiet neighborhood. And Charley Morrison was well-liked, even though he didn't socialize much," Mrs. Winslow said. "Kept to himself mostly."

I thanked the Winslows for their time. They seemed sorry to say good-bye. Probably not much company in their lives. I got in the patrol car, opened my note book and looked at what I had written. "Movement." Two hours with the Winslows and all I got was "movement." *Shit!*

FORTY-ONE

William Radcliffe

When Max and I got back from spring break, the investigation into the torching of Mr. Morrison's house was still going strong, at least if the police cars at the school were any indication. The story began to fade in the media, though, because there was nothing new to report.

And there won't be, I thought.

By this time, Max's and my parents had pretty much conceded that he and I were going to try to get into the same university, although, for some reason, my mother wanted to separate us. Anyway, she had lost that argument, so both Max and I spent some time over the break – me in New York, Max in San Francisco - talking to our parents about which schools we should apply to. Applications would not be due until late fall, but we still needed to decide where to apply and, so far, we had only seen Columbia University among the likely choices.

The list Max and I made ended up with five names – Columbia, Stanford, Yale, Harvard and Princeton. Our academic adviser, Peter Brant, met with us one Friday afternoon just after classes resumed in April.

"Your academic records here at Deerpark are excellent, boys. I have no doubt that any of the universities on your list would be delighted to admit you. Before you apply, though, I strongly encourage you to visit each of the universities. Introduce yourselves to the admissions staff, meet with academic counselors, if you can. Get a feel for each one. What you might think of as your first choice now could end up at the bottom of the list after you see the campus. It is important to know as much as you can about where you will be living and studying for four years."

Max and I thought this was good advice. It also had the benefit of resolving what we would do this summer. I would seriously consider offing myself if I had to spend another summer in Newport, and I think Max felt pretty much the same way about Napa. Neither one of us had any friends in these places and nothing really to do.

And so a plan emerged. At the end of term, we would fly to San Francisco and spend a week or so taking a look at Stanford. Even though Palo Alto is just south of San Francisco, Max had never been to the campus, so it would be a new experience for both of us. Then we would fly east and pick off Yale, Harvard and Princeton, and finally Columbia. Although we had visited the campus – at my mother´s insistence – a few years ago, we really hadn´t taken much of a look other than a walk around the courtyard.

The talk on campus, even two months after the fire, was all about Mr. Morrison, the arson and attempted murder as the authorities and campus staff continued to call it. The Greenwich police came back for more student and staff interviews, sometimes with their colleagues from Bridgeport, sometimes alone. A small piece of one of our tennis shoes had apparently washed up on the beach not far from where we tossed it, but I didn´t think it could possibly be of help, especially after a month or so in the Sound. This we learned at dinner one night where talk of the fire seemed to trump everything else. It was all speculation, of course, because there was nothing new. One of our hall mates told some of us he thought the flood in Mr. Morrison´s office and the fire at his home had to be connected, and that pointed to someone at Deerpark.

"Maybe it´s one of his colleagues," someone at our table said. "How would any of us know where he lived?"

"Bullshit," said another. "I looked him up on line. Address is right there."

"I hope you did it *after* the fire, dumb shit. Otherwise, you may be suspect number one."

Max didn´t like that the investigation seemed to be focusing on Deerpark students – if it was – but I reminded him there were six hundred fifty students and nothing to implicate us. Neither Max nor I was interviewed again by the police, although we were aware some of the students were interviewed twice or even three times. *Must have given stupid answers the first time around*, I thought.

Max and I tried to ignore all these conversations – they were gossip, really – and concentrate on our studies. We would be making college applications before the fall term closed, so this quarter really counted. We wanted a four point zero.

FORTY-TWO

Detective Stephen Olsen, Bridgeport Police Department

Deerpark´s spring term ended the last week in May, which meant all six hundred fifty students would be away from campus for three months, with the seniors not returning at all. Worse, we had made no progress in our investigation of the arson of Mr. Morrison´s house and his attempted murder. We had the shoe prints, and the only reason we had those was because they were different from the boots the firemen wore. They, of course, trampled all over the place, but we were still able to identify and mold two sets of distinct prints on the grounds leading to and from the house. We also had "movement" – *shit*! Sometime later, we found a piece of a tennis shoe in the Long Island Sound, but it was so damaged from being in the water for however long it was there, it could not be matched to the molds we had. It was likely from the perpetrators, I thought, but none of our forensic guys could tell us one way or the other. *Shit, shit, shit!*

On a Saturday morning in mid-June, I met with Jeff Johnson, a detective with the Greenwich Police Department. He was as frustrated as I was, maybe more so because we all thought Deerpark students were involved and this was his turf.

"Nothin´ man, and now the kids are gone. This will be colder than my ex-wife when fall term comes."

"I hear you, Jeff. Were you involved when someone flooded Morrison´s office – what, a couple of years ago?"

"Yeah, but that trail – if there was a trail – went cold, too."

"What about that incident where some student´s car was pushed into the Sound?"

"No, but others in my office were. You think there is a connection?"

"Shit, I don´t know, but it might be interesting to see a list of students who were on campus when the flood, the car theft and the arson took place. Might narrow the field."

"I like it, Steve. I'll get in touch with Deerpark on Monday and see what they can give us."

FORTY-THREE
Sylvia Radcliffe

Why, why, why did Will have to meet Maximilian Van Zuylen. Of all the people on the planet. *God!*

And William, Sr. will not hear of our trying to separate them. He thinks they are *good* for each other, for god's sake, and is *encouraging* them to go to the same university. *I can't believe it!*

"I love their friendship. I suspect they will be life-long friends unless one steals the other's girlfriend," he told me.

Every time I see the two boys together, I cringe. I feel nauseous, and it is getting harder and harder to hide. I don't know why William, Sr. hasn't noticed, but he is oblivious, thank God! Still, Marylou Whitney told me she thought they were twins when she and John came for dinner in New York one time and the boys were there for the weekend.

Aileen Mehle saw them together at "21" when she was with Nancy Reagan and the King of Spain and William and I had lunch with the boys before they left for their bike trip in Europe. She never misses anything. Worse, she is very good friends with some of the Van Zuylens, including Marie-Helene. God, this would be front page news, not just Aileen's column in *W*, although either one would be disastrous. *It's just a matter of time. I know it! Ruined! I am ruined!*

Now, Will is with us in Newport for two weeks before he flies to San Francisco to join Max for a tour of Stanford. Maybe they will go there, get away from the east coast. Yes, I will promote Stanford. It is a fine school. William, Sr. can't object and the boys will be away from New York. *Yes, that is exactly what I will do!*

FORTY-FOUR

Maximilian Van Zuylen

The third Saturday in June, I drove my red Blazer from Napa to Butler Aviation to pick up Will. We intended to get an earlier start, but his parents wanted him to attend some family function in Newport. Anyway, it didn´t matter. We had the whole summer to check out the universities we had on our list, and I was sure it wouldn´t take nearly that long.

Once Will was settled in my room in the penthouse, we took our laptops into the great room and began looking at websites for the five schools we had chosen, starting with Stanford. We had not had any time to do this in the final weeks of spring term because we were so absorbed with our upcoming final examinations. There was a ton of information and photos for each school, very reminiscent of the website for Deerpark Academy. Everything was written in superlatives, but in fairness, these were the five best universities in America so they had bragging rights. The photos of Stanford reminded Will of the Mexican architecture he saw in Mexico City when he visited Miguel. The website, however, referred to it as early California architecture. Whatever, they were nice looking buildings and very consistent architecturally, even among the newer buildings. There was one aerial photo of the courtyard, or quad as the website called it, which reminded me a little of the Columbia campus.

We had two appointments the following week, both with people my father knew from boards they served on together. One was with Dr. Alberta Siegel, a psychology professor "emerita" who had been with the school years before Will and I were even born. We were having lunch with her at the Faculty Club on Monday. The second appointment, on Wednesday, was with Dean Anderson, Stanford´s president. We were meeting with him in the morning and, in a call to my father, the Dean said he had arranged a tour of the campus after our meeting with one of the students there for the summer term.

With not much else to do until Monday, we hung out in the City, again riding the cable cars at Will's insistence, eating hamburgers at Tommy's Joint, and catching a sci-fi flick in the Marina. We also spent more time on the computers checking out Yale, Harvard, Princeton and Columbia.

Finally, on Monday morning, we got our grades via e-mail: four point zero and four point zero. We were ecstatic and couldn't stop high fiving and punching each other in the gut and the shoulder. One of the maids saw all the hijinks and called the chauffeur because she thought we were fighting. *Absolutely awesome!* This practically guaranteed admission to any of the schools on our list. Our adviser, Mr. Brant, had said we were shoo-ins to these schools, but this clinched it. Now we could apply to our first choice, whatever it turned out to be, and one other, just in case, and not worry about the others.

We left the penthouse at ten thirty for the drive to Palo Alto, not wanting to be late for our appointment. Dr. Siegel was easy to spot. She was waiting in the foyer of the Faculty Club and, anyway, my father had left a photo of her in my room from the annual report of the company on whose board they served. A heavy set woman probably in her early seventies, she had a big smile and an even bigger sense of humor. Both Will and I liked her.

We sat in one corner of the cavernous room and began to get acquainted over cokes for Will and me and ice tea for Dr. Siegel. At first, she didn't want to talk about Stanford at all, but instead to know about the other universities on our list.

"All excellent," she said. "You can't go wrong at any of these universities, and thankfully you have the grades to choose among them." We told her about knocking down four point zeros for our last quarter.

"Well, I know Max's father," she said, "so I am not surprised. I don't know your parents, Will, but you must be cut from the same stock." Over lunch, she went on. "I think Stanford might be a little more relaxed environment for students than some of your other choices, but they are all good. You should think about where you want to live for the next few years, because you will get the highest quality education America has to offer at any of these schools." Same advice we received from Mr. Brant.

"I like Stanford, Max," Will said when we were driving back to the penthouse, "and I know we are going to see a lot more of it on Wednesday. I´m a New Yorker and just not sure I want to go to school in California."

"I´m not either, but let´s see what we think after Wednesday."

As it turned out, Dean Anderson was a real hard sell. He down played each of the other universities on our list, insisting Stanford was where we should go. "Deerpark´s one of the best," he told us. "We would love to have you boys here at Stanford." He also asked us a lot of questions about what majors we might choose. Will told him we didn´t know and hoped to keep our options open, at least for the first year.

"That´s the best thing to do," the dean said. "Take courses in several fields and see where your interests lead." We talked for over an hour, or rather he talked and we listened. I was surprised he had that much time for us. Afterward, he introduced us to Bill Windsor, a junior from Canada, who took us on a walking tour of the campus. We didn´t see all of it, of course, but we did check out the undergraduate libraries, some of the class buildings and the quad with Stanford´s chapel centered on the west side of the quad. All very impressive, but Will and I were not convinced Stanford was where we wanted to go.

After our meetings with Dean Anderson and Bill Windsor, we drove to San Francisco, picked up our things at the penthouse and drove north to Napa, getting there in the late afternoon. We planned to spend a couple of weeks there, then fly to New York for our tours of the other universities on our list. I liked Napa when Will was with me because we had something to do. We played tennis, swam, and since we had "wheels" we were able to get out and go to the movies or whatever. My father was disappointed that we weren´t more enthusiastic about Stanford because of his associations with the school. To avoid any arguments, I told him we were keeping our options open until we saw all the schools. For some reason, Mrs. Radcliffe was also encouraging Will to choose Stanford, almost insisting, actually. We both thought that was strange, but we were determined not to let either of our parents push us into a decision we didn´t want to make.

FORTY-FIVE
William Radcliffe

In mid-July, we flew to New York where Jacob met us at Westchester Airport for the drive to Deerpark Academy where my car was parked. Jacob told me he was returning to Newport later in the day so we could have the garage in the townhouse. My parents stayed in Newport, and after some argument with my father, they agreed we could tour Yale, Princeton and Harvard by ourselves. We decided to visit Princeton and Yale first because they were the closest, although none of the schools was really very far away.

Mr. Brant made appointments for us at all three schools. Yale first, then Princeton and finally Harvard where we would spend the night in a hotel before returning to the City. The advisers we met with at Yale and Princeton were okay, but they did seem a bit full of themselves and spent way too much time, in my opinion, talking about each school's heritage and what an enormous privilege it would be to attend. Both Max and I liked Harvard and we really liked our adviser, Morton Gilman. He was probably in his sixties, very warm and friendly. He also gave us a piece of advice we hadn't had before: take a year off.

"Think about it, Will, Max. Except for vacations, you have been in school your whole life. I think every high school senior should take a year off – we call it a gap year – and do something different. Travel, get a job, do things you've never had a chance to do before. It will make you better students when you do enroll."

"But, how do we do that, sir, and still assure ourselves of admission?"

"It's called deferred admission. You apply now, or rather in the fall, and once your application is accepted, it is marked for admission the following year. Personally, I think every student should be required to take a year off between high school and college. It can be a very broadening experience."

That night in the hotel and on the drive back to New York, Max and I talked about little else. Mr. Gilman was right. We *had* been in school most of our lives. We *loved* the idea of doing something else for a year. But what?

"Relax, my man. We still have our senior year ahead at Deerpark and we have to choose a college. There's plenty of time to think about what we could do the year after."

"Do you think our parents will go for it?"

"Might, especially if we tell them it was recommended by the Harvard dude."

Back in New York, we spent two full days at Columbia. This was the only university on our list where my father had contacts. We met the admissions dean and one of the student counselors and also toured the whole campus. The university was built around a large courtyard with all the buildings facing into the yard. Still, it was an urban space and nowhere near as spread out as the other universities we visited. The dorms we visited were just okay. I told Max we could do better with our own off-campus apartment and he agreed. Barnard, the girls' college associated with Columbia, was right across the street. "A nice plus, Max."

One day we walked south from the campus on Riverside Drive overlooking Riverside Park and the Hudson River. I told Max the Park had been designed by the same guy – Olmstead or something like that – who built Central Park. "If we go to Columbia, we should live in one of these buildings, Max. Nice quiet neighborhood, nice views of the Park and the River."

We were both leaning more and more toward Columbia, but we decided not to tell our parents until after we applied and were accepted. We also decided to apply to Harvard as a back-up, but none of the others.

FORTY-SIX

Maximilian Van Zuylen

Early in August, I flew to San Francisco to spend a couple of weeks with my parents and get ready for our senior year at Deerpark. Napa was boring as hell, as usual, but I wouldn´t be there long. Will and I decided to broach the subject of a gap year as we thought it might take some convincing. To our surprise, both sets of parents thought it was a good idea, especially after learning the recommendation came from Mr. Gilman at Harvard. My father´s only caveat was that he wanted a plan. "I´m not in favor of you just sitting around for a year, Max." He also asked me to talk to Mr. Brant at Deerpark to see if he concurred that a gap year was a good idea after graduation.

Our academic schedule that fall was the lightest in all our years at Deerpark. That was to allow seniors plenty of time to meet with academic advisers, fill out applications to colleges, collect letters of recommendation and transcripts. We did meet with Mr. Brant who endorsed the idea of taking a gap year "as long as you have a solid plan for how you are going to spend the year." He sounded like my father. He also recommended we apply to three schools instead of two.

"Choate and Deerpark are the two best preparatory schools in the country, but they are not the only ones. Even though you have top grades from Deerpark and excellent SAT scores, there is plenty of competition out there. Remember, too, that these universities are now looking for diversified student bodies, meaning students from all over the world are encouraged to apply. *What happened to our being shoo-ins?* I wondered.

So, we applied to Harvard, Columbia and, at Mrs. Radcliffe´s insistence, Stanford. "Maybe she just wants me out of the way," Will said. "I´ve never heard her talk about the school before, and, as far as I know, she´s never been there."

The application process is complicated. In addition to the letters of recommendation and transcripts, we had to write an essay as part of each application, and we couldn't just write one and attach it to all three applications because each university had specific topics we were supposed to address. We got them in the mail, though, before the Thanksgiving recess. Then began the waiting game. Will got the first letter toward the end of January: Harvard. Accepted! Even though neither of us really wanted to go there, it was a relief to see the acceptance. Three days later, I got two letters, one from Harvard, the other from Stanford. In at both schools. At least we were both in at the same university, even if it wasn't our first choice. The same day, Will got an envelope from Stanford: Wait listed. *"What the fuck, man? How can you get in and I get wait listed? Our records are almost identical."* I thought it might have something to do with my father's connections to the school, but who knows? *"Probably waiting for some dipshit from Ethiopia to apply,"* Will said. It wasn't that much of a disappointment, though, because neither of us wanted to go, and Will said his mother would have to stop harping about Stanford.

Another week went by and we hadn't heard anything from Columbia. "What's their problem?" Will asked. We decided to talk to Mr. Brant to see if there was anything he could do.

"Just be patient, boys," he said. "Not all of the schools send out their acceptances at the same time. Give it another couple of weeks. If you haven't heard anything by then, I'll check with the admissions office."

Waiting was the worst. It was hard to think about anything else. We tried to concentrate on our studies because all of the acceptances were subject to receipt of final transcripts. Finally, just as we were about to talk to Mr. Brant again, the envelopes came. Both on the same day. We took them upstairs to our suite and just looked at them.

"You first, Max," Will said.

"No way, man. I went first with that Puerto Rican chick, remember? It's your turn to go first."

"What? I can't believe you are dragging that up. Open the fucking envelope!"

"After you, Will."

He tore open the envelope, read the first couple of lines of what looked to be a letter and let out a whoop. *"I'm in! Fuckin'A, Max, I'm in!* Now open yours." I couldn't. It would be so disappointing if we didn't get into Columbia together. We had spent so much time talking about the school, planning where we were going to live, all the things we could do in New York City.

"You open it, Will," I said, handing him the envelope. "I can't do it."

"You *wuss!*" Will opened the envelope, read a bit from the cover letter and said "Oh, no! Rejected!" I was shocked and really, really disappointed.

"Maybe I could appeal, Will," I said, then noticed he was trying not to smile. *"Give me that!"* I said, grabbing the envelope. "Welcome to Columbia" was all I read before jumping on Will. *"I will kill you, asshole. I will seriously kill you!"* We both started laughing – maybe crying a little, I am not sure. Our future was settled, at least for the next four years. What a humungous relief!

FORTY-SEVEN

Detective Stephen Olsen, Bridgeport Police Department

On an especially cold morning in January, I met with Jeff Johnson, the Greenwich detective who was working with me on the Morrison case. We met at a coffee shop in Greenwich and found an unoccupied booth at one end of the room.

"Any luck with that list of Deerpark boys who might have been on campus when Morrison´s office was flooded, the student´s car was driven into the Sound, and the arson fire took place?"

"It took a bit of work, Steve, but I´ll tell you what I have. First, I discarded all boys in grades seven through nine. I figure whoever torched Morrison´s house had to have a car, and that eliminates the younger boys." He went on, "There are about six boys in the tenth grade who were sixteen when the flood occurred, but you have to be a junior or senior at Deerpark to have a car on campus."

"Good. I like it, Jeff."

"So, just looking at the students who were juniors and seniors at the time, there are forty-three students who were on campus when all three events took place. Twelve of them graduated in June."

"Do we know where they are?"

"The school keeps pretty good track of its alumni, so I know where they are in college, at least where they were in September. We can take a look at these boys if you want to, but I think it´s more likely someone still at Deerpark was responsible. Why would anyone leaving school want to flood Morrison´s office and torch his house?"

"Still, it´s a possibility, Jeff."

"It´s also possible no one on this list had anything to do with any of the events, but it´s a place to start."

"Any roommates on the list? We know there were two guys out at

Morrison´s place."

"Most are roommates, Steve. The school lets juniors and seniors choose their roommates, so most students are with the same roommate the last two years. Take a look at the list, and let me know if anything pops out," he said, handing me a typed list of names. "Want to interview them?"

"Yes. Other than this, we got shit. Two sets of worthless footprints, a piece of a sneaker which may or may not have anything to do with the arson, and ´movement´."

"I´ll talk to the administration and see if they can set up the interviews for us."

FORTY-EIGHT

William Radcliffe

We spent spring break at home – Max in San Francisco, me in New York. We told our parents Columbia was our choice and we had been approved for deferred admission. My mother was upset we weren´t going to Stanford, why I don´t know, but there was little point in bitching about it since I didn´t get in. My dad liked Columbia, so except for housing, we were set.

There was plenty of room for us at the townhouse, but it was way too long a commute from East Sixty-Second Street to One Hundred Sixteenth and Broadway. It was my father who came up with the idea of buying a co-op apartment near campus, preferably on Riverside Drive. "No point throwing rent money down the rat hole," he said. I loved the idea and asked him to talk to Max´s father. Maybe they could buy something for us together. Max liked the idea, too, and began working on his father. By the time we returned to Deerpark in the spring, all four of our parents were in on buying a co-op, even my mother who said she would do some preliminary looking with one of the agent´s in Dolly Lintz´s office. "Dolly doesn´t do the west side, darling," she told me, "but she´ll find someone in her office who does."

Early in the term, Max and I were interviewed by Bridgeport Police Detective Stephen Olsen and Greenwich Police Detective Jeff Johnson. They were still fucking around with an investigation which I was sure was going nowhere. They were even trying to link the arson of Mr. Morrison´s house to the earlier flood of his office and – can you believe it? – the incident with Robert Montgomery´s car. Hard as it was, we tried to be humble and cooperative, essentially repeating what we had told officers in earlier interviews.

"Not very many of you on campus for all three events," Detective Olsen said.

"Well, that should help you find out who did it, detective, if it was one of the students." *Dick! Did he expect us to confess?*

Max seemed a little nervous as we walked back to St. Joseph Hall, but I told him to relax. "They don't have shit, Max, and they aren't going to have shit." And I really believed that.

Twice we went to New York for the weekend to look at apartments Dolly Lentz's associate, Mary McGuire, found for us. We saw six in all, four on the Drive and two on West One Hundred Ninth Street, both in the same building. The one we really wanted was a two bedroom penthouse on the sixth floor of a six story townhouse which had originally been a single family residence. The bedrooms were on either end of the floor with separate bathrooms. In the center was a combination living room / dining room / kitchen, and just off the foyer, a powder room on one side and a laundry room on the other. Best of all, big French doors opened to a terrace which ran the length of the living room and had awesome views of the Park and the River.

It was, of course, the most expensive of the apartments we saw and it took some persuading, but it helped that my mother liked it and saw all kinds of decorating possibilities. Max's father agreed and, subject to board approval, it was ours. I was afraid my mother had overdone it when she produced letters of recommendation from David Rockefeller and Henry Kissinger, but in the end we passed the board interview and the apartment was ours. "Lovely boys," one of the board members said. *Such bullshit!*

"Who was the young guy hanging out with the old lady at our interview?" Max asked me. "Erik Lowell, or something like that."

"I think he's the board chairman's grandson. Lives with her, apparently. She told me he is a decorator."

"Seemed kind of dim-witted. I thought he was gay."

"Dude, guy's a decorator. *Of course* he's gay."

"Well, I don't think we'll be hanging out with any of the owners in the building. But that's okay. The apartment is great and we're only four blocks from school."

FORTY-NINE

Maximilian Van Zuylen

It was the haircuts. If we hadn´t cut our hair for summer, we might never have known.

Brian Adams, my former roommate, came into our suite one afternoon to borrow some computer paper. "What happened to your hair, homos?" he asked.

"Cut it for the summer, Brian. You should try it. Might get less cow shit in it."

"Aren´t we the comedian. And look, matching tattoos."

"What the fuck you talking about, Brian? We don´t have tattoos."

"Sure you do, Will, right there at your hairline, just beside your ear. Oh, wait. Maybe they´re gang signs. You guys belong to some bad-ass New York gang?"

"Here, Brian, take the paper and get out. We gotta study."

"Bye, guys. I can´t wait to tell everyone you´re going steady."

Will and I just looked at each other. WTF? Since we didn´t have hand-held mirrors, we took cell phone pictures of the back of our heads where Brian said there were matching tattoos. Sure enough. Identical small red marks behind our right ears just on the hairline. Birth marks. No doubt about it.

"We couldn´t have the same birth marks, could we Max, unless …?" Will asked.

"Unless we´re related," I said, finishing his sentence.

We were quiet for some time. "So, are we Radcliffes or Van Zuylens?"

"Van Zuylens, I think, Will. You and I look like my father, not yours."

"Yeah, I think so, too."

We just sat there for quite a while without saying anything. Finally, Will stood up. I stood, too, and we gave each other a big hug. "Hello, bro," he said. "Hello, bro," I said.

I don´t know how long it took for this to sink in, maybe weeks, but it answered *so* many questions: why we looked alike, why we were alike, why we liked the same things. On and on. That my father was Will´s father didn´t actually seem very important. We were brothers, that´s what mattered. Neither one of us had a sibling and now we did. I came closest with Mike Smith, but Will and I were real blood brothers. *Awesome!*

I wanted to tell our parents what we knew, but Will wanted to wait until we had something we needed. "If word leaked my mother had a child with Frederick Van Zuylen, wow!" Will said. "This is a secret worth keeping, at least until we need to cash it in."

FIFTY

William Radcliffe

Discovering that Max and I were brothers was the most important thing that happened to us that year, or maybe any year. It overshadowed everything. The other big event, though, was our graduation from Deerpark Academy. Six years of our lives were coming to a conclusion. We had done some bad things – some *really* bad things – but we had never been caught, and now we were onto a new chapter: first our gap year and then Columbia University. It all felt good.

Graduation ceremonies were held in the student union auditorium on campus. There were probably four hundred or more in attendance – students, siblings, parents, grandparents, even some friends of the graduating seniors. I noticed Detective Olsen in the crowd. *Did he think the culprits were going to make an announcement during the ceremony? What a dick!* Mike Smith couldn´t come because his wife was expecting their first child any moment. Both my parents and Max´s parents were in the audience, including a couple of my relatives Max had never met. There were one hundred and eight graduating seniors.

The program started with the introduction of the graduates and the presentation of diplomas. That alone took almost two hours as Mr. Prendergast, Deerpark´s head master, had a few words to say about each student as he shook hands with us and handed us our diplomas. Normally, the class valedictorian would speak next, but we elected not to single out any one student among many who deserved the accolade.

That year, the commencement address was given by U.S. Secretary of State Myron Wilcox. Predictably, he spoke about public service, encouraging each of us to give something back to our country as we made our way through college and the professions we finally chose to pursue. *Boring as shit!*

The final event of the weekend was a dinner dance hosted by Deerpark Academy and Smithfield Girls Academy. It was a joint event for the graduating seniors of both schools held in the ballroom of the Waldorf Astoria Hotel in Manhattan on Sunday evening. Parents who chose to attend were seated in the balconies overlooking the ballroom floor where we ate and danced. Neither my parents nor Max´s elected to attend which was fine with us.

We were returned to Deerpark Academy and the girls to Smithfield in chartered busses around one in the morning. Deerpark gave us three days – until Wednesday of that week – to clear out of our suites so they could be made ready for the next occupants. We wanted to move directly into our apartment on Riverside Drive, but my mother was not finished with the decorating so we spent almost a month in New York at our town house while her decorator finished up.

We did go by, of course, several times and pretty much liked everything we saw. The flooring in the big room was now beige marble and the living room section was covered with a muted oriental carpet in grey and gold colors. There was a gray flannel couch facing a big screen television which was mounted on the wall above the fireplace and between the two terrace doors. "Awesome! I didn´t think she would go for the TV," I said. Beside the couch, there were two club chairs set at an angle to the television and covered in the same fabric.

At either end of the room, against the walls, were our desks. Just like at Deerpark, the decorator had put corkboard on the wall behind the desks so we could pin up notes, pictures, whatever. Between the kitchen and the couch was a small glass-topped dining table and four chairs. The kitchen was pretty standard for a New York apartment, but it had a dishwasher which was good. Our bedrooms were very similar and similarly furnished in a variety of blue fabrics. We each had a king size bed, a dresser and a comfortable chair. The bathrooms were pretty standard, too – stall showers, sinks, toilets. All the essentials.

Nothing had been put on the terrace, so I called my mother in Newport. We wanted a table out there, maybe a couple of lounges and some plants. "All coming, darling," she said. "Gregory has done this in record time, so have a little patience. I told him to save the terrace until last. I think he´s also waiting for your bedroom drapes unless they are installed already."

"No. No drapes, mom."

"Well, they should be there any day now. How do you like it?"

"We love it, mom. I think we´ll move our stuff in over the weekend."

"Send me some pictures, Will. Gregory has sent me a few, but I would like to see how the place looks once you and Max are settled."

"Sure thing."

Turning to Max, I said "I think she suspects. Why else is she being so agreeable, so nice to me?"

Who knows? She did seem awfully nice for a change.

FIFTY-ONE

Maximilian Van Zuylen

What to do during our gap year went through more than a few iterations as Will and I, and separately, both sets of parents, came up with ideas and plans for us. My father talked to Denise Hale who agreed we could work on her ranch under the supervision of her ranch manager, Rusty. After my few days on Brian Adams´ ranch in Montana, I was sure that was not what I wanted to do and Will had no interest either. One parent – I can´t remember which one – suggested a year with the Peace Corp in either South America or Africa. A good program, for sure, but not what we had in mind.

Finally, Will´s dad came up with something we both liked: crewing on a yacht in the Mediterranean and the Caribbean. It would give us some work experience which he liked and also let us do more traveling which we liked. The yacht, named after the New York restaurant La Caravelle, was owned by a Turkish man who Will´s father knew through his investment business. The yacht was based in Monaco and used by Mr. Anbar and his family only two weeks a year, at Christmas in the Caribbean, and it was available for charter the rest of the year. The plan was for Will and me to join the yacht´s crew in Rome for the months of August and September. Then, we would get six weeks off until we rejoined her in the Caribbean in November for the winter season.

We checked the on-line charter brochure for the yacht. She was beautiful and huge. Eighty-five meters, or just over two-hundred fifty feet, with four decks. A helicopter rested on the rear section of the top deck. On the main deck, photos showed a large aft deck, a grand salon, small library, a mid-ship entry with elevator and stairway connecting the other three decks. Forward of that was a formal dining room and the galley. On the bow was the master stateroom with twin bathrooms and dressing rooms. It looked like a floating palace. Below the main deck were four double staterooms which opened off the central elevator hall.

Quarters for eighteen crew were forward with the engine room behind sound-proof walls in the rear section. In the very aft was a garage for the boat´s tenders and toys like jet skis, wind surfers, water skis and the like.

Above the main deck was what the brochure called a sun deck. There were lounges on the deck and toward the aft section, a raised eighteen foot salt water swimming pool. Forward was the bridge plus four cabins for the yacht´s officers. There was also a bar / lounge on this deck. The top deck held the helicopter plus space for crew members not working to get some sun or rest.

We didn´t learn much about the crew from the brochure. There were apparently four men assigned to the helicopter – two pilots and two maintenance people. The remaining sixteen made up the crew who worked the on yacht, either as general crew or officers. There was a photograph of the captain, a Norwegian named Karlo Nielsen. We learned that Captain Nielsen had agreed to take us on after a phone call from Mr. Anbar. We would be deck hands responsible for keeping the yacht´s exterior clean. Our "boss" would be another Norwegian, Johan Jamiesen, who was responsible for the deck hands and the cabin boys.

"What do you think, Will?"

"We will be the grunts, that´s for sure, but it could be a cool adventure. Better than working a ranch or going to some godforsaken place in Africa or South America with the Peace Corps."

We used the two weeks we had before flying to Rome to move into our new apartment, not that we had that much to move. Just clothes, computers, some personal stuff. We went shopping for groceries and seriously over-bought at the local deli. "You want *how much* pastrami?" the counter man asked. "Having a bar mitzvah?" Anyway, it was kind of fun stocking up on things and getting our place organized. Gregory, Mrs. Radcliffe´s decorator, did show up with drapes for the bedrooms plus furniture for the terrace. We had a dining table plus four chairs and two lounges. He also brought some nice plants and left strict instructions about their care. The Radcliffes´ butler arranged for a daily to come in twice a week to keep the place clean. She could also water the plants while we were in Europe.

FIFTY-TWO
William Radcliffe

Max and I flew into Fiumicino Airport on August first. Before taking off for Rome, we had been given several instructions by Officer Jamiesen. We were very limited in what we could bring aboard. He suggested two, or "at the very most", three sets of street clothes, all casual. We would be given uniforms which were to be worn at all times on board La Caravelle. Officer Jamiesen also told us we would have five days to learn our jobs because charter guests were expected after that and we would have to know what to do without further instructions.

Officer Jamiesen – never Johan – met us at the airport for the drive to Civitavecchia, Rome's seaport where La Caravelle was docked and being readied for her next guests. From the moment we met him, Max and I knew he was a first class prick, a real stiff. He clearly hated the idea of having "green" deck hands on board and let us know we would be put ashore if we couldn't handle our jobs. *Nice welcome, dickhead.*

The yacht was even more beautiful than her pictures showed. Gleaming white hull with bright red trim, she certainly stood out in this busy commercial port with its freighters and tankers tied up at the docks. The first officer, Wayne Andersen – another Norwegian – was much friendlier. He offered to show us to our quarters and also give us a tour of the yacht. We took the forward stairs below the main deck and found ourselves in the crew quarters. There was a galley and two big tables for crew meals. Behind that area were the cabins, ten on the starboard side, ten on the port. The cabins were not grand or particularly spacious, but they didn't feel cramped either, and each had a rectangular window looking out to whatever view there was. Each cabin was set up for two men. There were bunk beds, a table with two chairs which could be used for dining or writing or using a computer if you had one. There was a closet with hanging space on top and drawers below and a bathroom, or "head", with toilet and shower facilities. Officer Andersen told us we would be responsible for keeping our cabin clean and showed us where crew cleaning supplies were kept. The laundry was in the very forward section of the bow, and there were two laundry crew who would take care of our uniforms but not our personal clothing.

Officer Andersen waited with us while we changed into our uniforms: white shorts, white tee-shirts with "La Caravelle" emblazoned across our chests in the same bright red as the trim on the yacht, and white tennis shoes. "You will be barefoot while working," he said, "because you will be cleaning the decks and using lots of water. You should wear tennis shoes, of course, when on the dock helping with the docking lines. Otherwise, you are free to go about the yacht barefoot."

"Johan tells me you are to report to him at eight tomorrow morning. In the meantime, after our tour of the yacht, he would like you to study the section of the crew manual which describes your job duties." A copy was on our table. Once we were dressed, Officer Andersen gave us a tour of the yacht. I can honestly say the pictures did not do her justice. If the crew quarters were utilitarian, everything else was just magnificent. The salon, the library, the dining room with its round table for ten and Baccarat – we were told – crystal chandelier. The master suite and guest staterooms were huge and sumptuous. I asked Officer Andersen if he knew what it cost to charter the yacht. "About four hundred fifty thousand per week," he said. "Better pray for good weather, right."

"Shit, I guess so."

Max and I thanked Officer Andersen for his time and retreated to our cabin where we unpacked our few belongings and checked our computers for e-mail. Strong signal here. I wondered if that would be the case when we were at sea. We went into the crew dining section where several crew were having their dinner. I wondered how much time the galley staff got off because it was clear crew members ate at different times depending on their jobs. The men at our table were older than Max and me, but not by much. I thought most of them were in their early to mid-twenties. They were friendly enough. A couple of the men asked us to let them know if we had questions or needed any help with our jobs, obviously having been told we were not experienced deck hands. So far, everyone but Officer Jamiesen seemed okay. *There's always one dick*, I told Max.

We went to our cabin after supper and began reading the crew manual. Every position on the yacht was covered in extreme detail from the Captain to the deck hands, which seemed to be the lowliest position on board. Our duties were pretty simple to understand: clean the hull and all exterior decks, including all "fittings", whatever that meant. What was not so easy to understand was how the two of us could possibly keep that much hull and deck clean. It was not until the following morning that we learned there were four deck hands aboard, Max and I and two others. Fortunately, they had been with the yacht for almost six months and could show us the ropes.

At just before eight the next morning, Max and I went up to the helicopter deck where Jacques and Cyril, the other deck hands, were already pulling cleaning supplies from a large locker where they were kept. We introduced ourselves and learned that both Jacques and Cyril were from Monaco where La Caravelle was docked when not in use. They seemed like good guys, very friendly and about our age. Jacques suggested we team up – one of us with him, the other with Cyril so we could learn the job as we went about our day. Officer Jamiesen showed up just after eight and told us once again we would be put ashore if we weren't up to the job. "Is he always such a dick?" I asked Jacques when he left.

"Never known him not to be," he said. "Thinks he should have been promoted to first officer and takes his disappointment out on the deck hands and cabin boys who report to him. A real shit."

"Just stay out of his way," Cyril said "and you won't have any trouble. All the other crew are pretty decent."

Jacques called the bridge to let the officer of the day know we were about to start the washing operation and all open doors and ports should be closed. An announcement over the yacht's loudspeakers followed immediately. We learned that washing a yacht follows a very particular routine. Basically, you start from the very top and work down so as not to get a clean deck wet by cleaning bottom to top. We didn't touch the helicopter – that was left to the helicopter crew – but we washed and dried everything else. Next, we tackled the sun deck. We were not responsible for any of the interior space on this deck or any of the others, but we were responsible for the decks, railings, ports – or windows.

We did work in teams after we finished the helicopter deck. Cyril and Max worked the port side and Jacques and I were on the starboard side. It was hard work, but not excessively hard and we were able to keep cool with all the water we squirted everywhere. By one p.m., when we stopped for lunch, we had finished the helicopter deck, the sun deck and the main deck, leaving the hull still to do. "That's the biggest job," Jacques said. "Usually takes two or three hours."

Jacques and I used the yacht's dinghy to clean the starboard side because we couldn't reach all of it from the main deck. Cyril and Max cleaned the port side, primarily from the dock where the yacht was tied up. By the time we finished up and put all the cleaning supplies away, it was four o'clock and Max and I just crashed in our cabin until about seven when we joined a few other crew members at the mess for dinner. Jacques and Cyril were at our table and told us what our schedule would be in the morning. "Tomorrow we polish," he said. "There's a lot of stainless steel, chrome and brass on the boat. Even though we washed everything today, we have to polish it up tomorrow."

"Just be grateful we don't have any teak on La Caravelle," Cyril said. "That's really a bitch to take care of."

"What do we do when we're at sea?" Max asked. "We can't very well wash the boat then."

"The hull, no," Jacques said, "but we can keep the decks and fittings clean."

"We end up with some slack time when guests are aboard because we can't very well go squirting them or cleaning around them when they are on deck. We always do as much as we can when we are in port and the guests are ashore."

"Do we get any time ashore?" I asked.

"Not much. A few hours once in a while, but mostly what you see is what you can see from the yacht."

Still, it seemed okay to us. The yacht was beautiful; we would be cruising in the Mediterranean for two months; and the crew was friendly and easy to be around, except for Officer Jamiesen.

FIFTY-THREE
Maximilian Van Zuylen

Our first charter party came aboard on Friday and that's when things started to go south for Will and me. The guests, it turned out, were Margaret and Stanley Mortimer, neighbors of Will's parents in Palm Beach, their twin daughters, age eleven, two friends the girls invited to join them, and two nannies.

Will was giving the aft deck furniture a last wipe-down before the guests arrived. As soon as Mrs. Mortimer recognized Will, she called his name and crossed the deck to give him a big hug. Mr. Mortimer came over, shook Will's hand and clasped his shoulder. "What a wonderful surprise!" she said. "You remember the girls, Will?"

"Of course." The twins joined their parents and Will kissed them both on the head. He was introduced to the girls' friends and also to the nannies who were now also on the aft deck. The Mortimers remembered me from a couple of vacations Will and I spent in Palm Beach. They talked to us for a few more minutes before being ushered to their cabins by one of the cabin boys. All this was observed by Officer Jamiesen who happened to be in the salon at the time. Shortly thereafter, one of the cabin boys told us we were to report to Officer Jamiesen's cabin.

"*What the hell do you think you are doing*? Crew are *never* permitted to associate with guests. That is strictly up to the yacht's officers."

"Officer Jamiesen," Will said. "The Mortimers are neighbors of ours in Palm Beach and good friends of my parents. What am I supposed to do? Ignore them?"

"Don't get smart with me, young man. Just do your job and stay away from the guests."

With that we were dismissed. "*What a fucking asshole!*" Will said when we went below to have lunch in the crew mess. When we told Jacques and Cyril what happened, Jacques said "Don't worry about it, man. Just do your job. He really can´t throw you off the yacht despite his threats. Only the captain can expel a crew member, and Captain Karlo is a very fair man. Besides, he is definitely not going to want half his deck crew dismissed with the charters we have coming up."

Jacques was probably right, but what Officer Jamiesen could do and did was make our lives aboard La Caravelle as unpleasant as possible. He was constantly finding extra work for us to do after we were finished for the day, and pointing out every spot or mark he saw anywhere on the boat as evidence we were not up to the job. "Spoiled rich brats" was one of the nicer things he called us. Jacques told us he thought one of the reasons Officer Jamiesen was such a jerk was because he was an insomniac and never got enough sleep.

"He goes up to the helicopter deck at two or three in the morning because he can´t sleep and smokes a cigar. He thinks it calms him down, but I think it just fires him up and makes it even harder to sleep." Will said nothing, but I knew he was beginning to form a plan to deal with Officer Jamiesen. I could just tell.

The Mortimers´ charter was for two weeks, beginning in Rome and ending in Istanbul. La Caravelle would call at the volcanic Italian island of Ponza, Sorrento on the Amalfi coast and three ports in Greece – Rhoades, Mykonos and Santorini. The last port before Istanbul was Kusadasi, famous for the four thousand year old city of Ephesus. The Mortimers would remain on the yacht for our two day stay in Istanbul and then fly to Palm Beach via New York. It was a nice, relaxing itinerary, Mrs. Mortimer said, with some fun ports for the girls and also some educational experiences in Kusadasi and Istanbul.

Will and I tried to keep to ourselves as much as possible without being rude to the Mortimers. It didn´t help. Everytime Officer Jamiesen saw either of us talking to them, he found something wrong with our work or something else for us to do. Until we got to Mykonos, every crew member was given at least a little shore time at one or the other of our ports-of-call. Will and I were not permitted to leave the yacht.

The blow-up came as we were pulling into the port of Mykonos late one afternoon. Will and I were wiping down the aft deck for our guests after a day at sea, and Officer Jamiesen was in the salon giving instructions to one of the cabin boys. Margaret Mortimer came out on the back deck. "Will, Max, Stanley and I want you to join us for dinner ashore tonight. Stanley knows a charming restaurant right on the water which he thinks we will enjoy. The girls will stay here with the nannies."

Officer Jamiesen overheard all this, of course, and came out on the aft deck. "Mrs. Mortimer," he said, "it is kind of you to invite the boys to dinner, but crew members are not permitted to socialize with guests." Will knew Margaret Mortimer and he knew what was coming. He said nothing, but gave me a quick wink.

"Officer Jamiesen," she said about as icily as anyone could. "You are working for me these two weeks, is that correct?"

"Well, yes," he answered hesitatingly.

"Then don't you *ever* tell me again who I can and cannot "socialize" with. *How ... dare ... you!*" I could actually see the color drain from Officer Jamiesen's face. Turning to us, she said, "Boys, Stanley wants to leave at seven so we can watch the sunset from the restaurant. We will meet here about quarter of."

She wasn't finished with Officer Jamiesen who seemed in some kind of a daze. "If I hear any more of your insolence on this cruise, I will ask Captain Nielsen to put you ashore. Is that *completely clear*?"

"Yes, ma'am," he managed to mutter. I thought she might slap him, but she just turned and walked toward the master stateroom. Officer Jamiesen gave us a furious look before he, too, turned and walked away.

"*Holy shit, Will!*"

"I saw her do that once before to some decorator who was trying to install something she didn't want in their Palm Beach house. Those are not cross-hairs to get caught in."

"I guess not."

After that, Officer Jamiesen laid off us, but I knew that would only last until the charter ended. I didn't want to think about what would happen when the Mortimers left us, but I knew Will was coming up with something. I just didn't know what, but knew he would tell me when he figured it out.

Will and I finally got to go ashore again on our first day in Istanbul. The Mortimers wanted us to accompany them on their tours of the Blue Mosque, Topkapi Palace and the Grand Bazaar. The following morning, they were to leave the yacht and I knew we were in for a whole lot of trouble from Officer Jamiesen who still fumed from Mrs. Mortimer´s rebuke.

In our cabin that night, Will announced the plan. I think I was shocked, but after a few minutes, I knew I was in.

FIFTY-FOUR

William Radcliffe

Once the Mortimers left the ship, Captain Nielsen announced we would dead-head directly to Venice where we were to pick up our next charter party in about a week. That meant we would cruise directly there without calling at any other ports. We would arrive in Venice with about four days to clean and provision the yacht. Ample time, the Captain said.

The plan was simple. We would have three nights at sea before reaching Venice. Officer Jamiesen continued his habit of going to the helicopter deck either very late at night or between one and two in the morning to smoke his cigar and try to tire himself enough to sleep. We would be waiting there and while he stood at the rail smoking, we would help him over the side. The plan seemed fool-proof and, in the end, it was. There was only one duty officer in the bridge late at night, and we all suspected he set the radar alarm and fell asleep or dozed from time to time in his chair. No one else was about late at night as the crew valued these hours when they weren't working or being responsible for charter guests.

Just before midnight, Max and I went separately to the helicopter deck to avoid suspicion if anyone saw us. We needn't have bothered. No one was around and no one saw either of us. We stayed in a little passageway just back of the stairs where the cleaning supplies were kept. An hour later, Officer Jamiesen had not shown up and I wondered if we would have to wait for the next night. Not so. He came out on deck just past one and walked directly over to the starboard railing where he pulled a cigar from his pocket and lit it. We moved quickly, but we didn't need to move particularly quietly because there was a pretty good wind which dulled any other noises. Max grabbed his left thigh and I took the right side and in a second or two he was over the side. If he made any sound on the way down, we never heard it.

Max and I stayed on the helicopter deck for maybe fifteen or twenty minutes, trying to slow our heart rates and calm down. We had never *on purpose* killed anyone before, so this was a first. We returned to our cabin separately, but again, no one was around and no one saw either of us. We both fell asleep almost immediately and stayed asleep until we heard the ship's alarm around seven. "*Man overboard! All crew to your assigned stations!*" came the announcement over the yacht's loudspeaker system. At the same time, the yacht slowed and made a sweeping turn, heading back in the direction we had been cruising since leaving Istanbul.

Man overboard instructions were written in our manual. Max and I were assigned amid ship positions on the starboard side of the main deck. Jacques and Cyril were in the same position on the port side. Other crew members were on the bow and on the port and starboard sides of the sundeck and the helicopter deck. Within no more than three or four minutes, the yacht came to full stop and we heard the rotor on the helicopter fire up. It made a horrendous noise as it spun faster and faster.

"*What the fuck, Will,*" Max virtually shouted into my ear above the din. "*They'll find him!*"

"No they won't, Max. It's been more than six hours. They can't know that." And, of course, the body was never found. We were way too far from any Mediterranean island for Officer Jamiesen to wash up. His body undoubtedly sank shortly after going over the side.

As we were in open waters, Captain Nielsen immediately called the Mediterranean Coastal Authority to report a crew member lost at sea. He also broadcast a VHF radio message to all vessels traveling in the area we had sailed through since nine the preceding evening which was the last time anyone on board could remember seeing Officer Jamiesen.

La Caravelle continued the search for nearly five hours with the helicopter returning to the yacht once for additional fuel and then continuing to search. Nothing. Finally, the search abandoned, we reversed course and continued on to Venice. The mood on board was a bit muted, but Officer Jamiesen would not be missed by many. The consensus was that he committed suicide. Most crew members thought he was depressed because he couldn't sleep. If anyone suspected foul play, neither Max nor I ever heard of it.

The one surprise we hadn't expected was that the story of Officer Jamiesen's disappearance had been published in the *International Herald*. Apparently, yacht crew or passengers lost overboard was such an unusual occurrence that it was news. Max was upset to see a full list of La Caravelle's crew printed in the article, but there was nothing to cast suspicion upon us.

We had four more charter parties that summer and got to cruise to some really interesting places. With Officer Jamiesen gone, the deck hands reported to Officer Andersen who was a cool guy and gave us a generous amount of shore time. Venice was truly amazing with its myriad canals and ancient palaces. We also got to tour Dubrovnik and the old walled section of the city, some of the Greek islands and the 4,000 year old city of Ephesus, much of which had been uncovered by archeologists working the area. We even heard a concert one night in Ephesus on the steps of the ancient library which had been unearthed in the excavation.

We flew home near the end of September and had the month of October and half of November to ourselves until we rejoined the yacht in Antigua, British West Indies for the winter season in the Caribbean. A very good summer once we rid ourselves of that asshole Jamiesen.

FIFTY-FIVE

Jeff Johnson,
Greenwich Police Detective

"Hey Steve, welcome to Greenwich," I said to Steve Olsen in a small coffee shop just off the main highway between Greenwich and Bridgeport.

"Fuckin' humidity. I sweat through my clothes on the way to the car."

"Yeah, well, good morning to you, too."

"Sorry, pal. My captain won't let me off this Morrison case. It's *dead, dead, dead.*"

"Maybe I have something. Maybe not."

"What?"

"Did you read about the crew guy who went overboard on a yacht in the Mediterranean a week ago?"

"No, why would I?"

"No reason, I guess. I've been putting the names of Deerpark students on Goggle who were on campus when all of those incidents happened to see if anything comes up."

"And?"

"And, Max Van Zuylen and Will Radcliffe came up as being on the yacht when the crew member went missing. Reported in the *International Herald.*"

"*Shit!* I remember those guys. Arrogant. What the hell were they doing on the yacht?"

"Crew members."

"Those rich assholes?"

"Taking a gap year before going to college."

"What the hell is a gap year?"

"Lots of graduating high school seniors are taking a year off between high school and college. Working, traveling, volunteering. Colleges are even recommending it."

"So, these two are off in the Mediterranean for their gap year?"

"At least for part of it. They were definitely on board when this Officer Jamiesen went overboard."

"Shit. You think they hosed the office, pushed the kid´s car into the Sound and set fire to Morrison´s house – and now killed a guy on the yacht?"

"Don´t know. Maybe so. Maybe they didn´t do any of it."

"*Shit!*"

FIFTY-SIX

Maximilian Van Zuylen

Will and I spent the first two weeks of our break at our new apartment in New York. We loved the place. The views of Riverside Park and the Hudson River were spectacular, and the walk separating the Park from Riverside Drive was a great place to run or jog. We also spent time in the Park throwing a football and even had a water balloon fight. Will insisted he won, but it was really a draw. The Radcliffes' cook put food in our freezer which saved us the trouble of trying to figure out how to cook anything, and the daily kept everything tidied up. All good.

We didn't talk much about Officer Jamiesen. I had no guilt or any other emotion about murdering him, and it was clear Will didn't either. I knew that said something about us, but I didn't want to know what that was and didn't really care. It was who we were, that's all.

I flew to San Francisco early in October to spend time with my parents and also attend the christening of Mike Smith's baby boy who he named Maximilian Smith. More than once I was tempted to ask my father about Will and me being brothers, but Will told me we should cash that check when we needed something, so I said nothing.

Little Max's christening was at Grace Cathedral. Like everything my mother organized, the christening and the dinner which followed at our penthouse was over the top. The section of the Cathedral where the christening took place looked like a flower shop. Roses and lilies and flowers I couldn't identify were everywhere. "They will go to the hospital tomorrow, darling," she told me. It was even more ostentatious in the penthouse. There were rose trees – *trees* – in the upstairs den where cocktails were served and also downstairs in the living room where two tables of ten were set up in the dining room and another two in the living room. Naturally, she had someone from the *San Francisco Chronicle* there to photograph everything. My father seemed to tolerate everything she did, but I don't think he really approved.

I didn't really get any alone time with Mike that fall. He had a busy law practice, a wife and now a baby. The days when we palled around in San Francisco and Napa seemed very long ago. I was happy for him, though. I think he was in a good place.

When I got back to New York, Will told me he had received a letter from Deerpark Headmaster Prendergast asking him to call Bridgeport Police Detective Stephen Olsen. The letter was sent to the Radcliffes' townhouse which was probably the only address Deerpark had for him.

"Here, take a look," he said, handing me the letter. It was short and to the point.

Dear Master Radcliffe, please contact Detective Stephen Olsen of the Bridgeport Police Department concerning the on-going investigation of the arson at Charles Morrison's home. Sincerely, Headmaster Prendergast.

There was a phone number and nothing else.

"What should we do, Will? I don't like it that he keeps coming back to us."

"Nothing. We do nothing. He can't make us talk to him, and anyway, we will be out of here for six months in another couple of weeks."

"Still, I don't like it."

"Look, Max, they don't have shit and they aren't going to have shit. Just forget the prick."

A few days later, my parents forwarded an identical letter which had been mailed to me in San Francisco. We decided to ignore both letters and heard nothing more from Deerpark before leaving for Antigua to rejoin the yacht La Caravelle.

FIFTY-SEVEN

William Radcliffe

Once you fly south of Florida and into the Caribbean, it is amazing how the water changes. Even from the air it is crystal clear with colors ranging from sapphire in the deep areas, emerald where it is shallow and pure white where it runs up onto the sand. Nothing like it in North America on either coast and nothing like it in the Mediterranean.

Max and I were glad to be back on the yacht. We knew our jobs well and we liked the crew now that that asshole Jamiesen was gone. He had not been replaced. The three remaining officers ran the yacht and supervised the crew. Officer Andersen continued to supervise the cabin boys and deck hands, but we were all seasoned, knew what to do, and were pretty much left alone. We were also given a lot of time off, especially between charters. Captain Nielsen always picked a nice anchorage off one of the Caribbean islands. We swam, snorkeled and checked out whatever was ashore, usually not much. Even though the work was hard, in truth this was more like a vacation than anything else.

Cyril was a dive master and taught us to dive with tanks. We learned spear fishing and even caught dinner for the crew a couple of times. Officer Andersen let us use the yacht's toys, so we did a little sailing, went water-skiing and rode the jet skis. "I can't believe we're getting paid," Max told me.

It wasn't all vacation, though. The deck hands were responsible for keeping the yacht clean whether or not guests were aboard. Jacques told us it gets much harder to clean the yacht if the salt is allowed to accumulate for a few days. Worse, he said the brass and chrome can pick up corrosion which pits the metal if left unattended. So, we were busy and often tired at the end of the day, but it was a good kind of tired.

Even though the deck hands were the low rung on the totem pole, Max and I thought we preferred that job to being one of the cabin attendants, especially when charter guests were aboard. These were the boys who waited on the guests hand and foot, serving drinks, meals, whatever they wanted. Fortunately, most of the guests drank too much and were usually back in their cabins sleeping it off by ten or eleven, but still, a hard job. The four of us, Max, me, Jacques and Cyril, pitched in whenever we could.

Most of our charters were for one week. At four hundred fifty thousand a pop, not many guests opted for a second week. Some did, but only a few. Our last charter in December ended December fifteenth so we could get ready for the owners´ arrival for their annual Christmas vacation aboard La Caravelle. Tension among the officers and crew was a little higher while we waited for the owner and his party. We were anchored in English Harbour, Antigua, where the Anbars would arrive by plane on December twentieth. The tenders went back and forth to shore almost constantly picking up food, wines, liquors and other items the Anbars would expect to find on board. I don´t think there was a square inch aboard the yacht which had not been washed, re-washed and polished. Everything had to gleam for their arrival, Captain Nielsen told us. And gleam it did.

I thought the Anbars would be difficult. Nothing could be further from the truth. They were gentle, even deferential. Mr. Anbar – I never knew his first name – was a slight man, mostly bald and somewhat stooped, but extremely gracious just like the rest of his family. His wife, Leyla, was almost shy. The two children, Alesta and Abbas, were quiet, reserved. Abbas, the boy, related to Max and me – and the other two deck hands – because we were about the same age. He hung with us when we weren´t working and asked us to go snorkeling and jet skiing with him. Captain Nielsen readily agreed because our sole job for these two weeks was to take care of the Anbars. It wasn´t hard.

Abbas reminded me of Miguel Sanchez, maybe because he put his hands on my shoulders and kissed me on both cheeks whenever we met and whenever we parted. He couldn´t have been nicer, and I realized I had a lot to learn about customs in different parts of the world. Those two weeks at Christmas – the only time the Anbars spent on La Caravelle each year – were definitely the best of the whole season. Max and I liked the whole family and were sorry when they left, although Captain Nielsen seemed somewhat relieved that nothing had gone wrong during their time aboard.

Most of the charter guests were nice enough if sometimes a bit demanding. You spend four hundred fifty thousand dollars for a week's vacation, you want whatever it is you want. Sometimes guests arrived with very specific itineraries in mind, some of which were hard or even impossible to accommodate given the one week time constraint. Those who had been to the Caribbean before all wanted to go to one group of cays, even if they didn't have anything else specifically in mind. These were the Tobago Cays, a group of protected, uninhabited islands south of St. Lucia and part of St. Vincent and the Grenadines. The Cays formed a rough circle with only one entrance so the water inside was especially calm. It was also shallow and allowed for spectacular snorkeling. La Caravelle cleared the bottom by no more than ten feet. Smaller pleasure craft could get inside the Cays, but cruise ships could not, so it usually was very private when we anchored there. One of our guests said it was like swimming in an aquarium and she was right. There is no more spectacular spot in the Caribbean that any of us ever saw.

Most of our charters involved six or eight guests. We only had one with the maximum number of ten. One charter was for three guests, a Mr. and Mrs. Rhinelander from New York and their teenage son, James. Why one couple and their son would want to charter a yacht the size of La Caravelle was a mystery to all of us. This was also our most difficult charter as the Rhinelanders were very demanding and their son was a complete asshole. He called the Captain and the officers by name, but the rest of us were "boy". Boy do this, boy I want that, boy the ice in my coke is melting, on and on and on. His parents never once called him on his rude behavior.

James wanted to learn to sail, so we got out the little sailing boat in calm water while we were at anchor in St. Lucia. Usually, with novice sailors, we tied one end of a tether to the sail boat and another to the yacht's swim step so we could pull the boat back to the yacht if the guest had trouble maneuvering. James would not hear of it. He drifted farther and farther away from the yacht. At one point, I thought he would capsize by tacking away from the wind instead of into it. Finally, Jacques and I took the jet ski out to the sail boat. Jacques went aboard to sail the boat back to the yacht. I stayed along side in case anything happened. James bitched and moaned all the way back, claiming the sail boat was broken, the steering didn´t work, whatever he could think of, even though Jacques sailed her effortlessly back to the yacht. He spent the afternoon complaining to his parents that we failed to give him proper instructions, that the sail boat was somehow defective, and that his father should complain to the yacht´s owner both about the crew and the equipment.

That night, I talked to Max about offing the kid, but he told me we couldn´t risk having two deaths on the yacht while we were on board. He was right, of course, but I still wanted to punish the brat. Our chance came when James wanted to go water-skiing, something he had never done before. I drove the tender while Cyril helped James with his skis and the line. I told James if he fell and his skis came off, he should hang on to the rope so we could pull him back to his skis. A skier who knows what he is doing will, of course, immediately drop the line if he falls; the boat will circle and pick him and his skis up at the point he goes into the water. By dragging James back to his skis, we were assured he´d get a good dose of salt water up his nose and in his mouth. And that´s what happened. He coughed up salt water for maybe twenty minutes, then decided he didn´t like skiing after all and told us to take him back to the yacht. Served the prick right.

Max and I were originally scheduled to leave the yacht at the end of May when she would cross the Atlantic for the summer season in the Mediterranean. Captain Nielsen asked us if we would stay until we reached La Caravelle´s home port of Monaco so we could help the other deck hands during the crossing. Even though we were at sea and cleaning the hull was not possible, we could take care of the decks, the stainless steel and the other metals in order to keep corrosion from salt to a minimum. We talked about it and thought an Atlantic crossing could be an adventure. Plus, we liked the men aboard. Not an asshole in sight for a change.

FIFTY-EIGHT

Maximilian Van Zuylen

The Atlantic crossing was amazing. Twelve full days at sea from Antigua, our last port in the Caribbean, to Arrecife in the Canary Islands, just off the West African coast. We could have made better time, but Captain Nielsen chose to conserve fuel as he said we were really in no hurry to reach Monaco. Some crew members bitched about all the days at sea, but, honestly, Will and I liked it. The seas were calm, we had no guests to take care of, and it was both peaceful and beautiful looking at the endless ocean.

I thought the only crew entitled to bitch were the cooks because most crew members had less to do than usual and seemed to hang around the crew galley waiting for the next meal or some in-between snack. I wasn´t sure the cooks got any time off. Will and I had assigned duties, for sure, but there is only so much you can do to keep a yacht clean while it is underway. We did clean the decks and the fittings, but that took no more than about four hours a day, so we had plenty of time to spend in our cabin or enjoy the sun on the helicopter deck. We played cards with Jacques and Cyril and watched movies fed onto the monitors in our cabin. There were bigger screens in the main salon and the upper deck bar, of course, but Captain Nielsen forbade us from spending time in the guest areas unless actually working there. No worries, though. The Captain allowed each crew member one glass of wine at lunch and two at dinner, so we often took our wine into our cabin at night and watched movies there with Jacques and Cyril while sitting on one of the bunks.

Much as we liked the Atlantic crossing, it was good to see land again. I noticed Jacques and Cyril both crossed themselves when we caught the first glimpse of Arrecife from the helicopter deck. We spent four full days and three nights at the island and Captain Nielsen gave every crew member time ashore. Will and I were given four hours ashore on two different days which we thought was pretty generous. Two of the engine room guys were brought home late the first night by police completely drunk. One had cuts on his hands and face, and the police told Captain Nielsen they had been in a fight in one of the local bars. The Captain was royally pissed and told the men they would be restricted to quarters and to their jobs on board until we reached Monaco. He would then decide whether to dismiss them. Will and I decided we didn´t need to hit the local bars.

It was hard work cleaning La Caravelle after twelve days at sea. The four of us – Jacques, Cyril, Will and I – spent most of our time cleaning the hull, the decks, the fittings and anything else which had been exposed to salt water for such a long time. I think we only managed about four hours total ashore, even though the Captain had given us more time, but that was okay.

In truth, there is not much to see or do on Arrecife. It is a volcanic island and there is lava everywhere – on benches and on walkways along the waterfront, in the undeveloped landscape and even in the statuary. What is of interest is the home, studio and museum of the artist Cesar Manerique, located just north of town. Will and I took a taxi there on our second day on the island. The house is built on top of a lava flow with the main floor being a very modern space with room after room of the artist´s paintings. I didn´t particularly like the paintings and thought Manerique might be more famous for his extraordinary house than for his art work. Anyway, from the main floor, stairs descend to rooms formed entirely out of lava tubes or caves. Here, there was a swimming pool, various living areas and other spaces for the display of more works of art. Will said the place was claustrophobic, but I thought it was cool.

Leaving Arrecife, we sailed for a day and a night to the port of Tangiers, Morocco in North Africa, where the Atlantic and Mediterranean meet. Once again, we were given time off to look around the city. Jacques told us Captain Nielsen was very generous with shore leave when we had no guests aboard. Will and I climbed the narrow streets of the medina. He wanted to find Barbara Hutton´s former home, which is within the medina, so he could send Miguel´s mother a picture. It is a four story white and yellow structure with a rooftop garden from which I imagine the views of the city and the sea are pretty spectacular.

Since the port of Tangiers is on the Atlantic, Will and I took a taxi up into the forest so we could see the beaches where the Ocean and Sea meet. On the way, we passed some spectacular estates, including one which, according to our driver, formerly belonged to Malcolm Forbes and was the site of his seventieth birthday party with Elizabeth Taylor as his hostess. There were other estates belonging to princes, kings and heads of state. You could not see much from the road, but the caretaker at one of these estates was a friend of our driver and we were allowed onto the property for a look. The gardens were lush and beautiful, so we thought there must be a lot of rain here. More impressive even than the gardens was the garage which held a Mercedes 600 limousine, two Bentleys and a race car neither Will nor I could identify.

Finally, on top of the hill, we could look down to one of the longest stretches of beach I have ever seen. Waves from the Atlantic rolled in on our left, and far to the right, waves from the Mediterranean broke near shore. Awesome!

Something was nagging at Will on the way back to the yacht. Finally, he asked "Max, has your father ever mentioned Malcolm Forbes?"

"Uh, yeah, he has. Went to a party on Forbes´ yacht *The Highlander* in New York harbor maybe eighteen or so years ago. Used to talk about it once in a while, not so much anymore. Why?"

He said "I think my mom went to the same party. She often talked about it when I was younger, especially when she was trying to impress someone, which is always."

"You think that´s where it happened, Will?"

"Don´t know. Had to happen somewhere, and the date must be about right."

We were quiet for a few moments, then Will said, "*Shit.* Well, I am *glad* it happened. You´re my best friend *and* my brother. What could be better?"

"Nothing, Will. Nothing."

We made only one more port, the port of Malaga, before deadheading to Monaco. We called at Malaga because it is the port closest to La Alhambra which Officer Andersen wanted to visit. All of the crew agreed that Captain Nielsen was a stand-up guy and did what he could to take care of his crew. He even met with the two engine room guys and while he did not release them from their cabin until the port of Monaco, he told them they could continue on La Caravelle if they promised not to repeat their drunken behavior on Arrecife. Everyone thought that was more than fair.

We spent two days in Malaga so all of the crew who wanted to could take turns traveling to La Alhambra. When it was our turn, the second morning we were in Malaga, Will and I went with Jacques and Cyril in a mini-van which took us high in the Sierra Nevada Mountains and many miles from the sea. We passed more than three million olive trees, according to our driver. He said the olive production is sold mostly to Italy where it is marketed as Italian olive oil. "Brings a higher price than Spanish olive oil," he told us.

La Alhambra is a vast complex of buildings high on a hill. We were told that the palaces, church, military buildings and medina, or town, were built beginning in 1273 with continued building taking place for several centuries. Many of the succeeding sultans built their own palaces, so there are now multiple royal residences throughout and gardens everywhere. Will seemed less interested in La Alhambra than I was. In truth, there were a lot of very old buildings, some restored, others not, and you would have no clue what any of them were without the guide to tell you. Still, I loved seeing it. We did learn that the Moors controlled La Alhambra until 1492 when King Ferdinand and Queen Isabella of Spain tossed them out and imposed Catholicism on the country. Same year as Columbus set out for the new world. Queen Isabella must have liked to shake things up.

Some of the crew wanted to spend a day or two in Barcelona before reaching Monaco, but at this point, Captain Nielsen was anxious to get La Caravelle to her home port and to begin preparations for the summer season of guests. Sailing along the coast of Spain, it took us two more days to reach southern France and the harbor at Monaco. Most yachts there dock "stern to" meaning that the yacht is backed up to the dock between other yachts already there. The fit is usually really tight. Because of La Caravelle´s size, Captain Nielsen preferred to anchor out and take our tenders to shore. It also made cleaning the hull much easier, as it would otherwise have been nearly impossible in such close quarters at the dock.

Will and I could have taken off once we reached Monaco, but we stayed for a few days to help our friends and fellow deck hands, Cyril and Jacques, "spit and polish" the yacht as Jacques liked to say. That took four days in all. Saying good-bye was harder than I thought. We really liked the crew and the experiences we had on board. The only dark spot on our time aboard was murdering Officer Jamiesen. Will really didn´t give a shit, and maybe I didn´t, either.

Captain Nielsen invited us to eat dinner with him in the officers´ lounge on our last night aboard. He thanked us for a job well done and told us we were welcome to come back next summer if we wanted to work on the yacht again. Will and I thought we would definitely like to do that. "We can always use a couple of experienced deck hands," he told us when we left the yacht.

FIFTY-NINE

William Radcliffe

I think our fathers were tired of sending their planes to fetch us, so Max and I took a bus to Nice, flew from there to Paris and on to New York. Jacob, my father´s driver, met us in the baggage area and drove us to our apartment building on Riverside Drive. My parents were already in Newport for the summer, Max´s parents were in Napa, and neither of us wanted to spend time in either place. Besides, we really loved our apartment and spent a good part of the summer hanging out, settling in, and enjoying the city. It is quieter in the summer because there aren´t the usual crowds. The humidity can be brutal, but we had air conditioning and our terrace was usually nice in the evenings with breezes off the Hudson.

We spent a fair amount of time on campus that summer, getting familiar with the place where we would spend the next four years, registering for classes and buying the text books we would need for our classes. We had a few more choices the first year than we were allowed at Deerpark, but class choices were still somewhat limited for freshmen. Max signed up for world history, English literature, some art / music class, and Spanish. My class schedule was similar, although we only had one class together, Spanish. I registered for an introduction to sociology, world history, contemporary American politics and Spanish.

"Why sociology, Will?" Max asked.

"Because it´s given across the street at Barnard. Chicks, man, chicks."

In August, we each spent an obligatory week at our parents´ homes – Napa for Max and god-awful Newport for me. I was pretty much a shit the entire week, and I am sure my parents were relieved when I left.

Ever since Max and I learned we were brothers, I thought about our relationship almost every day. It answered so many questions – why we looked alike, liked and disliked the same things, even talked alike. After six years on the east coast, Max was even sounding like a New Yorker. Of course, I gave him shit about that all the time. As the summer wore on, I became more and more convinced my mother new the truth. Much as I loved Max and was thrilled that we were brothers, I kept thinking my mother must have known and should have leveled with me. The fact that she tried to get my father to send me to a different prep school and wanted us to go to different colleges convinced me all the more that she knew.

"I'm going to confront her, Max."

"I thought you were going to wait until we wanted something. What are you going to ask for?"

"Max, my man, I am going to ask for whatever we want, whenever we want it, and for as long as we want it. My mother would die – I think she actually *would* die – if word leaked out that William Mortimer Radcliffe IV is actually a Van Zuylen. Her social standing, which is the only thing that really matters to her, *poof*, gone in a heartbeat. That society reporter, Aileen Mehle, would have a front page story. And the story after that would be the divorce papers filed by my father. See what I mean, Max? Anything we want forever."

"We're playing hardball, then?"

"Yes! And I think we should talk to her together."

"Okay, Will."

My parents returned to New York three days before Labor day, unusually early for them. There were two reasons for them to miss the end-of-season festivities in Newport. My father was taking off over the weekend with some friends for a fishing competition in Norway, and my mother was hosting a luncheon for Vicomtess Jacqueline de Ribes, of Paris, who would be in town to launch her fashion label at Saks Fifth Avenue.

How my mother knew the Vicomtess I don't know. Probably she didn't, at least certainly not well. Maybe she met her through Aileen Mehle or someone else on the New York social scene. In any event, the luncheon was set for the Wednesday after Labor Day. The timing was perfect. My father would be away, which he rarely was, so we could talk to her alone the day after the party. I told her Max and I were going to stop by on Thursday to pick up some of my things we wanted in the apartment. She paid absolutely no attention to me as she couldn´t stop talking about the party. "Aileen is coming and Nan – you remember Mrs. Kempner, darling – and Carolyn." And on and on and on. I told her we would see her around eleven on Thursday, but I was quite sure our visit would be a complete surprise no matter how often I told her.

On Thursday morning, we found my mother in her study on the second floor with her back toward us. She was at her desk talking on the phone and reading the *Suzy* column at the same time.

"I *so* wanted to include you, Marjorie. I´m afraid the guest list was strictly limited to the Vicomtess´ closest friends in Manhattan. Yes, you can read about the luncheon in *Suzy´s* column today."

Such bullshit!

"… So chic and her clothes are *elegant*! I am going to see the collection at Saks as soon as I can pull myself together. Yesterday was *exhausting…*"

Finally hanging up, she turned in her chair to notice us standing there. "Well, hello, Will and Max. What a lovely surprise!"

"It shouldn´t be, mother. I told you we were coming over this morning."

"Oh, yes, I do remember. I have been so distracted – *distracted* – by the party I hosted yesterday for the Vicomtesse de Ribes. Here, you can read all about it in *Suzy´s* column."

"I don´t want to read about it, mother, and that´s not why we´re here."

"Oh, and why are you here, Will? You hardly ever visit, and your father´s off fishing in Norway, of all places."

"I know that, mother. We´re here to talk to you."

"Goodness, this sounds serious."

Max and I sat in the two chairs facing her desk. "It is serious, mother. We want to know why you never told us we are brothers."

Just like that. I don´t think she could have been more shocked had I told her a Soviet nuclear warhead was on its way to take out New York City. She was stunned into silence, turned very pale, and I actually think she stopped breathing.

Finally, "*Will, for god´s sake, what on earth are you talking about?*"

"We *know*, mother. Frederick Van Zuylen is our father. Do you want to see the matching birthmarks?"

She sat there in silence, evidently unable to find words. Her face registered shock, of course, but mostly fear, I think. Her world just came crashing down. Her social standing, her ambitions, her marriage, all in ruins, or so she must have thought.

We waited for her to say something. When she spoke, she sounded like a very old woman. "Will, Max, you are both wrong! *You are not brothers! Definitely not brothers! I just can't believe this.*"

"Have it your way, mother, but we are brothers and you know we are."

"No, Will. No. No. No."

Finally, she asked the obvious question. "Who have you told about this entirely ridiculous idea?"

"It is not ridiculous, mother. You, of all people, know that. But, for now, we have told no one."

"Well, please don't! You would only make fools of yourselves."

"It would be a shame if this leaked to Aileen Mehle. She might be suspicious already, and I am pretty sure Marie-Helene de Rothschild thinks we are related."

"*For god's sake, Will, no! Anything. Just tell me!*"

"For starters, I think you and 'Dad' should double my allowance. Same for Max. After all, brothers should be treated equally, right?"

"You are *not* brothers, Will, but yes, I agree you both should have more allowance."

"You know where to send the checks. 'Bye for now, mother."

Max seemed a little shaken up when we left the townhouse and headed back to our apartment. Finally, he said, "Epic, dude!"

SIXTY

Sylvia Radcliffe

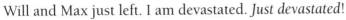

Will and Max just left. I am devastated. *Just devastated!*

Yesterday was perfect! *Pure perfection!* The Vicomtesse de Ribes, Aileen Mehle, Nan Kempner, Carolyn Roehm, Mica Ertegun, Annette de la Renta, and Brooke Astor – all right here in my dining room, and today it's *Suzy's* lead item. Now I am on the verge of ruin. *Ruin!* A *laughing stock* if this gets out!

How could they know? I've had my own suspicions but I've never *really* known. Maybe brothers know these things. *God!*

I could just kill those boys. Will always had a mean streak. How could he threaten me like this? *His own mother, for god's sake!* I think he *enjoyed* it! Something is definitely wrong with Will. Maybe with Max, too.

Oh my god, what am I going to do?

SIXTY-ONE

Detective Jeff Johnson, Greenwich Police Department

On a Saturday morning just after Labor Day, Bridgeport Police Detective Stephen Olsen and I met with FBI Special Agent and profiler Martha Stuart in her office at FBI Headquarters in lower Manhattan.

"It's very generous of you to see us, Agent Stuart."

"Not at all, detectives. Not a serial killer in sight this morning. Tell me what I can do to help."

Detective Olsen told her. "Maybe nothing, but we are pretty much at a dead end. We've got a series of crimes which took place over a period of some months in and around Deerpark Academy. We suspect student involvement but we have virtually no evidence at this point."

"What kind of crimes?"

"Vandalism, but serious stuff, not the petty kind. Flooding out the office of Deerpark's head of admissions causing thousands of dollars in damages, nearly destroying the car of one of the upper classmen, and, most seriously of all, starting an arson fire at the home of the admissions officer, possibly in an attempt to kill him."

"Well, you have my attention."

I added, "There were a limited number of students on campus for all three events. Of course, it may be none of them, but there were definitely two people involved in at least the arson. So we have opportunity among the students, but not motive that we have identified. Two of the students present on campus were also crew members this summer on a yacht in the Mediterranean where one of the yacht's officers went missing and was presumed drowned after a five-hour search of the sea by boats and planes. Coincidence? Maybe. Maybe not."

We sat in silence while Special Agent Stuart processed the information we had given her. "Are you sure two people were involved?"

"At least in the arson, yes," I replied.

"Bear in mind, gentlemen, that profiling is a very inexact science. Sometimes we get it right. We can, and do, also get it very wrong. The little you have told me suggests you may be dealing with psychopaths, or more likely one psychopath, whose crimes may be escalating. Vandalism to murder, if that is what is happening here, obviously suggests escalation. I would doubt it is two students, though."

"Why?" Stephen asked.

"Psychopaths tend to be loners. It would be rare that two high school students who formed a friendship are both psychopathic unless they are biological brothers with the same psychological profile. Even with brothers, the same profile would be rare. Possible, but rare. It is more likely, in my experience, that one of the perpetrators, probably the psychopath, is older, someone the younger man looks up to and follows willingly. Of course, I could be completely wrong. As I told you, profiling is an inexact science."

"Do psychopaths know right from wrong, Agent Stuart?" I asked.

"Yes, absolutely. They just don´t care."

I thought about that. "One more question if I may."

"Go right ahead."

"In an interview with a suspected psychopath, is there anything you particularly look for to raise or lower your suspicion that he or she might be psychopathic?" I asked.

"Most psychopaths don´t give very much away, and their outward appearance and behavior may not seem at all out of the ordinary. I try to look beyond the person sitting in front of me to whatever collateral evidence I have. For instance, is he or she a loner, lacking in friends, seemingly detached, maybe humorless. You can find all those traits in perfectly normal people, but they often manifest themselves in psychopaths."

"Well, Agent Stuart, thank you again for your time. This has been very helpful."

"Not at all, although I´m afraid I haven´t shed much light on your investigation. Do feel free to call or visit again if you think there is anything else I can tell you."

Out on the sidewalk in front of FBI Headquarters, the first word out of Steve Olsen's mouth was "shit".

"What now?"

"Want to pay the boys a visit?"

"You mean now?"

"Why not? Unless you have something better to do."

"You know where they live?"

"Yep. Upper West Side in the penthouse of a converted brownstone, undoubtedly bought by mommy and daddy."

"Figures. I wonder if mommy and daddy would like to adopt me?"

"Doubt it. Let's go."

"Okay, but you heard the Special Agent. Not likely to be the two students. They don't seem to fit any part of the profile."

"I heard her. She also said she could be wrong. You with me?"

"Okay, sure." And with that we rolled up the West Side Highway.

SIXTY-TWO

Maximilian Van Zuylen

On Saturday afternoon the weekend before classes began, Will and I were sitting on our terrace comparing class schedules. We tried to get all morning classes to leave the afternoons open for studying or just hanging out. Will ended up with one afternoon class on Wednesday and I had one on Thursday. We had no classes on Fridays which was great.

The downstairs buzzer let us know we had a visitor. This was odd because we hadn't yet made many friends in the neighborhood, and both the cook who worked for Will's mother and our daily had their own keys.

I heard Will answer the intercom but I couldn't hear the person who was calling. Will came back onto the terrace and told me "It is that dickhead cop from Connecticut."

"*What?*"

"You heard me. Wants to talk to us."

"*Shit. You think it's about Morrison? Now what?*"

"Calm down, Max. I told you they got shit and that's all they will ever get."

"I don't like it."

"Neither do I, but let's just stay calm and hear what they have to say."

A couple of minutes later, Will brought two men onto the terrace. We knew both of them from earlier interviews. One was Detective Jeff Johnson from Greenwich, and the other detective was Stephen Olsen from Bridgeport where Morrison lived. They sat down at our table.

Johnson spoke first. "Nice digs, boys. A big step up from Deerfield dorm rooms, right?" Will and I said nothing.

"What can we do for you, detectives?" Will asked.

Detective Olsen spoke next. "We want to ask you about the officer who went missing from the yacht you were on this summer." This came out of left field, but Will recovered right away.

"Johan Jamiesen."

"That´s the man. What happened to him?"

"No one really knows, detective. Captain Nielsen told us he went overboard at night when we were sailing from Istanbul to Venice, but no one on board actually saw anything so it made the search almost impossible because we didn´t know where to look. The Captain told us it could have happened sometime between eleven at night and around seven in the morning. You should talk to him. He would have more information than we do."

"Well, we´re here now talking to you. You worked on the yacht, is that right?"

"Yes. We were deck hands."

"And did you report to Officer Jamiesen?"

"Yes, we did along with about one-third the crew. Let´s see. There were four deck hands and four cabin attendants. We all reported to Officer Jamiesen. The engine crew and the helicopter crew reported to First Officer Andersen and the galley crew and chef reported directly to the Captain. There were also two security officers aboard. I am not sure who they reported to, but probably the Captain."

"Was officer Jamiesen popular with the crew?"

I chimed in. "No, he was not. I don´t think anyone liked him."

"Why is that?"

"The rumor among the crew was that he was pissed off at not being promoted to first officer. I don´t know if that´s true. I do know he was sick."

"How so?"

Will answered. "He had some kind of sleep disorder. Basically, he couldn´t sleep so he was up most nights, or at least he told us he was, and pretty cranky during the day."

"Were the seas particularly rough that night?"

"Not that I remember," I said.

"So it is unlikely he fell overboard, something which could happen in a storm."

"Probably not. Most of the crew who talked to us thought he jumped."

"You boys seem to have a lot of bad luck following you," Detective Olsen said.

"How so?"

"Let's see. You were at Deerfield when Mr. Morrison's office was flooded, when Robert Montgomery's car was trashed, and when Mr. Morrison's house was torched. And now you're on a yacht in the Mediterranean when your boss dies under mysterious circumstances. Odd, don't you think?"

Will said, "I don't know what you're suggesting, Detective Olsen, but if you have any more questions for us, please contact my father. He will refer you to our family lawyer. We are done here." Will stood up, the detectives stood also. We shook hands and Will showed them to the door.

"Two dickheads," he said when he came back onto the terrace.

"What should we do, Will?"

"Nothing, Max. Absolutely nothing. We are not going to hear from them again." I hoped he was right.

SIXTY-THREE

Detective Jeff Johnson, Greenwich Police Department

Leaving the apartment of Will Radcliffe and Max Van Zuylen, we drove north along Riverside Drive, cut west to Broadway and continued into the Bronx, finally picking up the Connecticut Turnpike which would take us to Greenwich where Steve had parked his car near my office.

"What do you think?" Steve asked.

"A penthouse like that on Riverside Drive overlooking the Park and the Hudson. Ten million maybe? Look, Steve, the boys are spoiled, obviously, and somewhat arrogant. Probably think they´re entitled to anything they want. They could have trashed the car, but I don´t like them for the flood or the arson."

"Why not?"

"Maybe the better question is why them? Morrison was the chief admissions officer at Deerpark. Both boys were accepted, maybe with some financial support for the school from their parents. Who knows? But they were accepted, they had a good academic record at Deerpark, and they got into the college of their choice according to their counselor at Deerpark. I just don´t see any reason why they might want to burn Morrison´s house down, or flood his office for that matter."

We drove in silence for a while.

"I think you´re right, Jeff, although I *really* thought we had something with those two."

"Don´t cross them off your list, Steve, but I think you and I ought to spend some time looking elsewhere."

"Shit. The only things we got are "movement" the old couple told me about and a worthless piece of a sneaker. *Shit, shit, shit!*"

SIXTY-FOUR
William Radcliffe

Max and I pretty much forgot about those two dickhead detectives from Connecticut as we started classes at Columbia. It didn´t take long to figure out we made the right choice of schools. We had a great apartment just four blocks from campus, much better than the dorm rooms we would have been expected to live in at one of the other schools on our list. We liked our classes. They were small, just as they had been at Deerpark. We both liked our professors except for the bitch who taught the sociology class I took at Barnard. The plus there was that I was one of two men in the class; the other eight students were women, and a couple of them were hot.

The year was off to a really good start. I knew Max worried about the Morrison investigation. In truth, I did, too, but I didn´t see how we could possibly be connected to the arson or to the other stuff we pulled on campus. Anyway, our lives pretty much followed a routine that year: classes in the mornings, only one in the afternoon for each of us, and Fridays off. We spent most afternoons studying on our terrace while the summer / fall weather held, then moved inside when it got colder. That was okay, too, because we had a nice fireplace in the living room. It was a gas fire, but the "logs" were really authentic and we could turn it on and off whenever we wanted.

The big surprise that year came in the form of a long e-mail from Miguel Sanchez. Instead of enrolling in college for the fall, he accepted a role in a Gael Garcia movie being filmed in San Miguel de Allende, Mexico, and he invited us to visit the set over the Thanksgiving holiday. Max and I would have four or five days off and, of course, Thanksgiving is not celebrated in Mexico, so the filming would continue throughout that weekend. We accepted right away. When I told my father, he told me to book commercial reservations. One phone call to my mother fixed that. I knew there was nothing she wouldn´t do to keep her secret. We could fly directly from Teterboro Airport in New Jersey to Leon, Mexico, about fifty miles from San Miguel de Allende. Miguel told us he would arrange for a car to meet us, and said we could stay with him in the Hacienda Nevada Hotel where he had a suite. He said the film crew had taken over the entire hotel for the filming. Max and I thought Miguel must be pretty important in the movie if he rated a suite. Whatever, we were stoked.

Max's parents didn't seem to care one way or the other where he spent the holiday, and I was pretty sure my parents were relieved I wouldn't be around to be my usual pain in the ass for them. Even the jet probably seemed like a small price to pay to be rid of me.

We cut our last class on Wednesday before Thanksgiving. Our other morning classes were about half full so we probably could have left earlier, but we were in the air by noon and on the ground in Leon five hours later, except Leon is an hour behind New York so it was only four o'clock when we landed and about five-thirty when we reached the hotel in San Miguel.

According to a travel book Max brought along, San Miguel de Allende is one of the old colonial cities in central Mexico. It was settled by the Spanish in the 1500's and the area was mined for its plentiful silver deposits, most of which were exported back to Spain. There were a great many buildings in the town which dated from the early Spanish days. The Hacienda Nevada Hotel, which was a collection of colonial era houses, was among them. Our driver led us to one of the houses which was the main reception area for the hotel and where, it turned out, Miguel's rooms were on the second floor overlooking the garden.

We hadn't seen Miguel in a while. For me, the last time was the Christmas vacation I spent with him and his family in Mexico City and Cuernavaca. For Max, it was when we both were in Acapulco, which was even longer ago. I think we were both slightly stunned when he opened the door to his suite and gave both of us the obligatory kisses on our cheeks. On our bike trip in Europe, Miguel was easily the smallest boy in our group with a very slight build. No more. Max and I were somewhere between 6'2" and 6'3". I always claimed to be taller, but Max said that was because I wore shoe lifts. It was an argument neither of us was going to win. Miguel was clearly taller than we were; he had filled out and now had a strong, muscular build. He was also the most handsome man I had ever seen – before or after. Dark, wavy hair, big brown eyes which seemed to look right through you, and teeth so white you wondered if they were fake. No wonder the girls loved this dude!

Miguel poured a glass of wine for each of us while we sat in his living room catching up. Max told him about our apartment in New York and our classes at Columbia. We both invited him to come stay with us whenever he could. Miguel said skipping college, at least for now, had been a hard decision, but his parents supported him – although his mother somewhat reluctantly – and he really wanted to try his hand at acting. When Gael Garcia offered him a role in the film after seeing his screen test, Miguel said that pretty much decided it for him. And now here he was in his first film role ever as supporting actor to the star Gael Garcia.

After stowing our bags in the adjoining room Miguel had rented for us, we went downstairs to dinner in the hotel garden. It was still early, but Miguel said he needed to be in bed by ten o´clock because he had to be on set at six in the morning. He planned to show us the set for tomorrow´s filming after dinner. I don´t remember what we ate. The menus were in Spanish, so I could make out some of it, but we were happy to let Miguel order for us.

During dinner, Miguel told us the story line for the film. It was about two brothers – Gael the elder, Miguel the younger – who lost their parents in an automobile accident near their home in Mexico City. The early scenes, he told us, were filmed in Mexico City while the parents were still alive. As I understood it, the story was basically about the younger brother growing up and the older brother playing the role of parent, brother and mentor to a somewhat troubled sibling. The two brothers moved to San Miguel after their parents´ death to get Miguel away from some bad influences among his friends. It sounded to me like a heavy role for someone like Miguel who had no real acting experience.

After dinner, we took a walk to La Parroquia de San Miguel Arcangel, the famous parish church in San Miguel. It is really an extraordinary structure. Built in the seventeenth century, Miguel told us the facade had originally been traditional Mexican architecture, but had been changed in the eighteenth century to Gothic by a Sr. Gutierrez, who was a bricklayer by trade and an amateur architect. Whatever, it is beautiful and apparently one of the most photographed churches in Mexico. Directly in front of the church is "el jardin", or garden, a square built in the French style with wrought iron benches where, Miguel said, locals tend to hang out during the day. It would be closed tomorrow as this was the set for the day's shoot. Miguel showed us where we would watch, along with the film crew. Max, especially, loved the idea of watching the movie being made. I thought it was pretty cool, too.

We walked along some of the cobbled streets a while longer, then returned to the hotel. Miguel needed to get to bed, and Max and I were tired from what seemed a long day. We also wanted to get up with Miguel and go to the set when he did, although he told us there would be a fair amount of waiting around. No matter. This is what we came for.

Miguel was right about the waiting around. We walked with him to el jardin just before six, and he went right into the trailer where, he said, they would put on his makeup and get him into his clothes. Gael Garcia arrived about ten minutes later and followed Miguel into the trailer. It was nearly nine o'clock before they were ready to start filming, but it was interesting watching all the preparation – the film crew coming and going, setting up their equipment, checking the lighting, the sound, and on and on and on. Gael and Miguel were the only two principal actors in the scene to be filmed this morning, but there were about a dozen extras who would wander in and out of the scene. The director, a man named Morales, seemed to be fussing over everything. I guessed he drove the entire crew crazy, but later Miguel told me, no, he was a great man and much respected.

Finally, they were ready.

Gael and Miguel were sitting on one of the wrought iron benches in el jardin. Extras walked from time to time along the sidewalk behind them. The dialogue was in Spanish, so Max and I only caught parts of it. Apparently, Gael was telling Miguel he was tired of being a parent; it was time for Miguel to grow up and be a man and stop being a screw up – or something like that. At least, that's what Max and I picked up. Finally, Miguel started crying. He was *actually* crying. The scene ended with the two sitting on the bench, hugging, Miguel still crying.

The director cut the scene, gave some instructions to Gael and Miguel and they filmed it again. They actually filmed it four more times. Miguel cried *each time*. I just couldn't believe it. With a lunch break, makeup reapplication, hair combing, etc., the director didn't call "wrap", or whatever they call it in Spanish, until almost four o'clock in the afternoon.

I know Miguel wanted to spend the evening with us, but he was obviously drained. We went back to the hotel together, he climbed into bed, and we didn't see him again until about five o'clock in the morning when he started to get ready for Friday's shoot, which was expected to be the last scene filmed for the movie. The set was the same as yesterday, only La Parroquia was in the foreground as Gael and Max walked away from the camera and from el jardin, arms on each other's shoulder. This was to be the closing scene of the movie and looked pretty simple to Max and me. It was not so simple to the director. He either didn't like the light or the sound or someone not part of the cast walked into the frame. Three, four, five takes beginning around eleven because the sun was high enough not to cast shadows at that time. Nothing satisfied him.

We broke for lunch and tried again in the afternoon. Finally, around two – about the last chance that day because the sun would soon cast afternoon shadows – Gael and Miguel were walking between el jardin and La Parroquia and Gael reached over, put his arm around Miguel's neck and gave him a nuggie on top of his head. Miguel smacked Gael on the side of his head and they continued walking, arms on each other's shoulder. The director *loved* it! Whatever he said in Spanish must have meant "That's a wrap" because there was a collective sigh of relief among the film crew and they all started dismantling their film, lighting and sound equipment. Gael and Miguel hugged each other – for real this time – and there were lots of high fives among the crew.

Miguel was flying high that night at dinner, and it wasn´t the wine. "Best damn experience I´ve ever had … except for Lola, of course."

"Who´s Lola?" Max asked.

"Lola´s his girlfriend. And she is smoking. *S-m-o-k-i-n-g!*" I told Max.

"I brought Will a girl, too, when he was in Mexico City at Christmas. He faded after only two or three hours. Can´t handle Mexican women."

I tried to punch Miguel, but he moved back from the table and all I managed to do was knock over a water glass. He and Max just laughed at me. I tried not to laugh, but that didn´t last long.

The next day, Gael and Miguel had to sit for "promo" photos for the movie. Some were taken in el jardin, some in front of La Parroquia and others inside an art gallery. That must have had something to do with the movie, but we didn´t know what. Max and I watched for a while, then took a walk around the central part of San Miguel. We stumbled on "el parque", a beautiful garden maybe a dozen blocks from el jardin. Young Mexican boys were playing soccer in an open space; others were running on a mini-track or doing other forms of exercise.

That night, Miguel invited us to the cast party, or "wrap party" as some called it. The evening was put on by the film´s director and was for everyone associated with the movie, family members and guests. It was a cocktail party and dinner held on the terrace of the restaurant La Capilla, located on the backside of the church and up a flight of stairs. "This used to be the nuns´ quarters," Miguel told us. I wasn´t sure I believed him, but he said he was serious.

The director, Sr. Morales, gave a short speech thanking everyone for their hard work on the project. He also managed to come by each table and say a few words to all of those present. Miguel introduced us to him. He couldn´t have been nicer, and he praised Miguel for an outstanding performance. *Wow!* I thought. He also invited Max and me to the movie´s premiere which was scheduled for Easter weekend in Mexico City. We both thanked him and Max promised we would be thrilled to attend.

"Only so I can meet Lola," Max said. Miguel just grinned.

We had breakfast Sunday morning in the hotel´s garden, then collected our belongings for the flight back to New York. Miguel rode with us to Leon, followed by his ever-present security detail. As usual, he paid no attention to them. The Sanchezes´ plane was on the tarmac beside ours waiting to take him and his guards home. We said good-bye with the usual kisses and promised to see him in Mexico City in April.

"I think he´s going to be even more famous than Gael Garcia," Max said on the flight home. I nodded in agreement. We just didn´t realize how soon.

SIXTY-FIVE
Maximilian Van Zuylen

Will was right. We did not hear from the Connecticut detectives again, at least not that year.

After Thanksgiving, we pretty much concentrated on our studies as we had final exams coming up before the Christmas break, only three weeks away. Again, we were grateful for the college prep we got at Deerpark. We were much more prepared for the workload than were some of our classmates, more than a few of whom seemed to struggle with the adjustment from high school to college. Anyway, we both thought we aced our exams, although Will was a little worried about sociology. I told him that was more likely because he hated the teacher than because he had trouble with the subject. We would find out in January when our first semester grades were due to be posted on-line.

I hadn´t been home for months and couldn´t think of an excuse, so I flew to San Francisco when finals were over to spend Christmas with my parents in our penthouse. Julius met me at Butler Aviation. Even after all the months away, it seemed neither my mother nor father could be bothered to meet me. The only plus I could think of was I would get to see Mike, his wife, Nancy, and Little Max as their baby was called. Mike and Nancy had moved out of the city so their child didn´t have to grow up in an apartment with no yard to play in. They bought a small house in Hillsborough, a really nice neighborhood just south of the city. I think my father helped Mike with the down payment and maybe the mortgage, too. I hoped so.

I am not sure my parents were particularly glad to see me. They asked a few perfunctory questions about my experience crewing on the yacht La Caravelle. My dad actually seemed somewhat interested in that. He also wanted to hear about the movie Miguel Sanchez was making with Gael Garcia, but I think that´s because he was interested in the fabulously wealthy Sanchez family. Whatever. Neither parent was apparently interested in what I was studying at Columbia, how that was going, etc., so our conversation petered out pretty quickly. I went to my room right after dinner, claiming to be tired from the trip. Truthfully, I was bored and wished I were back in my apartment in New York. Except for Mike, I had absolutely nothing to look forward to the next three weeks.

Will stayed in New York for the Christmas break, having refused to go with his parents to Palm Beach. Of course, his mother could never complain about anything he said or did because of the secret he held over her head. "When I saw her before they took off for Palm Beach, she looked like a rabbit staring into headlamps" he told me when we talked on Skype which we did every day. I almost felt sorry for her... but not quite.

I did spend one Sunday at Mike and Nancy´s. It was great fun and I got to play with my namesake, a cute little tyke who looked like Mike´s double. Christmas came and went, and I could stand it no more. Making excuses about getting ready for next semester, I left the day after Christmas even though there were still two weeks of vacation before classes started again. Neither of my parents seemed to care very much. While I was in San Francisco, they felt obligated to spend time with me, either missing their usual holiday parties or dragging me with them. Very much a lose / lose situation.

Will and I spent New Year´s Eve at Swifty´s, an Upper East Side restaurant very popular with its east side clientele. With us, we had Michele Saunders, a fellow student in Will´s sociology class at Barnard, and her roommate, Linda. Michele had been spending a fair amount of time in our apartment and seemed really taken with Will. Linda struck me as a girl who just wanted to have a good time with no attachments. Fine with me. The four of us went back to our apartment before midnight and drank most of a bottle of champagne on our terrace as we watched fireworks explode over the Hudson. From there, Will and Michele went to his room and Linda and I went to mine. No commitment on our part, just a good time. Happy New Year!

Miguel wrote us several e-mails in the new year, making sure we were coming to the premier of his movie over Easter weekend. One call to Will's mother and the Radcliffe jet was ours. Oh, yes, and we also got our allowance checks early each month. Nice work, Will.

Our first semester grades were posted on-line in early January. All "A's" for me and all "A's" for Will except for a "B+" in sociology. He was royally pissed, and I was sure he was going to enlist me to help fuck with the teacher. For the moment, though, he let it go. Most of our classes that year were full-year classes, so we had the same subjects second semester as we had first semester. The only difference was the art history class I had ended and the second semester was a music class.

SIXTY-SIX

William Radcliffe

The best part of that year was definitely our trip to Mexico City to see Miguel and his film. I had stayed with the Sanchezes in Mexico City before, but for Max it was a new experience and he was blown away. The Sanchezes´ house is really a walled palace with gardens, fountains and a main house bigger than our cottage in Newport. Miguel had a whole wing on the second floor. Max and I each had our own bedrooms and Miguel had his suite. We spent the first night in the company of Miguel, Mr. and Mrs. Sanchez, and Miguel´s sister, Maria, now four years old, and clearly the reigning princess. Dinner was served where I had eaten before, on an outside terrace with a fire going and candles in wall sconces providing the only light. The garden was also lit. Max told me later it was like being inside a fairytale, and I think he was right.

When we went upstairs to Miguel´s quarters, it was almost midnight. In his living room with an open bottle of wine on the table were Lola, Fabiola and a girl named Leyla. "Tens" every one of them. We joined them for some wine, Miguel telling me "I hope you are not too tired, Will." I could have done without the joke, but it all seemed good-natured. We paired up and went to our rooms leaving Miguel and Lola in Miguel´s suite. The next morning, actually early afternoon, I was the last one out of bed, the girls having taken off sometime in the early morning hours.

"I talked to Fabiola this morning, Will. She said you did much better this time." I threw a pillow at him. Max and Miguel were already dressed and ready to go, so I caught a shower and we headed out to lunch at an Italian restaurant Miguel liked in the Polanco district, an upscale part of Mexico City.

"So, what´s the drill for tonight?" Max asked.

Miguel was sipping on a cold beer. He was obviously very nervous. "The premier starts at nine o´clock at the theatre in the Zocalo. You remember going there, Will?"

"Yes."

"After the film, there is a midnight supper in the atrium. This is for the actors, the director and producer, invited guests and members of the entertainment press. Probably about fifty people."

I was surprised, thinking more people would be invited.

"No. This is mostly our chance to be seen and photographed by the press and to answer their questions about the movie. Too many people and that's not possible. I am so *fucking nervous,*" he said.

"Relax, buddy," Max told him. "We saw those two scenes you filmed in San Miguel de Allende. You were awesome."

"He's not just blowing smoke, Miguel," I added. "You really were awesome! I don't know how you could just cry like that on command."

"It's not hard if you become the character," he said. "For all the time we were filming, at least on set, I *was* the little brother, and Gael was my big brother."

"Well, it was impressive, I have to tell you," Max said. "Try to relax and enjoy yourself. If the press doesn't like it, we'll get drunk together."

"And if they do like it, we'll get drunk together," Miguel said, laughing.

The plan was for Miguel to go with two of his bodyguards in one car which would take him to the theatre's rear entrance. The director didn't want him talking to any members of the press before the screening. Mr. and Mrs. Sanchez and Max and I would go in another car with the driver, and a second car with their security detail would follow. It is pretty hard to be inconspicuous when traveling with the Sanchezes.

The Zocalo, one of the largest city squares in the world, was as fully lighted as it was the last time I was there. It is an extraordinary complex of buildings. I think the architectural style is Spanish, but I am not sure. Anyway, we arrived in the front of the square about eight forty-five and went directly into the atrium, or lobby, where guests were just beginning to go into the theatre and find their seats. Each guest carried an invitation card which had a theatre seat number on it, and ushers helped everyone to the correct seat. We four were together near the center of the theatre. I had no idea where Miguel was. He didn't seem to be in the theatre, then I noticed a balcony. Several people were up there, including Gael Garcia and Miguel. And others I did not know.

Sr. Morales, the director, came on stage and offered very brief words of welcome. He then left the stage, the curtain went up, the lights dimmed and the movie started. It was entirely in Spanish, of course, and there were no subtitles, so Max and I could only follow part of the dialogue. We were familiar with the story line, though, because Miguel had told us about it when we were together in San Miguel de Allende. The movie opened with the two brothers and their parents driving up the Reforma in Mexico city. I recognized the area because it is not far from the Sanchezes´ estate. A few scenes later, the parents were killed in an automobile accident, leaving the boys orphans. This is where, it seemed to me, the story really began with Gael Garcia taking on the role of parent and mentor to Miguel in addition to being his brother. Some of the scenes were quite emotional, especially when the boys learned of their parents´ death. There were also scenes where Gael and Miguel got into apparently heated arguments over Miguel´s behavior. Then came the decision to move to San Miguel de Allende to get away from boys whom Gael did not like and thought were bad influences.

The next to last scene, the one filmed on the bench in el jardin, was unbelievable. I could see some of the people sitting next to us wiping away tears. Then came the final scene where the boys were clearly united and where Gael gave Miguel a nuggie as they walked away together from el jardin, arms on each other´s shoulder.

The lights came on slowly. For a moment, there was complete silence in the theatre. Then, one person yelled "Bravo!" and the audience exploded with cheers, applause and a chorus of "Bravos!". Slowly, the applause died down and we and the other guests made our way to the atrium where cocktails were being served and tables had been set up for the midnight supper. Gael and Miguel came down stairs from the balcony to another chorus of "Bravos!" and much applause. They were accompanied by the two actors who played their parents in the early part of the film, by Sr. Morales, the director, and by someone I later learned was the movie´s producer.

We didn´t get near Miguel for at least half an hour as he and Gael were mobbed by reporters and by photographers. Dinner was served and Miguel took his place at the center table along with the other actors, the director and his wife and the producer and his wife. We were seated at a table for four which was fine with Max and me because we didn´t know anyone else in the room and the conversation I could hear was all in Spanish.

Guests at the center table left the atrium first which I thought was a good thing because the press and photographers were clearly not going to leave as long as Gael and Miguel were there. We left shortly afterwards and drove home with the Sanchezes and their security detail. Miguel was already upstairs in his suite when we got there. His parents gave him hugs and told him how proud they were of him. Max and I gave him high fives, slaps on the back and even kisses on both cheeks. Maybe I am becoming Mexican. When the three of us were alone, Miguel pulled out a bottle of tequila from his bar cabinet which we drank straight from small glasses, toasting Miguel´s success.

"I´ll get *really* drunk tomorrow if the reviews are good," Miguel said. "Tonight, I am just mellow." He took a few more sips of the tequila, put his glass down and promptly fell asleep in his chair. It was a big, comfortable chair with an ottoman and he was sleeping peacefully, so Max and I decided to leave him alone.

From the terrace off my room the next morning, I could see Miguel stretched out in a lounge chair beside the swimming pool reading newspapers. I put on swim trunks and a tee-shirt and went downstairs to join him. Most of the papers were on a side table. I picked one up, then noticed another paper in English. I took that one and read the entertainment headlines. "Brilliant performance by the young actor, Miguel Sanchez." Another called Miguel´s performance "the best ever by a first time actor". There were photographs of Miguel with the caption "Mexico´s newest heartthrob". There were also complimentary reports about Gael Garcia, calling his performance "brilliant", but it was Miguel who captured the most print and certainly the most photographs, maybe because he was so handsome or maybe because he was completely unknown until last night.

Max joined us a few minutes later. When Miguel stood up to pour himself some coffee, Max and I celebrated by pushing him into the pool, then jumping on him. We had mock water fights and generally horsed around until Mr. and Mrs. Sanchez came out on the pool deck with Maria. Miguel, Max and I calmed down, and once out of the pool we all sat around a large table where breakfast was served to us. Breakfast at noon. I supposed I could get used to the schedule if I lived here long enough.

Miguel took congratulatory phone calls from Gael Garcia and Sr. Morales. *"Best fucking day ever!"* he told us when we went upstairs for siestas.

And the rest is history, as they say. Max and I flew back to New York the next day. Two or three American reporters had been at the movie premier and we read their stories on-line. They used words and phrases like "awesome" and "blown away" and "amazing" when writing about the movie and, especially, about Miguel. "Come to Hollywood, young man," one of the stories began. "Your future is here."

The film, we learned from Miguel, broke all kinds of attendance records in Mexico. It was so successful, the producer and director decided to add English subtitles and distribute it in America. As famous as Miguel became, almost overnight, he never forgot his two American friends, and we stayed in touch always. I´ve been pretty much a shit most of my life. Max, too, although he got a later start on being a shit than I did. Miguel is truly decent, a nice guy. I wish I could be more like him, but it´s too late for that now.

SIXTY-SEVEN

Detective Stephen Olsen, Bridgeport Police Department

On a Friday afternoon in early May, Detective Jeff Johnson and I met with Charles Morrison at the apartment he was renting on the outskirts of Greenwich. He had decided not to rebuild his house in Bridgeport and the lot there was now for sale. The meeting was at Morrison´s request. We had met with him frequently in the months after the arson and, possibly, attempted murder occurred, but there was less and less to talk about.

"Thank you for coming to see me, detectives," he said as he led us into the apartment´s small living room.

"I wish we had something new to report," Jeff said. "Truth is, after all these months and hundreds of hours of investigation, we have essentially no evidence at all. We know the crime was committed by two people, but that is all we know. That and the piece of a tennis shoe we found near the Sound which may or may not have anything to do with the fire at your house."

Morrison looked older than when I first met him and very tired. "There must be something," he said.

Jeff just shook his head. "Nothing at all, really. We have interviewed all of the students who were on campus when the fire occurred, some of them more than once. We paid special attention to students who were old enough to drive because the perpetrators must have driven to your house. We also interviewed the Deerpark security staff, the gardeners, other staff and members of the faculty who you told us you might have had some disagreements with over the years. We interviewed your Bridgeport neighbors. Nothing has come of any of the interviews."

Morrison looked even more dejected than he had when we arrived. "I know you think about this all the time, Mr. Morrison," Steve said. "Does *anything, anybody* come to mind we should talk to?"

"No. I can't think Deerpark students were involved. They were *admitted* after all. The ones who were rejected? That is an impossibly long list, I am afraid. The others on campus? I really don't have enemies among them that I know of."

"We will continue to do what we can while the case remains open, Mr. Morrison, but in all honesty, I think our captains are about to close it."

"That's *terrible!*" he said.

"It doesn't mean we are giving up, just not working the case actively. If new evidence – *any* evidence – surfaces, no matter when, the case will be reopened."

Morrison sighed. "I understand, but it's a terrible thing to have someone burn down your house, maybe try to kill you."

"Yes, it is, Mr. Morrison. Yes, it is. We will stay in touch." With that, Steve and I said good-bye and let ourselves out while Morrison remained on his couch.

"It will be tough to let this one go, Jeff," I said.

"It's tough to let any of them go, but you and I both know we don't solve them all."

"Still, …"

SIXTY-EIGHT

Maximilian Van Zuylen

When we got back to New York, Will and I pretty much went into hyper study mode to get ready for year-end finals which were only weeks away. No more Michele or Linda for the time being. Michele was pissed; Linda not so much, which is one of the reasons I liked her.

Will's singular obsession was Priscilla Pettibone, his sociology professor. Can you believe that name? "*She's a fuckin' dyke*," he told me more than once. "*Hates* men. That's why she teaches across the street at Barnard." I didn't know her, had never even seen her, so I couldn't comment even if I thought Will would want my opinion which he clearly did not.

"I swear to god, If she screws me again, I *will* fuck with her. I *swear* I will." Translation: If she screwed with Will, he and I would fuck with her. That was always the deal. I really didn't want it any other way, but I hoped she would give him the "A" he wanted and thought he deserved. We really didn't need any more police sniffing around, no matter the reason.

Finals came and went and, of course, we had to wait for our grades. Will was in no mood to see Michele, who was more pissed than before. Linda had gone home to Wisconsin, so she wasn't in the picture any more, at least not until next fall. Our grades were published on-line the third week of June. Straight "A's" again for me; straight "A's" also for Will, except for another "B+" in sociology. He did everything but froth at the mouth. Any dog who acted that way would have been put down straight away. I knew there was nothing I could say, so I backed off and went into my room until he calmed down.

It took a while, but then he came into my room, icy cold. "I have a plan," was all he said. Then, he told me.

"*Are you out of your mind? You want to firebomb her office?*"

"Yes. Are you with me or not?"

"*Bro, I am always with you, and I will always be with you. But this is crazy!*"

"We won´t get caught. I have it all figured out."

"I´m sure you do, Will, but *think* about it. Those two dicks from Connecticut are already trying to connect the dots. I know their jurisdiction is Connecticut and not New York, but they´ve been down here to see us because they suspect we´re involved in some of the things that happened at Deerpark plus the fire at Mr. Morrison´s. What if they learn of a fire at Barnard? That the office of one of your professors was torched? You think they won´t suspect us and involve the New York police? And for what? It´s not going to change your grade."

Will sat on a corner of my bed, dejected.

"*Fuck!*" he said. "I have to mess with that lesbian bitch. She just hates men. That´s why she did it."

"Okay, Will. We will do something. Just not that and not now. Okay?

He didn´t say anything for a while, then looked up at me with eyes that could have been mine and said "Okay, but I´m not going to drop it."

"I know, Will, I know. And, I am with you, bro, just like always."

Will did let it drop, but I knew another plan would come up sometime. In the meantime, we had heard from Captain Nielsen, of La Caravelle, who confirmed our invitation to join the yacht as deck hands again this summer. We were stoked. It was hard work aboard the yacht, but we really liked the crew now that that asshole Jamiesen was gone, and we were sure Captain Nielsen would give us shore time so we could see some of the places La Caravelle intended to visit.

Most of the time, La Caravelle took aboard guests for a one week cruise, sometimes two weeks but only rarely because the weekly charter rate was so expensive. This summer, British friends of the owner and their twin teenage sons plus a second couple and their two sons were going to spend four weeks on the yacht, beginning in Dubai and ending in Jerusalem. Will and I were told to arrive in Dubai on July fourth so we could be aboard a week before the charter party joined the yacht. We had never been anywhere in the Middle East and it seemed like it might be a great adventure. Captain Nielsen told us Jacques and Cyril, our fellow deck hands, were still on board, as were most of the rest of the crew we had known from last summer.

I was really glad we were going, in part because I didn't want Will to come up with another plan to punish Ms. Pettibone, at least not right away. We made reservations on Air Emirates to fly from New York directly to Dubai. Mr. and Mrs. Radcliffe were using the Radcliffe jet to fly to Pebble Beach for the holiday weekend to visit friends who also owned a cottage in Newport. Will first told his mother she would have to make other arrangements because we were using the jet. I could only hear a few of her words on our end of the telephone, but it was clear she was on the verge of a meltdown. Will let her hang there for a couple of minutes, then relented and said we would fly commercial, but "only this once". I wondered how long Mrs. Radcliffe could avoid a nervous breakdown. We didn't want to kill the goose as long as she kept laying golden eggs.

Dubai is eight hours ahead of New York, and the flight time is about eleven hours. Our flight from JFK was scheduled to leave in the early afternoon of July third which would put us into Dubai between ten and eleven the next morning, local time. The morning we left, a beefy Middle Eastern man showed up at our apartment for the trip to JFK. He was extremely polite and insisted on taking Will's luggage and mine downstairs to the car which was a stretch Mercedes limousine with "Air Emirates" on the front door. Another middle easterner was at the wheel. "You sure your mother's not having us kidnapped and murdered, Will?" I asked. He just laughed as we climbed into the rear of the limousine and sank into the cushions there. At the international terminal, the man who carried our luggage got out of the car with us and took us to a VIP Customs and Immigration room and then drove us in a golf cart to a luxurious Air Emirates lounge. Our escort waited there with us until it was time to board the plane. Again, we got into the golf cart and were driven to the gate. There were check-in lines for business class and economy class and one line marked "Suite Class". No waiting there as we were the only ones booked into that section of the plane. A beautiful Air Emirates stewardess came down the ramp from the plane, welcomed us and offered to show us to our "suite". A steward collected our hand luggage and followed us onto the plane after we said good-bye to our escort.

"There´s more gold here than most people will see in a lifetime," Will said looking around the opulent interior. There were four suites in this section of the plane, but ours was the only one booked, so we had the whole cabin to ourselves. The stewardess led us to our suite which was made up like a living room. There were two comfortable chairs with a dining table which was hidden for now in space between the chairs. There were also two television sets in case we wanted to watch different movies at the same time. "Beats the shit out of our jet," Will said when the stewardess left us. "Maybe I will tell my mother we need one." The stewardess returned with a pot of hot, sweet tea which she poured into two gold rimmed glasses.

"I will make up one of the other suites for you to use when it is time to sleep," she said. "There are also two showers in the rear of this cabin which you are welcome to use whenever you want to freshen up." *Showers? No way!*

"I could live here," I told Will.

"No shit," he said.

Since Will and I were the only passengers in Suite Class, the steward and stewardess assigned to that cabin pretty much spoiled us the entire flight. They showed us how to work the chairs so we could bring up foot rests; they gave us Bose headsets to listen to music and watch television. Right after takeoff, they set up the dining table between us and brought us champagne to go with the cheese soufflé they served us for lunch. In the afternoon, we began to watch a James Bond movie which, according to the steward, was filmed in part on what is now known as James Bond Island off the north coast of Phuket, Thailand. Both of us fell asleep in our chairs part way through the film. When I awoke, Will was gone. When he returned to our suite a few minutes later, his hair was wet, so I knew he had taken a shower. "*Fucking awesome, man,*" was all he said.

The television sets had flight monitors just like the ones on our fathers´ planes. From New York, we flew across the Atlantic in a mostly southerly direction. It looked like we would fly into Dubai from the south, probably to avoid Syrian and Iraqi air space.

Hours later, our table was again set, this time for dinner. We started with green salads, then the main course of filet mignon, twice baked potatoes and asparagus. This time, the steward poured red wine. Between Will's parents and us, we agreed we got the better transportation deal. We re-started the James Bond movie after dinner and managed to stay awake through the film. Honestly, they're all alike, but pretty cool nonetheless. After the movie, the steward came in to tell us our sleeping quarters were ready. The space was just like our living room except in place of the furniture there, we had two beds with real mattresses. Pajamas, which neither of us ever wore, were laid out on the beds. We stripped to our undershorts, climbed between the soft sheets and were out in less time than it takes to say "good night".

The next morning was maybe the best part of the flight. The steward woke us up with hot cups of coffee which he placed on the table between the two beds. He brought us robes which he said we could wear on our way to the bathrooms and the showers. We could leave our clothes in the bedroom suite and put them on again after our showers. Will was right. *It was fucking awesome.* The bathrooms were pretty large as they occupied almost half of each side of the cabin. The showers, themselves, had windows looking out to whatever was below. I stood under the shower jets and let them beat into my shoulders and back, wondering if Will and I were using up all the water on board. Apparently not. The jets were going full blast when I finally turned them off. A shower at 35,000 feet! Hard to believe!

Once dressed, we returned to our living room suite and were served fruit and omelets for breakfast. I am pretty sure neither one of us wanted the flight to end or to get off the plane. We did land, though, and left the plane, again with an escort who took us to another VIP Customs and Immigration room where we were processed. Outside, First Officer Andersen, of La Caravelle, met us and gave each of us a big hug. Maybe he is part Mexican.

We collected our luggage and followed Officer Andersen to a nearby parking area. Once there, we got into a nine-passenger Chevy Suburban which Captain Nielsen had rented in part to provision the yacht and in part to accommodate our eight guests. The highway into Dubai is long and very straight. On either side is sand for as far as you can see. Absolutely nothing but sand, which actually looks more like dirt than sand because of its brownish color. Then, in the distance, the city came into view.

"*Max, look!*" he told me. "*It´s Oz.*" And it certainly looked the part. Extraordinarily tall buildings, which all looked new, in the middle of nowhere.

"See the tallest building there?" Officer Andersen asked. "It is the tallest building in the world with one hundred sixty nine stories. The ruling sultan lives in an apartment on the one hundred sixty-ninth floor." Will had lived in New York all his life among very tall buildings. He said he had never seen anything like it. When we got closer, it was obvious why the buildings all looked new. They *were* new, or most of them were, anyway. "Money means nothing in this part of the world," Officer Andersen said. "The rulers in this Emirate simply buy or build whatever they want without regard to cost." *Amazing,* I thought. *Just amazing.*

When we reached the yacht, Cyril and Jacques were on deck polishing some of the stainless steel. "About time," Jacques said with a big smile and a handshake. "Put your shit away and come help us." We were actually anxious to do that. It felt like home, or at least a home away from home. And we were among friends. I was pretty sure Will had forgotten about Ms. Pettibone, at least for now.

SIXTY-NINE

William Radcliffe

We spent the afternoon working alongside Jacques and Cyril but also greeting the other crew members, many of whom came by to say hello and welcome us back on board. At dinner that night in the crew mess, we learned about our planned itinerary in the weeks ahead. There would be less sea time than usual because the charter party wanted to spend quite a bit of time ashore at some of the ports we were going to visit. We would sail from Dubai through the Straits of Hormuz to Khasab, Oman, then Muscat, Oman. From there we would sail into the Gulf of Adan, bypassing Yemen. We would also skirt Somalia – and hopefully avoid the pirates – before entering the Red Sea and sailing past Saudi Arabia to Egypt. One stop was planned in Egypt before going to Jordan to visit the ancient city of Petra. We would return to Egypt to call at several more ports before joining a convoy for safety reasons and entering the Suez Canal with Israel our final destination for this charter.

Instead of the two security officers normally on board the yacht, there would be four former U.S. Navy Seals who would provide for our safety. The Straits of Hormuz, the waters off Yemen and, especially, the waters off the coast of Somalia are among the most dangerous in the world because of pirate attacks. We had on board razor wire to wrap around the lower sections of the yacht, we had some kind of sonar weapon which, apparently, would produce unbearable pain in the ears if pointed in your direction, and we also had the Seals who were heavily armed. Max and I thought those four guys could take out half a division if they needed to. Captain Nielsen was definitely not fooling around.

We had a full week before the charter party would join the yacht, so for the first few days, our workload was light. It was even lighter for the cabin attendants who could only dust the furniture and vacuum the carpet so many times. The group that worked the hardest those days was, as usual, the chef and galley crew. Because provisions were uncertain in some of the ports we would visit, the chef basically had to plan meals for a month for guests and crew and then go out with the galley crew to buy what he needed. They planned to pick up fresh produce and fresh flowers along the way, but virtually everything else, including premium wines and liquors, had to be purchased before we left Dubai. The galley crew would put whatever they could in the yacht's large freezers because meat and other perishables would not stay fresh for a month, even if placed in refrigerators.

Captain Nielsen told us we could leave the ship pretty much whenever we wanted as long as we got our jobs done. Both he and First Officer Andersen were real good guys, unlike that prick Jamiesen - gone but missed by no one. Max and I wanted to do two things before our charter party arrived. We wanted to have a drink in the cocktail lounge on the one hundred twenty-third floor of the Burj Khalifa, the one hundred sixty-nine story building we saw on our way into Dubai. We also wanted to drive to Abu Dhabi and see the mosque there which Officer Andersen told us is considered the most beautiful Muslim mosque in the world.

Normally, some component of the crew would be assigned to informal security detail when in port, especially when many crew members went ashore. This time that was not necessary because security was taken care of by the four Navy Seals who took turns going ashore, with at least two of them always on board.

Some of the crew joined a group traveling into the desert to a Bedouin camp where, Cyril told me, they rode camels, ate dinner on oriental carpets spread out on the sand, and watched performances by belly dancers. Cool! That was our second night on La Caravelle, and Max and I went to the Burj Khalifa instead. We each had brought along a sports' jacket at the Captain's request in case any of our guests wanted us to accompany them to someplace where a jacket is required. Good thing, because I don't think we could have gotten into the bar without one. We rode up to the one hundred twenty fourth floor in a completely silent elevator. For some reason, there is no elevator stop on one hundred twenty-three. We walked down a circular staircase and sat at a window table and ordered beer from the waiter who came by. In front of us, we actually looked *down* on sky scrapers. Max and I were used to high places because he lived his life growing up in a penthouse atop Russian Hill and I lived in New York City with some pretty tall buildings. Still, I had never been in anything this tall and didn´t like it when Max leaned against the glass and wanted me to take his picture.

The next morning, we hired a car and driver who would take us into Abu Dhabi and then bring us back to the yacht. Max and I had plenty of money now because of the extra allowance my mother sent both of us each month. On the way, we passed three extraordinary buildings. One was a commercial building constructed in the shape of a nickel or quarter, but huge. Perfectly round with a very small, square base. This one, our driver said, won an important architectural prize as the most futuristic building in 2008. We also saw a high rise condominium which was built like a cork screw, actually twisting ninety degrees from its base to the top. Finally, there was the look-alike Leaning Tower of Pisa, only this one leaned at a much greater angle. "Anything money can buy," Max said.

I´ve never seen anything like the mosque in Abu Dhabi. It is huge and built entirely of flawless white Italian marble. According to our driver, there are eighty two domes in the mosque and eleven hundred and ninety eight columns, most of which are covered with marble inlays in various colors, all shaped like floral displays and capped with twenty-four carat gold palm fronds. Our driver also told us the carpet inside the mosque is the world´s largest single carpet with two point four billion stitches. The chandelier, he said, is also the largest in the world, and it is covered with multi-colored crystals. Over the top, no doubt, but dazzling. Max and I were blown away, and if we saw nothing else this entire trip, our visit to Abu Dhabi alone was worth it and something I was sure we would never forget.

We were back aboard the yacht and back at work in the early afternoon. Our guests were arriving in four days´ time, so we were pretty much into full work mode, making sure the yacht´s hull and all of her decks were spotless. First Officer Andersen came by a couple of times and gave us a big thumbs up. What a difference from that asshole Jamiesen who found fault with everything we did. I was glad we killed him.

SEVENTY

Maximilian Van Zuylen

Captain Nielsen put on a little show for our guests' arrival. First Officer Andersen drove up to the dock in the Suburban and they all emerged from the car. A second SUV delivered their luggage. The Captain was standing at the foot of the gangway, and there was even a small square of red carpet which the guests had to cross before proceeding up the stairs. He greeted each one and welcomed them aboard. Several crew members, including Cyril and me, were standing beside the Captain and welcomed the party with handshakes or greetings. The chef was there, too, with a tray of champagne for the adults and juice for the boys. *What the hell?* They were spending a fortune for the cruise. I guess they deserved to be treated specially.

There were Robert and Margaret Bowman and their fifteen year old twin sons, Jason and Justin. The names were confusing enough. They were also identical, so we ended up calling them "J and J". The other couple was Jeffrey and Elizabeth Smythe. Their boys were a bit older. Jeff, Jr. was 19, and his younger brother, Mark, was 17. It seemed like a nice group, although time would tell. First Officer Andersen showed the adults to their cabins, and the cabin attendants took the boys to theirs and delivered the luggage. There were no plans for the first night as everyone seemed a little tired. The boys spent much of the afternoon by the upper deck pool while the parents remained in their cabins, probably resting from the journey from England.

Our guests had dinner that night on the aft deck. Will and I were below deck in the crew quarters and saw none of them again until morning. One of the cabin attendants told me the boys spent most of the night drinking cokes and playing video games on the big television set in the main salon. The cruise, we were told, was intended partly for fun for the boys and partly as an educational experience. The Bowmans and the Smythes brought along reading material so the boys could learn about Dubai, Abu Dhabi, Cairo, Petra, and the like, but apparently not last night.

Our guests took breakfast on the rear deck where they would end up taking at least half their meals. It is a wonderful, comfortable space with great views of everything around the yacht. Later that morning, they all left in a mini-van hired for the day for a trip to see the sights of Dubai. One of the boys – one of the "J´s" – told me later the Sultan of Dubai built a series of islands off-shore in the shape of many of the world´s countries. He thought it extremely cool that Rod Stewart bought "Scotland". Roger Federer owns a house in Dubai. Their guide pointed him out as he drove past the van in a bright red Mercedes convertible. Also very cool, according to "J".

La Caravelle remained at her dock in Dubai throughout the day and also the next three days while our charter party took in more of the sights of Dubai and also drove to Abu Dhabi to see the mosque there. On our last day in port, they returned to the yacht mid-afternoon after a late lunch at the Emirates Hotel in Abu Dhabi. Had they returned earlier, we would have left port immediately for Khasab, Oman, our first planned port-of-call after leaving Dubai. Captain Nielsen did not want to sail in the Straits of Hormuz at night, though, so the new plan was to leave the dock at six the following morning. That would put us into Khasab, Oman in the late afternoon, Captain Nielsen said, well before sunset.

We had smooth sailing that day and no unwanted visitors, although one of the "J´s" told me he and his brother hoped to see pirates. "Maybe later," I told him. Khasab is actually very near the tip of the Straits and only sixty-six kilometers from Iran. Most of us knew about the multi-nation blockade of Iran´s ports to keep foreign shipments from entering the country.

"Khasab is a mecca for smugglers," First Officer Andersen told us. The "J´s" interest picked up at this news, smugglers being almost as cool as pirates. "These fast boats you see in the harbor take electronic equipment and Marlboro cigarettes – only Marlboro – to Iran in exchange for goats." We all thought he was joking until we saw a small goat herd unloaded from one of the fast boats.

"Man, these guys are getting fucked!" Mark Bowman said. *"Goats? You gotta be shitting me!"*

"Any more of that, young man, and you will go below deck," his father told him. Nevertheless, I think we all agreed.

The port of Khasab is dry, bleak, and there is virtually no greenery. What is interesting are the fjords, spectacular sandstone and granite cliffs which rise straight up from the sea for up to several hundred meters. The Khasab fjords are known as the Norway of the Middle East. Captain Nielsen gave some of us, including Max and me, a couple of hours shore leave to see the fjords. That afternoon, we didn't get more than a quick glimpse, as it was getting dark, but I was glad to see what we did. Tomorrow, while our guests cruised the fjords, Max and I, together with Jacques and Cyril, would be busy on the yacht washing the hull and generally cleaning up after a day at sea.

We spent two full days in Khasab, then sailed the next day through the Sea of Hormuz to Muscat where we would spend several days before traveling on to Egypt. Muscat is a lively port, much nicer than Khasab, and home to the ruling Sultan. There is another beautiful mosque, apparently, which we were not able to see because of our duties on board. We did get to go to the souk there on our second day in port. Actually, Max and I were charged with babysitting the two "J's" while a couple of the cabin attendants took charge of Jeff and his younger brother, Mark. Jeff wanted to buy his British girlfriend some jewelry or some other trinket to take home. "Afraid she won't fuck you if you don't bring presents?" Mark said as we were driven to the souk. That earned him a serious punch in the gut. Then another one. I wasn't sure Mark could breathe, but he recovered in a few minutes and decided to sit quietly for the rest of the drive. Good choice. We were finding out that Mark could be a handful.

The souk is a huge labyrinth with stall after stall of everything you could imagine. There were spices, food, silk cloth, clothing, jewelry. There must have been thirty stalls for jewelry alone. It is a maze, and it didn't take long before we were lost and had no idea which way was back to the street and our car. The two cabin attendants had split off with Jeff and Mark some time earlier, and we had no idea where they were. A few people in the souk wore western clothing, but the great majority wore traditional Arab garb, the men in long caftans and turbans, or whatever they are called. Most women wore long, black bhurkas covering their entire bodies and faces except for slits where their eyes were. "How do you know which are the hot chicks?" one of the J´s asked.

"Don´t go there!" Will told him as we tried, unsuccessfully, to find our way to the street.

"They don´t date," I said. "In fact, until they are married, they are never allowed to be alone with a man unless it is their father or brother."

"Bollocks!" was his reply, whatever that meant.

It took us two stops at different stalls before getting the right directions to the exit to the street. We stayed aboard La Caravelle for the rest of our time in Muscat. There is a lot of work for everyone in the crew when guests are on board, and Captain Nielsen was generous to give us as much shore time as he did.

The original plan had been to sail from Muscat directly to Egypt, a five day sea voyage. Instead, Captain Nielsen decided to put into the port of Salalah, Oman so the galley crew could pick up fresh fruit and vegetables before our sea days. This turned into a two day stay in port, as Mrs. Bowman and Mrs. Smythe wanted to visit the souk there for more shopping. How they were going to get everything they bought back to England was not my problem, unless, of course, it became the crew´s problem. Finally, all was ready and we set out for Egypt. On cruises like this, you usually don´t get four or five consecutive sea days, and our guests all seemed excited about this part of the voyage. This was especially true of the two "J´s" who were sure we would encounter pirates someplace off Yemen or Somalia. If that happened, the Navy Seals were clearly at the ready. We had put up razor wire around the yacht just below the main deck level. Two of the Seals were on the helicopter deck at all times, day and night, rifles on their shoulders and binoculars around their necks. The two sonar guns were also there in a locker.

It happened one afternoon just as we passed from the Gulf of Adan into the Red Sea. The Captain sounded an emergency alarm and announced over the speaker system that two fast boats were approaching La Caravelle from the south east and the crew were likely Somali pirates. He ordered all guests and all non-emergency personnel below deck in the crew quarters. The two "J´s" were stricken. What they had hoped would happen was actually happening and they wouldn´t get to see any of it. La Caravelle picked up speed as we cleared the decks and went below. I knew she could do twenty-two knots which might even keep us ahead of the pirates. The Communications Officer did his best to keep us informed of what was going on. He said our pursuers were definitely pirates, and we were doing our best to stay ahead of them. I heard several shots which we later learned came from the Seals who took out the outboard motor on one of the pirate fast boats, quickly ending his pursuit. The other boat, we were told later, was newer, faster and had an inboard motor. After closing in and backing off for maybe thirty minutes, the Seals had had enough, especially after one of the pirates fired a shot at our helicopter, perhaps hoping to distract the crew with a fuel explosion. They shot the helmsman and turned the sonar gun on the rest of the crew. We could actually hear the screams below decks in the crew quarters. Amazing! It was over in about forty-five minutes.

When the Captain let us back on deck, the second fast boat was dead in the water in our wake about one mile astern. The first one was not in sight. Captain Nielsen assembled all the guests and most of the crew on La Caravelle´s rear deck and told us everything that had happened. Actually, we knew most of it already because the Communications Officer did a great job of giving us "live" coverage. The "J´s" were stoked. I knew for sure that this story would get more and more embellished as they told their buddies back home. The Saudi officials were notified by the Communications Officer because the incident took place in waters off Saudi Arabia´s coast and because there were now two disabled vessels, and at least one dead man, in the water. I think Mr. and Mrs. Bowman and Mr. and Mrs. Smythe got a little drunk that night and would probably embellish the story, too. Everyone congratulated the Seals and the Captain for their terrific response.

There were no more incidents, much to the boys´ disappointment, I am sure, and we docked safely in Safaga, Egypt three days later. The principal reason for this port-of-call was for our guests to enjoy the snorkeling and swimming in the crystal clear water there, and for the crew to re-provision the yacht with fresh fruit, vegetables and flowers. We also put some of the "toys" in the water and the boys tried their hand at water-skiing, kayaking, and sailing. This was clearly not the educational part of the cruise. The boys actually persuaded their parents that we should stay in Safaga for three extra days so they could enjoy the water and the sports. This was not a tough sales job, as some of the parents also spent a lot of time in the water snorkeling. Given the extra time there, most of the crew got some time-off, and Will and I did some snorkeling in amazingly clear water. Awesome!

From Safaga, we traveled to Aqaba, Jordan for a two day planned stop which turned into four days at the guests' request. The port itself is a busy commercial port with not much to recommend it to tourists. Cruise ships and private yachts like La Caravelle stop to visit two important places: the ancient city of Petra and Wadi Rum. The reason our stay in Aqaba got extended was thanks to the generosity of our guests who insisted the crew be given an opportunity to see these two extraordinary sites. Several vans were lined up for our stay in port. One day, the Bowmans and the Smyths went to Wadi Rum. The next day, they traveled to Petra. Most crew members stayed aboard La Caravelle those two days. Jacques, Cyril, Will and I spent our time cleaning the hull, the decks and polishing the stainless and the brass. The cabin attendants had plenty to do keeping up the yacht's interiors.

Our turn came the following two days. Some crew members opted to stay aboard because they had been to both places multiple times, so there was plenty of security aboard. For most of us, including the Navy Seals, who had never been to either place, this was a new adventure. It turned out the Bowman and Smythe boys wanted to visit both Petra and Wadi Rum a second time, so we left the port in multiple vans both days. Petra was the first place Will and I visited. We shared a van with the two "J's" and a couple of guys from the galley crew. That was good because they brought along some excellent lemon bars made just that morning.

The drive from Aqaba to Petra takes you through some of the bleakest landscape I have ever seen. It is desolate with almost nothing but a weed here or there growing. Our driver said nothing grows because there is no rain here. We saw a few Bedouin goat herders with small herds on the hillsides. There were also strange looking piles of rocks, maybe three feet high. When Will asked our driver what they were, he said "rock piles".

"Who builds them?" he asked.

"The goat herders."

"Why?"

"Because they have nothing else to do." Will said "*What the fuck?*" The boys just snickered.

Petra is a wonder. According to our guide, the city was built between 600 B.C. and 100 A.D. by an Arab tribe which settled there, later to be replaced by Romans. The centerpiece is probably the Treasury building, which is actually a mausoleum and a sacrificial site. It is forty meters tall and carved from solid sandstone. Other important sites in Petra include the three thousand seat theatre, also carved from solid rock, and the tombs. Our guide explained the tombs vary in size according to the importance of the person buried there with the largest tombs reserved for rulers. No one knows when the city was buried, or why, but excavation continues even now and new structures continue to emerge from the soil.

I think the Bowmans thought of Will and me not so much as deck hands but as companions / babysitters to their two boys, so we accompanied them the following day to Wadi Rum. The van took us away from the port into the interior of the country. Once there, we transferred to Jeeps which could manage the sand. Wadi Rum is a valley deep within the Jordanian desert surrounded by giant granite peaks forced up by movement in the tectonic plates thousands of years ago, and then shaped during the ice age. There is no permanent settlement in the valley, just a few Bedouin camps, some offering camel rides, which both "J's" took, and others selling clothing and souvenirs. A strange and beautiful site, especially to a couple of guys from San Francisco and New York who had never seen anything like it.

From Aqaba, we took a short sail to Sharm el Sheik, Egypt's principal resort on the Red Sea. Will and I thought it was Egypt's version of the Cote d´Azur, although a little down in the heel probably because of the massive economic problems Egypt had suffered during the last ten or twelve years. I don´t know how much time the four boys spent reading about our ports-of-call, but there wasn´t much studying done here. This is a playground, and our guests took full advantage of it, especially the boys. We were there for three days, and the crew each got one-half day ashore, at different times, to enjoy the beaches which are awesome! Will and I spent one afternoon at one of the hotels with Jeff and Mark Smythe who were intent on learning to parasurf. This is where you stand on a surfboard in a few inches of water while wearing a harness with a sail attached. The idea is to stand on the board and maneuver the sail so the wind propels you through the water. It is harder than it looks. Much harder. There were some seriously experienced para-sailors cruising back and forth in front of the hotel, but Jeff and Mark only managed a few seconds at a time before sliding off their boards. Will insisted on trying and did even worse. Good fun, though.

We spent the most time in Sohkna, our last port-of-call in Egypt. From here, our guests wanted to visit the Great Pyramids and the Sphinx at Giza, the Cairo Museum of Antiquities, and they also wanted to take an overnight trip to the Valley of the Kings to see the ancient tombs there. Once again, the Bowmans and the Smythes wanted to be sure there was time for the crew to take in some of these sites, too. None of us went on the overnight, but we did get to choose between the Museum and the pyramids. Not a hard choice, at least not for most of us.

On our second day in Sohkna, we hooked up with two of the Navy Seals and hired a mini-van to take us to Giza. On the way, we skirted central Cairo. The city is the filthiest place either Will or I had ever seen. Garbage is everywhere. In the streets, in the Nile, in the canals. Part of the problem, our driver said, is that Cairo was built to accommodate about six million people. Today, there are nearly twenty-five million, so it is way too crowded and there is no place for the trash. "I hope you guys had breakfast," one of the Seals said, "because you sure won´t want to buy anything to eat here." He was right.

Giza was somewhat cleaner, probably because there was no development in the surrounding area. We parked in one of the lots reserved for tourists and began walking toward the Great Pyramids. Our driver accompanied us to explain what he knew about the pyramids. He told us they were built in around 2,600 B.C. by twelve thousand paid laborers, not slaves as originally thought. The giant blocks of stone each weigh up to twenty thousand tons and were transported to the site from as far away as one thousand kilometers. What is not known, he said, and what will probably never be known, is how such massive stone was transported such distance and then erected into the giant pyramids. The Seals took pictures of Will and me in front of the giant pyramid and also the Sphinx, and our driver took photos of the four of us in front of these amazing monuments. On the way back to La Caravelle, I told Will, "We should have spent the day at the Museum."

"You´re such an asshole, Max" was all he said as he smacked me on the head.

The morning of our departure from Egypt, we joined a caravan going through the Suez Canal to the Mediterranean. Unlike the Panama Canal, which has a series of locks to raise and lower ships as they pass from sea level to about one hundred thirty-feet above the sea and then back down again, the Suez is a flat stretch of water connecting the Red Sea to the Mediterranean. It is not very interesting, to be honest. One of the "J´s" told me it looked like a "fucking ditch in the middle of the desert". I don´t know how many ships were in the convoy, but we had an oil tanker ahead of us and a cruise ship following. There were some military establishments and a couple of hotels on the banks of the canal, but otherwise just desert for as far as you could see. Still, it saved all the boats which used it a six thousand mile trip around Africa. Captain Nielsen told Will the fee for our passage was seventy five thousand dollars and up to three hundred thousand for some of the tankers and cruise ships.

Our charter party left La Caravelle three days after we docked at Ashdod, Israel, as scheduled. Even though they added unscheduled time in various ports, that was part of their plan so they could spend extra days in places they particularly liked. Will and I were sorry to see them go – I think all of the crew felt that way – because they had been so generous in giving us time ashore in some of the ports we visited. Before leaving us, however, they took day tours to Tel Aviv, Haifa and Old Jerusalem. The Bowmans saved Old Jerusalem for last. For some reason, the Smythes and their boys went there first, so it was just the Bowmans who were going to Old Jerusalem before leaving La Caravelle for their flight back to England. Will and I had not left the yacht since arriving in Ashdod, and as we had become friends with the two "J's", Mr. and Mrs. Bowman invited us to join them for a tour of that city.

We set out early the last morning with the four Bowmans, a driver and a guide who described himself as a "secular Jew" meaning he was born a Jew but wasn't particularly religious. It turned out he was somewhat of a comic. Our first stop was at the Mount of Olives from which the entire city of Old Jerusalem can be seen across a valley which is home to a Jewish cemetery. We got out to take photos. As we looked across at Old Jerusalem, our guide told us the city is really an airport because this is where Jesus and Mohammed ascended into heaven. He also explained the three requirements to be buried in the Jewish cemetery. "First," he said, "you have to die. Second, you have to be Jewish. And third, you have to pay forty thousand dollars. So," he said, "Jews have even found a way to make money from the dead!" The Bowmans, who are Jewish, thought this was hysterical. So did the "J's" who couldn't wait to tell their mates back in England.

Will and I had thought the mountain of luggage the Bowmans and Smythes now had thanks to all their purchases would be their problem. Wrong. It was ours. The next day, Will and I and two of the cabin attendants were asked to accompany them to the airport in Tel Aviv to make sure all the pieces got checked into their flight. First Officer Andersen drove the Suburban which we would turn into the rental agency before our planned departure from Ashdod the next day. Will and I and the cabin attendants followed with some of the luggage in the mini-van. We exchanged e-mail addresses with the "J's" and promised to stay in touch. We told them about our apartment in New York and, when their parents were out of earshot, all the hot chicks in New York City, and said maybe they could come for a visit next summer. That earned us a couple of high fives.

SEVENTY-ONE
William Radcliffe

The shit hit the fan when we returned to the dock. There were police cars, flashing lights, an ambulance, other medical personnel and emergency vehicles all over the place. Uniformed Israeli police officers posted at the foot of the gangway blocked our return to the yacht. First Officer Andersen managed to raise Captain Nielsen on his VHF radio and learned that one of the galley crew, a young Philippino named Cesar Marcos, had died on board about an hour ago, apparently from strychnine poisoning. Cesar had been ashore that morning picking up a few supplies the chef wanted and stopped for coffee and something to eat before returning to the ship.

When we were finally allowed aboard, we learned the taxi driver who brought Cesar back to the ship told Cyril, who was on deck cleaning the railing, that his passenger was sick and might need help getting up the gangway. Cyril tried to bring him aboard, but about halfway up the ramp, Cesar collapsed and died right there on the ramp. Apparently, strychnine poisoning leaves some very obvious clues, so when the ambulance arrived, the paramedic knew right away what was the cause of death. This freaked out everyone on board. Captain Nielsen said it was extremely unlikely Cesar contracted anything from our food supplies. No one else was sick, and the poison always works very quickly. Nevertheless, he ordered us to offload "anything you can put in your mouth". This included opened and unopened beverages, fresh, frozen and refrigerated food. He even told us to throw away toothpaste and mouthwash. An over-reaction, he said, but we were taking no chances whatsoever that the poison might have been in something on board. Everything we tossed was carted away in a truck and burned.

Cesar´s death, and especially the reason he died, put a pall on all of us, but the Captain wasn´t having any of that. We were assembled on the aft deck where Cesar´s roommate aboard La Caravelle spoke through tears and Captain Nielsen lead us all in prayer for his soul. Then he ordered us back to work. The ship had to be entirely re-provisioned since there was nothing on board which could be eaten or drunk. He ordered us to wipe down every surface with an alcohol sanitizer, even though it is extremely unlikely anyone could be poisoned by exposure to anything on the yacht's surfaces. Will and I thought what he was really doing was keeping everyone super busy, probably a good thing.

We stayed in Ashdod two days longer than planned in order to complete re-provisioning of the yacht and to clear our departure with both the port authorities and the police. That was okay, though, because we had ten days' time before taking on our next charter group, and we were meeting the new group in Athens, only a two day sail from Ashdod. What upset Captain Nielsen almost as much as Cesar's death was a fax the Communications Officer received midway between Ashdod and Athens. It was a copy of the *International Herald*, and a headline on one of the inside pages read "A Second Tragedy Aboard the Luxury Yacht La Caravelle". The story reported Cesar's death from strychnine poisoning and also re-told the story from last year of Officer Jamiesen's disappearance in the waters off Turkey. Most upset, of course, was La Caravelle's owner, who spent some time with Captain Nielsen on the yacht's satellite phone. Apart from being upset over Cesar's death, he was sure the news would affect La Caravelle's charter business. At four hundred fifty thousand a week, it was not hard to understand his concern. As it turned out, the news did not affect our next charter or any of the remaining charters that summer, and the yacht had a full complement of charters for the winter season in the Caribbean. It did, however, eventually lead to a telephone call to Captain Nielsen from that dickhead Detective Stephen Olsen of the Bridgeport Police Department.

SEVENTY-TWO

Detective Stephen Olsen, Bridgeport Police Department

On a Sunday evening in early August, I phoned Detective Jeff Johnson of the Greenwich Police Department at his home near Greenwich.

"Must be important, Steve. What can I do for you?"

"Did you see yesterday's *International Herald*?"

"Now, why would I do that?"

"Remember Martha Stuart, the FBI profiler we met in New York?"

"Of course. What is this, twenty questions on Sunday night?"

"Patience, my man. Anyway, Special Agent Stuart offered to enter William's and Max's names in the FBI data base to see if their names popped up on any of their search engines.

"And ... Bingo! The boys are again crewing this summer on the yacht La Caravelle. The *Herald* reported that one of the crew members, a Philippino cook, died a couple of days ago of strychnine poisoning. This was in Israel. A complete list of the crew was included in the story and both Will and Max are on it."

"Any link between our boys and the cook?"

"The story is pretty bare bones, but, no, I don't think deck hands normally work for the galley crew. Interesting to talk to the Captain, though. See what he says."

"Want me in on the call?"

"No. I'm not even sure I can reach him. Just keeping you up-to-date."

"Well, thanks for that, Steve, but unless there is a way to link a couple of mysterious crew deaths on a yacht in the Mediterranean where the boys are working to the arson at Morrison's house, I don't see how we could reopen the arson case."

"I know, Jeff. Straws. I'm just grasping at straws. I should let this go, I know, but my gut tells me something is very wrong here."

"I hear you, Steve. Let me know. 'Night."

I left a message for my assistant asking him to find out how to place a telephone call to the yacht La Caravelle which was cruising somewhere in the Mediterranean. *Straws! Fucking straws!*

SEVENTY-THREE
Maximilian Van Zuylen

For the rest of the summer, we had three short charters before Will and I had to fly back to New York. That was good because everyone stayed busy with guests aboard and we had little time to think about Cesar and the strychnine that killed him. The first cruise was Athens to Athens with stops every day at a different Greek island. Will and I only managed about four hours leave that week when we went ashore at Mykonos. All the houses and shops there are white washed with blue trim. There are a couple of houses which are actually wind mills. I don´t know if they produce useable power, but they are cool anyway. We anchored just offshore at most of the islands and took our guests ashore on the yacht´s tender. Will and I did get to cool off in the sea every day when our work was finished, so it was an okay week if a little busy with five couples aboard.

The next charter was also for a week. We were to sail from Athens up the Dalmatian coast and across the Adriatic to Venice. This was mostly a cruising trip as we only had three ports of call after leaving Athens – two in Croatia and then Venice. Again, there was very little shore time for any of the crew. Will and I did spend one hour walking around the old walled city of Dubrovnik which we had visited once before. This time, we saw the cathedral and the mayor´s palace, both magnificent and apparently undamaged in the 1992 Serbian – Croatian war. What Will and I remember most about this charter was a summons we got to the Captain´s cabin after we got back to the yacht from our hour ashore in Dubrovnik. I thought he might be pissed we went ashore at all, but I knew we had First Officer Andersen´s permission and we were back aboard when told to be.

Captain Nielsen´s cabin is on the starboard side of the yacht, directly aft of the bridge. While we had seen most of the yacht, we had never been inside the Captain´s cabin or those of the other officers –

except for Officer Jamiesen´s. The Captain´s cabin is quite large and divided into three sections. There is a work area with a conference table and a large desk where the captain keeps his computer and has other electronic equipment for his use. The center section of the cabin is basically his living room with comfortable chairs, a couch and a big screen television. Finally, there is his bedroom area which can be closed off from the rest of the cabin if he chooses to do so.

We knocked on the cabin door and he told us to come ahead. Inside, he pointed to the conference table where we took our seats across from the Captain. "Will, Max," he said, "do you men know … uh" he hesitated and looked at a paper on the table " …a Detective Stephen Olsen from the Bridgeport Police Department?" This came so far out of left field, I don´t know if I could have answered. Fortunately, Will is better at this than I am, and he answered for both of us right away.

"Yes, we do, Captain. He is the detective who was assigned to investigate a suspicious fire at the home of Deerpark´s head of admissions. Deerpark´s where Max and I went to boarding school," he added by way of explanation.

"He told me that much. He also said there are no suspects in that arson investigation although involvement by some students is considered likely, and that both of you were on campus when the fire broke out. Anyway, that´s his business, I guess, and not really why he called."

"He *called* you?" I blurted out, completely surprised.

"Yes, just this morning. Read about Cesar Marcos´ death in the *International Herald.* He also wanted to talk about Johan Jamiesen´s disappearance from the yacht last year. He wanted to confirm you both were part of the crew when these deaths occurred. I told him you were. Although he didn´t ask directly, I also told him it was impossible that you were involved in any way either with Cesar´s death or Jamiesen´s disappearance."

He went on. "Cesar died from poison he contracted at a coffee shop near the port of Ashdod. We all know Johan was mentally unstable and undoubtedly took his own life by jumping overboard after we left Turkey last year. I told the detective as much.

"Look, men. I don´t know what happened at your former school and, frankly, I don´t give a shit." *Wow! We had never heard the Captain curse.* "What I do know and what I care about is what happens on La Caravelle. I know you had nothing to do with Cesar or Johan. First Officer Andersen tells me you do excellent work and that you are well liked by your fellow crew members and by our charter guests as well. That is my observation, also, and I shared it with the detective. I also told him he had wasted his time and mine on what was probably a very expensive and certainly pointless telephone call. I do not expect to hear from him again.

"You will hear no more of this from me. That´s all, men."

With that, the Captain stood. We shook hands and left his cabin and did not exchange a word between us until we were back in our cabin.

"*Un-fucking-believable*" was the first thing out of Will´s mouth when we were alone in our cabin with the door shut. "I guess he told that dickhead detective where to stick it! Great news! Now I´m sure we won´t hear from him again."

"Probably not about Cesar and Officer Jamiesen, Will, but he´s obviously still interested in us. That´s not such good news."

"Relax Max. If he had us for the arson, we´d have been arrested a long time ago. This is over, man. Over!"

I wasn´t so sure.

SEVENTY-FOUR

William Radcliffe

Max and I had one more charter before returning to New York. This one was twelve days and the cruise was from Venice to Rome with several ports-of-call in between. Finally, we picked up some assholes. The new charter party was three couples from France, or "frogs" as some of the crew called them. They bitched about everything and everyone. There was just no satisfying them. They didn´t like the yacht, they didn´t like the food, they didn´t like the crew, they didn´t like the ports although, of course, they had chosen them. When their limousines finally pulled away from the dock in Rome and were out of sight, everyone on board let out cheers. I don´t think the Captain cheered, but he sure didn´t get on the rest of us who did. Even with the last unpleasant cruise, Max and I were sorry to leave the yacht. The crew was like a family, and I wasn´t sure we would see them again although Captain Nielsen invited us to rejoin the yacht next summer. I hoped we could do that.

We flew Air Emirates from Rome to JFK in the same suite accommodations we had flying to Dubai. One of the other suites had two people in it this time, but that left two empty so we again had a living room and a bedroom. Before landing, Max and I took showers. It is the most awesome experience taking a shower knowing you are in an airplane and looking out the window at clouds and the sea below. We went through customs in the VIP section and were met at the exit by the same man who had met us at our apartment in New York for the trip to Dubai. The driver and the Mercedes limousine were the same, too.

It was Labor Day weekend when we arrived in New York, and we had three weeks before classes began. We had thought about staying with the yacht for the Atlantic crossing, but Captain Nielsen was not sure exactly how long the yacht would be in dry dock in Europe, and he thought we would be cutting it very close to be back in New York on time. So, we were back in the City with three weeks to kill. Max decided to spend a week in San Francisco to "get it out of the way" and I went to my parents´ townhouse to have dinner one night shortly after their return from Newport. My mother had clearly lost weight and seemed nervous while I was there, although my father didn´t seem to notice. Neither one of them seemed to care much about my experiences over the summer, so it was a relief all around, especially for my mother, when I left shortly after dinner.

Michele was back in the City and began hanging out at my apartment with or without an invitation. I had had enough of her and broke it off. She was furious, but so what? I just didn´t want her around anymore. Max came back, so I had my best friend to hang with. We went up to Columbia, got the text assignments for our fall classes and bought books at the bookstore across the street from the University. As usual, we got a head start on the reading assignments. We also went down to the Village a couple of times for lunch at a restaurant we liked, and even went to a concert – Max called it a "retro-concert" - by Cher at this huge theatre in Brooklyn. Retro or not, it was pretty awesome, particularly for an old lady.

Classes finally started, and I think we were more than ready. I was not taking any classes at Barnard this year, just at Columbia. I told Max the place is full of lesbians anyway, so there is no one to hit on. He just laughed. Our second year at Columbia was like our second year at Deerpark. We were not upper classmen, but nothing was new or unfamiliar, so we got off to a good start.

Miguel came to New York for a week in October, primarily to promote the film he made with Gael Garcia, but also to sit with television journalists for personal interviews. He was a star, no doubt. Best looking dude I have ever seen, and he was hot, hot, hot. There were *fucking crowds* outside his hotel. Unbelievable! He spent the weekend with Max and me at our apartment. How he got there without press following him, I don´t know, but we had an uninterrupted weekend. Miguel wore a British racing hat pulled down low on his forehead and huge dark glasses whenever we went out. Even I couldn´t have picked him out of a crowd. We did stuff mostly on the Upper West Side because no one would think to look for him there. We spent one morning walking in Riverside Park. We ordered pizza in the apartment one night and ate it on our terrace. Max and I also took him to a local Chinese place where you were not allowed to order. The kitchen just brought you what they were cooking that night. Miguel loved it. Like I said, as famous as he became, he never forgot his two American friends.

I wonder what he thought when it came to an end for Max and me?

It was a good year for both of us, really good. We made a few friends on campus, did some casual dating but nothing serious for either one of us. We got straight "A´s" both semesters. I was still behind Max because that lesbian bitch fucked me with a B+ in sociology last year. I would screw with her, for sure, but I just hadn´t come up with a solid plan yet. I knew Max would be with me whatever I did, but I also knew we needed something solid and foolproof, so I kept thinking.

Max´s mother invited me to spend Thanksgiving with their family, so Max and I flew to San Francisco for the holiday. My mother did issue her perfunctory invitation for me to join them in Palm Beach, but I know she was relieved when I said no. I am her nightmare-in-waiting, and while I doubt I am ever out-of-mind, I am sure out-of-sight is what she prefers.

Mrs. Van Zuylen´s plan was for all of us – Mike, Nancy, Little Max, Max and me to spend the holiday in Napa. That was great because we could be outdoors without having to drive to some park in the City. Little Max was about the happiest kid I have ever seen. He was outside every waking minute, playing on the lawn, tossing his little ball to no one and then chasing it. We also took him swimming as Mr. Van Zuylen had jacked up the heat in the pool. We showed him the pond and introduced him to a couple of frogs we found there. I am not sure Nancy approved of that. Max´s parents played golf twice so the four of us plus Little Max were left on our own. Max and I played tennis and I crushed him. Well, not exactly crushed him, but I took two of the three sets we played. We had a big Thanksgiving dinner Thursday night, all of us at the table. Mike and Nancy and Little Max drove back to Hillsborough on Saturday as Mike said he needed to be in the office on Sunday. I don´t know if he really liked being a lawyer, but he sure put in the hours. Max´s dad drove us to the airport Sunday morning after dropping Mrs. Van Zuylen at the penthouse. He gave us both big hugs before we boarded the Van Zuylen jet. I think he suspects we are brothers. So does Max, but neither of us said anything.

The time between Thanksgiving and Christmas break is filled with studies and not much else because Columbia gives first semester finals during the four days before the break. We were spending most of the holiday in the City. I did fly to Palm Beach just before Christmas and stayed for a few days after that. I am really a shit, but you know that. One night at dinner, I told my parents Max and I were having dinner with Guy and Marie-Helene de Rothschild and the Van Zuylens at La Grenouille on New Year´s Eve. Max had told me the Baroness had bought an apartment in New York which would be the Baron´s legal residence, something to do with taxes in France. They would, however, continue to live most of the time at the Hotel Lambert where Max and I had lunch with his aunt during our bike tour of Europe.

I think my mother actually started trembling, so much would she like to have been invited to that party. Question followed question. Where is her apartment? How long will she be in New York? Can we arrange to entertain them? And on and on and on. Ridiculous. My father finally left the table, clearly annoyed. Weeks later, I was even more of a shit, telling my mother that Max and I took his aunt to P.J. Clarke´s for lunch and also went to see her new apartment.

New Year´s Eve was more fun than I expected. La Grenouille is probably the prettiest restaurant in New York with more fresh flowers around the room than you are likely to see in a florist shop. It is also stuffy with a capital "S". Not so that night. It was actually lively, although there were the usual share of old folks, at least a couple of whom were probably wondering whether they would make it into the New Year.

We had a nice table in the center of the main room. I really don´t know how to describe Marie-Helene. The word which comes to mind is dazzling. She is fun, funny, charming, and when she talks to you, there is no one else in the room. She is also quite beautiful, something not lost on her husband. He is many years her senior but clearly enchanted. He is also quite charming and actually appeared interested in what a couple of young men almost sixty years his junior had to say. I thought Max and I would cut out at some point and head to one of the bars in the Village, but we stayed at La Grenouille until well past one. Max's parents looked like they were ready to tuck it in, but Guy and Marie-Helene looked like they could keep right on partying. I did send my mother a photo one of the waiters took with my iPhone of all of us at the table just in case she should forget what a shit I am.

On Saturday after New Year's and just two days before our classes were to resume at Columbia, Max and I took a cab to the Rothschilds' new apartment. It wasn't a particularly fashionable address as it was on the corner of Lexington Avenue and Sixty-Sixth Street, away from the normal haunts of the rich on Fifth Avenue or Park. However, it was a nice enough looking building and the apartment itself was pretty spectacular. It was a duplex with a double height ceiling in the living room, lots of light, and ornate French furniture which looked like it came out of the Hotel Lambert. *Architectural Digest* had been there the day before to photograph the place, a magazine piece my mother would undoubtedly devour. The Baron had flown back to Paris on New Year's Day while Marie-Helene stayed behind to supervise some details of the apartment's decoration.

We took a cab to P. J. Clarke's. Marie-Helene said she was looking forward to a "grand adventure" but I wasn't sure she was ready for this place. It was always crowded, noisy, the waiters could be pretty rude when they got too busy, and the food was anything but grand. It's a joint. Not to worry. She *loved* it! She ate one of the small cheeseburgers and even the chili, a long-time staple on the restaurant's menu. She drank a glass of beer and pronounced everything "superb!" Later, Max told me he thought she liked it because it was the opposite of just about everything else in her life. She even seemed fascinated by the crowd and probably liked the fact that no one knew who she was. At lunch, she told us how handsome we were and how much we looked alike. "Like brothers," she said as she looked from one of us to the other. *She knows*, I thought. Later, Max told me he thought so, too.

Back at her apartment after lunch, she kissed us both good-bye and made us promise to take her there again on her next trip from Paris. She persuaded her doorman to take a picture with her phone of the three of us on the sidewalk. He also took one with my camera which I would, of course, send to my mother who knew nothing then about our lunch. I was sure she would have tried to join us if she had.

The second semester of our sophomore year started two days later, and we settled into our now accustomed routine: classes in the morning, homework in the afternoon, and most evenings free for television or just hanging out in our apartment, sometimes with friends, sometimes alone.

Nothing much happened for the rest of the school year, at least not until summer. We did get a phone call one Saturday from that dickhead detective Olsen. He said he was calling to say hello and see how school was going. *Dick!*

"I understand you called our Captain," I told him. "How did that go?"

"If you know I called, you know how it went, William."

"Are you still working on the Morrison arson investigation, detective?" I asked. I knew I should shut up, but I just couldn't resist sticking it to him. "When was that again, two or three years ago?"

"You know exactly when it was, William."

"Well, if you guys are still working on it, you must have a real light workload. Maybe I should consider a career with the Bridgeport police."

"We don't take on felons, William."

"I'm not a felon, detective."

"Maybe not yet. 'Bye, William. I'll be in touch."

Max told me I should have hung up on him and he was right. Pissed me off, though, so I gave him some lip. I shouldn't let that happen again.

SEVENTY-FIVE

Maximilian Van Zuylen

Will and I received a really nice e-mail from Captain Nielsen in April. La Caravelle was in the Caribbean, soon to head to Europe for the summer season. They would once again have the Bowmans and Smythes and their sons as charter guests. Captain Nielsen told us the "J´s" actually asked if we could be in the crew. I think they still had visions of coming to New York and meeting some hot chicks. Anyway, we were invited to join the yacht for a two month charter beginning on July first in Bordeaux, France and continuing north into the Baltic. It seemed almost too good to be true. The Bowmans and Smythes were really nice people, the crew was like family, and we could see some of Europe we had never before seen. We only had a rough itinerary, but what we saw indicated we would be going to some very cool ports, including Saint Petersburg, Russia. Awesome!

We put in a pretty intense month of studying in May, and we both thought we aced our final exams. That left us with three weeks before traveling to France. Will refused to go to Newport and I didn´t particularly want to go to Napa, so we hung out in our apartment in the City. That might have been a mistake because it gave Will a chance to come up with a plan for Ms. Pettibone. I had almost convinced myself he had forgotten about her, but no chance, of course. At least this plan did not include fire or flood. I had no idea if the New York and Connecticut police departments shared information about cases they are working, but I really hoped Will´s plan wouldn´t be a copy-cat of what we had done before. It wasn´t.

Ms. Pettibone´s office was on the third floor in one of the main classroom buildings at Barnard. There were other offices there, too, and some classrooms. The offices I saw there all had those big frosted glass windows on the upper half of the door, the kind you can´t see through. On Ms. Pettibone´s, Will wanted to spray paint "You Will Die, Bitch".

"Isn't that a bit childish, Will?" I asked.

"Not at all. This is a much more personal message than a fire or flood which might not be personal at all. It will be a long time before that bitch stops looking over her shoulder."

I couldn't think of a good argument against the plan, so we set about coming up with the details together. First was to figure out how much space we had to work with, that is how big the office window was. That was easy. Will had been to Ms. Pettibone's office after his two B+'s and told me all the office doors, including those at Columbia, looked alike with frosted glass windows that must be about the same size. I visited an art supply store near Columbia and bought a large sketch pad. Nothing suspicious about that.

Will then put together two pages from the book coming up with the approximate size of the window. He created about four of these double pages so he could try different arrangements with the words "You Will Die, Bitch". This he did with a pencil. The arrangement he liked best was one written at a slight angle with the word "Bitch" written on the first line followed by "You Will" in the middle and "Die" on the bottom. He tried to make the letters a little shaky. "When I use the paint," he said, "I want it to look like dripping blood." If the goal was to make Ms. Pettibone keep looking over her shoulder, I told him he was on the right track.

Getting the spray paint required a plan within the overall plan. We could have bought a can of red spray paint at the same art store where I bought the sketch book, but we thought that might be pretty easy to trace when the police started asking questions. Two guys buying one can of red spray paint at an art store a couple of blocks from Barnard. Way too dangerous. The sales clerk might even remember us. So, Will went to the New York Public Library one morning to use the library computers there. We obviously didn't want any search history on either of our computers or on any of those at Columbia. He was looking for paint and art supply stores out of our area in Manhattan. There were lots of them all over the city. What he finally chose was a huge paint and building supply store in Jamaica, Queens. We rode out there on the subway and bought all kinds of supplies we had no use for – sandpaper, wallpaper glue, a can of light blue interior house paint, paint brushes, some other stuff, and a can of bright red spray paint. Will found a dark color which he said would look like blood. We rode the train into Flushing, then found a dumpster where we threw away everything but the spray paint.

Now we had the paint and a template, although Will burned the penciled drawing paper once he decided how to place the words on the glass. We also threw the remainder of the drawing tablet in our trash chute at home, although neither of us could imagine how that could be a lead to anything.

Next step, of course, was to scope out the third floor of the Barnard classroom building where Ms. Pettibone's office was located. This is much easier than it probably sounds. Neither Will nor I ever found any of the Columbia classroom or administrative buildings locked. They were always open. This is probably because something is almost always going on at the campus – classes, students and teachers using the libraries, special lectures, and so on. The same is true across the street at Barnard. Everything was open, apparently all the time. I went into Ms. Pettibone's building and up to the third floor one weekday. My excuse, if I needed one, was wanting to check out the Sociology Department bulletin board for subjects which might be available next fall. Even though it was during the week, I only saw two or three students and no professors. There was one janitor cleaning the third floor hallways. Nothing else. There were no security cameras on the floor and – a bit of luck here – Ms. Pettibone's office was directly across the hall from both a women's restroom and a mens' restroom. The mens' room would give Will a place to duck into if anyone showed up unexpectedly while he was on the floor. We could always try again if need be.

We chose a Friday night about seven to carry out the plan. We thought that by seven on a Friday night, most people would be out of the building. Certainly the students taking summer classes would be gone, and we assumed the teachers and other staff with offices there would also have headed out for the weekend. Will would go into the building and up to the third floor. His excuse for being there would be the same as the one I had if stopped when I scoped out the third floor: he was going away for the summer and wanted to check out the Sociology Department offerings before he left. Simple enough, and at least half true. My job was to sit on a bench nearby and let Will know via text if anyone entered the building while he was there. My excuse, if asked, was I was waiting for a chick I met in a bar who wanted to enroll in Barnard and agreed to meet me there at seven so we could walk around the campus together. She would be a no-show, of course, and the only name I had was "Darlene". Not great, but probably good enough.

As usual, I was more nervous than Will who told me to stop being a pussy. I think that was his way of letting off some stress. Anyway, we went to Barnard separately. Will walked up Broadway; I crossed Broadway from the Columbia side when I saw him turn into the Barnard campus. Will was definitely alone, at least at that point. I saw no one at all until he entered the building. I sat on the bench and waited. I was sure it was taking much longer than it should and began to worry that Will had somehow walked into a trap or been apprehended. I swear it seemed like forever. I texted him once, "WTF", but received no reply. I worried even more, sure something was wrong, and thought about leaving my bench. A woman exited the building, but she looked like any other student on her way home. Finally, Will came out, hands in his pockets, walked to Broadway, then turned south in the direction of our apartment. He walked at an unhurried pace, although New Yorkers really never walk at an unhurried pace. I relaxed. Everything was okay. As planned, I re-crossed the street and began walking south on the east side of Broadway.

Will was beside himself. He kept high-fiving me, telling me her door was a masterpiece. *"She will shit!"* he said.

"Will, they might clean it up before she sees it," I told him.

"Sure they will, but they will not clean it up before they photograph it, and they will show the photograph to her in case she can help in the investigation."

We still had to get rid of the can of spray paint, and we did not want to put it down our trash chute. Will wanted to go to the Village to celebrate, so we took a subway downtown and tossed the can, which Will had wiped clean of his prints, into a dumpster on the street. I think we both got a little drunk that night, but I had to admit what we did felt good, even though I had no axe to grind with Ms. Pettibone. Will did and that's all that mattered.

We bought most of the New York papers on Saturday and again on Sunday. Nothing. Will was really disappointed. We didn't want to go up to Columbia on the weekend because we couldn't think of a good reason for being there, and we didn't want to get questioned if there were cops around. Then, on Monday, *the New York Post* had the story. The paper actually ran a photo of Ms. Pettibone's office door with the words "Bitch, You Will Die". They called it a hate crime and said the New York police were investigating. "Awesome!" Will said. More high-fives. I didn't see how we could be connected to the crime, but nevertheless, I was glad we were getting out of town for the summer.

On June 25, we took the Radcliffe jet from Teterboro directly to Bordeaux. Our only other choice was to take a commercial flight, like Air Emirates, to Paris, and then take a train to Bordeaux. One phone call to Will's mother and we had the jet.

SEVENTY-SIX

Detective Stephen Olsen, Bridgeport Police Department

Greenwich Police Detective Jeff Johnson and I met in his Greenwich office just before the July Fourth holiday. There had been a burglary in Bridgeport over the prior weekend. Someone had broken into a liquor store, stole some cash and also some beer. Because of the beer, and also because one of our police officers found a Greenwich Public Library card on the floor of the store, we suspected a kid from Greenwich, or possibly a couple of kids, might be involved. We wanted Jeff, or one of his colleagues, to run down the library card and talk to the person who apparently lost it.

"Will do, Steve," he said. "*Beer!* Why don´t the kids just leave a photo ID?"

"Well, there´s no photo on the library card, but the name should be good enough."

"Oh, it is. It is. I just hate to see kids get into this shit. You know we closed the Morrison arson file, right, Steve?"

"Yeah, I know. Remember those two Deerpark boys I thought might be good for it?"

"Sure."

"I called the Captain of the yacht La Caravelle because I had read their names on the crew list in the story which ran in the *International Herald* about the Philippino cook who died on board of strychnine poisoning. Captain Nielsen said the boys were great crew members, got along with everyone, blah, blah, blah. Couldn´t possibly be involved in the cook´s death or that other crew member´s disappearance last year. Actually chewed me out for wasting his time."

"You know I never liked the boys – what were their names, Max and Will? – for the arson. Made no sense to me."

"I know, and I guess you were right all along."

"Maybe, but here's something. Someone at Deerpark was pissed at Morrison, right?

"Yeah."

"Well, my wife reads that rag *The New York Post*. Why I don't know, but she does. So last Monday, the *Post* carried a story of a so-called hate crime where someone spray painted 'Bitch, You Will Die' on the office door of a professor at Barnard."

"So?"

"So, the NYPD thinks it was one of the students pissed at the professor."

"So, I still don't get it, Jeff. Barnard's a girls' college. What does that have to do with Max and Will?"

"Barnard and Columbia are right across the street from each other. Some of the girls take classes at Columbia and some of the boys take classes at Barnard. Those two boys go to Columbia, right?"

"Right."

"Might be interesting to know if they were taking classes across the street."

"Thanks, man. No harm in checking it out. Any straw, you know?"

SEVENTY-SEVEN

Detective Stephen Olsen, Bridgeport Police Department

It took several phone calls to the NYPD until I connected the next morning with a Detective George Marshall, the lead detective on the Pettibone investigation. I told him I had a case in Connecticut which had certain similarities and asked if I could talk with him.

"Sure thing, detective," he said. "This one's only a couple of days old and it is already colder than a well digger's lunch. If we can help each other at all, I'm in."

"Thanks, detective, and it's Steve."

"George here."

It turned out the NYPD had not yet interviewed Ms. Pettibone. In fact, they had a hard time finding her.

"Poor woman," Detective Marshall said, "this has really freaked her out. The *New York Post* story calling it a hate crime certainly didn't help. We're treating it as malicious vandalism for now."

He went on. "Miss Pettibone is a long-time sociology professor at Barnard. She lives alone in an apartment in Morningside Heights, not far from campus, and is afraid to stay there until we sort out what happened and find the person or persons responsible. For now, she is staying with her sister in Redbank, New Jersey, something she doesn't want spread around- I'm going out there to talk to her tomorrow about noon. Want to come along?"

"Absolutely."

Detective Marshall lived in the Murray Hill section of Manhattan, just south and east of midtown. I agreed to pick him up and drive him to Redbank because I had no place to leave my car in Manhattan and didn't want to pay the sky-high parking rates in the City.

We left Manhattan just after eleven in the morning, drove through the Lincoln Tunnel, connected on to the New Jersey Turnpike to the Garden State Parkway to the exit for Redbank, which is about thirty-five miles from Manhattan on the north Jersey shore. On the way, I asked what the NYPD had so far.

"Next to nothing," he told me. "There are no witnesses we have been able to locate. Barnard doesn't have cameras on campus, some student bullshit about invasion of privacy. We found exactly one student who was in the building Friday night when we think the vandalism occurred, and she saw nothing.

"The spray paint itself is a somewhat unusual color, a very dark red, probably used because it looks like blood. The brand, though, is very common and is sold probably at most paint stores in the country, so no help there. No physical evidence of any kind was found at or around the office."

I told the detective a little about the flooding at Deerpark and the arson at Morrison's house in Bridgeport. "No physical evidence there, either. I know it's highly unlikely that the Morrison and Pettibone cases are linked, but it's not often that there are crimes of violence against school administrative personnel or college professors, and even less often that there is no physical evidence at the scenes."

Detective Marshall thought for a moment and just nodded.

Redbank, New Jersey, is a New York commuter suburb and also a retirement community. It is mostly upper middle class with tract housing built on what was originally vast farms in the area. Ms. Pettibone's sister, Esther, a widow, lived on one of the few remaining farms. The main house, a large white clapboard building, was set back thirty or forty yards from the street. The area around the house was nicely planted with lawns, shrubs and flowers. Beyond that, the remaining property was pretty much in a natural state with an old gardener slowly driving a tractor and plowing under the weeds which grew everywhere else.

Ms. Pettibone met us at the front door just after noon. Her sister was nowhere to be seen. She was wearing what looked like hiking boots,

Levis and a man´s work shirt. There was nothing feminine about her, and she certainly didn´t look like a woman who could be intimidated easily. Looks deceive. She was extremely nervous and upset.

Even before inviting us in, she asked "Have you found him …or her … yet?" Detective Marshall told her no. Inside, she showed us in to the living room, a period piece which probably hadn´t been updated, or maybe even used, for years. All the furniture was in nice condition, or seemed to be, and looked like it might have been new in the 1960´s. Ms. Pettibone offered us water. We waited a couple of minutes until she returned with three bottles of Sparkletts Water. No cookies and coffee here.

"Ms. Pettibone," Detective Marshall began, "we have spent more than two days on Barnard´s campus looking for whatever evidence the perpetrator or perpetrators might have left behind. Frankly, there isn´t any. There are no witnesses that we have identified; there are no security cameras, as you probably know; and there is nothing about the spray paint which was used that leads us to anyone. We are here hoping that you can lead us in the direction of someone who might be upset or angry with you – upset or angry enough to write those hateful words on your office door."

"But, detectives, I don´t have enemies."

"Well, you have one," Detective Marshall said, "unless you think whoever did this sprayed the wrong door."

"No, of course not, but I just don´t understand why anyone would want to write those awful words on my office door."

"Nobody in the administration or the faculty?" Detective Marshall asked.

"No. Of course not."

"Well, then, what about students? Anyone you can think of seriously upset with the grades you assigned?"

"No, not really. Students who do not do well in any of Barnard´s classes almost always withdraw before the semester examinations are given. Understand, a "C" at Barnard is like an "F" anywhere else. You do not want it on your transcript because most of our students are destined for graduate school, and a "C" is a real black mark. They drop any class giving them trouble and then either take something else or re-enroll again next semester."

"Did you give any "C´s" this last semester?" I asked.

"No, detective," she said. "One or two withdrew from the class early in the year, but the others received grades ranging from B to A+."

I asked if it weren´t unusual to have a class of students receive such good grades. "No, detective. Remember, this is Barnard. One of the top academic institutions in the country, if not the world. There are no mediocre students at Barnard."

"Even among the students who received, well, "B´s", were some unhappy?" Detective Marshall asked.

"Oh, of course. As I said, the Barnard students are all academically gifted. I doubt any one of them thinks he or she is a "B" student."

"You said ´he or she´ Ms. Pettibone. Do you have men in your classes as well as women?"

"Yes, of course. We call them boys, but I suppose they are really young men. Not many, but some come across the street from Columbia to take classes at Barnard. Our girls go over there, too."

"Any of the young men in the last couple of years stand out?"

"Stand out? How so, Detective?"

"I don´t know. Trouble in the classroom, disruptive, that kind of thing. Maybe unhappy with a grade."

"Disruptive, no. I wouldn´t tolerate that for a minute. Unhappy with a grade? As I said, anyone in my classes who receives anything less than an "A" is unhappy about it."

"Let´s say one of your students received a "B" and thought he or she deserved an "A". Would he or she come talk to you about it?"

"Most would, yes."

"And that would be in your office?"

"Yes, I keep regular office hours. The students all know when they can come see me."

"Anyone come to mind in the last year or two who was particularly upset with their grade?"

"Detective, I don't know what the point is here. Every student in my class who receives less than an "A" is upset. Most come talk to me."

"Let me try something else, Ms. Pettibone, if I may."

"Please."

"Last year, how many male students were in the classes you taught?"

"Last year? None."

"And the year before that?"

"There were two or three male students in my Introduction to Sociology class."

"Did any of those students receive a grade lower than "A"?"

"I can't recall for sure, but I believe each of them received grades ranging from "B" to "B+"."

"Any reason you can think of why these students all received grades lower than "A"?"

"Of course I can. They come across the street to Barnard not because they want to study sociology, but because they want to study the girls in my classes. "

Now it's becoming more interesting, I thought.

"And did any of these boys complain to you about their grades?"

"Of course they did, but I didn't change any of them. I rarely do."

I asked Ms. Pettibone "Do you recall a male student in your class by the name of William Radcliffe or Maximilian Van Zuylen?"

"Yes," she said. "I have so few male students it is easy to remember their names, at least those in my classes the last two or three years. Maximilian Van Zuylen, no. William Radcliffe, yes. A nice boy. Comes from a very old New York family. Very polite."

"And do you remember what grade you gave him?"

"Yes, I do. I probably remember because he came to my office twice, once after each semester. He was very polite, even gracious. Tried to explain to me why he thought he deserved ´A´s´."

"And, did you change his grade, Ms. Pettibone?"

"No, as I said, I rarely do. Perhaps I remember William because he was so very polite, even when I told him his grade would not be changed. He thanked me for my time and for my consideration. Some students – particularly the girls, frankly – can get a little hostile if they don't like the grades I give them. But, I must say William accepted my decision with grace."

We talked for a few more minutes, but it was obvious this conversation was going nowhere. Ms. Pettibone didn't flunk any of her students; she couldn't identify anyone she thought might be worth talking to; and she couldn't think of anyone else in her life who might write hateful words on her office window.

At the door, Ms. Pettibone said, "I do hope you will find whoever did this dreadful thing, detectives. I can't sleep, I can barely eat, and I can't even think of returning to my apartment. Thank god I don't have to be on campus again until fall. Maybe by then …" Her words trailed off.

"We will do our best, Ms. Pettibone, and we will certainly be in touch. Thank you for your time this afternoon."

And with that, we drove away, neither of us saying very much on the drive into Manhattan. "So, you like the Radcliffe kid for your crimes in Connecticut?" Detective Marshall asked.

"I did, George. I really did, but everything I have been able to check out – and it's not much – tells me I'm way off base this time. The Morrison files – those are the two cases I've been working in Connecticut – are officially closed. We've got some other stuff going on in Bridgeport. I'm just going to move on. Sorry I can't help you with Ms. Pettibone."

"No problem, Steve. Just glad for the company this afternoon."

SEVENTY-EIGHT

William Radcliffe

We flew to Bordeaux on June twenty-fifth and had five full days before the Smythes and Bowmans would join the yacht. We were really glad to be back among the crew. There were two changes in the galley crew and all four of the helicopter crew were new – two new pilots and two new mechanics. We never had a problem with the helicopter crew, but they pretty much stayed to themselves. These four guys were no different. Everyone else was the same, including Jacques and Cyril, our fellow deck hands. Captain Nielsen and First Officer Andersen gave us warm welcomes before they told us we could stow our things and get right to work. It all felt good.

Bordeaux is inland from the Atlantic, located on the Garonne River in southwest France. La Caravelle was docked just about in the middle of town, so when we did go ashore, it was an easy walk to see everything in the central city. Jacques told us the architecture is all eighteenth century French, and there is certainly a uniform look to the city, from the apartment houses to the businesses, even the churches. Just a couple of blocks from the dock, there is a beautiful park with hundreds of ducks in the giant pond there, the little ones following their mothers with the fathers bringing up the rear. "The dads are riding shotgun," Jacques told me. We were busy preparing the yacht for guests, but not all that busy because we had a full five days so we got to see a little of the city before the Bowmans and Smythes arrived. Max and I bought a case of Bordeaux wine for the crew galley which earned us several high fives and even some cheek kisses. *So, it´s not just the Mexicans,* I thought.

The Bowmans and Smythes arrived at the dock in two limousines right on schedule. As usual, Captain Nielsen and First Officer Andersen, together with some of the crew, were lined up at the foot of the gangway to welcome them on board. It was much less formal than last time, though, as we all knew each other. It is hard to imagine a nicer group of charter guests. The "J's" could be a bit of a handful, particularly ashore and away from their parents, but there wasn't an asshole in the group. The Bowmans and Smythes treated us, for the most part, like members of their party. Once again, La Caravelle would be spending a lot of time in the various ports on our itinerary, or at least in some of the ports like Amsterdam and St. Petersburg where they hoped their boys would experience the culture those cities have to offer. So, we were off to a very good start.

We spent two full days in port after the Bowmans and Smythes came aboard as they wanted to tour some of the vineyards for which the region is famous. Mr. Bowman, who knows a lot about wine, told me the vineyards around Bordeaux have been producing Bordeaux wine since the eighth century and that Bordeaux is the world's major wine capital. The boys accompanied their parents on these trips, so it was a quiet time for the crew.

From Bordeaux, we sailed out to the Atlantic, then north to Brest, the western most tip of France. The crew didn't get any shore leave in Brest, but we did arrive in port during the International Festival of the Seas, a meeting of mostly old sailing vessels from around the world which gather there once every four years. The huge riggings on these old sail boats was really something to see. Jeff, Jr., the elder Smythe son, was studying oceanography in England and wanted to visit the Brest Oceanographic Research Center, so the plan was to spend two days in port. This, it turned out, was fine with the "J's" because both boys got seasick during our cruise north in the Atlantic and spent the entire two days "puking" as one of the "J's" told me.

The crew had almost no shore leave in either of the next two ports, Cherbourg and Calais. In Cherbourg, I heard Mr. Smythe ask Captain Nielsen why there were so many ferryboats in the harbor. He explained that Cherbourg is the main ferry line between France and England and also has service to Ireland and Jersey. Mr. Smythe joked he could "just pop home for a spell".

Everyone looked forward to Amsterdam, including the two "J's" who seemed fully recovered from their seasickness. We were going to spend a full week in port here as there was much the Bowmans and

Smythes wanted their sons to see and, as always, they wanted to make sure the crew had time ashore. The "J's" learned, probably from one of the crew, that Max and I had been to Amsterdam before on our bike trip, so they wanted us to show them around. "You know, man," one of them said, "the cannabis coffee shops, the red light district, all the good places." In other words, exactly what their parents would *not* want them to see. None of this was a problem the first few days we were in port because the Bowmans and Smythes took their sons to see Anne Frank's house, the Van Gogh Museum, the Rikjsmuseum, and some of the other important sites in the city. Finally, the "J's" broke away the morning Mr. and Mrs. Bowman went to visit the Amsterdam Stock Exchange, the oldest exchange of its kind in the world. Mr. Bowman is an investment banker in England, so he was particularly keen on seeing the Exchange.

That left us with the "J's" who were dying to see the seedier side of Amsterdam. Max and I flatly refused to take them to a cannabis coffee shop. "If the Captain detects any drugs on us, or on you, for that matter, we're gone, man. No second chance," Max told them. We decided to take them to the red light district, thinking the older women hanging out of the windows there would not be to their liking. *Wrong!* They never saw a prostitute they didn't want. We finally passed by a door where two women were hanging out. Mid-thirties, I guessed. Lots of mileage, no doubt, but not entirely over-the-hill yet. The boys soon struck a deal at what was probably double the going rate and went inside. Max and I waited on a bench nearby. About thirty minutes later, one of the "J's" came out, then the other a few minutes later. Both of them were visibly upset.

"Bitch gave me crabbies," one of them told us.

"Me, too," the other one said.

"I thought these whores were checked out," the first one said, now really distraught. "Our folks are going to kill us."

"Look, guys," I said, "we'll go to a pharmacy and get some lice shampoo you can use. No one will know."

"Can we go right away. These bugs itch like crazy!"

We took a taxi to a nearby pharmacy. The boys were embarrassed to ask for the lice shampoo, so Max and I went inside and bought what they needed. We were back on the yacht before their parents returned from the Amsterdam Stock Exchange. I think the boys spent the entire afternoon in the shower, shampooing and shampooing themselves to make sure every last bug was dead. They also shampooed the clothes they had been wearing

Then, they began worrying about other venereal diseases. "Didn´t you guys use condoms?" I asked.

"Yes, but I think they were old," one of the "J´s" said. "I´m pretty sure it split. Stupid whores!"

"Look, guys," Max said. "It´s very unlikely you picked up anything else. Just drink lots of water and piss as often as you can."

And that´s all they did for the next several days. Drink water and piss. I´ve never seen anyone drink so many bottles of water in one day. Finally, Mrs. Bowman noticed and asked why the boys were drinking so much water.

"Just thirsty, mom," one of the boys said. "Must be the climate."

The weather in Amsterdam was actually on the cool side, even cold in the evenings, but if Mrs. Bowman thought it strange her boys were drinking so much water, she didn´t say anything else. This was good because Max and I sure wanted to stay out of trouble. However, it was not long until we were summoned to the Captain´s cabin. We were very much afraid our misadventures with the "J´s" had been discovered and we were about to be disciplined, maybe even given the boot. Not so.

"I know what happened ashore with the two Bowman boys," Captain Nielsen said when we were seated at his conference table. "I know you were pressured to take the boys to the red light district and I want to thank you for handling the situation with such discretion. *Crabbies!* I hope they killed them all with the shampoo you bought. I am guessing the water consumption is to ward off VD, right?"

"Yes, sir," I said. "Sorry, sir."

"Nothing to apologize for, men. You handled a sensitive situation with as much discretion as possible. I thank you for that."

Wow! Another surprise from Captain Nielsen. Maybe we should forget college and become permanent crew. In all honesty, the idea appealed to both me and Max. And after what happened later, a much better plan.

The two "J´s" were definitely in our debt. I know they would have done anything for us. We owned them, no doubt about it. Problem was, under the circumstances, we couldn´t think of anything they could do for us. Nevertheless, it is always good to have people in your debt. What they didn´t know is that we certainly wouldn´t tell their parents which was, of course, their biggest fear. The Captain might not be pissed at us, but the Bowmans certainly would be. So, the incident was soon forgotten, except that the "J´s" kept bringing us stuff they bought ashore at the ports we called on. "Who knows?" Max said. "We might need a favor one day." Like I said, it´s good to have people in your debt.

Our next port-of-call was Hamburg, Germany. The principal reason for calling at Hamburg was for Mr. and Mrs. Bowman to tour the financial center, which, Mr. Bowman explained to his sons, has played an important role in European finance for centuries. It is also the second largest city in Germany, and there were other places the Bowmans and Smythes wanted to see, as well. Max and I stayed aboard, primarily to clean up the yacht with Jacques and Cyril after another rough day at sea.

We hoped to spend time ashore in Copenhagen, Denmark, our next port, and were not disappointed. The itinerary called for us to spend almost a week in Copenhagen because our guests said there is a lot to see and they wanted their boys to see as much as possible. The "J´s" had recovered their spirits, if not all of their exuberance, and did not ask us to take them anywhere. Captain Nielsen gave Max and me one full day ashore. Max found a "bicycle guide" on the internet, and we ended up booking with a guy named Josef for the day. He would arrange for bike rentals and would take us around the city to see some of the sites. Two members of the galley crew, young Philippinos, one named Juvi and the other something like Mahlo, came with us. I never quite got his name and it didn't really matter because neither of them spoke much English. They seemed content to go with us, though, and spent most of our tour snapping pictures with their phones.

Copenhagen is very much like Amsterdam. There is water everywhere, small parks, lots of flowers. It is definitely a bike-friendly city, like Amsterdam, with many more bicycles than cars. Best of all, almost everything the guide wanted to show us was nearby. In fact, we didn't really need the bikes because we could have walked everywhere we went.

Our first stop was at the statue of The Little Mermaid at Langelinje Pier. "The most visited place in all of Copenhagen," Josef told us. "She turned 100 two years ago in August." Josef took a photo of Max and me in front of the statue, and Juvi and Mahlo must have taken half a dozen photos in that place alone. Josef told us, according to legend the mermaid swims to the surface from the bottom of the sea every morning and night, sits on her rock and looks toward the shore hoping to catch a glimpse of the prince she loves. He said the story of the mermaid is based on a tale by Hans Christian Andersen.

Next up, the Stroget Shopping District which is located in the center of the city and is one of the longest pedestrian streets in Europe. Max and I were glad our mothers weren't along. We might still be there.

We rode our bicycles past the Amalienborg Palace, one of two royal palaces in the city, the other being Christiansborg. Josef explained the architecture of Amalienborg Palace is Dutch Rococo and that the palace was built in the 1700's. More pictures, lots of them, especially for the Philippino boys.

Our final stop, just after lunch at a bistro Josef took us to, was Tivoli Gardens. "It is an amusement park," Josef said, "but there is something here for everyone." And, he was right. It is full of exotic scenery, lots of gardens, and very exotic architecture. "It's best at night," Josef said, but we couldn't stay out that late as the sun was not setting until nearly midnight. "There are thousands of colored lights in the Gardens which create a fairy tale atmosphere. Perhaps that is why Hans Christian Andersen was such a frequent visitor. Even Walt Disney came here for inspiration when he built Disneyland."

We had two more days in Copenhagen, but Max and I stayed aboard while other crew members took their turns ashore. Again, the Bowmans and Smythes were very thoughtful of the crew.

From Copenhagen, we spent about two and one-half days at sea sailing north to Bergen, Norway. More rough seas, which meant extra work for the deck crew when we got to port, but no one seemed to get sick, including the two "J´s". There were two reasons for this port-of-call. Bergen is an international center for aquaculture, and especially subsea technology. Jeff, Jr. wanted to visit a couple of the institutes there. The more obvious reason is that Bergen is the gateway to the Norwegian fjords, the most famous fjords in the world, although Captain Nielsen said New Zealand might want to argue that point. After two nights and one day in Bergen, we headed north into the fjords. It is not far. From the coast, we sailed inland to the narrow fjord-arms Fjaelandsfjord and Naerayfjord. Just spectacular, particularly the glaciers hanging from the Jostedolsbreen Glacier. No worries about shore leave here. The best view was from the decks Jacques, Cyril, Max and I were cleaning.

From Bergen, we traveled south, rounding the southern tip of Norway, and then north again to Oslo. Here, we re-provisioned the yacht with fresh flowers, fruit, vegetables, meat and other supplies. The big draw here, at least for the Bowmans and Smythes, was the Munch Museum. Edvard Munch spent his youth in Oslo and returned there the last ten years of his life. Many of his works of art, including some of his most famous masterpieces, are located in the museum. Oslo is also where the world´s largest shipping companies are headquartered which made it interesting for Jeff, Jr., who seemed to love everything associated with the sea. Max and I spent a few hours ashore, but it was mostly to help the galley crew as there was quite a bit to load onto La Caravelle before our next major port of call, Stockholm, Sweden.

We had been scheduled to call at the port of Goteborg, Sweden, but the Bowmans and Smythes decided to skip that port in favor of a little more time in Stockholm. This leg of the cruise took two and one-half days as we sailed south from Oslo, Norway around the southern tip of

Sweden and then north again to Stockholm. The sea conditions were marginally better, but I think everyone on board was glad to be tied up to the dock once we arrived in Stockholm. Both of the "J´s" looked a little green while we were at sea, although neither of them complained.

Stockholm is the capital of Sweden and also the cultural and economic center of the country. Of particular interest to Mr. Smythe, for some reason, was the fact that Stockholm hosts the annual Nobel prize ceremonies. I heard him ask his younger son, Mark, if he knew why there was no Nobel prize for mathematics. When Mark said no, his father told him it was because Mrs. Nobel had an affair with a mathematician. So, there are prizes for science and a number of other fields, but not for mathematics. All four of the Bowman and Smythe boys thought this was hysterical.

Mrs. Smythe and Mrs. Bowman wanted to see the palaces in Stockholm, especially the Drottingholm and the Royal Palace. None of the boys was too keen on this, but they went along, probably because they had no choice. Mrs. Smythe, who said she hoped we could see the palaces, too, told us the Drottingholm has been the permanent home to the royal family since its construction in the seventeenth century. She was particularly impressed with the baroque gardens first laid out in 1681. The boys, not so much. They were a little more impressed with the Royal Palace, which is the official residence of Sweden´s King, and has more than six hundred rooms, making it one of the largest palaces in Europe.

What the boys really wanted to do was hire a RIB boat for a trip to the Swedish archipelago, a collection of thirty thousand islands off the coast of Sweden. As a special treat for us, the Bowmans and Smythes hired four of these boats, each one holding eight people plus crew, so the crew members of La Caravelle who wanted to see the archipelago could go along. It was an amazing experience. Max and I ended up in the RIB with the two "J´s" plus Jacques and Cyril and two of the helicopter crew. The "Captain" of our boat, Magdalena, was a Swedish beauty who told us we were going on a seal safari. One of the "J´s" had other ideas until the Captain threatened to pitch him overboard. He settled down after that. The seal safari was awesome. We would pull the boat up close to one of the islands or to rocks just offshore. Seals would swim up to us and we could throw herring to them from a couple of coolers on board. Magdalena actually made the seals come up out of the water and take the herring from her fingers. None of the rest of us had the guts to do that.

From Stockholm, we sailed overnight to Helsinki, Finland. We were in very calm waters, although Captain Nielsen told us the Baltic could be surprisingly rough, much like the Tasman Sea off New Zealand. Not for us, though. Our purpose in calling at Helsinki was fuel and provisions for the yacht. Captain Nielsen said he didn´t trust the fuel he would otherwise have to buy in St. Petersburg, our final destination on this cruise. It was a short voyage between the two cities, as St. Petersburg is only about 300 kilometers east of Helsinki. The plan was to dock there for ten days, as we were told there is much to see in St. Petersburg, and the Bowmans, Smythes and their sons were also going to fly to Moscow for four days during our stay.

On our passage to St. Petersburg, First Officer Andersen joined us in the crew mess for dinner. He is a bit of a history buff and is very keen on Russian history. He told us that thanks to our charter guests, the crew would once again have time to explore the city he called the "Venice of the North". The Bowmans and Smythes were leaving the morning of our arrival in port for their flight to Moscow, so we had several days to sightsee before their return to the yacht. Of course, our first job was to make sure the hull, the decks and all the fittings were once again clean. Because of the smooth sail from Helsinki, this wasn´t quite as big a job as it usually was when we arrived in port.

First Officer Andersen strongly advised all of us to take some kind of tour in the city. "It is the second largest city in Russia," he told us, "and there is much to see. A tour guide can really help." Max and I went on line and hired a guide and driver for a full day and talked our two Philippino friends from the galley crew into joining us, so there were four of us in the van plus a driver and our guide. Vladi, our guide, was in his late twenties, sort of humorless, but he really knew St. Petersburg. Max and I felt badly about the Philippino boys because their English was very limited and we were sure they understood little of what Vladi said. Nevertheless, they seemed content to ride along and take dozens of pictures of literally everything we saw.

Vladi explained that St. Petersburg is on the Neva River at the head of the Gulf of Finland on the Baltic Sea. In 1914, the City's name was changed to Petrograd, then to Leningrad in 1924. It has been called St. Petersburg since 1991.

This was our day to learn about Peter the Great, the founder of St. Petersburg. Our first stop was his "cabin" where he lived from 1703 to 1708. It is a small structure, built of wood in a combination of Dutch and Russian architectural styles. It is now a museum, open to the public, so we were able to go inside for a look around. The building is only sixty square meters according to Vladi, but it is completely restored to its original design.

One of Peter's major accomplishments was to build a fortress intended to protect St. Petersburg against possible attacks from the Swedes. Within the fortress is the Peter and Paul Cathedral. It is the burial place for all of the Russian Emperors and Empresses from Peter the Great to Alexander III. On top of the Cathedral is a golden angel holding a cross. The angel is actually a weathervane and one of the most prominent symbols of St. Petersburg. It is also the tallest structure in the City at four hundred four feet.

After a very forgettable lunch of some kind of Russian soup and hard bread, which Vladi washed down with vodka, we went to see The Hermitage, the largest art gallery in all of Russia and one of the most important in the world. It is located on the banks of the Neva River, and was the Winter Palace of the tsars for centuries. Originally built by Peter the Great for his daughter Elizabeth, she died before the Palace was completed, and Catharine the Great was the first Russian ruler to live there. It is a beautiful mansion, three stories high, built in the Baroque style, according to Vladi.

Inside, there are actually two point seven million exhibits displaying art and artifacts from all over the world. The Museum is most famous, of course, for its paintings. There are works by da Vinci, Michaelangelo,

Raphael, Titian, and a host of Impressionist painters, including Renoir, Cezanne and Pissaro. There are also bronze statues by Rodin. We saw only a small fraction of what is in the Museum that afternoon, and Max and I came back a couple of days later one morning to see some of what we missed. I have never especially liked museums, and Max gave me all kinds of shit for wanting to go a second time. I have to admit it was awesome!

Three days later, the Bowmans and Smythes returned to the yacht. Max asked one of the "J's" what he saw, and his reply was "Ugly women. Very ugly women".

"Anything else?" Max asked. "Oh, yeah, Red Square was cool." We could only imagine the Bowmans´ reaction if they knew what their sons thought of Moscow.

SEVENTY-NINE

Maximilian Van Zuylen

We stayed aboard La Caravelle doing our regular cleaning and polishing jobs until the day after the Bowmans and Smythes left the yacht. It was very hard saying good-bye because I was pretty sure we wouldn't be back. Captain Nielsen invited us to his cabin one last time where we had a farewell dinner with him and First Officer Andersen. The Captain encouraged us to consider a career at sea. "You are good workers, you get along well with the crew, and all of our guests have liked having you aboard."

"You mean except for our French guests," William said.

Both the Captain and First Officer laughed. "I don't think they liked each other, much less the rest of us," the Captain said. "Anyway, Will, Max, it's a good life. Let us know if you decide to give it a full-time try and we can set you up right here on La Caravelle or with any number of other yacht captains. They would be lucky to get you and I think you both could advance quickly."

Just before leaving the yacht, we all posed for a timed photograph. The Captain, First Officer, and all the crew. It sat on the mantel of our fireplace and was probably the last thing I looked at before I left the apartment that night.

Will and I talked about our time aboard La Caravelle often, particularly that last night in New York when we were walking down Riverside Drive for the last time. "Should have taken the Captain up on his offer," Will said.

"Too late," I told him. Will just nodded.

We flew to New York from St. Petersburg over the Labor Day weekend. Mr. Radcliffe didn't like our choice of airlines coming out of Russia, so he sent the Radcliffe jet for us. Much as we loved that summer, it was good to be home again. I hadn't seen my parents, or Mike, in a very long time, so after the weekend, I flew to San Francisco for a few days. My parents were just relocating to the penthouse after their summer in Napa and were pretty much occupied with whatever they did when they changed residences. I went to Hillsborough and had dinner with Mike, Nancy, and "Little Maxi" as Nancy began calling him, notwithstanding Mike`s objection. Mike was coming to New York in October for some securities law conference his firm wanted him to attend, so I made him promise to stay with us. Mike said he`d be busy during the day, but not have his usual workload at night, so we could be together in the evenings. I called Will later that night to let him know Mike would be coming to stay. He was stoked!

Mike´s visit was pretty much the highlight of our year, or at least most of it. I gave him my room and bunked with Will. We had big king-sized beds in both bedrooms, so it was no sweat sharing Will´s bed for a few days, and it was great having Mike around. Will and I kept our noses in the books every afternoon so we could go out with him in the evening. Mike had spent surprisingly little time in New York, so almost everywhere we took him was new. We went to the Village twice, both times having dinner at haunts Will and I loved. We caught a comedy show at one of the clubs there and walked around Washington Square Park afterwards. It is always a happening scene in the Park which is surrounded by New York University and haunted by students, bums and gawkers. We took him to the Chinese restaurant in our neighborhood where we had taken Miguel, the place where the waiters tell you what you are going to eat instead of the other way around.

Mike´s securities law course ended on Friday and his flight to San Francisco was not until Sunday, so we had all day Saturday to pal around. We spent most of the day in Central Park, just exploring and tossing a Frisbee. We bought hotdogs and cokes off a street vendor and ate them by the Reservoir. One of the best times I had with Mike in years.

What was not so great about the year was that our fathers began talking to us and sending us e-mails about choosing careers. Why they were both on the same page at the same time, neither of us knew. I was pretty sure they rarely talked. In truth, neither of us had any real idea what we wanted to do after college. "Maybe we should go to Wharton and study business," Will suggested. "My dad is always harping about getting an education in real estate and finance. I think he has visions of me joining him in his real estate development company. Not going to happen," he said.

My dad had similar ideas and wanted me to concentrate on something which would lead to a career. Problem was, I had no idea what I wanted to do with my life. Neither did Will. We were third year students at Columbia, got straight "A´s" – except for Will´s two "B+´s" in sociology – but we had not declared majors, something which one of the University counselors pointed out to us in letters we received early in the semester. So, we were getting pressured from all sides to decide what to focus on academically and what career paths to choose. Finally, and mostly to shut everyone up, we agreed to start taking business courses next semester and see where that led. My dad was pushing business school at Harvard. Will´s dad wanted him to go to Wharton. Everyone seemed to have a plan for us … except us.

Detective Stephen Olsen, Bridgeport Police Department

I sat at my desk on a Saturday morning in the fall going over my caseload and prioritizing what I would do the following week. Try as I might, I couldn't get the Radcliffe and Van Zuylen boys out of my mind. The Morrison cases were now long closed, both in Greenwich and in Bridgeport. I kept telling myself the same thing I always told junior detectives who were unable to solve what they were working on: "We can't close them all." I don't know why this one stuck in my craw, but it did. There were just too many coincidences.

The boys were on Deerpark campus when Morrison's office was flooded and when the arson, and possibly attempted murder, occurred at his home in Bridgeport. They had a car.

They were on campus when that senior's car – Robert Montgomery – was pushed into the Sound.

They were on the yacht La Caravelle in the Mediterranean when the officer went missing and presumably drowned in the Sea.

They were on the yacht the following summer when the Philippino cook died of strychnine poisoning.

The Radcliffe boy had taken a sociology class from Ms. Pettibone at Barnard, and was in New York when her office was vandalized.

Way too many coincidences. I had opportunity in every one of those situations. What I lacked was any physical evidence or any motive, other than the two "B+s'" in sociology. Both the Van Zuylen and Radcliffe boys got into Deerpark, did well there academically, and then got into their first choice for college. Hard to see why they would have been pissed at the Deerpark admissions officer who not only accepted them at Deerpark but provided one of the letters of recommendation sent to Columbia.

No one seemed to like Robert Montgomery. A few of the students we interviewed called him an asshole. Even the administration officials said he could be arrogant and was tough on lower form students. No limit to the suspect pool there.

When I spoke to Captain Nielsen on the yacht La Caravelle, he practically chewed me out for even asking about the boys. He said they couldn't possibly be involved in Officer Jamiesen's disappearance or the death of the Philippino, Cesar.

That left Ms. Pettibone and the vandalism in the form of hate speech sprayed on her office door.

On a chance, I picked up the phone and called NYPD Detective George Marshall. Like me, he was at his desk on a Saturday morning lining up his case priorities for next week. "What can I do for you, Steve?" he asked.

"The Pettibone case," I told him. "Anything new there?"

"Nothing at all. In fact, it's closed." I told him I was surprised it was closed after just three or four months.

"Nothing there, pal," he said. He told me the NYPD had talked to her neighbors in her building in Morningside Heights. She didn't seem to have friends there, but no enemies, either. Lived quietly, kept to herself. Her colleagues at Barnard said pretty much the same thing. She had no real friends among the faculty, but no enemies they could find. One of the professors they talked to said she was quite respected in her field, and that her sociology textbooks were used at a number of colleges and universities in the country.

"She spends a lot of time at her sister's place in Redbank," George said. "Told me she likes to drive the tractor and get her hands in the soil."

He went on. "We have a lot of shit to deal with in Manhattan. The Pettibone matter has been dead from the get-go. My Captain didn't want me to spend any more time on it. Closed it a month ago, in fact."

I thanked him for his time and hung up. Another dead end. Not even a straw. *Give it up, I kept telling myself. Give it up.*

CHAPTER EIGHTY-ONE

William Radcliffe

Max and I spent Thanksgiving in New York. I flatly refused to go to Palm Beach, and Max told his parents he had too much to do to get ready for finals. A lie, of course, but a convenient excuse. Max's aunt, Marie-Helene, was in town to spend a couple of weeks with her husband before they both would fly to Paris for Christmas. According to Max, the Baron had to log a certain number of days per year outside France in order to avoid some pretty horrendous tax penalties in that country. She called one day and asked Max if we would take her back to P. J. Clarke's. The Baron wanted to go, too.

We borrowed Jacob, our chauffeur, and the limousine and picked up Max's aunt and uncle at their apartment on Lexington Avenue for the short drive to P. J. Clarke's at Fifty-Fifth Street and Third Avenue. I don't know if the Baron was more surprised by the crowd, the noise, or the waiters, one of whom pointed to a table in the corner and said "Take that four top over there". Marie-Helene was loving it, and the Baron pronounced the cheeseburger he ordered "the best I have ever tasted!" We were clearly the odd group in the restaurant, a couple of college students and a very elegant, rather formally dressed foreign couple. No one paid the least attention, though, except for a photographer who showed up from somewhere and snapped a picture. I think Max was right. They liked P. J. Clarke's because it was different from practically everything else in their lives.

The photo appeared at the top of *Suzy's* column the next day and we were her lead item. It read, in part, *The Baron and Baroness de Rothschild dined at P. J. Clarke's, the midtown saloon which attracts anyone and everyone, but not Barons and Baronesses until yesterday. Cheeseburgers, of course, and champagne all around. Their guests were their handsome nephew, Maximilian Van Zuylen, from San Francisco, and his equally handsome college roommate, William Radcliffe, of the New*

York Radcliffes... There was more, but I stopped reading at that point, thinking about my mother's likely reaction when she saw the column. She had the New York papers sent to her in Palm Beach every day, and I was sure *Suzy* was the first thing she read when she got them. Despite all her social-climbing efforts, she had never managed to meet either the Baron or Baroness, and here we were having lunch with them in a saloon in New York. *Infuriating,* no doubt.

On Saturday night, a week later, we were invited to the Rothschilds for dinner at their apartment. The interiors had been featured in Architectural Digest a few months ago, but I am not sure the photos do it justice. Everywhere you look are the colors red and gold. Silks and damasks cover the sofas and windows. What you clearly cannot see from the photographs is the fact that everything in the apartment is comfortable – the chairs, the sofas, the ottomans. Max said it is kind of homey once you get past all the glitz and glitter. I'm not sure about homey, but it is very comfortable. Everything seemed to be set up with the Baron's comfort in mind. His writing desk was in the living room with an old-fashioned ink well and writing tablet on top. His favorite drinks were in bottles set out on top of an antique liquor cabinet, rather than stored away inside.

We had dinner in a fairly small, tented dining room, also red, with candles the only lighting. Marie-Helene was charming and funny and flirtatious, as usual, and the Baron seemed to enjoy the company of younger people. "How delicious," Marie-Helen said, "three of the most handsome men in New York at my table. That is why I refused to invite anyone else." It was easy to see why the Baron had fallen for her.

There was no getting out of it at Christmas. I was stuck going to Palm Beach and Max to San Francisco. Palm Beach was every bit as boring as I expected it to be. The only plus was the weather was decent for a change, so I did some swimming in our pool and also in the Atlantic. Apart from that, I really had nothing to do and no one to do anything with. My parents were out most evenings attending either a benefit of some kind or a private dinner. Mercifully, I was not required to go to any of these. They did host a dinner one night for about sixty guests. Cocktails were served around the pool, and dinner was served at six tables for ten on the terrace. I was placed at one of the tables next to a highly bejeweled old woman who, fortunately, was so deaf conversation was impossible. On my other side was an elderly gentleman who wanted to know how much sex I got in college. *Un-fucking-believable!*

I did have lunch alone one day with my mother while my father was out playing golf with some of his buddies. She wanted to talk about THE subject, of course.

"I hope you have stopped imaging that you and Max are brothers," she said. "It is so ridiculous. Even laughable."

I had had enough. "Mother, Max knows we are brothers. I know we are brothers. You know we are brothers, so let´s cut the crap."

"*William! Such language. I will not permit it.*"

"Whatever. Look, mother, your little secret is safe with me, at least for now. You can stop worrying about what you might read in *Suzy´s* column or the *New York Times*. I am not going to tell, but I might change my mind if you keep denying the obvious. Max and I know the truth, but we want to know what happened and when. It´s not right to keep the story from us. Not right at all."

She actually started to cry, and I think she would have cried more except it was probably ruining her makeup, so she stopped and dabbed at her eyes with her napkin. "All right, Will," she said finally. "I will tell you the story – you and Max – but not here, not now. When we are all back in New York, I will come to the apartment and tell you both everything." With that, she left the table, probably to repair her makeup.

My Christmas present that year was in the driveway with a big bow around it. A metallic red BMW five series. "Your mother´s idea," my dad said. *Yes,* I thought. *I bet it was.* "Jacob has the keys to your Explorer and will find someplace to keep it until you decide if you want to sell it. I know you only have one space in your apartment and I am sure you would rather keep the BMW there."

"*Thanks, dad, that´s really great! Thanks, mom!*"

How ironic, I thought, remembering Robert Montgomery′s metallic blue BMW five series which we drove into the Sound.

I called Max and told him my mother promised to tell us the story of our being brothers. He was skeptical, but then said, "She probably doesn′t think she has a choice." Max was right. No choice. I also told him about the BMW and asked him to fly to Palm Beach instead of New York so we could drive it back together. He was good with that plan and anxious to get out of San Francisco. Mike and his family had gone to Nancy′s family′s home for Christmas, so they didn′t have much of a chance to get together. He was as bored as I was, and made plans to fly to Palm Beach on the twenty-seventh. We would spend one night in Palm Beach, then start the drive north.

EIGHTY-TWO

Maximilian Van Zuylen

We left Will´s family´s home in Palm Beach early in the morning on December twenty-eighth. We weren´t going to make lots of stops on our way to New York because, after all, the most fun was driving the new car. What a difference from the Ford Explorer! Will and I agreed BMW´s advertising slogan "The Ultimate Driving Machine" was not just the usual bullshit. *What an amazing car!* "Definite chick magnate!" Will decided.

We did stop in Charleston, South Carolina, and spent one night in the historic district there with its beautiful southern mansions and restored public buildings. We also stopped for a night in Baltimore and took a long walk along the restored waterfront, now a popular residential and commercial area. We were going to stop at either Rehoboth Beach, Delaware, or Asbury Park, New Jersey, but it was the wrong time of year for the beaches this far north, so we continued driving to New York, taking the Lincoln Tunnel into Manhattan and the West Side Highway to the Upper West Side and our apartment. A twelve hour day. We ordered take-out pizza and promptly fell asleep in our chairs in front of the television.

I think it was sometime after Christmas that things started to fall apart for us, although we would not know it for a while.

Will´s mother did come to see us on a Saturday in early January. She said she and Max´s father attended a party hosted by Malcolm Forbes on his yacht, The Highlander, just over twenty years ago. She told us she had had much too much to drink as the yacht circled Manhattan and only remembered going below deck to one of the cabins in order to rest. She "thinks" she and Frederick Van Zuylen got together there, something she quickly pushed from her mind. Then, she was pregnant and thought she and William, Sr. were going to have the baby they wanted and had tried to conceive for more than two years. She said it never occurred to her Frederick Van Zuylen could be the father until she saw the two of us together at Deerpark. She told us a mother notices these things more than anyone else and knew right away what had happened, although she tried to convince herself it wasn't true. She started crying – "For real this time," Will later told me. He gave her a hug and, of course, she cried even more. I think it was a relief for her to get it out after keeping her secret for twenty years. She used Will's bathroom to freshen up.

"Don't worry, mom," Will said "we just wanted to know", bringing on more tears. Finally, she kissed both of us and left.

I asked Will if he was really going to let her off the hook. He looked at me and said "not entirely". I wasn't sure what he meant.

As promised, we took a couple of business courses in our second semester that year. I took accounting, which was boring as shit, and Will took real estate finance which he didn't really like but found easy enough. We both met some girls that semester, brought some of them back to the apartment, but there was nothing serious going on. Then, in the spring, Will met a young woman from Fordam University who lived with her family in Morningside Heights and used the Columbia Library to study because she shared a small apartment with her parents and younger sister and told Will it was never quiet there.

When I first met Lila, I thought she must be in high school. She was small of stature, timid and seemed way too young to be in college. She was pretty, though. Will liked her and began bringing her to our apartment after classes. They spent time studying, for sure, but also time in his bedroom. I knew Will thought this was just another lark, but it seemed to me Lila was taking everything much more seriously. Then it hit. I came home from jogging in Riverside Park one afternoon in May to find Will sitting on our living room couch utterly dejected. "Bitch says she's pregnant," was all he said.

I said nothing. "It gets worse," he said. "She will not consider an abortion. Catholic. Says her parents will kill her. Wants to get married. Shit!" Will got up and went to his room slamming the door before I could say anything. Not that I had anything to say. He was in there for hours. When he finally came out, he told me he would figure it out. Scared the shit out of me.

EIGHTY-THREE

Stephen Olsen, Bridgeport Police Department

Charles Morrison was on medical leave from Deerpark Academy. The incidents at his office and his home clearly took a serious toll on him, and as he told me, he just wasn´t fit to continue in his job. I felt very sorry for him but wasn´t sure how I could help. He continued to call, at least every week or two, to ask if there had been any progress in our investigations. I was reluctant to tell him the cases had been closed months ago, but always told him we had no new news.

One day in late May, he called to tell me he might have something of interest. I was beginning to tire of these calls and was prepared to tell him so.

"Detective Olsen," he asked, "do you remember the Radcliffe and Van Zuylen boys?" he asked. I sat up straighter in my chair.

"Yes," I answered.

"Well, this may not mean much, or anything, detective, but there were rumors the boys might be brothers, or at least half-brothers."

"Go on," I said, now fully alert.

"Yes, it was just rumor, of course, from other students, but it got me thinking. Both boys came from extraordinarily wealthy families and both had some – uh – discipline issues in their backgrounds before they came to Deerpark."

"What kind of discipline issues, Mr. Morrison?"

"Mostly pranks you would probably call them. I recall talking to the Van Zuylen boy about an incident involving the nuns at St. Mary´s Country Day school, his grammar school in San Francisco. It was included in the materials we received when he applied to Deerpark."

"Go on, please."

"Well, it sounds harmless enough. He put a water balloon underneath a cushion on one of the nun´s chairs so when she sat down in her classroom it burst and it appeared … well, it appeared she had urinated on herself."

Mr. Morrison was clearly embarrassed to talk about such a delicate subject.

"Maximilian Van Zuylen was beaten in front of the class for his transgression, which he admitted when the class was asked who was responsible. I do give him credit for that."

"Were there other incidents?"

"Nothing specifically linked to him. I did follow up, though."

"What about the Radcliffe boy, Mr. Morrison?" I asked.

"William went to The Brook, a very prestigious grammar school on New York´s Upper East Side. Nothing was ever attributed to him, but there were a couple of incidents while he was a student there. One of my friends is the dean of The Brook, so I checked with him after learning that the boys might be brothers or half-brothers, not that that might mean anything, of course."

"What did he tell you, Mr. Morrison?" Finally, *something*. Or nothing.

"There was one fairly serious incident during William´s time at The Brook. It involved the theft of an expensive textbook from one student´s locker which was later found in another student´s locker. The boy whose book was stolen was a senior and the locker in which the book was later found belonged to another senior. They had been best friends, got into a serious fight at school, and eventually received disciplinary marks which resulted in their not being admitted to the boarding schools of their choice."

"But, William was not involved?"

"It was never determined who was involved. The dean believed neither of the senior boys was involved, but the culprit, whoever he was, was not identified, either."

"Is that it, Mr. Morrison?" I asked, growing weary of this conversation.

"Well, there was the incident with the frogs?"

"Frogs?"

He explained to me the science experiment with the frogs and the fact that someone in Will's class had mutilated them in a way that the frogs could not be traced back to the individual students responsible for their dissection. "No one confessed," Mr. Morrison said, "and the frog dissection was thrown out as part of the grades assigned to students in the class."

"But there was no evidence William was personally involved?"

"No, detective," he said. "No." As usual in these phone calls, he sounded dejected when there was really nothing to tie anyone to the crimes committed against his office and his home.

"Well, thank you, Mr. Morrison. I will add these notes to our file. Who knows? It may lead somewhere."

I sat back in my chair and thought. *Opportunity. Always opportunity. Never anything more.*

Shit!

I dismissed the water balloon incident as a childish prank. I also dismissed the stolen book incident at The Brook as Morrison had told me there was nothing to link William Radcliffe to that incident. The mutilated frogs interested me, though, so a couple of days later I phoned FBI Profiler Martha Stuart at her office in Manhattan. It took her another day to return my call.

"What can I do for you, detective?" she asked when we finally spoke.

"Do you remember the questions I asked you some months ago about the possibility of psychopaths being involved in some crimes I was working?"

"Yes, of course, I do."

"Well, this is probably nothing, but I wanted to run something more by you."

"No problem, detective. Most of what I work on turns out to be nothing."

"You told me it was unlikely the two young men I was looking at were psychopaths unless they were related. Do you remember that?"

"Yes."

"Well, would your answer be different if I told you they were brothers, or half- brothers?"

"I believe I told you it would be unlikely two young men who were not related and who had formed a bond were psychopaths because such persons, in our experience, tend to be loners and would not form friendships easily or at all. If they are genetically related, yes, that could change my opinion, although as I told you at the time, profiling is a very inexact science. We get it wrong often. Way too often, in fact. But, yes, if they are related, the chances of them both being psychopaths would increase."

"What about animal mutilation?" I asked.

"A classic sign," she answered, "particularly among juveniles."

I explained the frog mutilations, possibly carried out by one of the boys.

"Young psychopaths," she said, "often carry out mutilations on small animals like cats, dogs, rabbits. The fact that these frogs were already dead and were mutilated to cover up which frog was assigned to which student weakens the possibility of psychopathic behavior."

"But it doesn't eliminate it altogether."

"No, detective, it doesn't eliminate it. But, I have to caution you. Young people who mutilate animals, dead or alive, are most definitely not always psychopaths. The most interesting thing you have told me is that the two boys are related, or may be related. That bears looking into."

I thanked her and hung up the phone. *A straw.* I decided to visit William and Max once more.

EIGHTY-FOUR
William Radcliffe

About a week after Lila said she was pregnant and wouldn't have an abortion, I went into Max's room at night when he was just getting into bed. I stretched out on the other half of the bed and began telling him what I had in mind. I knew he wouldn't like it, but I also knew he would be with me just as I would be with him no matter what. Max said nothing while I described my plan.

"Jesus, Will, we've got to stop killing people. We got away with it in Gibraltar and also in the Med, but that dickhead detective must suspect us of killing Jamiesen, among other crimes, otherwise why would he have called Captain Nielsen? And now another one? I don't like it."

"I don't like it either, bro, but I'm not going to marry the little bitch. It's her fault, really. Told me she was on the pill. I think she *wanted* to get pregnant. William Mortimer Radcliffe IV, gravy train. It's not going to happen, Max. *It's just not going to happen!*"

"I'm in, Will, you know that. But let's make sure there are no holes in the plan. It needs to be perfect."

I relaxed, actually fell asleep on Max's bed. I woke up at two in the morning, still there, and went into my own room and slept solidly through the night. It was Sunday morning, we had no classes, so we sat on our terrace drinking coffee and going over details of the plan. "How do you know Lila hasn't told someone?" Max asked me. "Her sister, a friend, anyone?"

"She's terrified to talk to anyone because she is afraid her father might find out. Hasn't gone to a doctor, either, but she told me she's never been even a day late and she just missed her second period."

"What about the people who see you together at the library at Columbia?"

"So what? She hangs out at the library, probably talks to a lot of people."

"You take her out anywhere?"

"Just here. Never ran into any of our neighbors, though, if that's your question."

"I'm just trying to cover the bases, Will, that's all."

"I know. I know."

"So, will she go out with you Friday night?"

"I'll ask her tomorrow at the library, but yes, sure she will. I'll tell her the priest is meeting us at the beach in Connecticut because it is easier to get married in Connecticut than in New York."

"Is that true?"

"Who knows, who cares? We're not getting married in Connecticut or anywhere else. Besides, she will believe anything I tell her."

"So, you expect her to leave her apartment to get married with no clothes, no suitcase?"

"I'll tell her we will drive back to New York after the ceremony and tell her parents together. Then she can pack some belongings so her parents aren't suspicious before hand, and come back with me to our apartment."

"And I am along because …"

"You are our witness. It's perfect, Max, *perfect.*"

I knew Max wasn't entirely convinced, but something had to be done soon and neither of us could come up with a better plan, so I met Lila in the library on Monday afternoon and told her we would get married on Friday night in Connecticut. I cautioned her not to tell anyone, but that seemed unnecessary because she certainly didn't want her parents to know until after we were married. She told me if her sister knew or any of her friends, it just might get back to her parents and ruin everything. We were good to go.

It was nearing time for finals so Lila said she would not have any trouble getting out of the house Friday night to study at Columbia. Max rented a Chevy sedan earlier in the day because we didn't want to take the chance that someone night pay attention to a bright red BMW out by the beach which is where we were headed. Lila was waiting on the corner of Broadway and One Hundred Tenth Street as agreed. We didn't want to pick her up directly from campus in case anyone noticed. From there, we headed north to Connecticut and to a stretch of the Long Island Sound where we had taken the Smithfield girls several years ago. This part of the beach was nearly always deserted which is why we had chosen it with the girls. It was deserted again, as far as I could tell.

Lila asked about the priest and I told her we were fifteen minutes early. "I hope my parents will still be awake when we get back to New York," she said. "It's already nine o'clock."

"It won't take long, Lila, once we get started."

I fell slightly behind Lila and Max pretending to pick something up from the beach. I came up behind her quickly and slipped the cord I had in my pocket around her neck and pulled hard. She struggled, of course, but it was all over in seconds. Lila's purse was still in the car, but we checked carefully for any identification she might have in a pocket before pulling her into the shallow waters just offshore. We knew she would be identified eventually, but there was no point in that being done any sooner than necessary. Less than fifteen minutes later, we were on our way, having changed into dry pants and shoes we had stowed in the trunk of the car. A few hundred yards away, we tossed Lila's purse into the Sound and watched it sink in the moonlight. After that, it was back to New York where we tossed our wet shoes and pants into a dumpster in the Bronx, turned in the rental car, and took a cab back to our apartment.

I poured each of us a tall snifter of brandy which we took out on the terrace. We were both lost in thought and didn't say very much. Finally, Max said he was tired and wanted to go to bed. I gave him a long hug and said only "thanks, bro." He hugged me, too.

EIGHT-FIVE

Detective Jeff Johnson,
Greenwich Police Department

I got the call about three in the morning because I was the detective on rotation. A girl's body found in the Sound not far from the Smithfield Girls Academy in Guilford. Probably strangled, according to the police officer on scene.

I dressed and drove to Guilford, arriving about forty-five minutes after the call. There was a heavy police presence at the shore where the body was discovered by a couple of kids who were parked there, probably making out. It's a pretty deserted part of the shore which is the reason it attracts kids in the first place. What our victim was doing there was anyone's guess at this point.

I found the County Medical Examiner just finishing up his preliminary examination of the body. This would be followed by an autopsy in his laboratory once the body was transported there by police ambulance.

"What did you find, Sam?" I asked him.

"Strangled. Maybe some kind of cord or garrote. Might have been pregnant. We'll know more once we get her to the lab."

"Judging from the approximate age, she could be one of the Smithfield girls. I'll send one of the officers over there in the morning to see if anyone's missing. Anything else, Sam?"

"Yes, just this." He pulled a plastic evidence envelope from his coat pocket and handed it to me. "I was going to give it to one of the police officers before I left. It appears to be a photograph, although it is hard to decipher. It was in her bra on the left side of her chest."

A picture she kept over her heart. Interesting.

I studied the photograph through the plastic bag. It was small, maybe two by two. The face had been washed away, probably by the sea. What was left was a picture of a shirt and part of a hand. Both were badly blurred, but the shirt and the hand appeared to belong to a man, not a woman. I would take it to our forensics lab to see if they could do anything with it.

Before leaving, I talked to the policeman on scene. He had already let the two kids go who had discovered the body. The boy said they were going to be in "deep shit" with their parents. The officer had phone numbers in case we needed to follow up.

The police officer's name was Bradley. I asked about any identification on or around the body.

"Nothing, detective," he told me. "Either she didn't have any on her or the perp took it. We got three good sets of shoe prints. From the size and tread, looks like two men and the girl. We also got tire tracks. The forensics boys are working on it."

I thanked Bradley and drove home. Nothing for me to do until we had a little more to work on.

I slept for a while and went into the office about eleven. The reports started rolling in. The victim was not a student at Smithfield. All their students were accounted for. We would check the other high schools in the area, but Smithfield had been our best bet because of its proximity to where the girl was found. Sam confirmed for me that the girl had been pregnant. "Probably six weeks, no more," he said. He told me whatever type of garrote was used was thin. "Not a rope because there is no hemp in the wound. Not a wire, either."

I asked my assistant to run a missing persons report for the tri-state area, our standard procedure when an unidentified victim shows up on our turf. A day later, we got a hit. Missing woman from New York City, age 19, student at Fordham University. The family was called and the father took the train to Greenwich police headquarters that afternoon. I saw him after he made the identification in the morgue. He was probably in his fifties, but looked decades older. Tragedy will do that to you.

"My Lila, my Lila" was all he kept saying over and over again. "What kind of an animal would do this?" he finally asked me. "That's what we are going to find out, sir," I told him. Nothing I could say offered any solace, of course, as I had learned over many years. *Sometimes it really sucked.* This was one of them. I tried to cover some of the basics – friends, boyfriends, neighbors, people she knew at school, that sort of thing. He did his best, I knew that, but we would have to meet again, probably several times, to get what we needed. I didn't want him to go home alone, so I sent one of our officers with him on the train with instructions to make sure Mr. Jacobs got back to his apartment.

Yes, sometimes the job really sucked.

Two days later, I got a look at the photograph found on the victim's body, enhanced by our forensics group. Still no face. The hand was somewhat clearer, although probably not enough to make an identification. The shirt I thought I recognized. I decided to drop by the apartment of William Radcliffe and Maximilian Van Zuylen.

One of the boys answered the intercom and let me in. I am not sure which one. They sounded just alike and I suspected they really were brothers. William answered the door when I pressed their buzzer. "I thought I told you to talk to my father's lawyer, detective," he said.

"Just a couple of questions, William. May I come in?"

"No."

"Take a look at this photograph, then," I said taking a copy of our evidence photo from my coat pocket. "That your shirt?"

"The photo's fucked up, detective, in case you haven't noticed. But, no. It's not my shirt." He started to close the door.

"I think it is," I told him just before he slammed the door. I could hear the lock snap into place.

Got you, I thought, but I knew I really had nothing. It might have been a mistake going there. If the shirt really was his, it would be gone before I left the building. *Shit! Dumb fucking detective,* I thought.

EIGHTY-SIX
William Radcliffe

Two weeks later, Max and I had all but forgotten about Lila. We were into study mode again with finals beginning in less than a week. The phone call came out of the blue one evening. Max answered. "Some guy named Jacobs," Max said.

"*Holy shit! Lila's father!*" I took the phone.

"Hello."

"*You fucking animal. You killed my Lila. Why? How could you do this?*"

"Mr. Jacobs ...," I said.

"*Don't lie to me, you bastard. She kept a diary which was under her mattress. You slept with her, you prick! I am going to the NYPD right now. They are going to arrest you for murder.*"

I hung up the phone and turned to Max. "It's over, bro."

He just looked at me and nodded.

We had time, at least some time. Mr. Jacob would go to a local police station, most likely. They would contact the homicide squad which in turn would probably contact the detectives in Connecticut. We had one or two hours, but not much more. It was a chilly night, odd for this time of year. We both put on windbreakers and took the elevator to the street. We crossed Riverside Drive and headed south along the Drive about ten blocks. We stopped just south of One Hundred Third Street. There was no street entrance to the Park here. It was quiet and dark. Max and I hoisted ourselves up on the wall and sat there facing Riverside Drive, the Park behind us. It was a good forty feet down from there to the granite bedrock under Manhattan.

I pulled out two small brandy bottles from a coat pocket and gave one to Max. We drank them and put the bottles back in our coat pockets. A couple walked by, hand in hand. A single guy walked by, then nobody.

"Any regrets, Max?" I asked.

"No, Will. It´s who we are, right?"

"Right, Max. It´s who we are."

We sat there for a few more minutes, not saying anything. We could hear sirens coming up Broadway, getting closer. I looked at Max. I put a hand on his shoulder and we both leaned back.

EPILOGUE

Detective Stephen Olsen, Bridgeport Police Department

Almost a week after the deaths of William Radcliffe and Maximilian Van Zuylen, I sat at my desk on a Friday evening looking at the file I had on the two boys. It now dated back several years with no real answers to any of the puzzle. I was surprised at the amount of press the boys' deaths generated, but then again, I had not realized just how prominent and well known were their two families. An associate of mine had picked up papers from one of those newsstands in Manhattan which sells all the national papers plus some of the foreign ones. Speculation about William's and Maximilian's death was all over the place. They were victims of a heinous double homicide, a murder / suicide, a double suicide, or a tragic accident. Take your pick.

Some of the newspapers speculated that the boys were brothers. This included the society columnist Aileen Mehle, who reported that the boys were likely brothers and that William Radcliffe was actually a Van Zuylen. The Van Zuylen boy's aunt, Baroness Marie-Helen de Rothschild, said flat out that they were brothers. "Mais, bien sur," she was quoted in *Paris Match*. "Garcons magnifiques! Quelle tragedie!" *Of course they were brothers. Beautiful boys. What a tragedy!* The Radcliffes denied this in the strongest possible terms. The Van Zuylens in San Francisco had no comment. A family friend, Denise Hale, was quoted in the *San Francisco Chronicle* as saying it was no one's business but the family's.

I put the newspaper articles in my file and closed it. William Radcliffe and Maximilian Van Zuylen, a mystery in life and a mystery in death. Were they brothers? Psychopaths? Were they responsible for the events we and the Greenwich police investigated at Deerpark Academy – the flood in Charles Morrison's office, the arson at his home in Bridgeport, the near destruction of the student Robert Montgomery's car, the deaths of the officer and cook aboard the yacht La Caravelle, the murder of Lila Jacobs? And, in New York, the hate speech sprayed on the office door of one of William Radcliffe's professors. So many questions. And now, there would never be any answers.

I sat in my office a while longer, wondering why the two boys held my interest as they had. Was it because they were rich, smart, good looking, had all the privileges this world could offer? Now, I would never know the answer to that either.

Made in the USA
San Bernardino, CA
20 January 2017